Green Hell

Book Two in the series

Death of the Jaguar

A novel chronicling the discovery,
dissipation and decimation of the
last "original people" of the
Amazonian rain forest,
in three parts:

The Jaguar People,

Green Hell,

and

Turn from the Jaguar.

By Robert Wolley

ISBN 1-59457-573-8

Author's notes: This is a work of fiction. *Masaki,* the name of the Amazon tribe central to this story and all characters and incidents spring from the author's imagination. Any resemblance to actual persons, living or dead, is coincidental.

For those who speak Euro-based languages, Amazonian Indian names are difficult if not impossible to pronounce. Therefore, in keeping with the story as it unfolds, from the opening page, the Indians' names have been anglicized.

GLOBAL BOOK PUBLISHER
NORTH CHARLESTON, SC 29418

BOOK DESIGN BY HAYS PENFIELD

RECENT BOOKS BY ROBERT WOLLEY

Testament (with Gobin Stair)

The Pranks an' Enlightenment of Frank an' Me

Between Sisyphus and Me

Seniors in Love

A Companion for Seniors in Love

The Jaguar People
     (Book One in the Death of the Jaguar Series)

And forthcoming in the Death of the Jaguar series:

Turn from the Jaguar (Book Three)

v

From Book One, The Jaguar People:

Masaki means "the only people on earth," or "the chosen people" or "the special people," and the forest is their mother. When three people, survivors of an airliner crash months earlier, emerge from the forest and enter the Masakis' lives, the Masakis are dumbfounded. It is inconceivable that other people exist. That the three are white skinned compounds the event beyond comprehension. The Masakis' immediate individual emotions range from abject fear to zestful curiosity. The whites pose no physical threat; and once Wasmaggi, the medicine man, announces his belief that the three are white because the forest made a mistake when coloring them, much of the fear dissipates and is replaced by the Indians' insatiable desire to touch and know the color white.

To Wasmaggi, color is of less concern than the whites' sicknesses and injuries. He examines each injury. He can do nothing about Connie's internal damaged rib bones pressing against her heart and left lung. Her life is in the hands of the forest. He gives her a liquid to ease her coughing and shakes his head. Next he examines Anna's infected cuts and gashes and wonders what kind of ignorant medicine man tried to repair her. He cuts and cleans her; she will live. And last, he examines Widel's torn shoulder and broken leg. It's too late to repair the leg; the man is crippled for life. No wonder all three are undernourished; the man cannot hunt.

For his final ministration, Wasmaggi administers liquid medicine for the many bugs and worms that live on and inside each white. His purging will take several days. If the whites live through that ordeal, they might have a chance for long lives.

Oral communication was impossible; language differences were unbridgeable, but it soon became apparent to the Indians that the whites wanted to become part of the village. They had, in fact, reached the end of their endurance in their failed attempted walkout from the rain forest. When the whites realized the Masakis know no other people, the whites became aware of just how far they were from any other human contact. They agreed: their journey had ended.

1

That first day, because she wore the scars of a jaguar attack and because she gave the village the jaguar's claws, Connie received special attention from the jaguar hunter, Tomaz, one of the oldest of the Masakis. The jaguars and the Masakis are the forest's special creatures. They coexist because the Indians admire, perhaps even revere, the ethereal qualities of the jaguar and would possess those qualities if they could. Jaguars are killed only when they threaten the Masakis, the killing the sole role of the jaguar hunter. For reasons he never would or could explain, Tomaz decided that first day to train Connie as his replacement.

And for reasons he later could and would explain in detail, Wasmaggi made a similar decision, to train Anna as a medicine woman.

To the Masakis, the whites were ugly, not only because of their color but because of the copious amounts of pubic hair. And they were ignorant; they ignored or violated tribal customs. Especially, the hunters were upset; the women less so. In Anna, over time, the women had a major female support figure. The children noted only that Connie took time to play with them and teach them songs and games. They became Connie's devoted followers, awed all the more because she was Tomaz's special pupil.

No one paid much attention to Widel. He was not a good hunter; his crippled leg made the silence necessary for successful hunting impossible. The hunters achieved a solution; they taught him the craft and art of making blow guns and other weapons. He became especially good at making bows.

From the beginning, it was assumed that Anna and Connie were Widel's women. The three shared a shelter and a cooking fire and behaved as a family unit, but neither woman shared Widel's bed and thus neither woman became pregnant, much to the disappointment of the Masakis for whom children were the forest's greatest gift. From the time of the plane crash, Widel honored his silent pledge never to compromise the girls. Many times he choked on that pledge, but he never broke it. Somewhere in their travels, the girls had agreed with each other: they would manage a relationship with Widel. It never happened.

After years with the Masaki, when Connie and Anna became aware they had absorbed all Masaki knowledge and could survive in the forest successfully on their own and perhaps walk out of the forest, they consciously decided to remain with the Masakis.

And they decided they would make Widel marry them, forging a Masaki family. On their way to inform Widel of their decision, Connie was struck by an alligator's tail, the ribs damaged many years before piercing her lung. What was to have been a joyful union instead became Connie's death and burial.

O N E

Widel Ranford treasured the midday siesta as the most precious hours of daylight. Even though the Amazonian sun was directly overhead, its light was diffused by the forest canopy and filtered down on the village rather than beat down as a gigantic heat lamp. The canopy covering the Masaki village was only slightly less dense than elsewhere, a blessing which he had taken for granted for a long time. As hot as it was, Widel had become accustomed to the midday heat and rarely thought about it.

He was in a particularly philosophical mood as he moved his hammock from the palm roofed house and stretched it between two trees, something he did every day when the weather allowed. His behavior reflected much of the calm that issued from the village itself. After all the years of hurt, struggle and loss, he still was amazed that the primitive houses and the tan people who inhabited them could be his whole world.

From his relaxed perch, he reviewed the village and its people, reaffirming in his mind everything that had come to be his home and his family. He studied each house, counted them and reassured himself that each was present and in its appointed place, not that they were likely to disappear or be moved, but for reasons he could not fathom, he felt a physical and emotional comfort, a profound sense of well-being, knowing that each house stood secure in its own space.

He checked off each man, woman and child in the village in a mental attendance record book. Those he could not see or those whose activities he could not immediately account for he noted especially, worrying about them. Some were napping inside their houses; some were hunting or gathering roots and nuts; some were at the stream bathing or relaxing. Widel had no guardianship role other than that which was self ordained, yet, in assuming the role, he was doing what came naturally to each and every Masaki, manifesting the Masakis' total concern for and commitment to the village. Without it being spoken, every other member of the village had noted the whereabouts and activities of every other member. If at times such concern seemed to violate privacy, he knew that privacy could be obtained with a single word or a simple gesture. What at first seemed nosiness, once he and the girls had understood it, had proved to be a consuming concern for the welfare of each Masaki and for the whole village. Life was too tenuous and too precious in the equatorial rain forest to be left unguarded.

But Widel felt something deeper than mutual custodianship; he felt a connection, a bond, to life itself. He sensed that connection as he watched the widowed Mansella instruct her son, Oneson, in the art of fire making; as he saw Tonto's old wives, Pollyque and Lucknew, carrying water from the stream; as Joshway did Sarahguy's work because after years of miscarriages she finally had given birth; as Lurch and Contulla played with Blue, their son snatched from the jaws of a jaguar. He felt the bond just seeing Hackway and Magwa and other women bending over the meager crops in the cultivated patches of the forest, seeing Walkin repairing his house of palm leaves, knowing that Soomar and Joqua and Mike were on separate hunts for meat.

He smiled when he wondered how a *civilized* visitor might react. Probably think it quite primitive and quaint, he told himself. He wondered if a visitor would see the essentialness of the play, the gathering, the hunting, the basic eloquence of the struggle to exist. And what would a visitor say in the midst of such a calm, prehistoric scene if it were revealed that he, Widel, had killed several men, that Connie had carried the marks of a savage jaguar attack, that Anna had those marks, that he displayed the scars of a spear and a knife, that Blue had been dragged into the forest in the jaws of a jaguar, that Connie had killed a man, that Connie had been killed by an alligator? Would the scene seem so quaint then? Or would the visitor be repelled by the forest's harshness, condemn its people as savages and pronounce the rain forest a living green hell?

It had been that, he admitted to himself, and he trembled slightly, remembering much of the brutality of the forest. Was he fooling himself when he focused on the harmony of the forest? Was he deluding himself when he felt his sense of atonement with the Masaki and with the forest? Was he ignoring the primal baseness and brutality and evil in this place? He didn't think so, but he wondered if he had become so much a part of it that he could not see the evil.

He did admit to bad things, but he chose not to rehearse them. He knew them well enough without having to enumerate them, just as he knew the good things. He was tempted to begin a list of such things, but he knew what they were without cataloging them.

Nevertheless, he went back to reviewing the village and its people. From his hammock he had a commanding view of every house and every cooking fire, and slowly, very slowly, he examined each house and each individual.

Only when he had completed his check list, could Widel settle back and enjoy the siesta. He never told anyone about his daily survey. Once in a while he asked himself why he took it, admitting that the business of counting the houses was an irrational compulsion for which there was no explanation. It was, quite simply, something he needed to do. He never mentioned it to anyone; especially, he never mentioned it to Anna.

He looked down at her now as she bent over the cooking fire, and as happened from time to time, he could feel the water build up in his eyes. What a sentimental old fool, he said to himself as he tried to focus on her through the mist. He nearly was overcome by the waves of love that flowed through him, not, he reflected happily, the waves of outright lust which had burdened him for so long.

Once, a long time ago, he had had a vision of Anna as the *All-mother* as she and Connie, naked and filthy and covered with blood, slaughtered an alligator in the eerie forest darkness lit only by a feeble fire of savannah grass. Now, looking down on Anna, the earlier image was reinforced.

Impulsively, he jumped down from the hammock and knelt beside her. He rubbed her back and kissed her on the back of her neck.

"What's that for?" she asked, turning her face up to him.

"I just felt the need to do it."

"I'm glad you did. A woman needs a lot of reassurance at this time." Anna turned around and stroked Widel's face, then kissed him. "Do you really love me, all fat like this? And growing fatter each day?"

Widel reached down and placed his hand on her growing belly. "I do, Anna, more than you can imagine. No, a thousand times more than you can imagine." He rubbed her stomach again.

"A few more weeks, Widel. I wish it would come now. I'm rather uncomfortable, all bloated out like this. And I can't wait. So many dreams will come true."

Laughing, Widel reached out and lifted a heavy breast. "Well, the baby should be well fed."

Anna started to push him away, then wrapped her arms around him. "Tease me if you want, but I'll find a way to get even."

"I suppose so. Every time I look at you, you tease me."

For a time they held hands by the fire, Anna occasionally turning a piece of meat on the spit and rearranging a yam like root at the fire's edge.

They ate in silence. They had come to practice the Indians' conservation of words. There was, however, a constant flow of communication, visual and physical; at these times their eyes seldom strayed beyond the other's.

The meal finished and the waste scraps consigned to the fire, Anna went into the house to nap. Widel returned to the hammock. He might close his eyes and even catch a short catnap, but he never remained asleep for long. After all these years he was on guard duty still, just as he had stood guard since he and Anna and Connie had first crashed into the Amazon jungle.

For some reason, perhaps because Anna was approaching her birthing time, he thought back to an earlier time when his guardianship was more real than symbolic, when being on guard was the whole measure of simply staying alive. He smiled inwardly, wondering if guards ever performed their duties swaying in fiber hammocks.

And he chided himself for using the thought "jungle." That's what it was in those early weeks: a confused, tangled, hostile, threatening jungle, irregular, without sense, the vines and roots and trees and the countless other growing things an interminable, impenetrable wall of a million hues, all of it inhospitable. And the creatures, not only the alligators and the jaguars but the gnats and chiggers and bees and a thousand other tiny, unseen annoyances. How they had struggled. Connie and Anna, in the innocent awareness of youthful idealism, had brought into the jungle a concept of natural harmony. Never was it more needed than during their early months of struggle.

When they ceased to fight the jungle and deliberately sought its cooperation, they began their true survival. And when they met the Masaki, they found a people so much a part of the forest that the people and the forest coexisted as a unity. For reasons Widel never could comprehend fully, Connie and Anna were swept up in that union, Connie as the jaguar hunter and Anna as medicine woman. In their roles, the girls became a part of the forest, just as the Masakis were a part of the forest. For a long time Widel had felt that he was a tagalong.

Why today, he wondered, did these thoughts occupy his mind? But he didn't shut them out. Instead, he allowed the thoughts to take him wherever they would. He had asked once why the Masaki villages were so small and so far removed from each other and had been told that the rain forest (he didn't think the rain word had been used) could support only a few people in one place and that only a few could live together in one place in the forest without damaging it.

From that recollection, his mind focused on the land itself. The ground, and hence everything that sprang from it, was the most important element in Masaki existence. The Masakis didn't worship the ground, but they treated it with reverence. There was no sense of ownership because the Masakis believed the land and the forest which grew up from it owned them. Without ever knowing the words, the Masakis had a profound awareness of the entire ecosystem and of being an essential, natural part of it.

The girls had understood that, too. The girls had understood a hell of a lot more than he had.

When the plane crashed and burned and the three survivors gathered their wits enough to make a fire and to tend to their wounds, Widel had accepted the relative ease with which the girls adapted to the jungle. Innocence born of childish ignorance, he had thought at the time. Not that he knew anything about the Amazon jungle; indeed, he was, as was soon proved, more ignorant than the girls. They, at least, had spent nearly a year studying and learning about South America and its Indians in preparation for their year as exchange students in Peru. What he had contributed was limited medical knowledge. As crude as that knowledge was, it had been adequate to the immediate emergency, but it had not been sufficient to treat either Anna's facial disfigurement or Connie's life threatening internal injuries. His knowledge hadn't even been enough to treat his own crippling leg break. Yet what he had accomplished, and in a sense it was remarkable, was enough to save their lives.

From the first day the girls had expected to be rescued, and when rescuers failed to appear, they began what they believed was their walkout from the jungle back to civilization. For months they crawled and scratched their way through the jungle. And when, after months of harrowing struggle and reluctantly accepting their imprisonment in the jungle, the girls began to plan their lives as forest dwellers.

Connie and Anna never gave up; they set the example; Widel followed. Once all hope of rescue was abandoned and the likelihood of walking out of the jungle became remote and then impossible, Widel was not sure what goals the girls had set, if in fact they had a goal.

For a long time he wondered if the girls kept moving only because to have stopped would have symbolized defeat. Perhaps their goal was to find a goal, and the only way to find something, anything, was to keep moving. Nevertheless, then and later, he had a sense of purpose in the girls' movements.

That undefined purpose, together with the girls' placid acceptance of the harsh facts of existence, led them on. It allowed them to accept the brutal attack on Connie by the jaguar, to suffer days without food or water, to give up all their clothing, to willingly attack and slaughter an alligator. The girls went through a metamorphosis, from their lives as comfortable, sheltered, protected New Englanders to bruised, naked, thirsty, starving aboriginals living only by their wits. More than once Widel had wanted to call it quits, had wanted to cease the endless, pointless march.

Then, when the old Indian summer camp finally was found, he was certain he had reached the end of the line. He would make some kind of arrangement with the girls and they would live out their lives as....

Widel did not know it was there the girls had defined their goal, not to be rescued because that was beyond hope and probably not to walk out of the jungle because that hope dimmed with each passing day, but to become a family unit. The idea was vague and unorthodox, but it was a logical possibility born of the girls' need for unity and solidarity and stability.

Widel had reached the same conclusion but for a different reason. As did the girls, he thought they could hack out an existence in the jungle and survive. And as did the girls, he knew they could survive only if they were united. But in Widel's mind, union meant something more and different. Crudely put, it meant physical sexual union.

Widel didn't finish the thought. He knew why he had continued the journey. He had been a dog in heat. The question was, why he had not acted on his basest instincts? What had there been about the girls that had stopped him from acting on his lustful impulse?

T W O

Following Connie's death, Widel and Anna had stayed at the summer camp. Their grief seemed to hold them there. It was a private grief which for a time they could not share with the Masakis. They held and comforted each other. Whatever Anna felt, and for a time she seemed drained of all emotion except remorse, Widel knew what he felt. On top of all the feelings of loss and despair, he felt impotent. When he looked at Anna, he was devoid of any sensuality. For the first time since he had opened his eyes after the plane crash, he had no sexual feelings toward her whatsoever. But more than that, far more than that, he felt utterly helpless, even to offering suitable comfort to Anna.

Even when Anna said she wanted to marry him and to have a child, Widel felt nothing, and when Anna said they would wait an appropriate time before marrying, Widel was relieved.

Later, when Anna stood before the Masakis and recounted the story of Connie's death, she told also the story of their wanderings and of their struggles, of their love and of their intention to make a family. And when she told the Masakis about her feelings of loss and of her love for Widel, she seemed to drop her burden of grief into the fire.

That night everyone expected Widel to retell the story as he had experienced it, but he said little, mostly cursing the forest that had produced the alligator that had been the ultimate instrument of Connie's death.

The Masakis comprehended nothing of what Widel said and nothing of his attack on the forest and its creatures. To them it was natural that Connie would seek the alligator, and it was natural that the alligator would strike back. It was heartbreakingly sad that

11

Connie had been killed, but sometimes the forest was harsh when it reclaimed one of its own. That was natural, too. As saddened as were the Masakis, and they were moved deeply, many to prolonged tears, their sense of life's unity left no room for blaming the forest. Of the three whites, Connie had understood best that sense of unity.

Connie had found the heart of the Masaki existence and had merged it with her own deep faith. To some extent it was a matter of semantics, she said, never bothering to explain the gymnastics of the words. Connie took seriously the Indians' belief that each person came from the forest and that each would return to the forest. "I am," she had said in what for her was a remarkably long theological statement, "born of the forest; I am the forest. And when I die, I will become the forest and a part of all of the life of the forest. I was and am and will be each piece of the forest; I was and am and will be all of the forest."

When neither Widel nor Anna responded, Connie looked at each of them. "You don't understand, do you? The forest is God, creator and giver of life. I am born of God, and God will receive me when I die, and I'll be with God; I'll be a part of God.

"Don't you see? Don't you see the unity? Don't you see that we always were and always will be? No, I won't come back as I am now, but I'll be here as part of the forest, part of God, always. Even if I go to the ends of the earth, I'll be a part of everything. Right now it's the forest, but maybe for someone else it's a mountain or a plain or the ocean, but wherever it is, everyone is forever part of God's world."

Widel had wanted to say something, thought better of it, and remained silent. If what Connie had said raised other questions and doubts, they would remain unspoken. The sense of life's unity which Connie felt, however, reflected his own, and he would carry always her passionate belief in that unity.

He knew himself well enough to know that he would not bother to create a systematic set of beliefs. He supposed Connie's religious upbringing made the need and the ability to do so natural. His regret was not his failure to have a clear concept of life and his insignificant role in it but that Connie had not lived long enough to help him deal with the bad things that happened, her death being the worst of the bad.

Widel put off marriage to Anna for months, and the months turned into a whole year. They shared the same house, shared the household duties of husband and wife, even talked about marriage as some vague event somewhere in the future, but Widel made no overtures and, strangely for him, completely eliminated from his speech and vocabulary any word or phrase that might hint however slightly of romance.

Anna busied herself in her medicines; Widel worked endlessly on his blowguns and bows and arrows. A whole year passed in that fashion. Outwardly polite, solicitous of the other's welfare, sharing gossip, sharing the daily chores, they never spoke of becoming a family.

There were enough emergencies and events of importance to justify continued postponement of the marriage, or so each rationalized.

First, within weeks of Connie's death, Mike was mauled badly by a female jaguar. Through his own carelessness, he had stumbled upon the tiger just after she had delivered two babies. His momentary distraction with the newborn gave the mother the time she needed to attack. The attack was savage, and Mike was torn open in a number of places, but apparently before killing Mike, the mother broke off the attack to check on her babies. Mike had time, although no one could imagine how he did it, to thrust his spear and kill the cat.

Somehow, Mike managed to reach the village. Anna, with Wasmaggi's help, saved the boy's life. For several weeks, Anna attended Mike day and night, leaving him only long enough to attend to her most personal elemental needs.

Sarahguy, desperately hoping to hold on to her unborn child after years of miscarriages, had become ill. When she was not actually treating Sarahguy, Anna worried about her, and that occupied her for several weeks. And when the baby was born, it was less than healthy, and Anna focused her attention on it.

When at last the village seemed well and healthy, Anna was summoned by Tomaz. In the simple, dignified manner that always

13

had marked the jaguar hunter, he told her he was going to die. He didn't want to trouble anyone, but he needed one last favor from the medicine woman; he wanted her to be the one to tell Hagga.

"Tonight," he said, "Wasmaggi and Tomaz walk into forest. Only Wasmaggi return."

Anna nodded; it was the way.

"Wasmaggi will comfort me, and I'll go back to the forest. It is as Tomaz has wanted for a long time."

"I know. Anna will remember Tomaz as a good man and as a dear friend."

"And Tomaz will go remembering An-na...and Con-nie."

Anna remembered well. On that first day on the beach when Connie and Tomaz had examined each other's jaguar scars, Tomaz had welcomed Connie to the Masaki tribe as someone special. There was a kinship between the old hunter and the young, white child-woman that neither could or would ever bother to explain, and when Tomaz choose Connie to replace him as the jaguar hunter, he seemed to absorb her completely into the life of the Masakis, and Connie, for her part, became every inch a Masaki. Yes, Anna said to herself, remember Connie, Tomaz. Of all of us, she was the most Masaki of all.

"Yes," Anna replied after a while, "Connie will welcome you wherever she is."

Tomaz smiled. The thought of being a part of the forest with Connie was pleasing. She had not disappointed him, ever. In fact, he thought, in every way she had surpassed the teacher. What more could he have wished?

But Tomaz had a more pressing concern, and he needed Anna's cooperation and assurance. "Will An-na tell Hagga that Tomaz has returned to the forest? Of all Masaki, you one she respect most."

"Anna will tell Hagga."

Anna sat with Tomaz for a while. When she heard Wasmaggi approaching, she leaned over and kissed Tomaz on the cheek. He smiled and thanked her.

Anna sat by her own fire, positioning herself so she could see Tomaz's house. When in the dark shadows she saw Tomaz and Wasmaggi leave for the woods, she got up and walked to Hagga's shelter.

"May Anna sit by Hagga's fire?"

"Stupid woman let own fire go out?"

"No. I thought I might visit with you."

"When you use hammock Hagga make? An-na slow in everything, Hagga think."

When Anna made no reply, Hagga said, "Know why An-na come. Hagga learn too long mean tongue. Too late change, but maybe Hagga love An-na. Say mean things and still love. An-na believe Hagga?"

"Yes, Anna does believe you."

"Hagga know Tomaz go. We say goodbye. When Tomaz gone, Hagga go. You here because Tomaz ask. Glad you here." Hagga crawled around the fire to Anna. "Like An-na hold old woman."

Anna cradled the ancient figure. She could find no words but she knew that none were necessary. Hagga fell asleep. Anna did not move her. For some time Anna held the old woman and stared into the fire.

Suddenly, Hagga bolted upright. "It is over, An-na. Wasmaggi comes."

Anna heard nothing, but presently Wasmaggi was standing by the fire. "The forest...," he began.

"Has taken Tomaz." Hagga finished the thought. "Have you brought me anything?"

"I return with Tomaz's jaguar spear."

"Then I shall have it."

"Hagga!"

"A scratch, An-na. Just a scratch."

As she spoke, she flicked the point of the spear across the inside of her wrist. A few drops of blood appeared.

"Will you hold an old woman again, An-na?"

Hagga said nothing more. She appeared to sleep in Anna's arms. She woke up once, spoke Tomaz's name and patted Anna's cheek. Then she went back to sleep.

Hagga died that night, her final resting place in the forest arranged by Spiker, her son.

The next day, Wasmaggi called Anna to his fire. "An-na...."

"No explanations, Wasmaggi. You and Tomaz and Hagga planned well. I don't want any details."

"Wasmaggi no kill. Know An-na think so, but Wasmaggi no kill."

"Then why protest? Did Anna say anything?"

"No, but know what An-na think, and An-na wrong. An-na medicine woman; only An-na have medicines for life and death."

"Yes, but you were the medicine man for a long time. Just because I do your job now, you still have all the knowledge."

"Now you medicine woman. Wasmaggi not use knowledge unless An-na ask. Is true. Wasmaggi not interfere, ever, even with Tomaz and Hagga. No matter what An-na think, Wasmaggi Masaki of honor. No lie to An-na."

It was true that Anna believed Wasmaggi had used his knowledge to help his friends leave this world. There was nothing she could do about it even though it bothered her, and so she said nothing. But why was Wasmaggi making an issue of it?

"An-na listen to Wasmaggi. Tomaz, Hagga and Wasmaggi last of old Masaki. Now only Wasmaggi. Tonto next, but him not know everything. Old Masaki have power of life and death in mind. Not need weapon or medicine if want to die. When Wasmaggi's time come, will think of it, and it will be as I say."

Somewhere Anna had heard or read of people, primitive people usually, who had the power or whatever it was to will themselves to death, but she had no knowledge of that ability other than a vague recollection of having had it brought to her attention.

"Hagga and Tomaz wanted to rejoin forest," Wasmaggi continued, "and it was as they wished. An-na no have that power. But much of Masaki life is believing in power. Is in head. No

16

medicine for head. If person think die, no medicine help; if person think get well, medicine help. An-na understand?"

Anna understood enough to recognize Wasmaggi's insights into the relationship of body and mind. She had long since recognized Wasmaggi's skills as a mind doctor as well as a doctor of the body. He was giving her a lecture on psychosomatic medicine, having skillfully diverted her attention away from any part he might have had in what she believed to be the suicides of Tomaz and Hagga. He had turned it all into a discussion of medicine. But what was the point? And now of all times?

"An-na wonder why Wasmaggi say this now? Because without old ones, Masaki lost. No direction, no roots, like leaf in stream. Only Wasmaggi left, and time short. Then Masaki look. See only An-na. An-na is Masaki. An-na give Masaki reason to live or all Masaki lost."

Shit almighty, Anna said to herself. How can he jump from dying to psychology to saying I'm the only hope of saving the Masakis - and saving them from what?

If there were answers, they would have to wait. Wasmaggi entered his house and left Anna standing alone by the fire, puzzled and amazed and strangely tired, as though she was as old as the old medicine man.

One night at the village fire, it was announced that it was nearing the time for summer camp. This year the camp would be in a special place where few had ever been.

"The journey will be long," Wasmaggi told the Masaki, "longer than all others. Some will not return it is so far, but it is a place all must know, a secret place. Wasmaggi will lead you because one day you may need to know the place. Ask no questions; Wasmaggi will say no more until it is time to speak. But we must prepare now for long time walking. Extra food, extra hammocks, extra arrows."

True to his word, Wasmaggi said no more that night or in the days that followed. Everyone seemed to understand the seriousness of his request for preparedness, and for weeks hunting and gardening and weaving were intensified. Widel worked from sun to sun fashioning arrows and finishing bows and blowguns.

The whole thing could have been one big joke, a super tease if it had not been for Tonto's pressure on everyone to comply. And, to add to the intensity, he announced that all shelters would be burned days in advance of the planned departure. No trace of the village was to be left. The immediate trails were to be covered, especially the trail to the stream, and to accomplish that, small trees and bushes were transplanted, a strenuous task for people with no digging tools.

Anna tried her best to learn something, anything that would clarify the seriousness of the labor. Wasmaggi said only that he was doing what he should have done long ago.

It was left at that. The medicine woman had no say in those matters decided by the hunters. That the hunters had not been consulted didn't seem to matter. What mattered was that Wasmaggi and Tonto and Tonto's wives agreed.

Tonto announced the burning of the houses several days before the journey began, saying that the houses would be burned in a planned order, the house of the youngest first, the house of the oldest last. Widel's and Anna's house would be among the first razed. Anna's medicines would be stored in Wasmaggi's house, the last house destroyed.

Widel helped move Anna's medicines, and then he and Anna packed their few belongings. Their house was to be burned in the morning. Among their possessions was the baby hammock so artfully woven by Hagga. As Anna studied the hammock, she was overcome by the passions and longings she had so carefully repressed.

Clutching the hammock, she kneeled beside Widel. "Make love to me, Widel. Before they burn down this house that was supposed to be a home for our family, make love to me. Please."

She pushed him down and half covered him with her body. When he did not respond, she reached down between his legs. Widel was flaccid.

Anna moved away. Nothing had prepared her for this. At first she was embarrassed, then confused, then angry. Without thinking, she slammed her fist into the side of Widel's face. He threw both hands over his face to ward off another blow. But she didn't strike him again. Instead, she drew her knees up to her chest, clutched the baby hammock over her head, and cried.

Widel wanted to leave, but he couldn't. He reached over and touched Anna lightly on the shoulder. "I'm sorry, Anna. Honest to God, I'm sorry."

Anna's body shook with each sob. Widel was at a total loss as to what he should do. He kept stroking her shoulder, knowing if nothing else he had to maintain touch with her.

After a long while, he reached for her hand and held it tightly. Later he kissed it. It came to him that when things were the worst or they had managed somehow to escape a major disaster, the three of them would hold hands, a symbol of their unity and of the strength each gave to and received from the others.

Then he forced Anna's other hand away from her face and attempted to kiss her.

"I can't explain it, Anna, but it's all right now."

"No, Widel, I don't suppose it is."

There was a prolonged pause. Finally Anna said, "Twice, I remember, Connie told me what a tragic thing it was to waste love. The first time she was talking about Tomaz and Hagga. The second time she was talking about us, about the three of us."

Anna rose and walked from the house. It began to rain; raindrops penetrated the canopy and fell with full force on the village floor. At first, Widel was reluctant to go after Anna, but when thunder sounded overhead, he followed behind. An Amazonian thunderstorm is a mighty and fearsome event if and when it is directly overhead. The likelihood of serious danger was remote; Widel could not recall the lightning ever striking the village, but he had seen evidence of its happening.

In one way, he thanked the storm. He needed an excuse to go after Anna, an excuse to touch and hold her and to reassure her that everything was all right, even if he knew it wasn't.

Anna was in no hurry; she walked aimlessly around the village as though she was not certain either of destination or direction. For a while Widel simply kept pace, but when Anna headed toward the river, Widel hastened to catch up. With a torrential rain, the river could rise as much as ten feet. More than once it had surprised the Masakis by its height and by the force of its currents.

Widel reached Anna just as the broad path from the village met the small beach. He was surprised how much wind the storm generated; within the growths of the forest floor, wind seldom is apparent.

Reaching Anna, he grabbed her arm. "Anna, it's not safe here. Where are you going?"

"Nowhere. Just leave me alone. I'd like to be alone."

"Yes. Okay, Anna. But let me lead you to some place that's safer."

"What do you care, anyway?"

"Oh, Anna, you can't know how much I care."

"Damn funny way of showing it."

"I'll say, especially for someone who spent years unsuccessfully trying to repress the irrepressible. Honest, Anna, I don't know what came over me. I'm not sure what I've been feeling these past months."

As he talked, he gently led Anna away from the river. He knew that she would balk at being led back to the village, so he guided her toward one of the several small knolls that in miniature resembled the undulating foothills of New England. The knolls were favorite resting places when the forest was exceptionally hot. Close by the river, they often caught faint breezes. Such places had been used for centuries and were well worn, not only by the Masaki but by the forest creatures as well. Nothing would be using them now. Humans would be in their shelters and the animals would be in theirs.

Anna was silent as they sloshed over the soggy forest floor. Only those who knew the forest well could navigate in the near darkness, but the lightning came in prolonged series and illuminated the entire area. Finally, on the knoll Widel knew to be the highest around, he kneeled and drew Anna down beside him.

"This is a safe place, Anna. If you want, I'll leave you alone."

Anna made no response, and Widel was left wondering what he should do next. Perhaps by doing nothing he was doing something; he didn't know. He wasn't asked to stay, but he wasn't asked to go.

He decided to wait as long as was necessary. Anna would have to determine his next move.

With that thought, he realized Anna had made a move, a substantial emotional move he had rejected. Anna had given herself to him, begged him to take her - and he had responded with no response whatsoever. He hadn't even touched her.

Widel began talking to himself, silently rehearsing the events of the past years, his feelings when he saw the girls naked and had had such little success hiding the fact he was aroused, and when he had burst with jealousy and rage seeing the girls embrace, and when every ounce of self-control was needed night after night as he viewed the girls in the firelight, and when, finally, all control and sensibility were unleashed. Somewhere in the reliving of his tensions, he began speaking out loud.

He seemed not to realize he had an audience. Anna listened with rapt attention. She knew of Widel's emotional distress only in the most vague way; now, unwittingly, he was setting before her a disjointed story of mental and visceral torture, and she understood for the first time just what anguish Widel had suffered.

But why, when all that frustration could have been healed at last, had Widel been found impotent? As Anna listened, her own confusion and anger diminished. She could see that she and Widel were pathetic figures, huddled as they were on the flooded forest floor, each locked in some kind of mental prison which neither understood and which, apparently, neither could control. How little I know, she said to herself, and how little I understand. But to Widel she said nothing.

He became quiet. When he began speaking again, almost whispering, Anna had to listen carefully to make out the words, and what she heard distressed her almost beyond endurance. Widel was talking to Connie. Over and over he proclaimed his love, begged her to love him, and in the end, begged her forgiveness for having killed her.

Right after that a particularly strong and brilliant flash of lightning jolted Widel to attention. He looked directly at Anna as if he was seeing her for the first time that night. When he spoke, Anna was aware that nothing that had transpired during the past hour was remembered by Widel.

"Do you want me to leave, Anna?" he asked.

"No, Widel. We must talk."

"Of course."

"What do you think we should talk about?"

"Me, I guess."

"Well, later perhaps. I think we should talk about Connie."

"Why? Is it necessary?"

"Yes. She's come between us, Widel."

"No. How could she? She loved you, and she loved me. She said so. And I know you loved her, and...I loved her."

"Yes, but it's not loving her or being loved by her that's the matter."

"What, then? You don't want me to remember Connie?"

"I want you to remember Connie, but Jesus, Widel, I don't want you to keep blaming yourself for her death."

"I...don't....do that."

"Do you remember what Connie asked us to do before she died?"

"She...asked us to get married and to have children."

"Yes. Why would she have asked us to do that?"

"Because she...loved us?"

"I'm sure of it. We had her for a long time, Widel, a lot longer than we had any right to expect. You know that. Can't we just give thanks for what we had? And get on with our own living? And remember Connie for the wonderful gift she was?"

"Anna, everything you say is true, and I know it in my mind. I know Connie had no right to survive the plane crash and probably shouldn't have done most of the things she did, but she lived to do them, and killing the alligator was just as natural to her as breathing. I know all that. I know it was the alligator that got her, but I also know, and here's the rub, that she was on that trail and met the alligator because she was on her way to me."

"We were on our way to you."

"Of course; God, I don't intend to leave you out, but you were not killed."

"Do you wish it had been me rather than Connie?"

"Oh, Anna, no. No! I didn't want either of you to die."

"But...."

"I could take it if I wasn't involved in the chain of coincidences. If Connie had been killed by Sampson, I could have handled that. If the jaguar had killed her, that, too. I would have hated it and yelled and screamed and cried, but I could have accepted it in the end. The same if you were killed. But to be a part of the puzzle, a piece of the.... Can you understand what I'm saying?"

"Oh, I understand, Widel. I just don't know how to deal with it."

The storm's intensity increased. The lightning became continuous, and in the light it was possible to see the rising water. They were marooned temporarily on an island. Widel had chosen the place wisely; the water was not an immediate danger. Far more dangerous were the lightning strikes. One strike was less than a hundred yards away on the opposite river bank where the trees were somewhat taller. Their knoll shook; they felt the surge of electricity; their bodies moved in minor spasms as the electrical charges passed around them; they could smell wood burning, although they could see no fire, and mixed with the wood smell was a hint of sulfur.

Other strikes were nearby, but none as close as the one across the stream, yet each subsequent strike jarred them. Once, Widel looked at the hairs on his arms; they stood out and reminded him of quills. He tried to look at Anna, but he couldn't seem to get her into focus.

There was nothing wrong with his eyesight. From head to toe, Anna was shaking in fright. It took Widel several long seconds to realize that, and when he did, he reached out to hold her.

In that instant another bolt slammed into the nearby trees and Anna and Widel, clinging together tightly, were thrown from one side of their tiny island to the other.

"Mother!" yelled Widel. "Why did you leave me? Why wouldn't you let me in the house?" He buried his head in Anna's arms.

As scared as she was, Anna had enough awareness to realize that Widel had uncovered some ghastly childhood experience. She

23

tried to stifle her own fears and to comfort Widel.

"I was afraid, Mother. You left me. Why do you always leave me?"

"You're here with me now, Widel," Anna said softly, not really knowing what to say.

"Leave me. See if I care. When I'm big, you can go. I won't care. And I won't be afraid. Do you hear me?"

"I hear you. You won't be afraid."

"No, I won't."

Other lightning with its horrendous thunder touched the forest, but the storm finally began making its way elsewhere.

What should I do, Anna wondered? Widel was holding her so tightly it was beginning to hurt. She tried to relax his grip, and when that failed, she spoke to him. "Widel, you're hurting me."

"Hold me tight, Connie. Don't leave me. For God's sake, don't leave me."

The tears came to Anna as strongly as the rains had come to the forest. "Oh, God. Oh, God," she repeated over and over. "I never did have you, did I?"

Suddenly Widel loosened his grip and broke free. "Anna! Anna!" he yelled as he ran around the tiny island in the darkness, bumping into one tree after another. He fell into the water, and half submerged, he shouted, "Anna! Don't leave me!"

Only because Widel had managed to grab one of the tree roots was he still connected to the island. The river's current was powerful and sucked along with it everything that was not attached firmly to the land. There was no more lightning by which to see, and Anna found Widel only by the sound of his pleading.

When she had him back on land, he crawled toward the center of the knoll. "What happened?" he asked.

"We had quite a storm."

"No. I know that. In the middle of the storm, what happened? Who was here?" Widel was confused and disoriented.

"No one was here. We are very much alone."

"Anna, my mother. I saw her. She left me out in the storm. That bitch left me out in all that lightning. She knows I'm afraid.

She wouldn't let me in the house."

"I know, Widel."

"But, Anna, I'm not afraid anymore. I'm not a little boy. I'm not afraid anymore."

"No, Widel."

"Then why am I afraid, Anna. I'm shaking like a leaf."

"What are you afraid of, Widel?"

"That you'll leave me, I think, just like Connie left me."

"Connie left because she had to; it was time for her to go."

"Yes, time to go. But it's not your time, Anna. Why am I petrified that you will leave me, too?"

"There is no reason, Widel. I'll be with you always, even if...."

"Tell me about my mother."

"She left you out in a storm, and you were afraid."

"Tell me about Connie."

"She left you because she died."

"My mother left me because she didn't want me; Connie wanted me but she had to die."

"It's about like that, I guess. Only you left out one thing."

"I did?"

"You left out that Anna is here and that she wants...that she is not going to leave you."

"No, I didn't leave you out, dear Anna. You're here, in my heart. I know I've got something in my brain that I've to get straightened out. Maybe I see a little of what it is. Maybe it's *Physician, heal thyself.* But whatever it is, Anna, the thoughts of you fill me with love. Unfortunately, the thoughts are not always pure. I mean, I have to work out an accommodation to the fact of Connie's dying. I've not handled that well at all.

"What my mother has to do with all this, I don't know. But I do know that I must find a way to forgive myself. Not excuse myself; forgive myself."

"I suppose I know the answer, Widel, but what have you to forgive?"

"I don't know. Really, Anna, I don't know. Sometimes I think that it's just that I failed both you and Connie."

"But how?"

"I don't know."

"Maybe I do, and I'll tell you as crudely as possible because I can't think of any other way. You think you let Connie down because you never had the opportunity to make her a mother, something she dearly wanted. But I know you, Widel, and I know that at least part of Connie's memory is that you didn't get from her what you wanted. Maybe you failed her because there wasn't time, but you really failed yourself. You threw the chance away."

"What a terrible thing to say."

"Somehow, Widel, I'm going to knock some sense into your head. You're so screwed up, you're sick. You think you're the only one suffering; you don't give a damn about anyone except yourself. Poor little Widel, afraid of a big, bad storm, afraid his mommy will leave him out in the rain. Big boy? Shit. You're a baby. Connie? Christ, you're using her an an excuse to be a little boy again."

"Anna, so help me...."

"You'll what? Leave me? You already have. But you've no place to go, do you?"

"What do you want from me?" Widel was angry, and he reached out to grab Anna, but being unable to see her in the darkness, he failed to reach her.

"I want a man, Widel. The man you were all those months and years before Connie died. Sometimes you were totally obnoxious; sometime you were exasperating, but you were a man. You were strong; you made us go on when we would have quit; you were brave."

The rain continued. Although the storm and lightning had left the immediate area, the rain continued. Widel hardly noticed. Perhaps the total absence of light made talking about his fears and failures and about Anna's disappointments easier. He knew he hadn't been strong. And for certain, he knew he hadn't been brave. Actually, more than once, he wished that he had died in the plane crash. If there had been strength and bravery, it had come from the two girls. Only later, when he realized they might never leave the jungle,

26

did he work at being a man, and then, he acknowledged, it was because he wanted both girls and sensed that having them was possible, if he behaved himself and if he had patience.

Just when he stopped lusting after them and began loving them, he could not say, but when he recognized his love, he began to act as he knew the girls hoped he would act. He wanted them to believe he was, in fact, what they wanted him to be, strong and brave, someone they could love.

He didn't tell Anna any of this, finally replying, "I was those things because you made me believe I was, and I wanted you to think of me that way."

"Well, whatever, but we thought of you as brave."

"And now you know that I'm weak, just like any other man. Weaker, perhaps, than any other man."

"Maybe. What I know is that you are so full of self-pity that you can't see anything but yourself. For a while I figured it was natural, but it's been a year, Widel, and if anything, it's worse."

"So you're going to play mind games with me?"

"Actually, I wish I knew how; I wish I could help you get free of your mother and of Connie, put them in their proper places in your mind. I wish I knew enough to help you."

"Yes, I know you do, and to tell the truth, I need help. I more or less deal with my mother's memory, her hatred - no, I guess she didn't hate me; more like unlove. My anger only pops up once in a while after all these years, and then it goes away. And it's like a dull toothache when it does surface.

"But Connie. That's harder. Can we talk about Connie?"

"Oh, yes, I wish we would."

"We never have, have we? All the time we wandered, all the time we spent with the Masakis, you and Connie had each other. I never had anyone to talk to, to share my feelings with. I used to talk to myself a lot, but after a while that's just one idiot talking to another idiot.

"I used to think I'd go mad with frustration, with lust. God, you can't believe how you two tortured me, how close I came to raping you. Instead, I kept promising you that nothing bad would

27

happen; a million times I wanted to break that promise. But I couldn't talk to anyone about it. And I promised myself, and kept remaking the promise, that I'd see you both to safety. When we got to the Masaki village, things happened so suddenly, and you and Connie became so wrapped up in the Masakis, I began to believe I had lost you to them. I was jealous and angry and hurt, and I couldn't tell anyone."

To this moment, Anna had been unaware of Widel's isolation. Only now did she begin to comprehend so much of what had gone on. Connie had been Anna's safety valve, as she had been Connie's. They had shared everything right down to their most intimate thoughts and feelings. Widel had had no one. But full comprehension was still in the future, proved by Anna's question.

"But we talked about being a family."

"But it was just talk. I'd look at you at night, and I'd see two girls sleeping in each other's arms, and I could see there was no room for me. You had each other. How was I going to break into that? And then Connie would go off with Tomaz, and you'd go off with Wasmaggi, and when you weren't off like that, the two of you would talk and giggle. I was left out, or at least when I talked with myself, I and myself agreed that we were not needed."

"And most of the time we were talking about sharing you."

"I didn't know that."

"No. I can see now that you didn't, and the truth was that we kept asking ourselves why you didn't want us."

"Of, Jesus, did I want you. It ate at me until actually I was physically sick. My only salvation was to elevate the promise I had made to myself not to molest you to such a height that finally I was able to stop thinking of you both. Maintaining your virginity became so important to me. That and protecting you from all harm.

"And that horrible night when I lost all control. Every promise I had ever made to you and to myself had been broken. I had betrayed myself, and I had betrayed you. The only thing to do was to get as far away from the both of you as possible."

The storm had passed and the first faint rays of the sun slanted along the stream. It was obvious that the river was in full flood; it would be several days before the stream was back to normal. In an area where ten feet of rainfall is normal, no one gave particular concern to occasional floods. But as Widel looked out over the flood, he knew that they were trapped for at least another day or two.

"I don't imagine they'll burn any houses today," he offered. "There's no place to go. And we're stuck here for a while. The currents are too strong to take a chance swimming."

"Can we drink the water?"

"Have to, I guess, if you're really thirsty."

"We'll be missed in the village."

"Probably. But they'll know we're okay." After a long pause, Widel asked, "Do you mind terribly having to spend the day here?" He wanted to add *with me* but thought better of it.

Anna answered with a simple negative. She stretched out on the wet ground, propped her head on her hand, and studied Widel. "Widel," she asked at last, "if we had to go through all this again, what would you do differently?"

"You're not serious, are you?" Widel had to laugh at the question because its implications revived so many of his earlier fantasies.

"Don't make fun of me. I'm serious. I want to find out what we did wrong, Connie and I?"

"I'll give you a serious answer because I've thought about it. And the answer is this: when we found out that the Masakis were at the end of the earth, and we knew we had gone as far as we could, and we decided we would make our home with the Masakis, I should have...."

"Married us?"

"Well, that, too, whatever it would have been called."

"How did we let the opportunity slip by?"

"I can't answer for you. I didn't see any sign from either of you, but by then I was picturing myself as some kind of medieval knight guarding the chastity of two lovely maidens. I was on a mission, or at least I talked myself into that idea."

"We were so dumb. Connie and I were so stupid. We couldn't understand why we turned you off."

"Well, the fact is, I never was turned off. I just had found ways not to show it."

"It used to show pretty good sometimes."

"Yeah. That bothered me a lot."

"And you used to watch us a lot."

"Couldn't help it. One or the other of you was the first thing I saw in the morning and the last thing I saw at night."

"You haven't looked at me for a long time."

"No. It was hard to teach myself that, but after we found the Indian camp, I worked on it. I got so I could see you without really looking at you, and if I didn't look, I didn't get all excited."

Anna got up and stood directly in front of Widel. "Look at me now."

"Anna...."

"Let's start over, Widel. We're on this island. No one else is here, just you and me. There's no one to rescue us. We're marooned, maybe forever. There's no promises, no rules, nothing but two people who love each other."

As she talked, Anna swayed slightly from side to side, her breasts moving in a rhythm that mesmerized Widel. She spread her legs slightly as she leaned forward and drew Widel's head toward herself.

Widel let the sight and smell of Anna's body sweep away every thought except the familiar pain in his lower belly. He reached out and encircled her hips. Anna's swaying increased, and when he could bear it no longer, he pushed her down to the wet ground and forced his way between her legs. She drew her legs up and welcomed his entry.

Widel had no thought other than his own relief, satisfied with three or four savage thrusts. "Now," he said breathing deeply, "you know there's nothing wrong with me."

Anna made no reply. Widel's roughness and abruptness shocked her. She wiped tears from her eyes, but she offered no resistance when he began to fondle her.

"I'm sorry, Anna. I don't know why I did it like that. Selfish, I guess, and.... Now I want to make love to you the way it should be, slow and passionate."

Widel was gentle and soothing, and when he kissed her, she returned his kisses, not as eagerly as she might have done before, more tentatively, wanting to but fearing the risk. In spite of herself, she rocked in a harmony of desire and felt tingling feelings cruising throughout her whole body. Her whole body shook. She became aware that Widel was no longer touching her, but the spasms continued. She opened her eyes; Widel was smiling down at her.

"That's for you. The rest will be for us, for my beloved Anna and me."

He drew her close and hugged her; the spasms began again, and she pulled Widel down. He was slower this time, almost too slow. She reacted almost immediately, more intensely if that was possible, and she sensed a great calm sweeping over her.

When he was quiet and motionless, she gently rolled him off and rolled on top of him, once more offering her breast. When he had taken it, she reached down to hold him. He was growing soft. She pulled away.

"It's natural, Anna. A man has only so much, then he has to rest. Not that I want to, but it takes a while for a man's body to recuperate."

"I thought.... Oh, Widel, I'm so ignorant."

"And I'm sorry about the first time; that was not called for."

"Maybe I deserved it. But it's over. The rest was too wonderful to let anything tarnish it."

They washed in the muddy waters of the swollen stream. In some ways, the torrential rains had washed each of them. It was not a thorough cleansing of the mind; each knew that, but it was a beginning.

They rested. Neither had much to say. The only conversation of substance had to do with the slight bleeding Anna experienced and Widel's words of assurance that like everything else in the forest, it was natural.

In mid afternoon, Anna bathed again, embarrassed by the stains. Her foot slipped in the mud and she uttered a tiny cry. Widel had turned his back; no Masaki ever watched another bathing. When he heard Anna's squeal, he turned and reached out for her. No words were spoken, and they held each other tightly in reassurance that nothing could ever separate them. They coupled again. Time and place and circumstance had no meaning; only the prolonged enjoyment of their mutual fulfillment mattered.

"If I had known what this was like," Anna confessed, "we would still be in the woods somewhere."

She meant it as a little joke, but then she frowned. A serious thought in her mind. "I wonder if I could have shared you after all. If I knew that Connie.... I'm jealous just thinking about it. How could you do that with Connie, with her when you knew I was waiting and wanting to and...? It wouldn't have worked, would it, Widel?"

He was silent. For the moment, one woman was enough; one woman was all he wanted; only Anna filled his mind. For the first time ever, he thought exclusively of Anna. Even when Anna spoke Connie's name and drew forth her memory, he thought only of Anna.

"I have to know, Widel. I don't know why I have to know, and I don't think I want to know, but I have to. What was I suppose to do when you made love to Connie? Fight her? Hate her? Die in a jealous rage? Help me with this."

THREE

Widel never did get to answer, a fact for which he gave thanks later. He had no answer anyway, singularly focused as he was. It had never occurred to him that Anna or Connie might be jealous of the another, that their sexual tensions might destroy the very arrangement he had fantasied for so long. Equal opportunity, he once had told himself in a moment of machismo, revealing an insensitivity to all other related concerns. The females would be pleased with the male. Period.

Widel didn't get to answer Anna because of Walkin's and Spiker's frantic shouts. "Ran-ford! An-na!"

The river was still high and flowing too rapidly to chance a swim to another knoll, but as the voices came closer, it was apparent the Indians were doing just that. "An-na! Ran-ford!"

"Here, on the hills by the river bank," Widel yelled back. "We're okay. Don't try to come closer; it's too dangerous."

"Ran-ford!" It was Soomar's voice. "Do you have your spear?"

Widel couldn't see any of the men in the near darkness. They must have worked their way from knoll to knoll all around the village and only now were working the riverbank knolls.

"Ran-ford! Much danger! Snakes! Watch out for snakes!"

"We have no weapons."

"We come."

Anna started to shout a protest, but Widel hushed her. "It won't make any difference, Anna. They've got it in their minds now. You're too important to these people for them to take a chance on losing you."

In the Amazon twilight, Widel and Anna could hear the men splashing through the water. More than once Anna wanted to tell them to turn back. There were long periods of silence when she was sure something had happened to one or all of the hunters, but then the noise would come to her ears again.

"Look!" Widel pointed. "They're coming down on us with ropes.".

Three hunters were swinging in the current on their tethers. Somewhere up stream, they had tied a line and from it they were able to swing and swim from one knoll to another. Tying off at each knoll, they repeated the routine until, just before complete darkness, they reached the medicine man and the weapon maker.

"You choose good place," Soomar offered. "But why here?"

"We got caught in the storm," Anna offered by way of explanation.

"Know better than that. Village only safe place in storm."

Spiker was right, of course; they did know better, but then, they were not going to reveal the real reason for their foolishness.

Walkin quietly studied the tiny island, what he could see in the fading light. Finally he walked up to Widel and poked him in the ribs. "Ran-ford enjoy?" he asked. When Widel failed to respond, Walkin poked him again.

Widel came close to swooning when Anna spoke up. "Ranford enjoyed, and because I know you'll pester me the whole night through, Anna enjoyed."

The three men let out a whoop that could be heard for miles. "Family! Family!" Spiker shouted into the forest.

It was too dark to see; Anna was crimson, only slightly more so than Widel.

"Joy! Joy!" yelled Spiker, and immediately he began to make up a story song. "In the rain," he began, "lightning strike/An-na and man/see the man/fast as lightning/boom, boom, boom." Spiker worked his thoughts out loud over and over.

But when Soomar said something to him, Spiker became quiet. Soomar placed Widel and Anna in the center of the knoll island. "Stay very quiet. No noise. Must be silent. Snakes come; seek warm land. Too much flood, so snakes come."

Walkin couldn't resist. "And no make love, either." He chuckled quietly, but it was obvious in his nervous laughter that serious business was at hand.

Anna couldn't stay the question. "But how can you hear a snake?"

She was startled when Soomar replied. "Can't hear. Feel. Snake look for warm place, and where feet are is warmest. Snake will find our feet. Then know have snake and quick kill him or throw in water."

"Jesus," was all Anna could offer, but when Soomar spoke so matter-of-factly and Walkin and Spiker gave every appearance of being on an every day snake hunt, she tried to reassure herself that what the men were doing was nothing out of the ordinary.

It was out of the ordinary, of course, but neither Anna nor Widel wanted to think about it.

As the men stood quietly, they used their spears to etch light, broad semi-circles in the mud. If a snake approached, they hoped to touch it ever so gently. The snake would not strike, assuming it was being touched by a twig or something similar, but it would coil up, just in case its senses were wrong. Then, if the hunter's own senses were adequate, he could flip the snake back into the water.

It was a long night. Occasionally one could hear the sounds of a hunter, but what those sounds meant no one knew. Of all things, Anna hoped no one would be bitten. She had none of her medicines at hand, and in the darkness, it would be impossible to do anything.

With first light, they were surprised at how little the water had receded. That, said Soomar, was natural. They were surprised, too, to see how many snakes had been killed and how many marks indicated other snakes flung away. There had not been enough noise made for either Anna or Widel to have counted so many.

"Much food," Spiker observed. "Now need An-na look at Spiker's foot."

"Oh, Spiker, you've been bitten. When did this happen?"

"Not know. Much dark."

"Big snake? Little snake?"

"Think not big snake."

Anna studied the hunter's foot. It was so swollen she could not find the fang marks immediately. It would, of course, have to be lanced and the poison sucked out. That was the first thing. Then medicine to counteract the poison. And warmth and dryness. And medicine to help Spiker breath and medicine to regulate his heart.

"Rope," she yelled. "And a clean knife." Clean meant only that a knife was dipped into the dirty water and wiped with a hand.

Tying a tourniquet just below Spiker's knee, Anna had Widel tighten it. When she was satisfied, she punched through the swollen upper foot, making two holes. Spiker said nothing, nor did he as much as wince.

"You know what to do, Widel." Anna bent over the foot and sucked hard, spitting out as much blood and poison as she could manage. At best, she knew it was of limited help.

"Soomar," she directed, "we must leave. We must get Spiker to the village and to my medicines." She added "immediately," but that was redundant. Everyone knew that time was against them, just as everyone knew that Anna would give her life before letting Spiker die. But for the moment, Anna was helpless.

Soomar took charge. Anna was the medicine woman, but it was Soomar and Walkin who were responsible for moving Spiker. "Ran-ford go now. Go village for help. Use rope to help swim. When get three islands up, must swim."

Widel took time only to reflect on the Indian's decisiveness. He had long admired that ability. Here were people, seemingly carefree and at times indolent, people who had no sense of time, outwardly people who shuffled through time, but always, when faced with a crisis, they sensed the right moves and acted without hesitation. Even as he started off, he knew that Soomar and Walkin, without ever speaking to each other, had planned both the escape route and the means by which they would move Spiker should he become unable to help himself. And he knew that above all, they would provide for Anna.

Widel plunged into the water, half swimming, half dragging himself along the rope. He reached one island and found a second

36

rope. He moved to the second island and then to the third. He was close to the dry, high ground of the village. Across the remaining water, he could see the eddies caused by the flood's currents, and he paused to choose his route. There was no rope linking this island to the village beach.

It was well he did pause. He counted at least three alligators anchored by their tails on the far shore, their heads in the current. If they wanted him, there was no way he could make it.

He had never practiced much, but now he needed the high pitched cry of the Masakis, the cry that would be both a warning and a cry for help. His voice trembled, but he was successful.

Half of the villagers appeared at the water's edge. He searched for the face of one in particular, and when he saw Tonto, the old hunter, he addressed him. If anyone knew what to do, it would be Tonto.

Amazing, he said to himself, how quickly they understand. Widel had only to indicate an emergency, that he must cross the water, that the alligators posed an insurmountable threat, and within seconds Tonto had understood and had organized an attack on the reptiles. Every hunter, and Widel was astonished to see several women, too, stalked the alligators.

The three that were visible didn't have a chance, and even as they were being killed, Widel had begun his swim. As he entered the water, from the other shore women entered the water to meet him, forming a human chain linked by branches they had torn quickly from the trees and brush.

Never ones to waste food, Widel noticed that two of the women had organized the children and that they were securing the dead alligators with ropes so they would not drift away in the flood.

On shore, Widel blurted out the essential facts: Spiker was injured and Soomar and Walkin and Anna were bring him in. They needed help because they needed swift medication for the stricken man.

There was no debate, no discussion, no questions. The women left. They would have fires and water boiling in the old airplane vat. They would have all of Anna's medicines next to the fire.

Wasmaggi would be ready to help. They would have food and fresh water for everybody. It was not spoken, but it would be done.

Already Lurch and Amstay were on the first island. Mike disappeared, and returned with a fishing seine; it was ferried to the island. As quickly as possible, Spiker would be wrapped in it. He was to expend no more energy than absolutely necessary.

Within minutes, the village population was strung out either in the water or along the tiny islands. Widel could remember hearing no commands, no spoken orders, but if anything, order prevailed. Even the smallest child seemed to know where to go and what to do.

Widel had done his part; now he seemed to be in the way. He wanted to wait for Anna, but he knew she would have no time for him, so he waited on the sidelines, hoping that someone would give him a task.

As he waited, he felt a hand touch his shoulder. It was Xingu. "Ran-ford, Wasmaggi want you. Come, please, quick."

As Widel hurried to the old man, he wondered what Wasmaggi could possible want.

"Ran-ford," the old medicine man said, "An-na medicine woman, but maybe need help?"

"She will, Wasmaggi. Spiker was snake bitten, hours ago. Don't know what kind of snake. Anna lanced the huge swelling, but it didn't help much. Too much time has gone by."

"Tell Wasmaggi. Quick. Must be ready."

With an economy of words that did him credit, Widel described the snakes that had been killed, described the wound, Spiker's color, and Spiker's reactions and behavior. Wasmaggi asked about fang marks. Widel had to tell him that the foot was too swollen to make them out with any certainty. He also said that Spiker thought the snake was small.

As they talked, Wasmaggi led Widel and Xingu to Anna's shelter. He pointed to certain medicines and Xingu separated them into a single lot. She had laid out Anna's cutting tools and stitching materials previously.

Now she paused to ask Widel's forgiveness for having entered his house. Forgiveness was expressed with a touch. Xingu and Widel carried the medicines to the fire that had been built by other women. Widel was glad to see the water boiling. Wasmaggi examined Anna's cutting knives carefully, laid them out on a banana leaf, and then arranged Anna's medicines in some kind of order known only to him and the medicine woman. When that was done, Wasmaggi laid out flat and closed his eyes. Widel wondered how the old man could fall asleep.

With nothing to do except wait, Widel asked Xingu how she had come to know Anna's medicines.

"An-na friend, most friend of Xingu. When Con-nie go, Xingu say An-na need someone help. Xingu that someone."

"And a good friend you are, Xingu. Anna is lucky to have a good friend,"

"Maybe more?"

"Of course, say whatever you like."

"Hope maybe one day Armot be medicine man. One day when An-na get old will choose new medicine man or woman. Would Ran-ford agree?"

"Ranford would agree, if it works out, but I won't have anything to say about it. That will be Anna's choice, you know. But I'm glad you think well enough of Anna to want your son to follow in her footsteps."

"Joqua think Xingu not right in head. Armot should be hunter, he says."

"Armot should be a hunter. That doesn't mean he can't then become the medicine man, if that's the way it works out. Wasmaggi was a hunter before he became a medicine man."

"Ran-ford wise."

Sure, Widel thought. The easiest way to be thought wise is to agree with someone.

Wasmaggi didn't stir until Spiker was being rushed to the fire. A look of worry lined Anna's face. "Oh, Wasmaggi. I knew you would be ready to help a woman who needs help." She bent down and kissed his forehead.

"Wasmaggi too old for such foolishness, An-na. I leave you now. Everything is ready."

"Please. Two of us will be better. Spiker needs both of us."

Wasmaggi was pleased. The years seemed to roll back, and he had an energy that was not present before. Together the two studied Spiker's foot, talking in such low tones no one could hear what was being said.

Wasmaggi mixed powders and liquids and forced Spiker to drink. Spiker had not lost consciousness but he was without energy and was barely to move.

As Wasmaggi mixed other powders, Anna took her knife in hand. She looked doubtful.

"Is well to think," Wasmaggi said, "but is not good to question self."

Anna still hesitated. Wasmaggi pointed to a spot on Spiker's foot and traced two lines with his fingers.

The operation had begun.

Widel squatted to watch. He knew that Anna and Wasmaggi were severely handicapped by not being able to identify the kind of snake. They were even more handicapped by the passage of time. Yet, the fact that so much time had elapsed served them in one way; there were a score of snakes whose bites could be eliminated from consideration. To have been bitten by one of those snakes would have meant certain death within an hour or two. At least four hours had passed and maybe as many as eight.

Anna cut carefully under Wasmaggi's watchful eye. She made two lines across Spiker's foot, parallel and about four inches or less apart. Then she connected the lines, making the letter H. She was seeking to uncover the two major blood vessels that crossed the top of the foot. If one of those had been punctured directly, it almost was certain Spiker would die.

Widel was impressed, impressed that Wasmaggi knew so much about the human body, impressed that he could have given that knowledge to Anna, impressed that Anna could do what she was doing, never having done it before, and impressed that in all the

40

blood and swollen flesh, Wasmaggi and Anna could make a meaningful examination.

"See," said Wasmaggi, "fangs here. Very short. Either snake not sure he should bite or snake very little. Young not mean no poison, but Spiker lucky."

Anna worked rapidly with wads of kapok, sopping the blood and staring intently at the opened would. "Look. Here's the vein. The fangs almost straddled it. Just a nick, but enough to kill Spiker if we're too late."

Anna sprinkled some kind of powder on the open wound and drew the skin back over it.

Wasmaggi spoke to one of the women. "Is almost ready," she said.

She left, returning with a large woven framework which was slid under Spiker. He was rolled onto his stomach and rested on a bed inclined some thirty degrees.

Anna felt just below and behind Spiker's knee. She rubbed a spot with her thumb and then drew her knife across the flesh, making two incisions parallel to the main artery. She made a third cut, this time forming the letter U. She cut deeper into the flesh, exposing the artery. At the top of the main incision, she pressed down hard on the artery, and as she did, Wasmaggi punched a tiny hole in the artery and inserted a thin reed. To that reed he attached one slightly larger, and then he added a third, creating a small funnel. Slowly, he poured a reddish liquid into the reed.

At a signal to Anna, she jerked the reed out of the artery, removed her thumb, and placed it over the tiny hole.

"Well, for Christ's sake, if that doesn't beat all," Widel whispered.

Anna made a pressure bandage of boiled and carded kapok and placed it over the artery, checking it from time to time. Very little leakage was evident. When she was satisfied, she closed the incision with a series of stitches. She would check this area at regular intervals for days.

Satisfied for the moment that that task had been done as well as possible, she had Spiker rolled onto his back. She turned to

Wasmaggi. "How long?" she asked.

"Not take long. Color should show now."

Anna returned her attention to Spiker's foot. She laid back the flesh once more, mopped the blood away, and studied the open wound. Particularly, she wanted to see what came out of the fang nick in the artery. "Yes," she said suddenly. "See the color, Wasmaggi. See, the red is darker. Maybe we've done a good thing."

Wasmaggi didn't bother to look. He knew what would happen. Now there only was waiting left, and as Anna closed the wound, Wasmaggi went sound asleep, curled up on the village floor next to Spiker.

Sarahguy bent over Anna. "Now?" she asked.

"Oh, yes. Right now."

Without commotion, food appeared. "God, Widel, I'm famished. Two days, at least. And look what the women have done. Come on. Might as well eat while we wait."

As incongruous as it seemed, the whole village appeared and picnicked around the semi-conscious Spiker and the slumbering Wasmaggi. Anna had taken time only to wash her hands; now she was stuffing herself, gorging herself on freshly cooked alligator meat.

She leaned over to Widel and whispered in his ear. "Sometime we'll try living on love."

For all its outward appearance, this was no party. Spiker's life hung in the balance between a mysterious snake and the skill of Masaki medicine. Saymore hovered over her husband, touching Anna from time to time, looking into her eyes, pleading.

Wasmaggi awoke a couple of times, spoke Anna's name, and each time they carried out a careful examination of their patient. Late in the day, Wasmaggi said, "Think An-na won. Think Spiker be as you say, okay."

Filled with Wasmaggi's reassurance, Anna sat beside Saymore. "I think," she said, "you'll have your hunter back this time. He's a very brave man. When he's well again, love him with all your heart."

"Thank you, An-na. I ...." She couldn't continue and burst into tears, throwing her arms around Anna's neck.

Anna hugged her back. "Now, Saymore, go to someone who needs you as much as Spiker does. Go and tell Sayhoo her father will be well."

Throughout the day, Soomar and Walkin had checked on their companion, but at no time had they stayed long, knowing there was little they could do. Now that Spiker seemed out of immediate danger, Widel went in search of the hunters. He found them sitting by Walkin's fire.

"I want to thank you for coming for Anna and me. It was very brave. I'm only sorry it has caused Spiker so much pain."

Soomar looked at Widel. "Not worry about you. Not worry about An-na, either. Worry about medicine woman. That most important. Ran-ford hunter. Not always good, but hunter. Take care of self. An-na hunter, too. Should not be, not woman's place to be hunter. Not good. But An-na hunter and know danger. But An-na medicine woman. Masaki need medicine woman more than need hunter. Worry medicine woman."

"Yeah, I see what you mean. You're right, of course, but anyway, I wish that Spiker had not been hurt."

"Spiker not think about it," offered Walkin. "His only thought find medicine woman. He not think about you or me, only village. Spiker not mind hurt if help village." Widel was humbled by the expression of selflessness. The village, the tribe; above all things the common welfare. He hoped if it ever came to it, he could act as nobly.

The flood postponed indefinitely the promised mysterious journey to a new summer camp. Had it not been the flood, Spiker's illness would have been sufficient cause. Now the village would wait for whichever took the longest, for the waters to recede or for Spiker to get well. Everyone counted the village's good fortune for not having burned down the houses.

The villagers waited two more days to be sure of Spiker's recovery before building the community camp fire. Surely there were stories and songs to be told and sung about the storm and about Spiker and, especially, about Anna and Widel who had left the village as the storm raged.

The retelling of the storm was mercifully brief; the people had other things on their minds. Even Spiker, speaking from his cot about finding the couple and about the snake watch, was brief. He knew he would have plenty of opportunities to recall that adventure, just as he knew he was a minor player in a much larger and socially important drama.

It was Walkin who got the Indians' attention. He began by describing a jaguar hunt, leading his audience along the marks left on the trail. Just before the descriptions became tiresome, he told his listeners that now they were searching for two jaguars, a pair. There was no mistaking the imagery as Walkin led his hearers to the knoll by the flooded stream, nor was the imagination left to fill in the blanks when he described the signs on the knoll's surface.

Walkin continued to speak, but all eyes were fastened on Anna and Widel. Even when Walkin ceased his story, every man and woman present stared at the two whites.

From his sickbed, Spiker began his song. He had not had time to polish it, but refinement was unnecessary. Even before he finished what little he had composed, the Masakis were shouting for Widel.

The last time he had stood before the Masakis, he had confused them by cursing the forest and had disappointed them by blaming Connie's death on the forest.

Not so this night. "I am Ranford," he began, "and I am Masaki. I came from the forest and I'll return to the forest one day. It is natural. And it is natural I have a Masaki wife." He was interrupted by cheers.

He looked down at Anna. When the sounds stilled, he continued. "It is natural that I have a wife who came from the forest and who will return to the forest."

There were murmurs of approval. Widel broke into the sound. "It is natural for a man and his wife to have a Masaki family."

"Yes, yes," shouted the Masakis, cheering loudly.

"Who will be Ran-ford's wife?" someone asked.

"An-na! An-na! An-na!" the Indians replied in full chorus.

Widel held up his hand, begging for silence. "A man must ask a woman. Ranford has not asked. I'm sometimes stupid. I did not remember to ask. Now, before you all, I ask Anna if she will be my wife."

He reached down and took Anna's hands and drew her to her feet. He cupped her face in his hands and whispered, "Will you, Anna? Will you truly marry me?"

Anna threw her arms around Widel's neck and kissed him hard and long. When she realized that the Indians were patiently and silently waiting for her answer and that kissing still was strange to them, she took her lips away. "Oh, yes, Widel. Oh, yes."

She spoke loud enough for the Indians to hear. As they shouted their approval and joy and sang refrains of joyous songs, Anna whispered in Widel's ear, "But you'll have to learn to control yourself."

Widel slumped to the ground, annoyed at his loss of control, embarrassed by his lustfulness. If the Indians noticed, and there were few who did not, they accepted Widel's erection as natural.

"In three days," Anna told the village. "Anna must prepare herself."

Three days. The village wondered if it could find enough adequate diversions to wait that long.

That night, Anna and Widel slept on the same bed, the oversized one the hunters had made for them so very long ago. That night they repeated as much of the Christian wedding ceremony as they could remember. They kneeled on the bed facing each other and recited their vows, each promising to the other love and fidelity and caring, each accepting the other's vow as seriously as it was given.

F O U R

Spiker recovered fully within weeks, but the forest did not. Rain continued to fall in amounts never before experienced. There was no summer camp at the mysterious location promised by Wasmaggi. To move the entire village was considered too dangerous. Wasmaggi and Anna consulted often. Certain medicines could not be replaced until the forest floor dried and the flowers were able to bloom. And Wasmaggi, Tonto and the hunters consulted, too, worried that extensive hunting in the immediate area would deplete the meat supply.

Already parties were hunting far beyond their normal range. Anna took two day trips into the sodden forest in search of plants and roots. Usually Widel went with her, but the food situation became so desperate that sometimes Anna took some of the women with her because Widel was needed to hunt. So wet was the surrounding forest the jaguars had gone elsewhere, but not the snakes or the alligators. They became an even greater threat.

Some months later, Wasmaggi approached Anna. She assumed he had come to ask about her medical supplies, and was stunned when he asked the question on many people's mind, why she hadn't become pregnant. "Not for lack of opportunity," he reflected. "Ranford and An-na like cats in season." Wasmaggi has lost none of his directness.

"It isn't time," Anna answered. "You know how you say it; it is natural."

"Wasmaggi think not natural. Wasmaggi think An-na take medicine. That not natural."

"It's none of Wasmaggi's business."

"Is business. Wasmaggi gave An-na knowledge. But An-na misuse knowledge."

"I have my reasons."

"Afraid have child? Maybe think Ran-ford no want child? Maybe not want be family after all."

"No, none of that. Oh, damn, Wasmaggi. You'll keep after me until I say something, won't you? All right, I'll tell you, although there's nothing you can do about it." She drew a deep breath, held it for a long time, and let it out as one extended sigh. "It's Connie."

"Con-nie? Wasmaggi no understand."

"Well, not Connie exactly. Widel still thinks about her, and when he does, he gets morbid. He still blames himself for her death."

"So?"

"He thinks of her."

"That natural."

"No, it's not, not when it interferes with my marriage."

"How so?"

"He feels guilty. And sometimes when he makes love to me, I think he is making love to Connie. If you say that is natural, I'll strike you."

"You hit old man?"

"Oh, Wasmaggi. Don't you see?"

"I see An-na unhappy. I talk with Ran-ford."

"No. No! Don't do that."

"Maybe man talk."

With that said, Wasmaggi shuffled away. Anna knew he would search for Widel, and she wished for once that the ancient medicine man would mind his own business.

On the other hand, perhaps it would help. Widel would not talk with anyone on his own volition, so maybe some good would come of it.

Widel was working on a new blowgun. As weapon maker for the village he had a steady job, and since it took many weeks to make a single superior blowgun, he had to work a good part of each day to maintain his stock.

"Ran-ford talk with Wasmaggi?"

47

"Of course. It would be a welcome interruption to talk with Wasmaggi."

"Wasmaggi no, how you say it, beat bush?"

"I think the expression is *beat around the bush.*"

"Anyway, Wasmaggi ask why An-na no have baby."

"Well, you aren't going to waste time, are you? The plain truth is, I don't know. As I suppose you know only too well, we've given it every chance to happen. Guess it's just not meant to be, at least not yet." Widel could not resist the urge to titillate the old man. "But you can rest assured that we'll keep trying."

When Wasmaggi failed to react, instead looking at Widel with concern, Widel asked, "Is there something I should know, something the matter with Anna?"

"Wasmaggi old man; know should not interfere, but him old medicine man, too. An-na take medicine so not have baby."

"What? Why, for crying out loud?"

"Because of Con-nie. An-na think you really rather have Con-nie. But Con-nie dead."

Widel was silent for a minute or two. Then, "Damn it, Wasmaggi, this is my own problem."

"No. Ran-ford wrong. Is An-na's problem."

Widel thought for a moment. "Yes, I guess it is."

"Wasmaggi help?"

"Wish you could. It all boils down to the fact that I can't get it out of my head that somehow I'm responsible for Connie being killed. I know it's foolish, but every once in a while the feeling comes back. I'm better than I was, but apparently Anna doesn't think so."

"What Ran-ford seek is happiness with self."

"Exactly."

"And how Ran-ford find such happiness?"

"I wish I knew."

"Maybe Wasmaggi know. Maybe Ran-ford look wrong place. Should remember Con-nie. But Con-nie almost dead when come to Masaki. Only Wasmaggi keep her alive, and maybe Tomaz help, too."

48

"I know."

"She love you very much."

"I know that, too."

"Wasmaggi say why not Con-nie and An-na go to Ran-ford? No answer. Con-nie and An-na waste time till too late for Con-nie. Not Ran-ford's fault maybe. Look at him sometimes and know he ready."

Widel said nothing. The ancient one was rehearsing all that had been said before, many times, too many times. But when he asked if Widel loved Anna, he added a twist.

"Why not think An-na both women? Two women really one, so much alike. Not look alike, both ugly, really, but think alike, talk alike, hope alike. Even love alike."

Then Wasmaggi added a sobering thought. "If An-na take no baby medicine long time, she never have baby, even without medicine. Medicine for little time. Bad take too long. Ran-ford think about that."

After Wasmaggi left, Widel did think about it. At whatever cost to himself, Widel knew he had to turn the corner on his obsession. He needed help and went looking for Walkin's wives, Desuit and Yanna. Of all the people in the village, they were the ones most recently remarried after the loss of their husbands. He wanted to know from a Masaki what rationalizations they had made in order to cope with the sudden loss of a loved husband.

First, Widel had to talk with Walkin. It was one thing to talk with another's wife, in this case wives, about something as general as the weather and to share gossip and small talk. It was quite another thing to pry deeply into feelings and emotions. So Widel needed Walkin's approval of the conversation.

"Walkin no mind. Desuit and Yanna tell Ran-ford what he want to know."

"Thank you, Walkin. You can listen in if you like. I don't seem to have any secrets."

Walkin politely refused, but Widel knew Walkin would receive a full report from the women anyway. For some reason he didn't mind.

Yanna summed up the women's position at the end of the conversation. "When husbands go back to forest, forest goes on. Forest goes on forever. Forest mothers us, provides for us, loves us because we forest's children. And we must love someone alive, so we love Walkin. Make him happy. No forget husbands, but now Walkin husband, and to make him happy makes us happy."

To make the point, Yanna called to her son. "Ran-ford, this child of first husband. Not named when father die; not named until Yanna marry Walkin and we new family."

Typically, Widel had not given the child's name much thought. Now it became obvious. Twoman was named to honor both his father and his stepfather. The boy approached Widel, and Widel smiled at him. Impulsively, he reached out and hugged the boy.

"You and Con-nie and An-na gave name to my baby," Desuit announced.

"We did?" Widel was puzzled. He had had few conversations with the two women other than idle gossip. "How did we do that?"

"Hear you ask Walkin about threesome. Not know what word mean, but know mean love of three people."

"Yes," Widel said thoughtfully, "the love of three people. It's a perfect name."

Widel's mind began to wander. The women had chosen their children's names carefully it seemed, both to hold something of the past and to acknowledge the present. And in the present, they were happy. They made it seem so simple. If only it was.

The next day as Widel walked out of his house, every one the hunters was waiting for him. Tonto, as the oldest hunter, greeted him. "Hunters have need for Ran-ford in forest," he said, leading Widel by the arm.

Widel had no idea what was wanted of him, but neither did he seem to have a choice. Far from the village, the party stopped, forming a circle around Widel.

"We draw straws," said Westman, "to see who speak. I lucky one and speak for all hunters to friend." Westman smiled at Widel, attempting to reassure him that there was nothing sinister in the meeting. "When Masaki true friend, we call him brother. You true Masaki and true friend of all hunters. We address you as brother. But when brother, if thing wrong, we have right to speak to our brother. And now thing wrong. We hear from Wasmaggi maybe no family; we hear from Walkin maybe not love enough for An-na. Now we hear from you, because all brothers want help."

Dumbfounded did not describe adequately Widel's reaction. He stood blank and speechless.

"Ran-ford," Mike said after a long wait, "all hunters know something wrong. We hear from you and fix." Mike's eyes pleaded for his friend to speak. "Not know trouble; not know how help."

The hunters squatted on the ground, prepared for however long it took Widel to unburden himself. He looked at them, hunters whose only purpose at that moment was to help him resolve whatever was preventing him and Anna from becoming a family. He knew no one was there because of idle curiosity; each was present because of genuine concern, and he was touched and moved by the demonstration. And he knew also that while the hunters did have a sincere and deep concern for him, it really was Anna who was uppermost in their minds. Yet he was the key, and the Masakis seemed to know that.

At first, he simply thank them. Then all of a sudden he couldn't stop repeating his story. As he retold it, tears came to his eyes, and he was amazed to find his listeners crying, too. He went through everything, even to the fight that had led him and Anna to the island during the big storm. He didn't know whether a single man had any grasp of what was being said, but he withheld very little, and the little he did withhold, his first love-making with Anna, the men could fill in for themselves.

He retold the wedding ceremony which each had witnessed, leaving out the vow taking and giving he and Anna had shared privately. He told of his joy and of his sorrow and tried to explain his obsession with Connie. And he tried to explain Anna's jealousy, if that was the proper word, and his own misbehavior, and Anna's fear that Connie's ghost lay between them. He knew that certain words had no meaning, ghost, for instance, but he didn't bother to explain, hoping the Masakis would understand the gist of his telling.

When he completed his story, he thanked the hunters for their concern, telling them it was the first time he had shared the whole story with anyone.

If Widel doubted their understanding, he was wrong. The hunters were well aware of the effect Connie had had on them, Lurch and Amstay, especially. They admitted their feelings and told how jealous their wives had been. They even seemed to understand something of Widel's emotional struggles, and they seemed to understand completely Anna's doubts and fears.

There was no resolution of Widel's problem, but it was recognized. In turn, each man offered encouragement. Each man evidenced a measure of pure empathy for both Widel and Anna.

For Widel, the session was a catharsis. To say he felt better because of it was understatement at its best. It didn't remove all doubts or guilt, but for the first time it gave him a sense that he was not fighting alone. No longer would he have to deal with a desperate sense of isolation; he had brothers on whom to lean.

If he did not tell Anna everything, he conveyed a new spirit, a renewed and healthier outlook, so much so that Anna set aside her contraceptive drugs.

It would take time for Widel to completely free himself of his specter, but gradually it would disappear, surfacing only when he was careless or failed to be on guard. He could talk about Connie without breaking down; only when her memory pounced on him unannounced did he falter.

It seemed that every male in the village took some credit for Anna's pregnancy, not the actual physical act, but the fact that Widel was going to be a father bonded the hunters closely. Each brother believed he personally had helped make that possible.

Some of the women were upset by the men's talk, and for a time the women were aloof and uncommunicative. They saw in Anna an object of their husbands' affections, and they were upset and jealous.

It was not until Fraylie announced his intention to marry Sayhoo that the women's reserve was broken. An obviously pregnant Anna was consulted by Sayhoo's mother, Saymore, Spiker's wife, and by Fraylie's mother, Magwa, Hakma's wife.

The women did not want a medical opinion; they wanted a genealogical report. Saymore and Magwa were Wasmaggi's daughters, making Sayhoo and Fraylie first cousins. Since Anna was responsible for knowing the lineage of each family, she had to be consulted.

This was the first time as medicine woman that Anna had been involved in a village romance. It could very well be her last. If the women became angry enough, Anna and her medicines would be neglected. Shunned was the word that came to her.

Anna made no bones about her decision. The children should not be allowed to marry. But if they did marry over her objections, Sayhoo should not be allowed to have children.

Anna knew the tribe disapproved of first cousin marriages. On that she was on solid ground, and she was certain Wasmaggi already had reminded his daughters of the prohibition. But he no longer was the authority in this matter; the authority was Anna.

Knowing Fraylie and Sayhoo had frequent sex, Anna supposed they would continue to do so; she left the marriage door open but with the strongest demand that no children issue from the marriage.

The mothers indicated no emotional involvement whatsoever, indicating that Wasmaggi had already told them the outcome of the consultation. They could have been talking about two strangers when they spoke of their children until they asked about contraceptive measures.

Reluctantly, Anna admitted that she had taken such measures for herself until the hunters had talked Widel into persuading her to stop.

The women did not know that. Suddenly, it became clear why the men had behaved as they did. They had not been fantasizing relations with Anna; they had been urging and wishing Widel on.

A bit sheepishly, Saymore and Magwa admitted their mistake. To rectify it, they would forbid the marriage, affirming Anna's wisdom.

"But that's not the reason you should discourage the children," Anna said. "I appreciate the fact you think you have to make up to me, but the reason Fraylie and Sayhoo should not be married is the Masaki way that says first cousins should never marry."

It was agreed, and not long after, the two mothers were seen moving from house to house, spreading the word about the revelations they had received from Anna.

When Sayhoo came to see Anna, she seemed to come as a little child seeking a pat on the head. "Can Sayhoo sit with An-na?" she asked.

"Of course. Anna welcomes it."

"My mother has told me of your decision."

"I'm sorry it has to be this way."

"My mother said you were very sorry. She also said you would know about love."

"Your mother is generous with her words."

"She said I could marry Fraylie if I did not have children. Is so? Is a way?"

"I did not say you could marry Fraylie. What I said was that if you did, you should not have children."

"If I marry Fraylie anyway?"

"Then there is a way."

"May I have way?"

"No."

"But you said there is way."

"I said there is a way. I did not say I would give you the way."

"Why is An-na so mean? Do you think Fraylie and Sayhoo will not marry just because of you?"

"No. I think Sayhoo and Fraylie will not marry because there should be no children, and because if there are children, they will be allowed to die. It is the Masaki way, and you are a Masaki."

Sayhoo ran away, crying that Anna was evil and only wanted to hurt her and Fraylie.

Not long after, Fraylie appeared, upset and angry. He asked the same questions and received the same replies. But for him, Anna had one last question of her own.

"Does Fraylie want a child?"

"Of course, many children. That is what is family."

"Then Fraylie knows that to marry Sayhoo means no children?"

"But...."

"Fraylie, believe me when I tell you that Anna knows you love Sayhoo. Sometimes love means giving up what you love and finding someone else to love. I know you and Sayhoo have made love many times. For your sakes, I'm glad no child has come of it. You know that such a child would be given to the forest, not because you and Sayhoo are not married but because you are first cousins, and you will not be allowed to have children. You know that is the Masaki way, and you are Masaki."

"I am Masaki."

"Are you a Masaki hunter?"

"No, but one day soon."

"Anna says that when you become a Masaki hunter you will find a wife to love and have many children. Will Fraylie want for that day?"

"Fraylie must...." He did not finish his thought. He got up and walked toward the forest.

Anna wondered if Sayhoo waited along a trail, if Fraylie and Sayhoo would make love for the last time, if there would be a time when either of them would find another love.

She had had so much trouble getting her own love life straightened out that she wondered at her audacity in giving advice to anyone else. But she shrugged her shoulders, and feeling the burden of her pregnancy, retired to her house to rest.

Toward evening, Anna came out to cook the meat provided by the hunters. Not feeling well, Widel did the cooking. She ate very little; instead, she related to Widel the unpleasantness of the afternoon with Sayhoo and Fraylie. She concluded, "As Connie used to say, it's a shame to waste love."

"It's especially a waste," Widel reflected, "when nothing can come of it but grief."

FIVE

Lucknew and Pollyque, by age the ranking women of the village, had prepared Anna well for the birth. She had a thousand questions, and once the two women got over the fact that Anna was completely ignorant about the birthing of a child, they attended to her full education with a determination that would have given a medical school credit.

"One thing," asked Lucknew. "How can be medicine woman if not know how baby comes out?"

"Well, I kind of practiced with Sarahguy's and Xingu's babies, and I had the help of all you women, of course."

In truth, Anna was an observer at the actual births and at the last minute was shoved into the background. Neither Pollyque nor Lucknew mentioned that fact.

Pollyque laughed. "Now you find is not same. One thing see other become mother; different when you mother."

Widel had been no help. His limited medical schooling had neglected birthing, and he and Allie had had no children. Anything he knew, and it wasn't much, he had picked up second hand. His total contribution was to ask, "Didn't they teach you anything in those high school health classes of yours?"

"God, no. They were focused on keeping us from getting pregnant. They never did acknowledge an accident." Anna smiled. "Can you imagine what one of those classes would be like if I was there to tell them about this? Jesus, they'd freak out."

Widel was prepared to share more of the lighter side of the impending birth, but Pollyque shoved him aside. "No time husband now."

For a week the women came at siesta time to help Anna. They helped her select whatever medicines she might need by revealing what might happen. Some of the possibilities were distressing to Anna, and she became apprehensive.

"Too late," counseled Lucknew. "Baby come out, but baby no go back in."

Indian women had been assisting in the birthing process since the dawn of time. It was as natural to them as any other female function. Every woman would be present. Not all would assist, but each would observe, make mental notes, and be better prepared for the next birth, and when that woman's time came to assist, she would have the entire knowledge of the Masaki tribe. Men, of course, and that included Wasmaggi, were banished.

Lucknew and Pollyque told Widel the baby could come at any time; Anna sensed that birth was imminent.

"Will you stay with me this afternoon, Widel?"

"Of course."

"But when the baby comes, you'll have to leave, you know."

"The ladies have told me that a thousand times. Do you know that not even Wasmaggi has seen a baby born? The women have the baby birthing business all locked up. They even have a union, the MMU, the Masaki Mid-wife's Union."

Anna laughed. "You're probably right. When I was reading, getting ready for the trip to Peru, I read about the Incas. They had a medical system that included professional mid-wives."

"Undoubtedly so, although I never heard about that specifically. But a couple of my medical school professors were awed by what the Incas accomplished with their medicine. Brain surgery, for instance. You and Wasmaggi sew people up with the fibers made from palm, but the Incas used human hair. Maybe you should try that sometime."

"Could I let my hair grow?"

"I'd like that. Better than the Masaki haircut."

"Tell me more."

"Well, they set broken bones with plaster they made from feathers and tree gums and resins."

"Wasmaggi and I do that."

"Yes, I know. The Incas removed teeth, not the way you do it, but by yanking them out. I don't know how, though. And they amputated limbs."

"Thank God, I haven't had to do that, but Wasmaggi has given me complete instructions."

"And when the limbs were cut off, the Incas cauterized them."

"I don't think Wasmaggi knows anything about that. He just saves the flaps of skin to fold over the wound."

"Cauterization, I think, would require some kind of metal that could be heated to sear the flesh. It's a horrible treatment. Frontiersmen used it; it was the battlefield treatment of choice during the Civil War."

"You mentioned it once," Anna said , with a momentary flashback to their first days.

"Yes, it was a last resort."

"And the Incas knew all about the heart and about the circulation of blood."

"Indeed they did. Their priests learned all that from their unholy business of human sacrifice. I wonder which came first, the medical or the religious purpose? But on a happier note, they had a fanatical belief in taking a daily bath and in washing every part of one's body. Do you know that the Europeans found that strange? Europeans seldom took baths, the reason why the perfume trade was so big. I even remember that Napoleon asked Josephine, not much more than a hundred years ago, not to take a bath because he liked her raw odors."

"God, Widel, is that true?"

"Supposedly he was coming home from battle somewhere and requested that in a letter to the smelly one."

"Well, I won't ever make the same request of you."

"Nor I you."

"Widel, do you find similarities between the Masaki and the Incas?"

"Gosh, I don't know, Anna. I'm too ignorant about the Incas to make any guesses. Nothing survives here by way of artifacts. There is no stone, no metal, everything is made of wood or bone that rots away quickly. But what I do find puzzling is a lack of history, anything before Wasmaggi and Tomaz and Hagga."

"They had to come from somewhere. Maybe they're a lost tribe."

"Like the lost tribe of Israel? Now, that would be something. But they have been lost a long time, long enough to have forgotten any roots or origins."

"Widel, wouldn't it be crazy if we were part of something big?"

"Oh, I'm sure we're part of something much larger that we cannot see or understand. Again, I don't know enough to assume anything, but, for instance, we have what the Indians call the fever bark, quinine. Originally, as I remember it, quinine came from the bark of the quina tree and was called quina-quina, the bark of barks. And do you know where it was found? In the Andes, not in the rain forest."

"Well?"

"Well, hell. Malaria is not a South American disease. It was brought here by the Europeans, along with smallpox, tuberculosis, yellow fever, influenza, and the three kids' diseases, measles, mumps and whooping cough. When quinine was first discovered, it was one of the greatest exports back to Europe and Africa, right after gold."

"I didn't know that."

"Anyway, my point is, malaria got here less than five hundred years ago. Assume that it took a while for the disease to get to the Indians and another while for the Indians to begin using quina, then another while for our Indians to learn to transplant the quina tree and make it grow in the forest here, and we're talking a relatively recent history, not ten thousand years ago but a few hundred years ago. Maybe our Masakis brought the medicine with them when they came out of the mountains."

"If they came out of the mountains."

"I stand corrected. But think of it this way: Columbus finds the so-called New World in 1492; by 1500, there are a few white settlements up around Panama; by 1535, the Spanish have finished off the Incas; by 1600, ninety percent of the known Indians are dead, slaughtered or from diseases brought to them from Europe and Africa.

"The Inca civilization lasted about five hundred years, we're told, and during that time the Incas waged war on other groups, maybe the Masaki who might have been here, or somewhere, all along. A thousand years ago at best."

"But maybe the Masaki were here before the Incas."

"Maybe. But they do have a history, even if they don't know it. In some ways they are so primitive; in other ways they are remarkably sophisticated, your medicine, for instance. They have an ethical system. some levels of which would shame a Christian monk, but they have no religion as far as I can tell, although there is something about the jaguar. Speaking of which, the jaguar was an important symbol in Incan and Mayan and Aztec cultures."

"Very mysterious."

"Does give you something to think about during your waiting time, doesn't it?"

"I do think about it from time to time."

"Yeah, so do I, more than a little."

"Especially sometimes because of Wasmaggi. I'm certain he knows more about the past than he knows he does, or more than he wants anyone to know. I keep hoping he will open up for me. Sometimes he seems ready to."

From time to time, the whites speculated about Masaki beginnings and history. There seemed to be no knowledge of anything before Wasmaggi's time. To the whites, it seemed impossible that Wasmaggi, trained to carry the Masaki history, would not have extensive knowledge. If he did have an oral history, he never spoke it.

A ray of sunshine fell across Anna's face. "Widel," she shouted, "the Incas were sun worshipers."

"Yes, that's been quite common throughout history."

"No, that's not what I mean. The sun here is not all that present. Oh, it shines every day, and the Masaki certainly acknowledge it, but they don't worship it like a god or anything."

"Okay, but what's your point?"

"If they were Incas, they would have some kind of sun worship."

"Or maybe, when they came to the forest and lived under the canopy, they gave it up. A lot happens in four or five hundred years."

Both knew they were at a dead end. Each time the discussion arose, it ended in a dead end, not that they expected otherwise. Today's discussion was as shallow as any other day's discussion; they simply did not have any evidence for an explanation. They could speculate only.

But in one way, speculation served a need. It helped keep their minds sharp, and by recollection of their own history and by supposition based on what they knew, they exercised their powers of deduction and reasoning. Never mind that they might be wrong; the important factor was that they did not let their minds grow stagnant.

For Anna, the present discussion had a serious side. She wished, she said, they could give their child a sense of being a part of an ongoing history. The forest gives and the forest takes was not enough for Anna. She needed the long reach back into beginnings and she needed a hopeful sighting of the future.

Anna came to the forest with only a casual and superficial religious foundation. It proved inadequate. Unlike the Masakis, and probably Widel, she asked, who am I, looking for more than her immediate existence as a Masaki in the Brazilian rain forest. She accepted that she lived in the forest and would die in the forest. That did not bother her. What bothered her were the basic questions asked by people since time began: who, what, how, why? For all her superior schooling, she did not know Descartes or Kierkegaard, Spinoza or Emerson, Abelard or Bertrand Russell, or any of the philosophers from ancient Greece to her own generational contemporaries who sought answers. No one had told her that the poets e.e. cummings and Shakespeare and Tagore, that the playwrights O'Neill and Sophocles and Maxwell Anderson, that the novelists Steinbeck and Galsworthy and Camus, that composers, scientists, explorers, and archeologists had and were engaged in the same search for answers. No one ever told her because few teachers were aware of the singular purpose of philosophy and the play, philosophy and the novel, philosophy and the poem. Each speaks to life; some try to answer the questions. Anna did not know that and so she ignored a storehouse of wisdom within her own brain.

She felt isolated and adrift, when, in fact, she had numerous lifelines. She had read Camus and O'Neill, Shakespeare and Emerson. She had learned a line from Anderson, "On this hard-star adventure, knowing not...." That would have been a place to start. "To be or not to be, that is the question, whether...." But she did not make the connection; for all the knowledge and good intentions of her teachers, not one had helped her make the connection: all human life is a search for the meaning of being.

Anna's labor began sometime after dark. She reached for Widel. "I think this is going to be very quick," she told him. "Once the first pain came, all the pains are close together. Get Pollyque and Lucknew, please."

"God," Widel said on his way out, "just like a white woman. The Indian women have their babies in broad daylight. Why do white women always have to have theirs when its pitch dark?" He didn't wait for an answer.

It was polite to awaken Tonto first and to ask him if he would allow his wives to attend to Anna. "Good thing Tonto old, Ran-ford. Might have women in bed." He laughed at his little joke as he awakened the women. "Now Ran-ford have to stay here. No man allowed. Don't know why. We put in; don't know why can't see what comes out."

No other women had been called, but it seemed that every woman heard the call. Widel remarked that the gathering was a convention of mid-wives.

"So many hands," said Tonto, "baby will run for life."

All the villagers heard the new born baby's first cries. Pollyque returned within minutes. "An-na have baby girl, very strange color, all red."

Widel dashed from Tonto's fire. It struck him suddenly that white people had white or pink babies. What if the Indian women thought something was wrong with the baby? During the few seconds it took to cover the distance, all sorts of nightmares overran him. Reaching his own house, he shoved the women aside.

"Widel, what's the matter?" Anna asked, agitated that he would break a Masaki tradition.

"The baby's white!" he shouted.

"Well, I should hope so. What did you think it would be?"

"But these women have never seen a white baby!"

"So they haven't. Do you think I would have sprung that on them?"

"But...."

"But nothing, Widel. Get out of here. Let the women do what women do." Widel turned to go. "Widel, the baby is beautiful."

As if to reinforce her mother's opinion, the baby cried louder. Immediately, she was placed at Anna's breast. With little fumbling, she started to nurse, and one by one the women congratulated Anna, and one by one each woman announced her contribution to the birth.

"Widel," Anna called in parting, "I love you."

Pushed beyond the women's circle, Widel had to shout, "I love you, Anna. And the baby."

The happiness of the village knew no bounds, and for two days most activity ceased as each member of the village looked at, admired and was puzzled by the white child. Even if the villagers had been warned about the baby's color, her whiteness was beyond comprehension. Had the forest made another mistake?

Once again it was Wasmaggi who spoke the truth or at least what he perceived to be the truth. He had solved the mystery of the whites' whiteness when they had first appeared, and it was natural that the village turned to him to explain the baby's whiteness.

He had studied the matter, he announced solemnly, and there was but one explanation. The forest had liked the color, not that all babies would be white, witness Sarahguy's and Xingu's babies, but there was a place in the forest for white babies, although he thought

63

maybe only Widel and Anna would have white babies until the tribe became accustomed to them. To him, that seemed natural.

Since there was no other possible explanation, Wasmaggi's seemed natural to the Indians, too. There was no more talk about color among the hunters, even if some of the women expressed an interest in having a white baby. For a time, they asked Anna how she had accomplished it, but she replied only that it was the forest's doing.

The matter of color vanished as time went on. As the child grew, she was tanned by the sun, and while she never would be as brown as the Indians, like her parents she darkened sufficiently so as not to stand out as someone dramatically different.

By Masaki tradition, naming the baby was delayed, anticipating that something unique about the child or some event or other inspiration would help determine a suitable name. No event occurred, but Anna did have an inspiration.

She spoke of it to Widel. "Do you know the name of the first baby born when the Pilgrims landed in the new world?"

She didn't wait for a reply. "Well, her name - catch this - was Peregrine White. Think of that for a minute. White. A color of mystery to the Masaki. So, what was the name of the first white baby born to the Masaki?"

"Not Peregrine, for heaven's sake."

"You don't like the idea, the perfect symbolism?"

"Well, I believe your Miss White was born on the *Mayflower*."

"A mere technicality."

"And Peregrine? Do you know what the word means? Peregrinate: to wander from place to place, maybe from one foreign land to another. The Whites in 1620 must have turned the verb into a noun."

"Or they named the child after the falcon."

"Okay. That's a possibility, too."

"But I like the first explanation better."

"Okay. I'll tell you what. Let's compromise. Name the baby Peregrine, but let me call her Penny. I kind of like that name. Has a nice ring to it. Penny Ranford."

It was settled quickly. Widel had added to Anna's concept of the name. Peregrine at once established both a tie with her former homeland and spoke to her and Widel's journey to the Masakis. The name was perfect, and if they shortened it to Penny, why, that was all right, too.

Again that day, Widel sensed the Masakis' telepathic powers. From the time in midday when he and Anna had chosen the baby's name, not only had they not told a solitary person, but Widel had not left the hammock from which he viewed the village. He had held Penny while Anna cooked their simple evening meal. Never did he observe other than normal activities. He even remarked to Anna how quiet and peaceful the forest and the village were. If anything, there seemed to be fewer forest noises and less than the normal murmur from the dozen or more cook fire conversations.

Yet, when the darkness became complete, the meals finished, the personal needs of the Masakis met, the villagers gathered around the community fire, waiting, it seemed to Widel, with eager anticipation. He asked Anna what was going to happen; she did not know. Together, with Penny sucking noisily on Anna's breast, they stepped toward the fire and sat down behind Joshway and Sarahguy. As far as they could tell, every man, woman and child was in attendance.

"What's going on?" Widel whispered to Joshway.

"Not know," Joshway whispered back.

"Did someone ask for this fire?" Anna asked.

Sarahguy turned. "Not know; just come. Have to come to fire but not know why."

"No one says anything; everyone looks equally mystified; they all show up. I tell you, Anna, they have a level of communication that science says doesn't exist."

"Perhaps they're here just the way we are. A crowd gathers, and onlookers gather."

Then, somewhere beyond the furthermost reaches of the feeble fire light, somewhere in the dark recesses of the forest beyond the village was heard the unmistakable beat of a drum, unmistakable, that is, to Anna and Widel.

Except for Tonto and Lucknew and Pollyque, it was a brand new sound. To them, it uncovered long forgotten fears. They stood, shaken and terrified, so frightened they were voiceless. Tonto opened his mouth to speak or to shout, and nothing came out. He gestured wildly. At best, Lucknew and Pollyque managed the most pitiful squeaks.

For a moment there was pandemonium, mostly questions without answers, and confusion as hunters raced to gather their weapons. If Tonto, Pollyque and Lucknew did nothing else, they stirred the village to frantic action.

In less time than it took the three old people to express their fear, the Masaki hunters had secured their weapons, had taken strategic positions throughout the village, and were ready to defend family and village from an unseen enemy. Women scooped up their children and with them hid in the shadows, not, as Widel noticed, in their houses. An attack, he realized, would have been directed at the houses. They would have been death traps. The Masakis knew this. But attack from whom?

Widel backed Anna and Penny away from the light. When he had hidden them, he walked back to the fire, having delayed only long enough to pick up his favorite weapon, a very short bow and a bundle of arrows.

The bowstring on this particular bow was fashioned from woven jaguar gut. It could be fitted with an arrow quicker than any other bow. Widel already had an arrow half drawn. His right hand rested against his hip; his left hand held the bow a couple of feet in front. He had taught himself to shoot from the hip with amazing accuracy, and even without fully drawing the bow, he knew that at thirty yards his arrow would completely penetrate a man.

The drum sounded again, close enough for Widel to know its direction. He turned slowly toward the sound, moving slightly to his left. He did not want the fire at his back. He never would be able to say why he was doing this, but he could say in all truthfulness that he was not afraid. He knew that whoever came out of the

66

darkness, one man or many, would be killed, if not by him then by the hunters.

He waited. He might not be a first class hunter, but he was the first line of defense, a fighting machine defending his family, his home, his people.

In all the years in the jungle, he had stood guard. For months he had guarded his women against jaguar attacks which never came, against anacondas he never saw, against alligators which he fought but once, against piranhas which never appeared, against men who had appeared. He had stood guard, as faithful to his duty as was humanly possible. And he stood guard now, ready to fight and to die.

Noises came from the undergrowth just beyond the circle of Masaki houses and beyond the light. Widel wanted to let loose an arrow but feared that it would be wasted. He needed something for a target.

Once more the drum sounded, so closely that Widel jumped. He heard a twig snap to his left. He didn't move his feet or hips or shoulders, but in an almost imperceptible movement, he slid his left hand more to the left and at the same time let the bowstring slide off the first two fingers of his right hand. He didn't wait to hear if he had hit anything. Even before the first arrow struck, he had fitted another to the bowstring, and before he heard his name shouted, he had let fly the second arrow.

"Ran-ford! No!"

A third arrow was on his bowstring before he recognized the voice. It was Wasmaggi, now shouting as if his life depended on making as much noise as possible.

"Ran-ford! Ran-ford! I Wasmaggi!"

Wasmaggi tumbled into the firelight. In front of him he carried a log almost a foot and a half in diameter and about four feet long. In the dim light, one could see two arrows impaled in the log, either of which would have killed Wasmaggi had he not been holding the log as a shield. Widel was awash in a cold sweat.

The entire village achieved a kind of controlled panic. Its beloved medicine man had come close to death; he held an object only Tonto and his wives had ever seen or heard, and the sound of that object had sent them into immediate frenzy.

Every hunter admired Widel for his solitary stand by the fire; each admired Widel's ability to shoot his arrows with such speed and accuracy; each was incapable of expressing his distress at the nearly perfect killing of Wasmaggi; each admitted being ready to kill with his weapon.

Only gradually did the panic give way to mere confusion. No one seemed to know what to say or to do, and so everyone tried to talk at once. For some reason, the situation seemed to call for a lot of nervous jumping.

In the midst of the disorder, Anna shouted above the noise. "Wasmaggi, what the hell do you think you are doing?" She didn't wait for an answer, although the rest of the village did. She turned to Widel. "Do you know you almost killed Wasmaggi?" she yelled. And then in turn she berated each man, first Wasmaggi, then Widel, then back to Wasmaggi. When finally she exhausted herself, she looked at each man. "Well?" she asked.

After a prolonged silence, Widel began, "Anna, I didn't...."

"Goddamn it, didn't you ever hear about the whites of their eyes? Jesus, Widel, you almost killed Wasmaggi!"

Widel opened his mouth, but nothing would come out. He accepted Anna's tirade and blame for what it was, uncontrollable relief that no damage had been done.

But Anna wasn't finished. She glared at Wasmaggi. "How dare you?" she began. "How dare you threaten this village with such a stupid stunt? Of all the asshole things, Wasmaggi. You deserve...." Anna dissolved into tears and slumped to the ground, completely overcome.

Within seconds, the women kneeled beside her in a demonstration of solidarity, and as the women cried out their relief, the men quietly shuffled their feet in the dust.

Whatever Wasmaggi had intended to do or to show was lost in the commotion. When Anna stood up at last, she looked at Wasmaggi and shook her head.

"You dear, precious, old fool," she said softly as she walked toward him. "Oh, Wasmaggi," she cried, throwing her arms around him and burying her face against his neck.

"An-na...."

"Not tonight. Time enough tomorrow to explain." Anna turned to Widel. "Take me home," and more softly, "and hold me. I'm so scared."

Only the very young were able to sleep that night. As Anna and Widel looked at the other houses, all the adults were outdoors beside their small cooking fires. Throughout the night one could hear the subtle din of conversation as family after family tried to make sense of what had happened. Wasmaggi rested by the village fire, his head propped up on the log he had dragged from the forest darkness. He had broken off the two arrows and held the feathered ends in his hands.

Tonto's entire family had gathered around his fire. Not only were his daughters and sons-in-law there, Tilla and Moremew, Janus and Soomar, but the grandchildren and great grandchildren. Anna remarked that that one family represented a third of the village.

"What happened, Anna?"

"Honestly, I don't know."

"God, I could have killed him. I'm still shaking."

"I'm so afraid, Widel. I can't explain it: I have an awful fear that something terrible is going to happen, to us, to the Masakis, to the whole world."

Anna reached for Widel's hand and clutched it tightly. For a long time they sat beside their fire without speaking.

SIX

Under the rain forest canopy darkness comes quickly; the morning light seems to come much more slowly. The darkness gives away to a period of almost light in which objects are seen in a magical setting. Perhaps it is the forest mist that creates this period. There is evidence of light, but it seems reluctant to struggle to its fullness.

This is a period of great activity. The creatures most active in the dark hurry to reach their daytime hiding and resting places as the daytime creatures start their hours of business. Bird and monkey noises begin to overwhelm the insect noises.

For a brief time between full dark and full light there is no noise at all. The length of that noiseless time varies considerably; sometimes it is but a few seconds and at other times it may last fifteen or twenty minutes. However long the period of silence, it is a time of astonishing beauty, when all the senses become visual. If the mist is not too heavy and is slow leaving the forest floor, everything appears to be wrapped in gossamer, and if the mist lingers, one can watch certain flowers open, their blossoms greeting the light in slow motion.

Even the Indians who have witnessed such times for thousands of years are captured by the beauty, and they will stand and stare as if seeing it for the first time.

Then, suddenly, the spell is broken. A macaw or a howler monkey will shout at the new day, and as if on signal, the mist will evaporate. Women will add twigs to their fires, children will play, hunters will enter the forest. It's a new day, a day as old as Masaki time. It's a day to live, a day to survive.

Only today is not like other days. Today is a day of unsolved mysteries. With the sound of the first screeching macaw, Tonto, followed by his wives, and behind them the rest of the family, strode toward the supine Wasmaggi. Tonto carried his spear.

In all likelihood, Wasmaggi heard Tonto's approach, but he did not move. His eyes remain closed. Savagely, Tonto thrust his spear into the ground beside Wasmaggi's head. Wasmaggi did not move even then; he opened his eyes and looked directly at Tonto, but he did not move.

Tonto glared at the former medicine man. "Once," he said roughly, "we agree never make sounds of drum. Why does Wasmaggi make now the sounds of killing? Does Wasmaggi bring death to the Masaki?"

"Is time, Tonto. Time to be Masaki."

"Never time, old man. Last time of drum many die. Promise never hear drum again."

"But drum also for life. Time Masaki live."

"Drum brought death."

Tonto and Wasmaggi began to argue, drawing the predictable crowd. In front of the people, the two men revealed bits and pieces of Masaki history, all new and unknown to everyone except Lucknew and Pollyque. Only they and Tonto and Wasmaggi were old enough to remember.

The argument was hard to follow, but out of it came a compelling and dramatic story.

Sometime before the time of the jaguar hunters, when Wasmaggi, Tonto, Pollyque, and Lucknew were young and before any living others of the village were born, the tribe was attacked. Wasmaggi was a hunter, not the medicine man; Tonto had just concluded his boyhood test, having been alone in the forest for three days during which he had fended for himself; Lucknew and Pollyque were still children. That meant that Tonto was ten or twelve years old and the two girls who became his wives were seven or nine. It was hard to figure out.

That Tonto had just been accepted and initiated as a hunter was clear enough because he was allowed to participate in an important event: the gathering of all the Masaki hunters from each of the five villages. It was the last time such a gathering took place.

The meeting took place almost a month's walk from the present village. The number of Masakis, said Tonto, equaled the number of birds; the campsite was several times larger than the village, many times larger he indicated with a sweep of his arms.

One day all the hunters gathered to hear from the five medicine men; the women gathered a short distance away. Each group had its own fires and feasts. Each group exchanged gossip, told stories and sang songs. For the hunters there was the business of redefining hunting boundaries. The medicine men exchanged knowledge and experiences. Single men sought potential wives from other villages. Articles were traded. Newborn children were shown off. New hunters were honored. New marriages were celebrated.

In mid afternoon the drums sounded. *Boom. Boom.* Men fell, their blood flowing into the ground. Bellies were opened, heads were burst, arms and legs were torn from their bodies. *Boom. Boom.* Women screamed, babies cried. *Boom. Boom.* The drums beat over and over, louder and louder. *Boom. Boom. Boom.*

Creatures appeared. At first they looked like men, but they had no toes, no private parts, no belly buttons. *Boom. Boom.* The creatures tore through the hunters and attacked the women. Old women were killed by the long drums, and babies and small children. The young boys were killed. The creatures dragged the girls and the young women into the forest, Pollyque and Lucknew among them. All afternoon the drums sounded.

So many killed, so many wounded, so many many creatures who looked like men sometimes.

Not all hunters were killed or badly wounded, but the toll was high. Of all the hunters from this village, only a handful survived, among them Wasmaggi and Tonto. And Tomaz, although Tomaz was not yet of this village. He came to work with this village's hunters, and it was Tomaz who galvanized the hunters to action.

It took no great effort to determine the creatures' route. Even if they had the skill to cover their trail, the women they abducted left many signs. Tomaz divided his force in half. One half followed the creatures, doing what it could to kill them or to recapture the females. Wasmaggi was in that group. The other half, with Tomaz in the lead, raced through the forest in an attempt to cut off the creatures' escape route. From time to time, Tomaz dispatched an individual hunter to watch the creatures and, if possible, to harass the enemy. Tonto had been one such solitary warrior.

When night came, Tomaz and his hunters were in position. He had fewer than a dozen men, having sent eight or nine on their separate missions.

Behind the creatures were twenty hunters led by a fierce hunter, Markway, Sampson's grandfather. When his hunters joined Wasmaggi and the others who followed the creatures, Markway sent several hunters forward to reinforce Tomaz. The creatures were surrounded.

Nothing would be done until the faintest light of dawn shown above the canopy, but in the darkness each hunter moved silently toward the creatures' campfires.

There were two fires, both many time larger than anything the Masakis would have built. The two fires threw much light, which was probably why they were so large. The creatures stayed between the fires and within a protective ring of girls and young women all bound together. Any attempt to attack the creatures first had to go through the ring of females. It was obvious that a frontal attack would mean the death of the thirty-two women captured.

Tonto had not been in touch with either Tomaz or Markway. He had a sense of what would happen; if he acted, it would be on his own initiative. As he told the story, he admitted his doubts. From his vantage point, he studied the fires, the women, the creatures, and when one of the creatures walked toward him, he was beside himself with fear.

In the semi-darkness, he watched the creature reach into his skin and pull out his penis. When water flowed, Tonto's spear went completely through the creature's neck. The only sound was a dull thump as the creature fell to the ground. From the rings of firelight, other creatures shouted.

With extreme care, Tonto removed his spear and backed into the forest. He heard several loud drum beats, but nothing happened. He waved quietly at bothersome mosquitos.

Several creatures stretched out by the fires. Tonto supposed that all creatures had to sleep. When the first light of day came, however, he was surprised that some of the sleeping creatures did not wake up, even when other creatures kicked them. He would learn later that one of the hunters had carried a blow gun and had used all of his darts on the sleeping forms. They were dead.

With full daylight, the creatures did not behave as had been predicted. It had been assumed they would continue their escape, but they did not try to leave the spot. No Masaki hunter wanted to expose himself. The drum beats meant injury and death. The Indians squatted in the undergrowth and waited.

At mid-day a woman was untied from the rest. One of the creatures pointed to the forest and pushed the woman from the circle. At first, she was uncertain about what to do. She took a few faltering steps, then began to run. Before she had taken more than three or four running steps, drums sounded and the woman fell, her back ripped open. Blood covered her and the ground around her.

The object lesson was not lost on the Masakis. Each of the women would be killed one by one if the Masakis did not withdraw and allow the creatures to escape. As if to punctuate the lesson, drum after drum sounded. Two hunters looked at themselves in total bewilderment. One felt a burn of fire on his hand. When he lifted his hand to see what had caused the pain, he found his middle finger had been taken away. The other felt a burning in his thigh; he had two holes not more than inches apart.

Markway left his group and found Tomaz. The tribe could afford no more losses, either hunters or women, nor could the tribe give up most of its childbearing women. Moreover, some of the women belonged to the hunters surrounding them. If the united tribe did not act soon, there was no telling what individual hunters might do.

Tomaz and Markway devised a plan. They would attack. The signal for the daylight attack would come from the creatures. If the creatures set another woman free, when the creatures pushed the woman forward, all hunters on the side of the fires away from the women would attack. When the creatures turned to meet the attack, the rest of the tribe would attack.

If no woman was released, then the signal would be, Markway said, pointing to a tree's shadow, when that shadow reached, and he pointed again, another tree. It was agreed.

Markway would find and inform the hunters on one side of the creatures' circle if Tomaz would do the same on his side. They would meet again with Markway's group to confirm the plan.

Tonto and Wasmaggi, of course, learned many of the details after the fact. They only were told what to do and when to do it.

Neither Wasmaggi nor Tonto could say much about what followed. Each had his eyes on the shadow creeping toward its appointed mark. As the shadow touched the target tree, the hunters swooped out of the forest. The women flattened themselves on the ground, both to be out of the way and to let the hunters leap over them. Drum noises could be heard repeatedly over the grunts and shouts of hunters and creatures. Now and then a scream sounded over the other noises.

Then it was silent. Even the birds and monkeys had moved to safer havens. Most of the creatures were dead, and those which weren't were killed quickly. Three hunters had been killed; six had been badly wounded, among them Markway. Not one of the women had been hurt.

The uninjured hunters untied the women, picked up the dead Masakis, and helped the wounded. They touched neither the creatures nor anything associated with them. They and their belongings were left to the forest.

When the hunters arrived back at their meeting place, they discovered just how much destruction of life the creatures had caused. One half of the entire tribe had been killed; several of the wounded would die during the next few weeks, including Markway.

The medicine men worked frantically on the wounded. There were no village designations; each man worked on whoever most needed his attention. Their supplies of roots and herbs and barks, their liquids and powders, their tools were used up long before the wounds were treated. The untreated had to take their chances.

The dead were placed in long rows, each row representing a village. Five medicine men gathered to make sense of the tragedy, to plan for the immediate future and to plan for the life of the tribe.

First, they drew lines on the ground, five lines representing the five different directions to the separate villages. Along those lines, the people would dispose of their dead. As hunters, Tonto and Wasmaggi had to help in that awful task. Their village gave back five hunters, seven women, and eight children and babies. They counted themselves lucky. Other villages returned more to the forest.

The medicine men came to a number of conclusive decisions. Never again would the tribe meet together in one place. Villages would be moved so as to put more distance between them. Drums would never be heard again, a symbolic honor accorded to the more than one hundred Masakis killed. This dishonorable disaster would never be spoken of again, nor would the existence of the creatures be acknowledged. Ever. Only from this time forward would the Masaki have a history.

And there were lesser details upon which the medicine men agreed. So great was the disaster and so real the possibility that one or all of the medicine men could have been killed, each medicine man immediately would select an apprentice. Thus it was that Wasmaggi became an apprentice and later the medicine man. And because hunters were more valuable than ever, there might be medicine women, reviving an older practice or tradition in which women had fulfilled that role.

Men and women were encouraged to find new mates before the tribe went its five separate ways. The medicine men knew that to do so now would only add to the agony, but above all, family and tribe were vital.

There were hunters without wives, women without husbands, and children without parents. It was only a suggestion, the medicine men could not force anything on any one, but this was the last opportunity for choosing.

There were a few arrangements made, very few. It was not time. Wasmaggi took a young girl, but that had been settled before the creatures arrived.

One more thing, the medicine men said, there would be no more no-baby medicine. The tribe now must hope for children, hope to replenish itself. In that spirit and because children were universally adored and desired, the orphans of the wholesale slaughter were adopted quickly. None went to Wasmaggi's village but not from a lack of being wanted.

When Tonto and Wasmaggi completed their astounding story, the Masakis were speechless, stunned by the revelation of wanton destruction, unable to voice horror or even comprehension of such an act. The existence of creatures who killed was beyond imagination. That such creatures roamed the forest was unbelievable.

"Guns," Widel said. "The drums they thought they heard were guns."

"And what they thought were creatures were the infamous *tropas de resgates.*"

"Translation?"

"Slave hunters."

"Whore hunters, I think. Do you have a phrase for that?"

"No, but of course you're right." Anna paused for a moment, then asked, "Do you think they called them creatures because they didn't want to acknowledge the possibility of other people?"

"I think the creatures wore shoes or boots, hence no toes, and clothing, interpreted as skin. As Tonto said, one of them reached into his skin. The Masaki have never seen clothing, and everything must have happened so fast or in such utter confusion that no one took time or had time to examine the creatures."

"None ever came back?"

"Apparently not. It must have been a private, what's the word?"

"*Bandeir*, if you mean expedition."

"Yeah. So no one ever came looking for the men."

"How long ago?"

"Thirty, forty years. Tonto was only eleven or so; now he's a great grandfather. Given they start families when they are young, it has to have been forty years ago."

Tonto and Wasmaggi were still arguing. They had agreed on most points in the retelling of the story. The one point of disagreement was the drums.

"Tonto's mother and father killed that day. Does Wasmaggi forget?"

"Wasmaggi not forget. Does Tonto remember that Wasmaggi gave his mother and father back to the forest - and his brother and sister?"

"Tonto remember."

"But Wasmaggi not think. Remember but not think about Tonto and Pollyque and Lucknew. Forget to remember. Women and Tonto relive bad time; much afraid. Over years put bad time away but never forget. Drum make memory come again. Drums not silent to honor dead; drums silent because they sound of killing. Sound, almost, of end of Masakis."

"You think Wasmaggi remember wrong?"

"Wasmaggi remember wrong. Drums speak death, so no drums. Even wives say that."

"But women not...."

"Not know? Lucknew and Pollyque were taken by creatures. How they forget?"

Wasmaggi reflected on Tonto's words. "It is as Tonto remembers."

"Then destroy drum."

"No. It is time. Hagga gone. She once captive, too. Tomaz gone. Only Wasmaggi left from then, and you and wives. Only Tonto and wives and Wasmaggi left. Time now give Masaki back life."

The entire village had listened and watched in rapt silence. It had heard a story it had never heard, not even in its wildest nightmares.

Soomar asked the question on everyone's mind. "How many other stories you not tell?"

Wasmaggi looked at Tonto. "Is time for Masakis to become Masaki."

Tonto shook his head no, but he said yes. He looked at his wives. They nodded agreement. It was time.

Anna pulled Widel from the crowd. She was shaking from head to toe, and at first Widel thought she was ill. But as he studied her, he could see that she was sick with fear. She had a hard time holding Penny, and Widel took the child from her arms. Reaching their home, Anna did not stop to sit by the cooking fire; she headed directly for their sleeping platform.

"Widel," she murmured, her voice quaking.

"What is it, Anna? What's wrong?"

"Widel? Can't you feel it? Don't you see it?"

He didn't know whether to say yes or no, not sure what it was that Anna feared. During the past hour, listening to Tonto and Wasmaggi, he had accumulated his own fears and doubts. But he worried about voicing them because just asking the questions meant a completely new way of looking at their lives, and the doubts which filled him were, at the moment at least, threatening his entire existence. Perhaps Anna was in distress for the same reasons, but if it was for some other reason, he didn't want to add to her obvious burden.

"Oh, Jesus, Widel. Do you know what's running through my mind?" She reached out and buried her face in his chest.

He could feel her shaking. He took the leap. "The creatures?" he asked.

"Other men, with guns. Widel, if they found the Masaki once, they could find us again!"

"I know. Maybe we aren't so far from civilization as we thought."

"That's a damn funny word to use."

"You know what I mean. Nearer to other people."

"At first the story distressed me, all the killing, the taking of half the tribe, people like these. Then I realized I was more distressed by the reality that we were within reach of others. If they could come to the Masaki, we could go to them."

Anna took a deep breath. "Widel, I don't want to go to them. If the creatures had been a flock of angels, I wouldn't want to go to them. This is my world; this is all the world I want, ever."

"And it is, Anna, and it will be."

"No! No. You don't see, do you? There are two worlds, this one and the other one. And the other one wants to kill this one."

Anna was inconsolable. The only difference between Anna and me, Widel muttered to himself, is that she lets it out. "It was a long time ago," he said out loud.

"It will happen again, Widel. I can see it, just as plain and real as I see you. We must make plans, Widel."

"Yes, Anna, we will make plans."

"This is our home. We must protect it."

Sometime during the day it was decided, again Widel wondered by whom, that there would be a waiting period before Wasmaggi and Tonto told more stories from the days of the drums and before that.

Widel supposed the two old men had decided that, but no one remembered hearing either suggest as much. Nevertheless, three days were to be devoted to an intensive hunt for meat by the hunters and a concentrated harvest of the gardens by the women and children. And although it was not a favorable time of year, there would be an intensive fishing party.

How many times before, thought Widel, had these people whose entire organizational system seemed to be one of pure anarchy, been organized, commanded and led and always without an apparent word of direction by anyone. One moment the Masakis looked totally vague about any kind of action, seemed without ability to grasp even the slightest concept of a problem, and the next moment, without hint or suggestion of any kind, they had defined the situation, organized the solution, divided the numerous tasks, and were hard at work.

Widel stood aside to watch what he had come to believe was a mystical process. Hunters gathered their weapons and by twos and threes entered the forest. Other hunters prepared the fishing nets and the scooping hoops. How did a hunter know if he was to hunt or to fish?

80

Some women went into the tiny gardens while others prepared the woven racks on which to smoke the fish and the meat and others stretched out the fishing nets that needed repair. Who told which woman to do which task?

Who told him to prepare arrows, to makee new darts, to sharpen spears? No one, yet that's what he was doing, working frantically. And why? Not because he was told to but because he knew that his weapon making skills were needed, not tomorrow or next week but now.

And who told the children what to do? Who told Oneson to race back to the village with the first macaw feathers so Widel would have fresh feathers for the arrows? Who told Armot to cut fresh, straight branches from the ironwood tree? Or Blue to harvest oak resin?

Yet is was all happening as though it had been rehearsed and rehearsed again, just like the defense of the village from Sampson's attack, just like his and Anna's rescue from the flood, just like the unified attack of the Masakis upon the creatures.

During the three days neither Wasmaggi nor Tonto left the village. They had a hundred small tasks to complete, often together, and they talked at length.

Since only on a hunt or under the most extraordinary circumstances did anyone eat at another's cook fire, each house was abuzz with speculation. There was more talk in one evening hour, Widel told Anna, than during an entire year.

One night, Anna and Widel invited Wasmaggi to eat with them.

"Cannot," Wasmaggi said, declining the invitation. "Know you will ask questions Wasmaggi cannot answer."

"No questions," Anna promised.

"Cannot. Everybody want Wasmaggi tell before time to tell."

"Then," Widel asked, "will Wasmaggi answer one question that's not about the time before the creatures?"

"Ran-ford ask. Wasmaggi will decide if answer."

"Months ago, just before the flood, before Anna and I became a family, before our baby was born, you were prepared to take the

Masaki on a walk to a special, secret camping place. We prepared for that walk, just as we have prepared now. We never made that walk, never went to the special place. Why?"

"Because as you say, the flood, then Spiker ill, then you become family, then An-na pregnant, then child born. Spiker get well but not An-na and Ran-ford. They need help. Cannot help on trail. Then, joy, An-na grow fat. Cannot risk medicine women. Then baby come. Happiness covers Wasmaggi's eyes. I not see what must be done because happy, but always know must find place of secret hiding."

"But we haven't."

"Will. Soon. Very soon. Now say no more."

By the afternoon of the third strenuous day, meat and fish smoked over the fires, roots hung from a hundred branches, fishnets were stored, broken arrows were stripped of their feathers, spears were sharpened and hardened over the fire, darts were dipped and placed in fresh containers, kapok was carded, fresh medicines were compounded, scores of minor, irritating wounds were treated; the village was ready.

For what?

Long before the final rays of sunlight left the village on the third day, the Masakis surrounded the village fire. The circle had been left open. Into that opening marched Wasmaggi and Tonto and the two old women, Pollyque and Lucknew.

Wasmaggi was carrying his log drum; Tonto, Lucknew and Pollyque each carried two or three small packages wrapped in banana leaves.

Wasmaggi placed his log before the fire and squatted behind it. He turned the log end for end, and one could see that it had been hollowed out. Such work must have taken weeks of intense effort. At best, Wasmaggi had only bone knives with which to work.

When he was satisfied that everyone had seen the hollowness, he rolled the log over, revealing a split about a third of the way along the log.

There was no verbal explanation; Wasmaggi only gestured and pointed. He took two sticks and beat on the log. *Boom. Boom.* The noise that had so upset Tonto and his wives sounded again. Today Tonto did not appear afraid, nor did Lucknew and Pollyque.

Boom. Wasmaggi beat on the log again. Both he and Tonto shook their heads. Carefully, so everyone could watch, the two men began to extend the split. Every inch or so, Wasmaggi struck the log. Ever so slightly, the pitch was changing, growing more resonate.

At last, Wasmaggi spoke. "This is as we remember it."

Tonto and Pollyque and Lucknew nodded in agreement.

Anna whispered to Widel. "A split log drum. Very ancient."

"Drum not heard since time of creatures," said Tonto. "Once drum important. Masaki people of music. Still sing songs, but no drum. Wasmaggi convince Tonto time for drum again."

"Time use drum now, for naming of babies." Wasmaggi struck the drum four times.

During the years since the three whites arrived, only three babies had been born in the village, Joqua and Xingu's second child, a daughter, Joshway and Sarahguy's only child after years of miscarriage, a daughter, and Widel and Anna's daughter.

Threesome and Twoman, the sons of Desuit and Yanna had been born in Sampson's village. While the women had given them names, with Walkin's approval, of course, they had not been named by the tribe.

For that matter, neither had Barkah or Blue, Armot or Oneson or anyone else in the village. As Wasmaggi explained it, only he, Tonto, Lucknew, and Pollyque had been named formally in the ancient manner of the tribe.

The situation demanded a hunters' conference then and there. Except for Tonto, no one had the slightest idea what Wasmaggi was suggesting, but when Hakma said that he didn't want to be treated as a baby, the hunters agreed that whatever it was Wasmaggi was proposing be confined to the three babies, Love, Coanna and Penny.

Typically, the mothers and other women were not consulted. It wouldn't have matter anyway. Even if the all the mothers of small children had joined forces, they wouldn't have been heard, much less listened to. The decision was made, and it was final.

83

The naming of each child was simple and touching. Wasmaggi had spent a brief portion of each of the past three days instructing Anna in the medicine woman's role in the ceremony, but since her baby was to be named, Anna deferred her part to Wasmaggi.

Not that Anna had a choice. Wasmaggi obviously was going to use the naming ceremony for purposes which went far beyond.

"Not since before the creatures," he began, "have Masaki named baby."

Joqua and Xingu stood before the old medicine man. Their child was the oldest and would be named first. Wasmaggi took the little girl in his hands and held her up before the villagers. "What name?" he asked.

Names were not chosen lightly or on the spur of the moment. Some children were not named for years, their parents waiting for inspiration. But whatever the name chosen, the parents had to explain it and its significance.

Joqua and Xingu had chosen the name *Coanna*, they said, because Connie and Anna had saved their son, Armot, from drowning. They wanted the Masaki to remember forever, and they wanted to remember forever.

There was approval. Wasmaggi held the child and hugged her. "Hello, Coanna," he said. "I am Wasmaggi, and I will know you forever."

He passed the child to Tonto. "Hello, Coanna. I am Tonto. I will protect you as long as I live."

Coanna was passed from hand to hand. Each member of the tribe, even the children, greeted her with "Hello, Coanna, I am...," and each made a commitment to the child's life. The commitments were not given lightly; they were sincere pledges of solidarity and would be honored even unto death.

Joshway and Sarahguy were next. When it came time to explain their daughter's name, Sarahguy spoke. She told of the difficulties of bearing a child, of her many miscarriages, of losing hope. She told of Anna's support and medicines before the baby was born and of the care both she and the baby had received from Anna after the birth. She wanted to name the baby Anna because of her love for the medicine woman. But never had a Masaki taken the name of another. She quickly noted that Joqua and Xingu's name choice was not the name of another but a new name.

She rehearsed all of the names she and Joshway had tried, names to express their thanks for the child, names to honor the village, names reflecting years of disappointment. For one reason or another, the names fell short of their happiness and pride. But in every event leading to the birth of their daughter, one word kept appearing. Until the whites came, it was not spoken as much as it should have been. The word, she said, and the name of their daughter was *Love.*

"Hello, Love. I am Wasmaggi, and I will love you forever."

"Hello, Love. I am Tonto, and...."

When Widel and Anna stood before Wasmaggi, Wasmaggi was crying. "They are old man's tears of happiness," he explained. And then hurriedly, "What have you named the baby?"

Widel spoke for the parents. "We have named the girl *Peregrine*, although we call her *Penny*."

The name, of course, meant absolutely nothing and met with no response whatsoever. Widel had to improvise. "It is a word we made ourselves. It means that the forest made us white; it means that we wandered a long time looking for our home; it means that we found our home and our loved ones here with you; it means that the forest gave you to us."

This the Masakis could understand. "Hello, Pere...."

"Penny."

"Hello, Penny. I am Wasmaggi. I loved you before the forest gave you and will love you until the forest takes me back."

"Hello, Penny...."

If ever there was a seal on Widel and Anna's place in the tribe, it was this moment. Not that they needed another sign, but if it was possible, they felt an even stronger bond to the village.

When the passing around of Penny was finished, each child was given a gift by Tonto's wives.

And as the oldest women in the village, they performed the final act, the bonding of the oldest to the youngest. No one had witnessed this before. It was known only to Wasmaggi, Tonto, Pollyque, and Lucknew. It was from a time before the time of the creatures. It was from a time when the drums represented the heartbeat of Masaki life, before the drums represented the last heartbeat of so many lives. It was from a time when the drums sang the rhythms of Masaki life.

The two old women moved back from the fire. All traces of sunlight had disappeared and the dancing flames of the fire added drama and mystery to the proceedings.

The women drew a large, heavy circle in the dirt. They needed one more woman and selected Magwa, Wasmaggi's daughter. She would hold Penny. Lucknew held Coanna; Pollyque held Love.

Wasmaggi beat on the split log drum, two quick staccato beats, a rest, another beat, a rest, and a final beat. Ever the musician, Anna listened with intense interest to the 4/4 meter of the rhythmic measures. She noted the first beat as a short eighth note upbeat leading into the meter.

The women moved around the circle, slowly at first. It took Magwa two or three measures to catch on. Two quick steps, stop, lift the baby, stop, lower the baby. Two quick steps, stop, lift the baby, stop, lower the baby. Over and over, faster and faster, the three women raced around the circle, and as they raced, their two quick steps were made to turn them so that they moved in tiny circles around the larger circle.

The villagers began to clap in unison with the drum, faster and faster. And when it seemed that the women could go no faster, when it seemed that they would become dizzy and fall, the drum stopped.

The women put the children on the ground on the path they had beaten into the dirt and went to their places in the circle opposite the babies. The drum beats began again, slowly and softly, and the women moved with the beats toward the babies.

"How absolutely perfect the symbolism," Anna exclaimed. "The circle, unity. The women crossing the circle to embrace the children, bonding age with youth."

As the drum continued its rhythm, the women, still in step, still raising and lowering the infants, presented each baby to its father.

86

Magwa returned to her place; she was not needed now.

The two old women, great grandmothers, long beyond their childbearing years, danced alone in the circle. Now the movements were different. Two quick steps in place, a rigorous thrusting forward of the pelvis, and its withdrawal. Two more steps, a thrust, a return, faster and faster. And still in harmony with the drum, the old women reached out a hand to the mothers, drawing the mothers into the circle and to the dance.

This was no celebration of child naming; this was erotic dancing; this was child creating dancing, and as the old women and the mothers danced around the circle, the old women reached out to other women and drew them into the circle, ever expanding the circle until all women, even the young, immature girls, were moving in frenzied motions.

Tonto joined Wasmaggi at the drum, beating a countermeasure of sometimes conflicting, sometimes unified beats. In the dancing there was no uniformity. The beats remained, but the beats were reflected in numerous, individual ways. The beats became intoxicating. Some women held and pulled on their breasts, others stroked themselves, all in rhythm to the beats, all oblivious to the men who stood mesmerized, their own arousal showing and some keeping time with the drum.

Then, without warning, the drum stopped. Pollyque and Lucknew sat where they were and signaled the women to sit.

Off on another side of the fire, Tonto drew a circle. The beat began again. Two eighth notes, a rest, a quick double beat, a rest, a beat. Tonto pantomimed the throwing of the spear: two quick steps, rear back, throw.

He mimicked the shooting of the arrow: load, raise, pull, let fly. All to the beat. He duplicated the hunter's action with the blow gun: load, sight, draw a breath, blow. Over and over the old man worked the three hunters' actions into a well choreographed dance, and from time to time he drew other hunters into the circle.

Even Widel joined the circle, and as the circle of hunters moved faster and faster, he felt himself swept up in the hunt and in the killing. In spite of his attempt to resist the feelings, he sensed the killing. This was a war dance. Such an image would have been lost of the Masakis, but Widel felt a savage pleasure in the dance. He wondered if it was something he alone felt, something in his own nature that caused the feeling.

Just as suddenly as with the women, the drum beats ceased. Would Tonto begin a male's erotic dance? It did not happen. Tonto returned quickly to Wasmaggi's side.

Wasmaggi indicated that the fire was over for now. Tomorrow, he said, he would take the Masaki on a journey.

"Unbelievable," Widel said as Anna placed Penny in her sleeping hammock. "Utterly unbelievable."

"Wasn't it. Every day seems to unleash a revelation. And what about the drum. Did you feel anything?"

"God, Anna. Every man felt something. Didn't you see it?"

"I'm not sure. I didn't see anything in particular. What do you mean?"

"Oh, God, Anna, when the women were dancing, at the end it was so, so sexual. Christ, every man was aroused. You didn't see it?" Widel wondered about that. "What did you see? How did you feel?"

"At first? At first I thought the naming of the children was just beautiful. 'Hello, Penny. I am....' And then the promises, to love, to protect, to remember. Everything. And with such pride and caring. Always the children. I wanted to cry, I was so happy. And you know what I wished? I wished I had more children so they could be Masaki."

Widel grinned. "When you women were dancing, I figured the whole tribe would get a good start on a baby boom."

"When the mothers danced with Pollyque and Lucknew, I had only one feeling. No, now that I think about it, maybe I had a lot of feelings wrapped up in one. At first I was uncomfortable, shoving my...well, you know...out like that. But I wasn't alone, and pretty soon we were all doing it. I felt a totally uninhibited freedom. I was with all the women, but I was me, expressing me. I never really felt like that before. As the drum beat faster and faster, I felt as though I had gotten my whole body synchronized with my feelings. For the first time, I was connected. Everything was connected: my head, my legs, my breasts. I wasn't made up of parts; I was whole. Most of my life I was angry because I was top heavy, that that's what people saw of me. Look at them now. They're twice as big as ever. They're filled with milk and they sag, only tonight.... I can't describe it. I was whole and I was free...and, Widel, I was.... If the drum hadn't stopped...."

"If the drum hadn't stopped?"

"Let's leave it for a minute. Tell me when you were dancing, what did you feel?"

"Savage. That's the only word that comes to mind. I went through the motions of shooting the arrows, blowing the darts, throwing the spear and all I could think of was killing something. And I know that's not what I was supposed to feel. Probably, I was suppose to feel the hunter as provider of food, to feel the duty of protecting family and tribe, but I felt like going to war, like killing. Killing, raw, savage killing. Like there is something in me that has to kill, a beastly brutality I never knew existed."

Widel shook his head. "And you probably will worm it out of me sometime. I wanted to go on dancing; I wanted the men to do what the women had done, to arouse you as much as you aroused me."

"But you did. You want to know what I felt when the drum stopped? I wanted you right there, anywhere. And then when the men danced. You might think you were acting out hunting and protecting, but that's not what came through. What came through were a dozen ways for a man to make love to his woman. I could feel your hands, your mouth, your...."

Anna never finished her thought. She kissed Widel with wanton abandon, parted his lips with her tongue and drew him between her legs.

From the first day, Anna said, stories seemed to bind the villagers together, and the best of the stories were made into songs. Would the old people sing the old songs? Did the four old people remember the songs?

Whatever her fears, and her fears were very real and always near the surface, she shook as she prepared the morning meal, not out of fear now but out of anticipation. She sensed she was about to enter a realm where few had been, She was eager and apprehensive at the same time.

"I wanted a history for Penny," she told Widel. "Now, I wonder if what I want is really what we should have. What if...?" But she did not complete the question. "No, I will not anticipate or try to guess."

"We can't, Anna. We'll just let it flow, and we'll join all the others who are just as blind and ignorant as we are."

Widel was surprised at the number of people on the tiny beach. Usually when he and Anna took Penny to the beach for their morning baths, there were few families present. While everyone would take a morning bath, bathing was stretched out from sunrise to mid-morning.

Not today. Everyone was in a hurry to perform the usual chores and to get on with the business at hand.

A bath always is a semi-private affair for adults. For a people who paraded through life entirely naked, washing one's private parts is not done in public view. If two families happened to reach the beach at the same time, they go to opposite ends of the sandy beach and deliberately turn their backs. There are husbands and wives who would not wash in view of their mates. Widel always found that a wonderful contradiction. He and Anna were such a couple, or at least Anna was. She always washed in private, sometimes waiting for hours for the beach to become deserted. If several families appeared at the beach at the same time, some always withdrew until the others were finished.

Not today.

SEVEN

The beach was buzzing with questions and speculations. There were few displays of modesty. It was impossible to turn one's back on everyone when one was surrounded by people. Even if a bather did find a private corner of the beach and a momentary measure of solitude, neither lasted long.

It was the custom to keep one's eyes focused on the sand or the water if others were present during the morning baths. Today, that custom was honored only in the mind. One would never think of speaking to another bather, but today people not only spoke but examined each face for a clue as to what others were thinking.

Women often bathed together, and at such times there was a lot of talk and giggling. So, too, when men bathed together. Community bathing had an entirely different set of rules, only now there were no rules and no observable conventions.

No wonder it did not matter. Whatever one saw was of no importance. The only sense that was operative was that of hearing. Tonto and Wasmaggi had promised a full day; each person waited for the signal calling the village together.

When the sound of the split log drum was heard, there was a universal shudder. With all the excited anticipation, one would have assumed a mad dash from the beach to the village fire or a wild bursting forth from Masakis houses to the fire. Instead, without exception, each man and woman walked slowly, walking as though they dreaded what was to happen.

There was no dread showing on Wasmaggi's face. He was, if anything, lighthearted and buoyant. He began by telling the Masaki that for most of his life he had carried a great heaviness in his heart and now that heaviness was going to be lifted.

He would tell the villagers about the time before they were born, about the great Masaki tribe which covered the earth. His arms swept around in huge circles to emphasize the size of the tribe and the vastness of the earth. His face was alive with his memories.

But he was serious when he told the people that he was preparing them for a journey. To make that journey, he said, the Masaki had to know where they had been, who they had been, why they had been, what they had been.

At first, Anna and Widel thought that Wasmaggi was speaking of a physical journey to the secret camping place; they were surprised that no one else seemed to think that way. Everyone else accepted the fact that Wasmaggi was speaking of an historical and spiritual and cultural journey, although those particular words would have had no meaning for the Masakis, that he was speaking of beginnings and that the journey was a journey of the mind from the beginning.

"I tell you now," he said, "because only Wasmaggi left from before time. Hagga, Tomaz could tell, but they no more. Only Wasmaggi left. Tonto not know all; Pollyque and Lucknew not know; only Wasmaggi. Time was when Wasmaggi say no tell; let Masaki go; let Masaki return to forest; let all Masaki go back to when no Masaki. Let Masaki end.

"But new life. Old die, babies come. So Wasmaggi say tell all. Wasmaggi make drum; drum speaks rhythm of forest. Tell no one about drum. Want surprise. Forget that drum once spoke Masaki death; forget Tonto and women. Much unhappy make Tonto and wives remember."

Wasmaggi looked at Tonto. "We talk. Agree Masaki should know about selves. We say, should have told when Tomaz and Hagga here. Say, Masaki people of forest. Forest lasts forever. Masaki must last forever."

Wasmaggi closed his eyes. As he spoke, he rocked back and forth. He seemed to be groping for the words and the images which would reveal what the words were intended to reveal.

He took his listeners back before the time of the creatures, back before the jaguar-men, back to a time when the Masaki were strong, before intratribal warfare, before outside attacks, back when shamans could draw power to the Masaki and make the Masaki strong in war, back to a time when there were no medicine men, back to a time when there was music, drums and flutes, dancing. Wasmaggi described a score or more of drums that had reverberated through the forest, speaking drums, singing drums, dancing drums.

He spoke so fast it was hard to keep up. Happening was piled upon happening, idea heaped upon other ideas, objects upon objects. He recited myths and legends from the dark past, most of them meaningless, disconnected recollections from his childhood.

As if in a trance, he recalled the rituals of medicine men who directed the taking of prisoners in war and prepared them for sacrifice.

The Masakis were stunned; they could not comprehend what Wasmaggi was telling them; they had no experiences against which to measure his words.

He spoke in halting words and phrases. His story was hard to follow, but the Indians were caught up in the cadence of his speaking. They were mesmerized, and when Wasmaggi suddenly shouted out the word *pachamainta, pachamainta* and fell over onto his side, they hardly seemed to notice.

Anna rushed to Wasmaggi. After a quick examination, she declared him exhausted by the effort of his speaking and by the memories he was calling forth. She administered a brew of coca and ordered Wasmaggi removed to his house. She asked Tonto to have Pollyque or Lucknew stay with Wasmaggi while she prepared other medicines. When that was done, if Wasmaggi did not go to sleep soon or became so uncomfortable that he could not sleep, she was to be called. In the meantime, she suggested, Tonto might think of postponing the storytelling.

The Indians did not leave the fire. They had a hundred questions and not a single answer. Widel and Anna had a hundred questions of their own.

"War, Widel?" Anna asked. "What was he talking about?"

"About the past, Anna, with all its warts and ugliness."

"But war against whom? And prisoners sacrificed?"

"We'll have to wait. I don't think he was talking about times he remembers, actually, not always anyway."

"Pachamainta. Twice he shouted out that word."

"Haven't any idea. Someone, something. I don't know."

Throughout the remainder of the day, the Indians hovered about the fire, leaving only for the most personal of reasons and hurrying back as soon as their needs were met. When children got hungry, mothers rushed to their food stores, grabbed what was necessary, and fed the children by the fire. It was, to say the least, an unusual scene.

There were periods of frenzied conversation and periods of absolute silence. With Wasmaggi temporarily unavailable, the Masakis focused on Tonto and the two old women. Lucknew and Pollyque and their husband were of little help. They knew the jaguar-mens' time; they had experienced the creatures first hand, but they knew little about the Masaki before the creatures. That would have to wait for Wasmaggi.

Failing with the old people, the Indians turned to Anna. What secrets had Wasmaggi passed on to her along with the knowledge of his medicine and the village genealogy? What secrets did she possess? When Anna replied that she had no secrets other than the medicine, the Indians reacted with a sullenness born of doubt.

It was not that the Indians disbelieved Anna, not enough, anyway, to accuse her of lying, but it was well known that the medicine man carried the tribe's history in his head. And since Wasmaggi had passed the job on to Anna, well, naturally, it was assumed he had passed on everything else in his head.

A rather heated debate arose about what Anna did or did not know, and sides were drawn largely on the basis of gender. Most of the hunters seemed to believe Anna knew more than she was telling; most of the women accepted Anna's denial.

During the argument, Contulla, defending Anna's integrity, got shoved. As she fell to the ground, she clutched her stomach and yelled something about carrying a baby. Lurch immediately was at her side. It was the first he had known about Contulla being pregnant.

When he assured himself that she was not hurt, he stood up, looking for the person who had shoved his wife. Under most circumstances, Lurch was a most peaceful man, a thoughtful man and a respected hunter. He also was capable, as he had proven with Connie, of savage physical reactions. When one of Sampson's men had attacked Connie, Lurch had thrust his fingers into the man's eyes and literally had torn out the man's brain.

The argument with and about Anna was forgotten. Now the village focused on Lurch as he sought retribution for the insults to his wife and their unborn child.

With all eyes glued on Lurch, no one noticed that Wasmaggi had emerged from his house until he shouted for Lurch to sit down.

Widel whispered to Anna, "God, I never thought he would live to see another sunrise."

"What did you say?" Anna asked with great excitement.

"I said I never thought Wasmaggi would ever see the sun again."

"That's it!" Anna shouted. "That's it!" She kissed Widel hurriedly and ran toward Wasmaggi.

Wasmaggi turned her away. He held up his hand and motioned for Anna to stand where she was. Then he commanded her to sit down. Anna sat alone, apart from the villagers, apart from her husband.

"This woman medicine woman," he said to the people, pointing to Anna, "but she have much past to learn. She not know all because Wasmaggi not tell. She how she sits alone. That medicine man; that medicine woman."

Wasmaggi studied every face to make sure that each Masaki understood what he was saying.

"Sometimes alone because only medicine man, medicine woman, know everything. Wasmaggi alone most of life. Have wives, have children, have family, but in head alone. Have given An-na much knowledge, but have not given An-na knowledge of time past, so she alone and not know why."

He hobbled to Anna and held out his hand, helping her to her feet. He led her to Widel.

95

"Here husband," he said, taking Widel's hand and placing it in hers. He took Penny from Widel's arm. "Here baby, here Penny," he said. "You family."

He stood with Widel and Anna and Penny and stared at the villagers. "We all family. No fight."

He waited until he was satisfied every Indian would heed his admonition.

"Now hear Wasmaggi again. An-na will be alone. Times not even Ran-ford will comfort her. You think An-na not tell what you want. This time she not know what you want, so cannot tell. But you blame anyway. Shame on you. An-na always tell truth. Who knows otherwise? But I tell you, some day she will know, and she will not tell, not because she does not love you but because she knows she must not tell. That why she will be alone. That why Wasmaggi sometimes alone. You trust An-na. I need not speak of this again."

With that, Wasmaggi went to Contulla and raised her to her feet. He put his right hand on the small of her back and his left hand on her stomach and rubbed both slowly and gently.

"The forest loves us and sends us another child. The forest bears us. Gives us life. The forest is our nourishing mother."

Wasmaggi continued to stroke Contulla. "Woman with child like center of forest. Woman with child like center of life." He took his hands away. "Woman with child source of Masaki life." He put his hand on Contulla's stomach again. "Here beginning."

Then he reached out and touched three or four of the children's heads. "Here life continues."

The object lesson was not lost on the Masakis. Forest mother, earth mother in other cultures, Anna would say later, and human mother were one and the same to the Masaki.

As Wasmaggi paused to let all he had said sink in, Anna spoke a word. "*Pachamama ,*" she said loudly.

Wasmaggi turned quickly, his face showing a deep scowl.

"*Inti* !" Anna yelled.

Wasmaggi fell to his knees.

"What the hell are you doing?" demanded Widel.

"I know what he was yelling earlier, the word that didn't make any sense."

"But look at him. He looks like you've shot him."

"No. I don't think so. I think he's stunned into remembering."

"Remembering what, for Christ's sake?"

"Where we came from."

Wasmaggi looked at Anna, the scowl replaced by an expression of utter wonderment. "Does An-na know?"

"Anna knows a little."

"Jesus, Anna, what's going on?"

Anna ignored Widel. "Does Wasmaggi believe?"

"Holy shit, Anna. What the hell are you talking about? The old man looks at you like a goddess."

"How An-na know name?"

"The name of what, for God's sake?"

"What does Wasmaggi remember about the name?"

"Old name of everything." Wasmaggi arms swept around his head, then he reached for Anna.

"Will you tell me what this is all about!"

"*Pachamama* is the Inca word for the earth mother; *Inti* is the Inca word for the sun. He combined them."

"Pachamainta," yelled Wasmaggi. "Our An-na is Pachamainta!"

"No, no, Wasmaggi. I only know about Pachamainta. Pachamainta is the earth and the sun, the mother and father of the forest, the mother and father of us all."

Once again the villagers were experiencing an incomprehensible revelation of great importance and didn't know what to make of it. It seemed to most villagers that Anna in fact did have more to tell than she had admitted, and they demanded that she tell them. Widel joined in the demands.

"Look, Widel, it's what I read and what we studied in school. You know, sun worship and all that."

With the Indians, she took a different tack. She asked them to sit down, and when they had, they looked like a class of eager children. She drew Wasmaggi down beside her, asking him to help with the story which she knew he knew much better than she.

97

Long ago, she told the Masakis, so long ago that no one remembers the time, mother earth had a name, Pachamama, and the sun had a name, Inti. Together, they made everything to grow. The Masaki saw how Pachamama and Inti lived and worked together, like husband and wife. One could not exist without the other. The Masaki began to think of them as one and gave them the name Pachamainta.

Anna had to improvise, hoping Wasmaggi would fill in the blanks and add knowledge and understanding, but he said nothing.

When the creatures came, Anna told the Masakis, skipping hundreds of years of unknown history, everything was disrupted. The people were so sad and afraid that they forgot many things. It was like trying to forget a bad dream, and if the dream is bad enough, one works hard at forgetting. After the creatures were killed, the medicine men did everything they could to take the nightmare of the creatures away. That meant that Wasmaggi and the other medicine men could not speak of the early times, could not tell the story of Pachamainta, could not tell the Masakis that Pachamama and Inti had to rest and that their son, the moon, looked over them and us at night.

Anna knew she was on shaky ground. She wasn't even sure about the moon part, and she didn't have a name for it. She said nothing about worshiping the earth and the sun, about worshiping Pachamama and Inti, and she said nothing about the Incas. What she said mollified the Indians, although in no way did she answer all their questions.

She figured she was home free when she returned to the theme of family. She figured wrongly. She was speaking about the earth and the sun giving birth to the variety and abundance of the forest and alluded to the size and generations of Tonto's family. That went over well enough, except that Tonto had a question.

"Remember when jaguar-men come, call Tonto *Mita*. Creatures use same word. When Sampson come he call Con-nie Mita. Always name mean trouble. Who Mita?"

Strange, isn't it, Anna thought, that the few words distinctly remembered from the Incas' Quechua language are the words that come now. She remembered in her reading how poorly South American Indians had fared when bonded in slavery and how a slave trade had failed because the Indians simply allowed themselves to die. They did not have the strength or the will to survive that the African slaves had had.

"Mita," she said, "is not someone's name. It is what people are called when they are slaves."

That word meant nothing, and Anna had to explain the entire concept of slavery, ending with the jaguar-men's intent to enslave the tribe, of the creatures' intent to enslave the women, of Sampson's intent to enslave Connie.

"Always," Tonto added, "word in head; always word make Tonto afraid."

"Yes. No one should be a mita; no one should be a slave. We are created to be free."

Again the language difficulties. The concept of slavery meant nothing; now, too, the concept of freedom was meaningless. Anna knew a demonstration was needed.

She chose Armot as a subject. "Anna will show what mita means."

She commanded Armot to kneel down in front of her, then commanded him to crawl around on his belly. Both of those things he did without protest, but when Anna told him to put his hand in the fire, he refused. She grabbed him by the hair and began to simulate beating him.

The hunters were incensed and moved toward her.

"No," she said, "Armot is not hurt." The boy nodded agreement when she asked him. "But this is mita. You bend before a master, someone who commands you, and if you don't do as that master says, you are beaten. Mita is wrong; mita is bad, as Tonto says."

She helped Armot to his feet and hugged him. "Masakis will not be slaves to anyone, to jaguar-men or to creatures. Masakis are free."

She turned to Soomar. "When do you hunt?"

"When I must; when I wish."

"Then you are free."

She looked at Janus. "When do you bath?"

"When I wish."

"Then you are free."

She spoke to Westman. "Why did you change your name?"

"Because I wanted to."

"Then you are free."

It was a beginning. "Freedom is to be Masaki, to hunt, to wash, to change your name if you wish to do that. To be a slave, to be a mita, means that someone tells you you cannot hunt, that someone tells you you cannot wash, that someone tells you you must put your hand in the fire. Being a mita means that if you don't do as commanded, you will be thrashed or starved or killed."

Some of what Anna said seemed to sink in. In time, much of what she said would be remembered. In time, mita would be a concept not even Anna could explain away.

Anna had held the stage for too long. She wanted Wasmaggi to get on with his revelations. She leaned down and whispered to Widel, "Get me out of this."

"Speak about the hunters, Wasmaggi," Widel suggested. It was the right signal.

"Yes, Wasmaggi must speak about the hunters." But Wasmaggi did not speak, not for a long time. He seemed to be remembering or trying to remember. Finally, only with great effort, did he speak.

"Must speak about women first. Long before hunters were women. Pachamainta make forest, then make Masaki. Women made first so babies come and Masaki grow much large. Women plant fields and have much food and many babies, all female. But then crops grow weak. Women say where food? Babies say where milk? Women die. Babies die.

"Then Pachamainta give hunters. At first hunters roar like jaguar, frighten women. But much food. No more dying, many babies, some female, some male."

Wasmaggi closed his eyes. Anna wondered if he would collapse again, but he only was trying to remember.

"For long time Masaki live without trouble. Then big trouble. Medicine men fight. Make hunters fight. Bad medicine men make jaguar-men. Good medicine men make more medicine men. Not fight. Wasmaggi become medicine man because... because... Wasmaggi want Masaki live without fight and death. When Sampson die, Wasmaggi know path is right."

Widel took Anna's arm. He was visibly excited. "God, Anna, I see it. I see it all. It was the woman, the planters, against the hunters. Classic stuff. The planters, I'll bet anything he means the Incas, were strong. Then the warriors, the army took over. Some medicine men championed the planters; some backed the army.

"And what were the Masaki when we got here? Both planters and hunters. Then Sampson came, a revival of the jaguar-men, the army, an attempt to take the Masaki back to a hunting society when the hunters dominated. Only Wasmaggi had led this village too far, and the Indians wouldn't go.

"Classic, Anna. God, what a book it would make! It all falls into place. We show up. Wasmaggi makes you the medicine woman. Woman, planter. Perfect. Tomaz makes Connie the jaguar-hunter. He was once a master, then he became a planter. But he still has doubts, and he expresses his doubts through Connie, Connie the hunter. But when it comes down to the nitty gritty, he sides with the planters.

"And the resurrected jaguar-men appear, led by Sampson. Either the tribe will take a great leap forward or a great leap backward. It's up to Tomaz to choose. In the hunting world the masculine male prevails; in the planting world the feminine female prevails. What will Tomaz choose? He chooses the female world, only he sees it not as female but as gardens and crops, agriculture. Textbook. Classic.

"And listen to this, Anna. In this village the women are the dominant power, all appearances aside, proved by your becoming the medicine woman and Connie the great hunter. Did Sampson just want Connie's body? No, he wasn't like me. He wanted control of the Amazonian female, the real power. Think about it. Connie was huntress, marked by the jaguar, a leader of hunters. Sampson had to dominate her, and to prove his true intentions, when he failed, he killed his own medicine man."

And all at once, like a gift from heaven, Widel felt his obsession with Connie's death and his own prolonged depressive doubts fall away. Connie had been real enough; he had no doubt about that, but suddenly, he recognized her as a symbol, the manifestation of the hunting culture. Connie the hunter was doomed as surely as was Connie the injured. Her death was inevitable, just as Anna's continued life was a manifestation of the planters, cultivators, and harvesters of an agricultural society.

Widel was a player in a cosmic drama, or so he imagined. His dramatization was overly exaggerated. He knew that. Still, he pictured himself as a figure in the transformation of a civilization, his role impossible to imagine.

If Anna heard anything Widel said, she gave no evidence of it. She was into her own deep thoughts, trying to draw some thought or other out of her own sketchy knowledge, something just beyond reach. What that thought was, she didn't know, but it had to do with making some order out of all the things Wasmaggi had said.

Widel continued talking a mile a minute; Wasmaggi talked on. Anna heard little or nothing of what either was saying. Her thoughts had returned to the first days in the hostile jungle.

What did she want to recall? And then there it was, the natural division of labor. Natural? Was it natural that she and Connie had looked for roots and nuts and water while Widel had looked for meat? That's what happened. And when Connie hunted the sloth? Was that a foreshadowing of the conflict within the jungle itself? And when they found the Masakis' summer camp, what was the first thing the girls did? They pulled weeds! Did Widel ever pull a weed? He watched, and then he hunted. Why was that the way, she asked herself?

She asked Wasmaggi. "Why do the men never work in the gardens; why do women never hunt?"

Wasmaggi thought for a moment. "Is way," he answered.

"Who made it that way?"

"Pachamainta."

"But in the beginning, when there were only women, didn't the women hunt?"

"Don't think so."

"When the men came, the hunters, they protected the women?"

"Yes."

"Against whom?"

"Against.... Wasmaggi not know."

"Think back, Wasmaggi. Think back to the old stories. The stories the old medicine men, the shamans, told, before they were medicine men."

"To the stories of the high places?"

"Yes, the high places."

"The medicine man would go to his house, burn the leaves, beat the drum. He could see whole world; he could see to the beginning and to the end. He saw high places; he saw low places. He saw the people; he saw the enemies."

"What enemies?"

"He saw other people; other people all dead. Other world gone."

"What other world?"

"High up world." Wasmaggi pointed toward the sky and waved his arm in a wide circle. "High up world gone. Only here, only Masaki."

So there were other people, Anna said to herself. Could high up mean mountains? If the Masakis were not the only people, could the notion that they are have been built on the premise that they were the chosen people?

"Were the hunters warriors?"

"Many fights. Old stories of fighting and killing and running and hiding. Old stories say Masaki kill all others, that Masaki alone chosen by Pachamainta."

Wasmaggi seemed extremely tired. He looked at Anna. "Does An-na wish to see?" he asked.

"Wasmaggi knows a way?"

"Wasmaggi not see for long time, but is way. An-na have way; maybe not know it."

"I have the way to see the beginnings of the world? To see the end of the world?"

Widel knew what Wasmaggi was saying. "No, Anna! Don't even think about it!"

"To see the beginning, Widel!"

"But you won't see what Wasmaggi sees. You'll see your own beginning and end, and all the badness that you ever imagined." Widel turned to Wasmaggi. "If you saw once, why don't you look now?"

"Wasmaggi see when young man. When Wasmaggi stop looking, he old man, frightened old man. What Wasmaggi see...."

Pollyque completed the unfinished sentence. "Remember when Wasmaggi made medicine man. Told us he was going on journey, find missing Masaki. He try fool us. What missing Masakis, we say? But he not go. He go only to house. Many days in house. When come out, like say, he old man. Never speak of it, but hard believe he Wasmaggi."

"Is true," offered Tonto. "Wasmaggi much changed; he much afraid."

Widel studied Anna's face. "Anna," he spoke sharply, "they're talking about when medicine men were sorcerers and conjurers, magicians and sooth-sayers, and they're talking about coke, cocaine, and other stuff in your medicine kit. Leave it alone!"

"Yes, Widel." Anna did not sound very convincing.

"Not journey for Anna," Wasmaggi said, bringing the discussion to a hasty conclusion.

But not a satisfactory conclusion for the men and women of the village, the people who for the first time in their lives were told that once, at least, people other than the Masakis had lived. It was a startling revelation that brought forth great fear and immense curiosity, a mixture of images both wonderful and horrifying.

The People or The *Only People* or The *Chosen People* once had shared the forest with other people! And what were high places, and low places? And if the earth and the sun had names, why didn't their child, the moon? Or wouldn't Wasmaggi and Anna reveal the name? What, or worse, who were the creatures?

In the days that followed, Wasmaggi revealed little more, refining his revelations somewhat, and to Widel and Anna, at least, unconsciously revealing that what he had uncovered obviously was far beyond his personal experience, probably a part of the oral tradition he was required to know as a medicine man's apprentice. Some things had impressed him deeply, certain words and vague concepts, for example, and the fact that there once were other people in the forest who now, to his satisfaction, were gone. According to Wasmaggi, his teacher had died early in Wasmaggi's apprenticeship, and before his death, Wasmaggi's teacher had failed to pass on to Wasmaggi much of Masaki history.

Which was why, apparently, Wasmaggi had tried the hallucinogenic drugs which, failing to reveal what the medicine man sought, had produced only images and visions of the darkest kind. Wasmaggi never had returned to them; his one prolonged experience to the depths of personal and Masaki hell had been enough. He had seen his own beast. It had not devoured him, but it had made him an old man before his time.

Without ever speaking of it directly, Wasmaggi and Widel were relieved that Anna gave no more evidence of wanting to take the same journey into the past. From time to time, Wasmaggi expressed regret for having made the suggestion.

It was not that Anna had forgotten the possibility, it was that she did not want to see the future. So fearful had she become of the Masaki's future, she shuddered at the possibility of learning what that future held. In her state of mind, she envisioned only evil things. Even though she knew no one could foretell the future, it took all of her conscious emotional energy to hold the unspeakable future at bay.

EIGHT

Masaki life settled down, following its ageless routine. Widel and Anna lost all track of time. Once they had marked the years by summer camps. They could remember six, but that number was not firm. Besides, they had begun to mark time from Penny's birth, from the time they were a true Masaki family.

One day, Widel climbed into the double hammock made especially for them by Contulla and Cutilla, and more out of habit than anything, he invited Anna to join him. Surprisingly, she did. Mostly she refused because, she said, Widel would start fooling around, and she didn't like public displays of their affection. He always told her the same thing, that it was natural, and she always responded with the same retort, "But not for me."

Penny was napping. When she awakened and saw her parents swaying gently in the hammock, she begged to join them. As Penny quietly nursed, her mother and father reflected on their family. They were upset with themselves when they realized they could not state with precise accuracy their daughter's age. Nine months? Ten months? She was old enough to imitate some of the forest sounds, old enough to take a few faltering steps, old enough to eat solid food, old enough to have developed her unique personality, old enough to be toilet trained in the Masaki way. But her exact age eluded them.

It was a short step from that time sense failure to their inability to determine how long they had been in the forest. They settled finally on seven years while acknowledging the meaninglessness of time.

They rested quietly. Penny sucked spasmodically, more for comfort and reassurance than for nourishment. With one hand she had a grip on Anna's breast. She held Widel's finger with the other. Now and then she looked up and smiled. And when she lost interest in Anna's milk, she crawled onto Widel's chest. It was play time.

Widel lifted her above his head and twisted her slowly from side to side. Penny giggled. When he lowered her, she begged for more, and once again he lifted her, this time twirling her faster and faster. He made little sputtering sounds with his lips, imitating some kind of engine he had heard a long time ago.

But when he stopped making his sounds, the sound continued. Clutching Penny tightly, for the first time since before the plane crash, Widel heard the noise of an airplane.

He thrust Penny into Anna's arms and leapt from the hammock. Panic grabbed at his chest. He could see nothing through the canopy as he tried to judge the airplane's location. He ran back and forth over the village floor. He was afraid, very, very afraid.

When the sound withdrew, and he stood still, Anna rushed to stand beside him. "Widel?"

"I don't know, Anna. Maybe just someone flying over. Awful low, though. I just don't know."

"Will he come back?"

"I don't know. I hope not. I never thought I would hate that sound."

"What will we do if he does?"

"I don't know that either, dear."

In the middle of the village, Anna and Widel stood locked in each other's arms, holding on to the child for whom the noises were meaningless.

Only when the villagers gathered around the whites did Anna and Widel realize that the noise was without meaning to the Indians. They looked to Anna for an explanation.

How did one explain to the only people on earth, a people who in their four remaining villages might number one hundred and fifty, that not only were there other people on earth but that those people were counted in the billions? How did one explain that such people came in red and black and yellow and brown as well as white, that some were very small and others were very large, that just one of their villages could cover all of the Masaki's hunting range? How did one explain that people who were believed never to exist had ten thousand languages? How did one explain airplanes when the Masaki had not even conceived of a canoe? How did one explain the twentieth and twenty-first centuries to a people who lived centuries before the first?

But was it necessary to explain anything at all? Maybe the airplane was a single phenomenon, a once in a million chance fly-by that meant nothing.

Anna decided to attempt no explanation. It was her considered opinion, she told the villagers, that the forest had made the noise, and while she didn't know what the forest was saying, she was sure the forest meant the Masaki no harm.

Since the noise did not return that day, Anna's explanation was accepted. It did not, however, still the apprehension everyone seemed to feel. These had been long, tension filled months: Wasmaggi's drum, Tonto and Wasmaggi's stories, Wasmaggi's revelations - and now an utterly new noise that upset the medicine woman and the weapon maker was almost too much to bear.

For weeks the Masaki listened for the noise's return, and only after weeks without hearing the noise again did the village return to normal.

Anna and Widel were not so easily calmed. For some reason the sound of the airplane lingered in their ears. Each had a feeling of impending disruption if not of actual destruction.

The Cessna 206 that made the noise had been flown by a Brazilian bush pilot, one of a hundred or more civilian pilots hired by the government of Brazil to take low level, wide angle photographs of the Amazon rain forest and to make rough grid charts of selected areas. The pilot of the Cessna was making his grids and taking his pictures when he flew over the village. He saw nothing that drew his attention; he didn't even spot the stream that ran near the village.

When the pilot's flight ended, he delivered his rough charts and his photographs to a minor bureaucrat of *Projecto RADAM*. In time, the photographs would be matched to the pilot's grids and studied carefully. Later, the grids and the pictures would be used for a more intensive survey of the area by side scanning radar planes. If anything of interest or of value appeared, the area would be explored by teams of scientists: botanists, geologists, foresters, and engineers.

It was three months before the sound of an airplane was heard again. This time the village was two days into the trek to a summer camp, the people stretched out in single file along a trail that had not been used for years.

It was impossible to see the airplane, but it was flying as low and as slowly as was prudent. For some reason he could not explain, Widel commanded the villagers to lie flat on the ground. Only when the aircraft had passed out of hearing did he permit them to stand up.

There was much confusion, and the demands for Widel to explain his orders and to explain the noises were so great that he had little choice but to attempt an explanation. He promised the Masakis that when they reached an overnight clearing where they could all be together, he would tell them what he knew.

Widel was stalling; everyone knew that, but they had little choice. Since they could not gather as one cohesive group along the trail; they had to wait for a suitable meeting place. By intent, Widel and Anna worked their way to the end of the line. They drew Wasmaggi back with them. That single act added to the worries of the Indians.

For days, the men and women of Projecto RADAM studied the images returned to them from the intense examination of the latest scan. So detailed were the images that the knoll where Widel and Anna had first made love stood out among other knolls. The village clearing was evident as an opening in the forest, but since the houses had been burned only two days before the radar scan, the frameworks were mistakenly identified as tangles of small trees. A summer camp had been found, but the original photograph confirmed that it had been abandoned for some time. The stream appeared but was judged so tiny as to be insignificant. The Cessna's original photographs did not reveal it, and thus the tiny bare beach went unnoticed.

There were items of interest. There were indications of a small network of trails, some of which led to abandoned camps. It was concluded that a small number of unknown Indians probably inhabited the area. A note to that effect was made.

But real interest in the area did not include a few Indians. What was of interest were precious metals and marketable timber. The area seemed to harbor neither, and when the report for the area was included in RADAM's *Survey of Natural Resources,* it was of such little interest that it was neglected completely.

Without knowing it, the Masaki world had been surveyed, mapped, studied, and then relegated to a cartographer's map book. The land was of such little commercial importance that it did not rate even the usual *Potential Use of the Land* report. Anyway, barring any unforeseen treasurers, already the use of the land had been determined. Much of it would, after further studies and examinations, be flooded by *Electronorte*, northern Brazil's state electric company.

Widel's attempted explanations were doomed to failure from the start. The Masakis simply refused to believe in the present existence of other people. Even when Widel told the Masakis that he and Anna and Connie were some of the other people, there was universal disbelief. Penny was not other people; she was born in the forest in front of every woman's eyes. Widel was playing a joke on them.

The only individual who nursed a doubt was Wasmaggi. When Widel gave up all efforts to explain, Wasmaggi spoke. "I have felt," he said to the Masakis, "something beyond. Many times when young went looking; nothing there. But Wasmaggi think. Maybe beyond next water, beyond next tree, beyond...see. But always more forest. Yet...." His voice trailed off.

"Wasmaggi make decide. Don't understand what Ran-ford says. Maybe are more creatures. Now Wasmaggi say must go to special camp. If what An-na and Ran-ford say true, Masaki in much danger.

Wasmaggi promise special camp; time to go. Ran-ford say no time waste. An-na say time.

"But An-na say Masakis must decide for self. Wasmaggi go to special place with An-na and Ran-ford. You come or not. You decide. We go now. Hope you follow, but if not...."

Since Wasmaggi did not seem able to complete the thought, Anna spoke. "Masaki, Anna has failed you. I cannot find the words to make you understand. But these words you do understand: I love you, all of you, and I hope...." Anna couldn't continue. "Help me out, Widel."

"Masaki, there are more creatures than you could ever count even if you lived forever. Some creatures are good; some are bad. Every day they come to the forest. One day they will come to the Masaki. Anna and I hope those that come will be good, but until they prove themselves good men and women, we believe we should disappear until we can find out.

"Whatever we do, we should do as one people. But you are free not to go with us. Penny and I are going with Wasmaggi. If some of you don't want to go, Anna says she will stay with you as your medicine woman if you want her. That's how much she loves you. She will give up her baby and her husband to prove that love.

"But you must decide tonight. Tomorrow Wasmaggi will lead some of us to a safe place. I love you, and the only way I can prove that is to give you Anna if you choose not to go with Wasmaggi. Decide tonight; after tonight it will be too late."

Choosing did not take long. There were no dissenters. Fear motivated the Masakis to follow Wasmaggi and Anna. In a world suddenly totally irrational, the two medicine people provided the only positive direction, whatever that was.

Without being aware of it and lacking the most rudimentary experience to understand if they had been aware, the Masakis' world was shrinking. If one stood off and examined it, one would have to wonder how the Masaki could had been overlooked for so long, being as it was less than a thousand miles from the mouth of the Amazon. Part of the answer was in its lack of major waterways, part was in its awesome swamps and its reputation as being useless, part was in its excessive heat, part was in the difficulties of penetrating it even for a few miles.

But, mostly, the answer about its neglect was the promise of the bigger and better rewards that drew generations of adventurers up the mighty Amazon. The currents of the river beckoned explorers and adventurers with a beguiling seductiveness to test its currents. Perhaps what was near at hand seemed too mundane, too easy. And if the river called, so did the mountains at its source, and the call was of priceless ores.

Too, there were those who searched for lost civilizations, secret cities of the race called *Atlantis* and the city prized above all others, the secret city of *Z*. Without ever leaving the Amazon for more than a few miles, there was more than enough to occupy most men. And when the Amazon disappointed, there were scores of other major rivers. And when it wasn't gold or silver, there were the savannas stretching from horizon to horizon on which to graze cattle, and ranches and plantations to build.

Brazil covers half a continent; the land of the Masaki is but a minute fraction of the whole, and up to now it had remained hidden in neglect. Projecto RADAM gave no one reason to revise the opinion about the area, so once again the world of the Masaki was ignored.

Since the fifteen hundreds, Brazil, especially the Amazonian basin, has suffered from an original sin, the assumption that Europeans in the beginning and European stock to this day have a divine right to the land - and to the native populations.

Portuguese and Spanish gold hunters were the first to act on that belief, followed by animal skin hunters and explorers, followed by rubber seekers. By the time the rubber industry became full blown, it was corporate dogma that business interests had inalienable rights to the land - and to the native populations. Since the native populations are mostly extinct, that question was becoming moot, but even now the original assumption dominates as individuals and huge corporations go about burning millions of acres of rain forest each day, as mining interests pollute the river and its tributaries with mercury, and as cartels poison land, water and life with insidious insecticides spread over the basin in megaton amounts, duplicating the destruction caused when smallpox and measles and other diseases were introduced five hundred years ago.

For centuries, the exploitation of the Amazon basin has been as natural as breathing. Indeed, not to attempt to gain from the land and its people is viewed in most circles with suspicion, as if one was committing a serious sin of omission.

NINE

In Manaus, the mighty river port at the junction of the Amazon and the Negro rivers, Alfredo Herrera was not going to commit that sin. Nor were Paulo Ferraz or Hans Wittenberg and others like them. There were riches to be taken, riches already being taken. Let the Devil himself suck the hind teat.

No one ever counted the thousands of small bars and hideaways that lined the waterfront of Manaus at the confluence of the Negro and Solimões rivers, the latter being better known as the Upper Amazon. Manaus is as international a city as exists anywhere in the world, although it differs from the great ports of the world in a hundred ways, most of the differences being negative.

Paulo Ferraz and Hans Wittenberg and thousands like them were not sailors; all of them had drifted to Manaus as the most logical place in the whole of South America in which to disappear while at the same time conducting enterprises which, however sleazy and contemptible and unlawful, employed their special and considerable talents.

To an extent greater than any will admit, that is the nature of Manaus. One time sailors are on the beach; small armies of wharf rats prey on each other and anyone foolish enough to walk the waterfront alone and unarmed; criminals of countless hues from petty thieves to gangland executioners slither through the shadows; prostitutes block the streets; dealers in everything from drugs to skins to human flesh hatch plots and conclude deals in uncounted alleys and byways. The waterfront belongs to the devious, the evil, the dregs of the world's societies, drawing them like so many rusty iron filings to the magnet of Manaus, a duty-free port and, within certain bounds, a totally open city.

114

There are good people in Manaus, many good people. Manaus is a cosmopolitan center of culture and has been since the middle eighteen hundreds. There are excellent schools and advanced hospitals, churches and uncorrupted police, and a world renowned opera house, the *Amazonas Theater*. There are scores of social agencies ready, anxious and willing to serve displaced Indians, dislocated seamen and health seeking addicts. There are missions and societies dedicated to helping wayward men and women mired in the depravity of the waterfront; they provide medical services for the wounded, food for the hungry and prayer for lost souls.

Only a few blocks up from the piers and wharfs on the waterfront is the city proper, the public buildings, the parks, the houses. Looking down from their mansions, the good citizens of Manaus can look down on the endless blocks of shacks that house the waterfront people and down on the *cidaae flutuante*, the floating city of over two thousand huts built on rafts.

Between the good and well intentioned citizens and the waterfront there is a wall. It cannot be seen, but it can be measured. It is a million miles long and a million miles high, and it is real even if no one can touch it. It separates the waterfront from the rest of Manaus.

Not always, of course. When the inhabitants of the waterfront find slim pickings among their own, they walk through the wall and prey on the rest of the city. Then the police get angry and retaliate with vicious swiftness. The guilty might not be punished, but someone is.

The police leave the waterfront alone in exchange for the waterfront people leaving the rest of Manaus alone. The unwritten arrangement is old, and most of the time it works, but when the arrangement is breached, the police move brutally against the waterfront, leaving no doubt as to the sacredness of the arrangement.

Whatever goes on along the waterfront is the waterfront's to deal with. Murder is the only exception, but even then police functions are limited mostly to body removal.

For the most part, the live-and-let-live arrangement has worked for several generations of wharf people and Manaus citizens because it is an arrangement that provides each with certain benefits. The good people are assured of few intrusions by waterfront citizens, and the waterfront people are assured of an absence of official law enforcement. For the people of the waterfront, this arrangement is especially meaningful. It has created a haven for the criminal and has assured his anonymity.

Surprisingly, the unloading and off loading of the hundreds of ships that arrive each year is accomplished with remarkable efficiency. There is no shortage of labor. There are no unions, so labor is cheap. The docks, the cranes and gantries, the railroad tracks and the rolling stock, the tractors and the cargo carriers, everything that physically pertains to the traffic of cargo, is owned by one or another of a half dozen international corporations or cartels. And that ownership extends to the upper levels of management. Company men are owned lock, stock and barrel, just as is each and every piece of machinery and gear.

The company men live on the upper side of the wall in Manaus's prime neighborhoods. They go to the waterfront only in the daylight and then only to oversee their particular part of the larger operation.

Those men are the top of the on-the-scene hierarchy. Beneath them are their subordinates, local men who do their jobs, sometimes with brutal efficiency. The company men never ask how the tasks get done or by whom. They don't care; they need only to know that each job is done as required and when required. If the local supervisor changes foremen or if the foreman uses impressed labor, then that was what is required. If fist or pipe are required, then so be it. There is a chain of command thoroughly understood by the company men. They don't want and they don't need to know the details. They hire men to get results; how the results are attained is of little concern.

So pianos and metallic mercury arrive from the United States, furniture from Sweden, marble from Italy, wine from France, silk from Japan, wool from the Falklands, and crystal from Ireland. So hardwoods, both raw and milled, go to London and Tokyo, Brazil nuts to Germany, and kapok to Holland. And so, too, do drugs go to the United States and young Indian and Brazilian girls to brothels throughout Brazil.

It is that last kind of cargo that excites Paulo Ferraz.

Ferraz spent two years of an imposed forty year sentence in prison. When he decided he had had enough, he stepped away from his prison work gang and into the forest and disappeared. His guard was fired from his job, but on suspicion only, and Ferraz became a statistic. Ultimately, he made his way to Manaus.

From the time he arrived, Ferraz stood out among the waterfront people. He was well spoken and fluent in English and Portuguese and, most surprisingly, in a score of Indian languages. It is unusual to find so cultured and well mannered a gentleman along the piers.

Ferraz is no ordinary man. He was born into a well-to-do family and was given the opportunity that money creates in Brazil to go to a university. He proved to be a brilliant student and earned degrees in both sociology and psychology at the university in Rio De Janeiro. His specialty was Indian culture and social systems and Indian thought. After two years of teaching at the university as he pursued a doctorate, he was called to the capital at Brasilia and given a department head role in the SPI, the Indian Protection Service.

The SPI had been created by the government for three very specific purposes: to pacify the Indians, to get the Indians to accept outsiders, and to convince the Indians occupying coveted lands to be resettled on reservations and to become *civilized.* That was necessary because timber, ore and agricultural companies were exploring and developing the Amazon basin; the Indians stood in the way. It was, let it be said, the alternative to the older practice of simply eliminating the Indians.

Ferraz was very good at pacifying the Indians and resettling them, so good, in fact, that in 1967, along with a number of others, he was tried and convicted of genocide, murder and slavery.

When his bookish theories failed to work and the Indians refused to leave ancestral lands, Ferraz deliberately introduced the Indians to such diseases as measles and mumps and scarlet fever, and when not all of the Indians died, he directed the murder of individuals.

Neither of these actions provided Ferraz with any satisfaction; indeed, he admitted it was the last resort of a desperately ambitious man, and he suffered occasional bouts of guilt and remorseful depression.

What gave him satisfaction as well as a handsome profit was sexual slavery. Ferraz developed a highly refined traffic in young Indian girls. To certain trusted assistants, he issued a standing order that females from age nine or ten to twenty were to be culled from every Indian population and sent to one of several special locations.

Ferraz and his cohorts established secret *training centers,* as he called them, in several provinces. Ultimately, when his enterprise was at its height, he was able to supply a steady stream of prostitutes to any area in South America where large numbers of men were working.

What gave Ferraz away in the end were not his murders and genocidal campaigns but, within a few years of providing prostitutes, the alarming flow into the cities of Brazil of Indian women with venereal disease. Venereal diseases were a European import, unknown among native Indian populations. With Ferraz's systematic supply of Indian prostitutes, the diseases became epidemic. It took a while, but the medical detective work of health workers from SUCAM, Brazil's public health agency, eventually traced the female carriers to Ferraz which led to further investigations and to his conviction.

That might have been the end of it had it not been for Alfredo Herrera. When Ferraz met Herrera, Ferraz knew immediately he was being set up.

Ferraz was drinking alone in one of the waterfront bars. Almost before he was aware of it, three men sat down at his table. If they were not actually bandits, they reminded him of the cangaceiros he had known in the sertão, the interior of Brazil. When Ferraz looked at his own bullies, he saw them accompanied by other, unfriendly men.

A minute or two later, Herrera walked in and walked to Ferraz's table. The three strangers stood and waited nearby. Herrera offered Ferraz a drink.

"Thanks. Do I have a choice?"

"It will make the conversation easier."

"And what will we talk about?"

"You, maybe. If I'm right, we'll talk about you. If I'm wrong, you've had a free drink."

"So?"

"Is your name Ferraz?"

"I've had many names."

Herrera was a little man. He was dressed immaculately, in sharp contrast to the bar's other customers. His hair and nails recently had had the attention of a professional. He spoke in a soft, somewhat squeaky voice but with the manner and vocabulary of one well positioned.

"I'll start again," he announced. "A man of your talents should not have been addressed in such a crude manner. Let me introduce myself. I'm Alfredo Herrera. I work for FUNAI."

When Ferraz and so many others had been tried and judged, the SPI had been dissolved, and a new organization within the government had been created, the National Indian Foundation, FUNAI.

"So what? That means nothing to me?"

"I'm responsible for preserving the Indian culture hereabout."

"Well, that's a joke. There isn't any Indian culture anywhere around here."

"No, that's not true, and if you were the Ferraz I seek, you'd know that."

"Look. I've had the drink. Is there anything more you want?"

"Yes, there is, and I'll give more than a drink. But have another, and that will give me time to say what I have to say."

"As long as I don't have to answer."

"Paulo. May I call you Paulo? Paulo, I've studied the career of Paulo Ferraz with great interest. I wanted to know what went wrong. I found out that Ferraz was...well, let me speak plainly, an asshole."

"You're taking a lot for granted for your drink." Ferraz was beginning to redden.

Without acknowledging the interruption, Herrera continued. "His ego got in the way. When his mind games with the Indians didn't work, he went nuts. All that killing. Very shameful."

"Do you have a point?"

"Yes, I'm coming to it. Ferraz had one thing right though, the women. That was a masterful stroke, or at least it would have been if there hadn't been a little disease control problem, what the business men call *quality control*."

To this point, Herrera had been talking to his liquor glass. Now he looked at Ferraz, staring directly into Ferraz's eyes. "I've invested years tracing your operation. I traced you all the way from your prison cell to this bar."

"And why would you bother to do that? Seems a waste of time to me."

"Because you had a good thing going."

"And you have taken all your time and trouble to find me and say that?"

"No. Everything you set up is gone, all your little schools, all your contacts. One by one they were found out and closed up. Everything has come to a conclusion except you."

Ferraz drew a sharp breath. Could this little man be a professional killer? Ferraz turned white, but he managed to control himself. He knew he wasn't wanted dead or alive just because he escaped from jail. Was this man here to take him back into custody? It took all of Ferraz's courage to ask, "And you have come here to conclude me?"

Herrera immediately sensed Ferraz's discomfort. "Oh, on the contrary. I could have had you taken back to prison months ago or had you killed as an escaped convict. Either way wouldn't have mattered if that's what I had in mind." Herrera let the threat sink in.

"I've gone to all the bother to enlist your cooperation. I'm in hope that you will join me and a couple of friends in a new enterprise."

Much relieved, Ferraz spoke loudly and rapidly. "In what, for Christ's sake?"

"In finding new products for new markets which my friends and I intend to open."

Ferraz hadn't a clue as to what was being proposed, but thinking of himself as having been snatched from the hands of an executioner, he was willing to listen to anything Herrera said.

What Herrera had to say was simple, familiar and preposterous. "I need your help, Paulo. Here, in Manaus. I've got a few women that work for me. I dare say you have enjoyed one or two of them. Anyway, I've men who will go into the sertáo and find more. My procuradores are very good at that sort of thing.

"But once they bring back the Indian girls, I need someone to train them in the finer arts of pleasure. From everything I've learned about you, you were especially good at that."

"Herrera, it's damn foolishness. Even if I was who you think I am, there aren't that many Indian women anymore, and it's impossible to move them around even if there were."

Alfredo Herrera was a very patient man. He ignored Paulo Ferraz's objections. He seemed not to take umbrage at Ferraz's forthright attack.

Ferraz continued. "Look, Herrera, if you've got some women, then be your own best customer and enjoy yourself, and when the ladies stop earning money, go back to Brasilia or wherever you call home and forget the whole thing."

"Paulo, now let's stop right here. I know where there are women, enough, I think, to last us quite a while. And I know where to sell them. And I know how to get them out of the country. What I don't know is how to train them, and other than you, I don't know anyone who does. That's my problem. You are the missing piece, to make a bad pun."

Actually, the training of the women was the easiest part. Any good psychologist could have done that, if the Indian women were young enough. That's why he had wanted them before they were out of their teens; they were the easiest to remodel. The older they were, the harder it became, and beyond nineteen or twenty, it just wasn't worth the effort. It was no secret, really. You had someone deprive them of every essential thing, especially family and village, and then you literally loved them back to health. You became their substitute family and provided them with all of the cultural accouterments their tribe had provided and rewarded them with everything they desired. If you were patient enough, if you had enough knowledge about a girl's culture and customs, you had a slave dependent on you. It was easy, then, to get the girl to work for you. She was not only physically dependent but emotionally dependent and anxious to please.

Ferraz smiled as he recalled some of the lessons for giving sexual pleasure. He had been careful to ensure that his girls received their maximum physical pleasure before he took his own. He rewarded them when they gave him pleasure, and he amplified the rewards, a technique on which he had stumbled accidentally, when the girls pleased themselves in front of him first. He made pleasure, both receiving and giving, the sole reason for the girl's existence, and it had worked.

Pleasure and reward, that was the combination. What had screwed it up was his failure to protect his girls from venereal disease.

Ferraz was not listening carefully when Herrera began to expand his ideas. "Back up, Herrera; I was daydreaming."

"It does interest you, Paulo?"

"Enough to let you buy me another drink."

"Excellent."

Ferraz leaned forward. Like an old if somewhat ragged war horse, he began to hear the trumpet calls and to sense the mounting charge. "Let me hear it all, Herrera."

"I was telling you that I know where the Indians are. I've people who can get the females out of the sertáo. And I know those who can take the women out of the country and, shall we say, place them."

"You have talked to those people already?"

"Not exactly. I can't offer certain goods unless I'm sure I can deliver. That's where you come in. You know what I mean? You would be the one to get the girls willing, ready and able to screw out a man's brains."

"But, my friend, that's the easiest part."

"For you, perhaps."

"Tell me how you are going to find enough Indian women."

As Herrera spoke, it was clear that FUNAI had at least one thing in common with SPI: prostitution. While FUNAI was making many honest efforts to preserve Indian culture and while it had no policies of *elimination,* certain of its agents, including Herrera, had not changed in their exploitation of Indian women. Ferraz's earlier operations had been confined to Brazil; Herrera's ultimate market was overseas. He was adamant that no Indian girl would ever work in Brazil, his own little brothel being an exception, thus avoiding the disease problems that had led to Ferraz's downfall.

"Now, how do I know there are women to be had? Did you ever hear of Projecto RADAM?"

When Ferraz indicated that he knew the initials but little else, Herrera continued. "RADAM is the agency that does the radar scanning and mapping of all of Brazil. Every pinprick, every hollow, every dung heap in Brazil is on one map or another. Everywhere there is anything of the slightest use or interest, men hike in or are dropped by helicopter, thousands of them, and they take tree and ore samples. You can't take a shit in the forest without it being mapped.

"Anyway, now those maps are available to anyone. Projecto RADAM has tens of thousands of pages of maps. The paper companies study them for their uses. CVRD, Companhia Vale do Rio Doce, in case the initials don't mean anything, studies them for its mining plans. Electronorte has been studying them because it wants to build a lot of dams for electric power."

"Yeah?"

"And I' ve been studying them because there are hundreds of thousands of square miles where no civilized man ever has set foot. Up to the northeast of here, where for centuries everyone said there is nothing good, only swamps and jungle shit. Electronorte has a secret document that says there might be a whole bunch of Indian tribes in that land."

"Okay, I'm following you."

"Three years from now, FUNAI is going to be in charge of opening that land, finding the Indians, and getting them the hell out of there."

"Yes?"

"Three years. We've got three years to get a head start, and maybe a couple of more years because it will take a few years to get to and move all the Indians. Say five years head start. By then, before FUNAI gets its job done, we've got all the little girls."

Ferraz knew of the planned damning of the Trombetas River. It was supposed to be a secret, but already half of the waterfront of Manaus was planning to move down the Amazon to Oriximiná or Obidos once the work began, not that many of the waterfront community planned to work, but the opportunity for fast money was a lure few were able to resist. Ferraz knew that long before the dams were built and the waters started to rise there would be Indians to cheat.

He knew also that once the lands were opened, hundreds of hunters would slaughter the animals for their skins. He had envisioned his own profitable trade in jaguar and alligator hides, and while his ideas and plans were not as grandiose as Herrera's, he had assembled a handful of men.

They were but common pistoleiros, but they were tough and hard, and as long as he regularly paid them a couple of thousand cruzeiros each week, they were loyal. They supplemented their ten or fifteen dollar pocket money with petty crimes, and once in a while with substantial crimes. Ferraz allowed them to keep almost all of that money, taking only for his expenses and a smaller than average share. It was the price he paid for his *army*.

"Paulo. I like to call you Paulo. I know a lot of people. I'm gambling that you still have the talent, and I'm ready to gamble that you want one last, big hit before you're too old or before the past catches up to you. You could walk away from this, but I don't think you will. So, what say?"

"I say that you have entertained me. You have even.... Let's say that I'm interested."

"I knew it! I knew you would be, Paulo."

"Let's suppose you find the Indian girls. Suppose, even, that I train them. What then?"

Herrera was so enthused with his success that he told Ferraz more than he had intended originally. "There are two Germans here in Manaus, Wittenberg and Lippstadt, that do a lot of smuggling. I think they will want to have our merchandise."

"You've talked to them?"

"Ah, no. As a matter of fact, I don't know them personally. Haven't had that pleasure yet. They have a certain reputation, somewhat violent. I don't want to offer something I can't deliver."

"That's understandable." Ferraz did not know the two Germans either, but he knew something of their operation. He also knew they were virtually unapproachable. Once he had sold them some furs. At the time, he had been paid by a Swiss by the name of Flims. Later, when he offered a second patch of furs and then failed to deliver the promised number, two men called on him, an Argentinean by the name of Jachal and an Irishman with the name Newcastle. They had beat him up while suggesting that he make no further efforts to do business with their German bosses. It was a suggestion he took seriously.

For a time he plotted revenge, became infatuated with revenge, but in the end he could find no way even to begin to approach Wittenberg and Lippstadt. They had isolated themselves and were so heavily guarded that Ferraz let the matter drop.

Herrera was taking an almost childish delight in detailing every facet of his plan. Names rolled off his lips, some foreigners, some Brazilians. Three of the Brazilians Ferraz know: Czura, Jaicos and Pavón.

When Herrera had finished talking, Ferraz said, "Well, you've told me a lot, a lot probably I shouldn't know. But I suppose you've done that on purpose. Either I go along or I'm dead meat."

"Paulo, you misjudge me. Don't even give me a final answer now. Think about it, say for a week, then we'll talk again."

Without waiting for a reply, Herrera left the table and the bar, followed by his henchmen. On the way out he paid the bartender, spoke to him briefly, and turned to wave to Ferraz.

When the bartender came to the table with another drink, he spoke softly. "All your drinks for a week are free. But you've chosen your friends poorly."

Ferraz said nothing. He knew that from the beginning when the three men first had sat at his table and his own men were covered by other rough characters. As congenial as Herrera had been, his show of strength and his open conversation were a threat. Ferraz was as good as dead whether he trained Herrera's Indian girls or not. He got up and left the new drink untouched, a minor show of independence, supposing someone in the bar would report it.

Keeping to the shadows, Ferraz slithered from one alley to the next. He was following one of his own men; two others walked a short distance behind. When they came to the first of the rafts of the cidaae flutuante, they entered hurriedly, passed through a tiny hut, and continued on through several more. On the outer edge of the cidaae flutuante, they were safe. Two candles provided all the light they needed.

"I want to know everything you can find out about Herrera. Two days. Spend whatever money you need."

The men nodded. They had questions, but they knew the answers would come in Ferraz's own good time.

"I also want to know just how Jóse Czura, Rafael Jaicos and Carlos Pavón are tied to Herrera and why. You have one more day for that. Three days. Understand?"

Ferraz had his information about Pavón, Czura and Jaicos the next day. They were animal hunters, and they were supplying Herrera with illegal skins. Ferraz knew what they did; he wanted to know how closely they were tied to Herrera.

"They work for money, Paulo. Whoever has the most money."

"Do you know them, Rangel?"

"I've met them."

"Would they work for me?"

"Not unless you have more money than I think you have."

"Rangel, I have to know if they are connected to Herrera in any way other than selling skins. I can't say why at the moment, but I have to know."

The next day Rangel reported. "I've lots of cousins and friends. Seems only Jaicos talks with Herrera. He is always the leader; the other two are not so smart. My information is that Czura and Pavón do what Jaicos says. My cousin on my mother's side, a third cousin maybe, is also cousin to Pavón; says Pavón would like to leave Jaicos; doesn't dare."

"Interesting."

"There's more. Czura and Jaicos had a fight the other night over some whore. Jaicos cut Czura in the fight, and Czura has threatened to get even."

"That's even more interesting."

"Oh, but it gets better. Seems that the fight was not fair. The whore belonged to Herrera, and Czura got cut because Herrera's men were holding him."

"Well, well, well. Trouble in paradise, and all over a trick."

"Well, Paulo, don't make too much of it. Fights and threats are common. Chances are this will be patched up like so many."

"I don't want it patched up. Understand? I want a falling out. No, let me put it directly. I want Jaicos out, permanently, and I want the other two working for me, only I don't want them to know they work for me. Have Eneas pick them up."

Rafael Jaicos was found floating in the river a few days later, or what was left of him anyway. The police talked with Jóse Czura but finally let him go for lack of anything other than a threat. It was easy to dispose of a man. Ferraz had seen to it many times.

The reports about Herrera were delivered on time. He was respected all over the hills of Manaus, knew his job well, and was a bandeirante.

That title had been around since the early colonial times in Brazil when armed expeditions of explorers sought gold and slaves. The expeditions had been called bandeiras, and now were so glorified in folklore that the term bandeirante was given as a rank of honor to those skilled in the jungle. Its North American equivalent probably was the honorary title of colonel given in southern states.

Herrera served the city in a number of ways, not the least being that he was a director of three banks. He lived very quietly, was seldom seen in public, and avoided all publicity. He never knowingly allowed his picture to be taken.

His ties to the waterfront were his sponsorship of two missions to the Indians, one that provided food to the needy and one that was staffed with priests with the outward appearance of working to convert the Indians to Christianity.

Rangel had done his checking carefully, and Ferraz praised him for it.

"Now, I've saved the best for last, Paulo. This bit you will not believe."

"I was hoping there was more."

"Yeah, well, there is. First, Herrera's women all stay in the mission. They even service some of the customers there."

"That figures."

"And the priests don't know a word of Latin."

"Oh?"

"I went to a so-called mass. I got sent to a Catholic mission school once. Hated it, but I did learn a little Latin from the Sisters. Ain't none spoken in the mission."

"Maybe you've forgotten. Maybe it's a matter of language."

"Shit it is. Those guys ain't priests. It's that plain."

"I don't know what to make of it."

"I didn't neither, so when one of those guys left the mission, I had him followed."

"And?"

"And Eduardo mugged him. Know what he found under the robe? A semi-automatic. And you know what else? Five thousand English pounds. Five thousand!"

"Maybe we should go into the mission business."

"Wait, there's more. When the guy got up, did he go back to the mission? No. He went straight to the food kitchen. And guess who was there."

"Herrera?"

"Right."

"And what did Herrera do?"

"That's the last thing. I don't know. He got into a big car and drove away. Eduardo and I covered the kitchen for a long time. The other guy never came out. He disappeared."

"With the other garbage, I suppose."

Ferraz was quiet for a time. He had what information was necessary, and he was a little scared having it in his possession. At last he said, "All right, Rangel, I want Eneas, Rogelio and Simón here tonight. And, Rangel, keep you mouth shut. You know more than enough to get us killed."

"Ain't it the truth."

If Ferraz knew anything, he knew he was in too deeply to ever come up for air. His one hope was that Herrera had underestimated him. With a network radiating from the food kitchen and the mission, that seemed unlikely, yet it was possible. It was, in fact, the only straw to which he might cling.

Rangel, Eneas, Rogelio, and Simón were all tough and experienced men, and the men they employed for their varied pursuits were tough. But when taken all together, Ferraz wondered if they had a brain among them. Besides the money, he held them together because he provided jobs. Not one of the four who sat with him had enough imagination to go out on his own.

However, he was backed against a wall. If he turned Herrera down, he was a dead man; if he joined him, he might prolong his own life for a few years, but he would be dead anyway and those few years undoubtedly would be a living hell.

And if he joined Herrera, he would be nothing, really, in the larger scheme of things. Thus, he could see but one avenue for escape.

As simplistically as possible for the benefit of his men, Ferraz told them most of what Herrera had said and what had been learned about Herrera. And he told them that now that they knew, they were in danger. He outlined the calculated risk he considered as the only way out.

And he added the other thought creeping through his mind. He would put Herrera's plan into operation. His men would obtain the girls, he would train them, and he would peddle them. If, and a big if it was, he could succeed, he and his men would reap a substantial bounty.

"Gentlemen, we have no choice as I see it. We must put Herrera out of business, and we have to do it within the next two days."

"Jesus, Paulo. Do you know what he must have for an organization? He must have a hundred men."

"Probably more, but we're going to take a chance that without the head the body won't work."

Ferraz was quiet while the men tossed the idea around among themselves. Without him to guide the discussion, it came to little.

"We've got two, maybe three days. In that time we can all light out of here, disappear. I've got enough money so all of us can hop a plane to somewhere. When you get there, you're on your own. Or, we can move against Herrera so fast that he won't know what happened. It means a lot of mess and a lot of killing, but it'll blow over and we'll be out of the woods. I'll leave it up to you, but we have to decide this thing tonight."

It was decided then and there. The promise of money and whores outweighed the risks, as if, Ferraz thought, there would be any question. Flash big money and a handful of tits in front of these men, and they would do whatever was needed.

Ferraz already had determined the major steps: burn the mission and the kitchen, kill everyone inside, and, if possible, kill Herrera. "And if it means," he told them, "that a quarter of the waterfront has to go down, then that's the way it is. And no one, and I mean no one, is to walk out of that area alive." How many people would be killed, Ferraz refused to estimate, but in his own mind he was prepared to guess the number would be in the hundreds.

It didn't take long to plan for a natural gas container ship to lay along side the nearest wharf. The initial explosion would destroy most of the target area. Other fires set at the same time would appear to be connected. A mountain of dynamite always sat on one pier or another, awaiting shipment to the mines in the Andes. It was a simple matter to have one shipment relocated. And the cangaceiros who worked for one or the other of the four men would be stationed where escape from the doomed area was impossible.

"I want knives and clubs," Ferraz told the men. "No shooting unless it's absolutely necessary." And Ferraz insisted that each person killed be robbed and stripped to make it look as though looters had done the work.

"And I know you know more about doing this than I do, but for God's sake, take positions so you don't get yourselves killed."

TEN

On Friday, November 30, 1983, more than a third of the Manaus waterfront disappeared in a series of explosions and fires that reminded those who remembered of the saturation bombing of Europe's cities during World War II. Airborne refuse showered Manaus, in some places almost three inches thick. The newspapers reported that the explosions had unleashed a wave of looting and killing never before seen in the western hemisphere. A hundred clergymen reviewed Armageddon for their Christian worshipers. The city was in shock.

On Saturday, in a bar far removed from the scene of destruction, Doktor Ferraz sat in a bar waiting for Alfredo Herrera. Most of the twenty men in the bar worked for Ferraz.

"Well, Paulo," said Herrera as soon as he approached the table, "I'm happy to see you were not among the many killed."

"No. Sit down, Herrera. Thank you for all the drinks you provided."

"I'm told you did not take them."

"No. I was too busy."

"Thinking, I hope. Have you come to a decision?"

"Yes, but last night made me stop and think. I think that you lost something yesterday."

"I did?" Herrera's eyes twitched slightly.

"I believe you lost your little whore house, the one in the mission."

"Well, you were busy, weren't you. Very cleaver."

"I'm thinking you might not have the money to start up a new business. I don't suppose you were insured."

"I've other resources, my friend, but my loss was substantial."

132

"I think you were five thousand pounds lighter just the other day."

"What?" Herrera stood up. "You damn fool!" he shouted.

"Sit down, Herrera."

Herrera composed himself quickly. "Do you know what you are doing?" he asked. "You stupid bastard, you're the one who destroyed the waterfront. Now I suppose you're going to kill me. You scratched the surface. Doktor, what do you think you will find when you dig deeper?"

Ferraz lost some of his confidence. Was there something else he should have found, something he should know? Or was Herrera playing a game, trying to save his own hide? "Do you want to enlighten me or, as I imagine, are you trying to bluff me? I wonder which?"

"When you kill me, you'll find out. If you don't kill me, you may never know. It's a kind of riddle, I guess, but it's my only play?"

"Either way?"

"Either way. If I'm alive, you'll never know whether I've an ace or a deuce. If I'm dead, you'll know that I had nothing less than a black-eyed queen."

"You've very cool, Herrera."

"Well, the fact is, I've two cards. I'll show you one. It's a black ace, the death card. But it's not for you. It was dealt to me some time ago. I'm not afraid of dying. In a way, I would approve of your killing me. You see, I'm ill, and I'm going to die soon anyway. I've come to terms with that fact, so your threat doesn't bother me very much. A quick death is to be preferred, don't you think?"

Another bluff? Ferraz's confidence was fast dissolving. Was there an alternative? He could think of none.

"Paulo, I'm leaving now. I could say I would withdraw, paying you off with my plan and the promise that I would neither interfere nor inform on you. I suppose you would not trust me; I probably wouldn't trust you. I've played my last card; unfortunately for you, it's face down on the table. Goodbye, my friend." Herrera walked to the door and out into the darkened alley.

His death shoved the waterfront off the front pages. Suddenly, all hell broke loose. Among other things, Alfredo Herrera left behind a number of ledgers outlining his activities and accounts with the food kitchen and the mission and his manipulation of bank employees and bank funds.

There was no mention of his scheme for the procurement of Indian women, and while he named scores of people on both sides of the Manaus wall, there was no direct mention of Paulo Ferraz, only vague references to certain expenses for a new *plan for pleasure* and *a special friend.*

Paulo Ferraz suffered no guilt pangs, wondering only for a moment whether he had misjudged Alfredo Herrera. He didn't spend much time worrying about it.

There was enough in Manaus to keep the police busy for months. Teams of special agents descended on the banks, investigators combed the waterfront, a thousand guesses were made about Herrera's "special friend," but in the end it all died down and life returned to normal, the good citizens on one side of the invisible wall, the waterfront community on the other.

The corporations took their losses in money and personnel stoically. People could be replaced and insurance companies took the financial hit. The banks, as is their nature, worked quietly to polish their tarnished images.

The waterfront carried the burden of the dislocation. The carefully constructed human system had to be restructured, new lines of authority had to be established, and rebuilding had to be done. But after the initial shock, what seemed most to disrupt the waterfront were the missing bars and the diminished stables of prostitutes.

Ferraz made no moves in Manaus for several months. His men scattered up and down the river or otherwise dropped out of sight. He risked a hasty, secret visit to Brasilia and obtained copies of Projecto RADAM's maps and reports. He was amazed how simple it was. He simply walked into the Projecto information office, studied catalogs, and ordered his information. The cost was seventy five cantos, about five hundred dollars.

Ferraz purchased far more than he needed and about areas in which he had no interest because he didn't want anyone pinpointing his area of interest should he be recognized or should inquiries be made about purchases of RADAM studies.

Ferraz's single area of interest lay east of the Trombetas River toward the Para River and north of the Amazon to the Northern Perimeter Highway, an area of over one hundred thousand square miles heretofore unexploited and largely unvisited by explorers and commercial hunters.

What excited Ferraz the most were two facts gleaned from the studies. There was little of commercial value in the entire area, and there was evidence of several Indian populations heretofore unknown.

Over a period of months, Ferraz allowed a plan to evolve. It would take much time, but if patience was its own reward, then it was possible for the rewards to be considerable. If men were willing to pay four thousand cantos for the Indian women available locally, what would they pay in other parts of the world for women trained in the highest skills of giving pleasure?

That was the one rub. Herrera had said that none of the girls in his plan should ever work in Brazil. Ferraz agreed that was a sound concept. But how to get the girls out of Brazil and into other countries was a problem. Herrera had suggested Wittenberg and Lippstadt. Allegedly, they were experts at both shipping and smuggling.

At some risk to himself, he would say later, he had managed to get a brief meeting with Wittenberg, It had gone poorly; that had been his own fault. He was sitting on something good and had allowed himself the stupid luxury of acting superior. The wonder was that Wittenberg hadn't gotten angry.

Not only that, Ferraz now realized that he had failed to complete his homework. Perhaps he was over the hill, too old, too long out of the serious cloak and dagger business. Years earlier, he would have known everything there was to know about Wittenberg. He knew nothing first hand other than the man's reputation and nothing at all about Herman Lippstadt, Wittenberg's partner. Such ignorance was uncharacteristic; his neglect literally could be the death of him.

There were those on the waterfront who knew Wittenberg, and some had dealt with him directly. No one, it seems, knew Lippstadt; no one even claimed to have seen him. He was a shadow, and on the waterfront shadows were sinister and dangerous. If nothing else about him came to light, everyone seemed to be afraid of Lippstadt.

During the first weeks of his investigation of the two Germans, Paulo Ferraz was afraid, too. What he was learning upset him, and at the same time, it gave him insights into the reasons for Wittenberg's and Lippstadt's success.

Wittenberg's and Lippstadt's grandfathers had been among those industrialists who had funded the Kaiser's rule over Germany and Germany's World War I efforts. They lost much with the surrender of Germany, but, having foreseen the defeat of Germany, they had hidden hundreds of millions of marks in gold in Swiss and South American banks. They were able, in the 1920s, to rebuild their heavy industries, and when Hitler came to power in 1933, they had been financing him since 1924. The two men, along with others, with money and large credit lines, financed the German Reich in its early years. They also assumed powerful behind-the-scene positions in the Nazi Party. As the two grandfathers aged beyond their ability to actively participate in business and political careers, Hitler rewarded them with appointed positions in Argentina. Each man had a son; each son was a loyal Nazi and Hitler supporter.

Sometime in 1943, before the Lippstadts could move to Argentina, the family was killed in an Allied bombing raid. The sole surviving member of the family was young grandson Herman, away at the time in a German Youth Camp.

Honoring the families' friendship of generations, the Wittenbergs "adopted" young Lippstadt. When it became apparent after the successful Allied invasion of France that Germany was going to lose the war, the two boys, Hans and Herman, were sent to Argentina as aides to grandfather Wittenberg. Sometime during the final assault on Berlin, the rest of the Wittenberg family disappeared. How or where or why was never known.

At war's end, Hans and Herman were living with the elder Wittenbergs in Rio. The boys became members of the German Party in Argentina. When Juan Domingo Perón became president of Argentina for the first time, in 1946, the elder Wittenberg had contributed substantial funds. Later, Perón rewarded the youths for that contribution by giving them land and position.

When Perón fell out of power in 1955, grandfather Wittenberg, then in his late nineties, died. There was some speculation about his death. Natural, suicide, murder? Nothing was publicly said, and in the turmoil of Argentinean politics, the question was dropped, yet immediately after the old man's funeral, Hans and Herman dropped out of sight.

Again, one can only speculate about their activities in the intervening years, but in 1973, when Perón reemerged, Wittenberg and Lippstadt were important figures, responsible, it would be claimed later, for the kidnapping, murder and disappearance of thousands of Perón's enemies. Among others, the two were charged by world opinion with the most grievous crimes violating human rights.

Sometime during Eva Perón's efforts to continue her husband's reign, the two disappeared from Argentina, emerging later in Manaus. By then they were well known for their shipping interests.

Wittenberg and Lippstadt were of the Manaus waterfront, but they were not considered criminals in the ordinary sense. That is, they had committed no crimes in Brazil for which they ever were charged. They existed in official limbo, untouched and apparently untouchable.

Ferraz saw two things in this. First, he was attempting to deal with two powerful and dangerous men, quite like himself in that they had little or no regard for human life.

And second, they had to have wide and substantial contacts in the Americas and in Europe and Asia. That Brazil had protected them from prosecution in Argentina by refusing extradition was proof enough of their power.

As Ferraz learned more of the Wittenberg/Lippstadt operation, two other names kept coming up, Jorge Jachal and Michael "Red"

Newcastle. Ferraz knew both men; they had beat him up once for reneging of the delivery of some furs. Jachal and Newcastle were Wittenberg and Lippstadt's local presence, and neither man was what Ferraz remembered as pleasant or reasonable.

Newcastle was an Irishman who had found Ireland too tame. A soldier-of-fortune, he once had been on the American FBI's most wanted list as a hired assassin; he had gone to South Africa but had left because killing black protesters, he said, was like shooting carp in a rain barrel; he had worked for the IRA, but when he killed an IRA member in a pub fight, he had departed Northern Ireland. Somehow he reached Manaus and fell in with the two Germans. He boosted that his nickname was not because of the color of his hair but was because he was able to make people bleed. All but a very few on the waterfront gave Newcastle a wide berth.

Ferraz didn't like him or trust him, not because Newcastle had administered a thorough beating and not because he was sadistic, but because he bragged. Bragging made a man too careless, made a man talk too much and made a man too ambitious.

Jachal was an Argentinean who, like the Germans, had been charged with human rights violations. He was a bully, too, but he had one redeeming feature: he was well educated, spoke several languages fluently, and could adapt to any gathering of men or women. He was as much at home in the Amozonas Theater as he was in the filthiest bar on the waterfront. He could charm a sea captain's wife with his conversation and gossip as easily as he could talk a whore out of her pay. And, Ferraz noted, he knew which was which.

If Lippstadt was invisible, only less so was the fifth member of the Wittenberg/Lippstadt hierarchy, Johann Flims. Flims was a Swiss banker, manager of the Bank of Switzerland in Manaus. The bank did not serve the general public. It served as depository for the international corporations and as the exchanger of currencies. In a way, it was unique in Brazil because it competed with the state banking system. It existed because Brazil found it necessary to protect its own funds in Swiss bank accounts and because the international corporations and cartels refused to use Brazilian banks, knowing that at any time they might be closed or, more likely, the money embezzled. The Bank of Switzerland was inviolate. The fact that the bank building itself was at least as secure as Fort Knox and that it was guarded by Swiss soldiers gave every depositor a sense of unflagging security. Indeed, since the rubber barons had arranged for its establishment, the bank had never suffered a loss of any kind.

The bank was an international money island ruled by Johann Flims. He treated corporation money with, he said, the same duty and respect he would were it the Corpus Christi. It was his religious duty. What he neglected to add publicly, however, was that also he was guarding, transporting and exchanging money from certain other parties, among them the proceeds from the shipping and smuggling interests of Herr Wittenberg and Herr Lippstadt.

The Germans had legitimate business enterprises. They owned most of the wharfs or piers along the waterfront; they had minor, and sometimes major, investments in a number of shipping companies and ships; they owned or were in partnership with others in owning tug boats; they provided many of the smaller crafts used by the river pilots; they owned a fleet of tugs and barges that plied the river system; they contracted with loggers and miners throughout the whole of central and western Brazil to ship cargoes.

For some, the latter business was an economic lifeline. The Germans found markets, arranged shipping, collected money, and brought in new equipment for hundreds of small miners and logging operators. They did so for unreasonably modest fees and tariffs, a fact no competitor could comprehend. Many tiny logging outfits would have failed had not the Germans been willing and able to consolidate the small rafts of individual loggers into huge shipments to Denmark and Japan, two of the most profitable markets.

Perhaps the other side of the shipping business subsidized that, the shipping of drugs, hides and artifacts. The drug business alone produced millions of dollars each year, dollars being the universal currency of the drug trade. Hides were in such demand, especially the skins of jaguars, that thousands of Indians and Brazilians spent their entire lifetime attempting to satisfy the demand. Indian artifacts were a small percentage of the smuggling business, and procurement involved mostly people in Peru, but hundreds of thousands of dollars were generated from the old Incan sites in the hills and mountains of Peru.

And, of course, there were people being moved surreptitiously in and out of Brazil. For those being *imported,* there was the guarantee of a safe haven. For those being *exported* with their money or their goods, there was a guaranteed safe delivery.

All this required a gigantic network and the cooperation of officials, sea captains and shipping dispatchers and receivers around the world. It also required the ability to secretly transfer unbelievable sums of money.

As Ferraz gathered his information and put together the extent of it, he was overwhelmed. He began to doubt the wisdom of his own plans. He was just about to give it up when he was summoned by two seamen to meet with Jorge Jachal.

ELEVEN

In the equatorial rain forest, what distinguishes the wet season from the dry season more than anything else is the rain's intensity and duration. During the wet season the rain is heavier and lasts longer, although there is hardly ever a day when the sun does not shine for a few minutes. Under the canopy, its shining is not always evident; the forest endures long periods of excessive dampness and heat. Always the heat.

If nothing else exists to control the forest, the mildew produced by the fungi serves to balance the growth and death of all organic matter. The wet season can be measured not only by the rise of the water in rivers, streams and swamps but by the amount of mildew covering everything: houses, hammocks, spears, blowguns, clay pots.

Anna suggested to Widel that perhaps a science fiction story she had read once might come true, that algae and mildew united and formed a living protoplasm that existed on people and took their forms, and when all the earth's people had been devoured, the protoplasm moved off into space, returning to earth in the hideous forms of the beings that had been eaten in other galaxies.

"For all we know," she concluded, "we are one of those hideous forms."

"More likely," Widel said, "we'll start turning white or green or black, like the mildew, and we'll all turn into some kind of fungus. With gills," he added.

The worst of the rainy season served the Masaki well. It promised that crops would be waiting to be harvested in the summer camps of the dry season.

And now there was speculation about the camp few had visited and which only Wasmaggi remembered or thought he remembered from long ago.

That last was his secret. Outwardly, he displayed an air of great confidence; inwardly, he wondered if he could find the camp, and if he did, what would be its condition. Would it support the village? Would it support the village for a long time? He could only hope so, if he found it. The inner doubts troubled him.

There were other doubters also, Anna and Widel. In Wasmaggi's vagueness, he had projected a trek of a month, give or take a factor of....

Of what? No Masaki had a measurement for time. A week, a month? What did that mean? Only Wasmaggi's suggestion that the travel would take twice as long as to other camps guided the whites' guess.

And herein the doubt. Neither Wasmaggi nor Tonto seemed capable of days of strenuous travel through the forest, and Lucknew and Pollyque were not much stronger. These four old people, the aged population of the village, could they endure thirty days of such laborious work?

They were not sick, and there was little Anna could do for them; certainly she could not reverse the passage of time. What to do with or about the elderly became a topic of conversation.

Wasmaggi reminded Anna that the old ones had secret places which, when they were no longer able to contribute and had become a burden to the village, would be their final resting place. Perhaps, he added, it was time for him to take his last journey.

When Anna protested, Wasmaggi assured her he was not ready. He had, he said, something more to give to the Masaki. When Anna asked what it was, he pointed to his head but would say no more.

Tonto and his wives had made their decision. They would continue on the journey, but if it proved beyond their capacity, they would camp along the way and do what hunting and food gathering they could. They promised they would not return to the village site.

Anna remembered the difficulties with Hagga on her last summer camp journey home. None of the present four represented the innate stubbornness of Hagga, but each did resemble her slowness. Nevertheless, Anna had made up her mind. The tribe would remain intact and complete the forest march as a unit, no matter how long it took.

If those four represented the oldest generation, then Saymore and Spiker, Hackway and Westman, Magwa and Hakma, Soomar and Janus, Mansella, Tilla and Moremew, Sarahguy and Joshway, Joqua and Xingu probably represented the next oldest, although there was a wide spread of ages among those fifteen Indians.

Contulla and Lurch and Cutilla and Amstay, along with Walkin and his wives, Yanna and Desuit, and Soomar's two unmarried children, Jappah and Jonquilla, were a third generation.

And Sayhoo and Fraylie, Merci and Manway, Armot, Oneson and Blue, and Barkah and Penny and Coanna and Love and Twoman, had she left anyone out?, were another generation, although their ages spanned ten years or more.

And somewhere in between was Mike. Actually, what started Anna thinking about the Masaki generations was her concern for Mike. It was long past the time when he might have taken a wife.

"Not marry, An-na," he said when she ventured to introduce the subject.

Mike's body was covered with the marks of the jaguar. To the Masakis that only made him more handsome. In fact, Jonquilla had done her best to capture his attention, even though Jonquilla knew that Mike was her half cousin and that Anna might not approve a marriage.

About that, Anna hadn't decided. It was not a clear cut issue, not like the requested marriage of Fraylie and Sayhoo. But so what? Unless Wasmaggi protested, Anna would give her approval.

But Mike would have none of it when Anna suggested it. It was enough that he was the jaguar hunter now. When Anna pressed him, he told her that he had loved once, and that was enough. Since Anna had known him since he was eight or nine, she wondered who he might have loved and who had rejected him. Immediately, she regretted the question.

"Mike love only Con-nie and An-na," he replied. "Not need love another." He trotted away without waiting for Anna's response.

143

Soon after that misguided conversation, Fraylie announced that he wished to undergo his trial. Sometimes a hunter's trial was a long period alone in the forest; other times, as with Mike, it was a particularly noteworthy manly performance in an adventure of danger. Sometimes the would-be hunter proposed his own trial.

Fraylie appeared before the campfire and asked the hunters to approve his trial. He would, he told them, find another Masaki village. He wanted a wife and he wanted to be a Masaki family. He convinced the hunters that his trial would serve him as well as serve the village. Among the hunters there was universal agreement not only to the trial itself but with Fraylie's promise to return with a wife.

The requested trial was so unusual that the hunters attached a qualification to their approval. Fraylie would be allowed to go only if he had a companion, a skilled hunter. They realized, the hunters told him, that a trial was supposed to be an individual test lasting a few days. What he had proposed might last forever, by which the Masakis meant a long time, and if another Masaki village was found, better two representatives.

Mike volunteered immediately, and it was well he did. He was the only candidate anyway, and since he carried the jaguar hunter's spear, he was the logical one to converse with another village.

With the first rays of light the next morning, the hunter and his apprentice were gone.

"Did you talk with them?" Widel asked Wasmaggi. "Do you know where they are going?"

"I talk, and tell them no hunter from this village knows where other villages are."

"You don't know, not even the direction?"

"Not even that. If knew, An-na would know. She does not."

"My God, how long will they travel if they don't find someone?"

"Maybe forever."

"A long time, you mean."

"Mean forever time."

"What if they give up and want to find us? We'll be at some place where they've never been? How will they ever find us? Aren't you afraid that they will be lost in the forest forever?"

"Wasmaggi think about that. Tell them all I know. Now Wasmaggi enough worry. Cannot worry more."

Jorge Jachal was dressed in a conservative business suit. The last time Paulo Ferraz had met him, Jachal was wearing the clothing of a dock worker. And the day Jachal and Michael "Red" Newcastle beat him senseless, Jachal was wearing a sport coat.

Today's meeting was planned carefully, Ferraz thought. Who else would have arranged a meeting on a ship? And in the captain's quarters?

"I thought this would be a private place," Jachal began. "We won't be disturbed."

Ferraz nodded. No, he thought, and if anything happens to me, who can help? Out loud he said, "It is comfortable."

"May I offer you something to drink? The captain has a much better selection than the waterfront bars." When Ferraz declined, Jachal continued. "No? Then perhaps we should get down to business."

"Yes, although I'm not sure what business we have."

"Doktor Ferraz, let's cut the bull shit. Have we met before?"

"You know we have."

"Yes. That was very unfortunate. As I remember, you made some promises and then failed to keep them, and there was a brief discussion."

"You and Newcastle kicked the crap out of me."

"Very unfortunate. Newcastle got carried away in the heat of the moment. I would not like the memory of that to discolor our talk."

"It's not something I'm likely to forget."

"I know it's a little late, but perhaps I can make up for it today."

Jachal seemed sincere, genuinely concerned with making a good impression and with setting Ferraz at ease. But Ferraz had his personal memory of the beating and an even greater awareness that Jachal had been a major figure in Argentina's *dirty war* of the seventies and eighties when more than nine thousand people disappeared and thousands of others were tortured.

Ferraz only had to look at himself to realize that nice clothing and cultured language and manners could mask diabolical intents. Jachal was a man to be feared, and Ferraz was afraid.

He remained on guard. "I doubt you have brought me here to apologize for the past."

"No, that's true. But if you can forgive the past, the present will be so much easier."

"Forgive? Forget? If you have something of interest, the past will not matter."

"Good for you, Doktor. I appreciate that. And I will, if I can, make up for the past."

"I take you at your word."

"Thank you. Now, let me get to the point. You went to some effort to meet Herr Wittenberg. As he remembers the conversation, you didn't say a damn thing. But you did get his attention and somehow you got his curiosity worked up. And when Herr Wittenberg's curiosity is aroused, well, that usually means a lot of work for me. You know, asking around, finding out certain things, and.... Well, you know what I mean.

"For instance, you've been doing a lot of asking yourself, and I guess that's really what my bosses want to know about. That and about Alfredo Herrera and your rather sizable organization of pistoleiros, and, of course, your sudden interest in the RADAM maps and reports."

"You have had a lot to do."

"It's kept me busy."

"And now you have come to a dead end?"

"How perceptive. But not really a dead end. Let's say that I've come to the place where I have to make a choice as to how I'm going to get the information I want."

"A choice?"

"I thought I might get whatever there is by talking with you. My alternative, Doktor, is to send Newcastle out to talk with some of your people, Rangel, maybe, or Eneas or some of the others."

"Quite honestly, Jachal, they don't have much to talk about."

"Perhaps, but then Newcastle isn't much for talking."

"I'm well aware of that." Ferraz also was aware of the fact that Jachal was fishing and didn't have the slightest idea what he was fishing for.

If Ferraz had felt uncomfortable up to now, suddenly he realized he was in control. Jachal would have done his homework well, and he would have realized that not one of Ferraz's men knew enough about the grand scheme he, Ferraz, had in mind to have been much help. So the men knew about Indian prostitutes and Ferraz's intention to obtain and sell them. Nothing unique in that. That's why Rangel and the others had not been hurt.

Jachal was at a dead end. There always was a potential for something big along the waterfront, and he couldn't get a handle on it. His meeting with Ferraz was an unconscious admission of that defeat. Ferraz wondered if Wittenberg and Lippstadt knew that Jachal was holding this meeting. It was time to find out.

"Jachal, I do have something, but not for you. I've some men and a modest means to do what I have in mind. But I'll say nothing about that except to Wittenberg and Lippstadt, and I mean to them directly. No intermediary."

The last thing Ferraz wanted was to get Jachal mad. He had to offer him something of substance, something that would make Jachal think that he had achieved a victory and at the same time lead Ferraz to the two Germans.

"I'll tell you this: I need Wittenberg and Lippstadt, and you and others. What I have in mind cannot be accomplished without you and your bosses. And I'm talking big, not big brags but big money. And I'll add this: even if you knew what it was, you couldn't pull if off without me."

And then Ferraz added what he hoped would be the clincher. "Herrera thought he could, but before he got a chance to find out, he died."

"Doktor, I'm going to let that last remark pass. It doesn't become you, admitting to murder. I don't take kindly to threats, if that's what you intended. But since Herrera was one of our competitors,

147

perhaps you did us a favor. In any event, you haven't given me much."

"I don't intend to. But your dead end can be opened easily. All you have to do is put me and Wittenberg and Lippstadt together."

"Christ, Doktor, I can't go to them and tell them that they should listen to you just because you say you've got something big. They'd have my head."

"Tell them I'm looking for a partnership."

"You're fuckin' crazy."

"Then tell them they don't need me; tell them I need them; tell them anything you want, but put us together. Tell them it's an investment of their time against the odds that they will add millions to their accounts. Better make that thousands. Don't want to promise what I can't deliver."

Jachal wondered how he had lost control of the meeting. What had he said or done that had turned Ferraz from a weak, scared wimp into a firm, secure adversary? Had he misjudged the man? And how was he going to report this development to the Germans?

Ferraz stood up. "Now, if you'll excuse me, I think our conversation has come to a natural conclusion." Ferraz started toward the cabin door, paused, and turned to face Jachal. "Perhaps before I go, you'll offer me a drink." He couldn't resist rubbing in his apparent victory.

"By.... Yes, by all means, please, have a drink." Jachal opened a cabinet. "What is your pleasure?"

"Do I see scotch there?"

When the drinks had been poured, Jachal raised his glass. "To your health, Doktor."

"Do I catch a bit of sarcasm in your toast?"

"No, Doktor Ferraz. As a matter of fact, what you sense is a measure of admiration. I was misled by our earlier encounter."

"I was at a disadvantage."

"And I misjudged you because of that. I should have realized that you would not have lost the skills of your earlier years. Just now you gave me something to take to my bosses."

"I did not intend to. What did I say?"

"Not what you said; what you did. You have balls. I rather like that, even if today you've rubbed my nose in my own lack of success."

As Ferraz walked down the gangplank, he was shaking, partly in relief and partly in victory, He had survived the meeting with his skin intact, and, he believed, he had managed to outwit Jorge Jachal. That fact, he hoped, would not come back to haunt him.

For all intents and purposes, Soomar had assumed the leadership role. With Tomaz gone and Tonto's age a severe restriction, it was natural that Soomar be regarded as chief hunter. Nothing was said; it was simply that the hunters looked more and more to Soomar for direction. So long in the shadow of his father, Soomar was uncomfortable with the unsought status. He sought counsel from Tonto and Wasmaggi and, surprisingly, Anna.

He had never known what to make of the two white girls. He had been bitterly opposed to the selection of Connie as the jaguar-hunter because he was firmly and completely convinced that the forest opposed women as hunters. Simultaneously, he admired Connie tremendously. In every way he had regarded her as his peer. Her tracking ability had been unmatched; her hunting instincts had been proven over and over again; her bravery had compelled him to praise and support her even when he knew she was wrong.

He didn't approve of Anna's hunting, either. If he had had his doubts about her becoming the medicine woman, they had vanished a long time ago. If anything, with her medicines, she brought something, he couldn't name it but he felt it, that Wasmaggi had never shown. And she had a wisdom about people and events that appealed to him, drew him toward her. He felt rather than saw many of the attributes Wasmaggi had sensed when he selected Anna to be his apprentice and the future medicine woman.

Several times Wasmaggi had said that Anna was tied irrevocably to the Masaki's future. Soomar had no idea what Wasmaggi meant; Soomar had little more than a vague concept of the future, but he did have a sense of Anna's importance to the village and to the tribe.

149

It was that sense that allowed him to tolerate the white women's appearance at the village campfires. Before the whites' came, women seldom were invited to the fire, and even less often were they allowed to speak. Anna, especially, had changed that, and women now not only sat in the front rows of the fire, they had taken to speaking. If others did not notice the change, Soomar did.

He was not making a judgment; he was noting that changes were taking place. And he was confused because all of the changes he noted could be traced directly to Connie and Anna. Yet, he had such respect for them that he tolerated the changes. He regarded Widel highly as the weapon maker and totally disregarded him as a hunter. If the changes had been traced back to Widel, Soomar might have reacted much differently.

This all came to a head a few days into the trek to Wasmaggi's special camp. Soomar had hoped that his daughter, Jonquilla, would be married to Mike. The way he approached the matter was to ask Anna if there were any hindrances to the marriage.

"If you mean," she said, "are there enough generations between them to gain my approval, there are not enough generations, but If they wish to marry, I've no reason to disapprove." Anna said nothing about Mike's earlier declarations, but she did add, "I thought the women usually made such inquiries."

"Is so. Janus make no effort. Says likes children at home."

"Jonquilla is ready to marry?" Anna wanted to say the child was too young, but that would have been her private valued judgment.

"Yes, but if not Mike, who her husband be?"

"I see the problem. She can't marry Fraylie for the same reason that Sayhoo cannot."

There was an awkward silence. Anna felt that Soomar really had had something else in mind when he first approached her. Not having the slightest clue as to what it might be, she would have to wait to see if it came up.

During the brief conversation, Soomar had stood in front of Anna. A man never sat down at a woman's fire unless he was invited to do so, and then he sat on the opposite side of the fire. If a man had more than a quick, informal conversation to conduct, it was customary for the man to ask the woman's husband for permission to speak. If the woman was unmarried, one or another of the parents had to be asked.

Often in her function as medicine women, the formality was neglected. Soomar had asked a question of the medicine woman, thus he had violated no custom. Anna had not asked him to sit, thus she had violated no custom. But since it was obvious Soomar had more on his mind than his daughter's marriage, Anna asked him to sit.

"Have not asked Ran-ford," Soomar said.

"He will understand."

"Would talk with An-na, but must ask Ran-ford."

"It is not necessary, Soomar. Sit and say what is on your mind."

"An-na is on my mind."

Oh, shit, Anna said to herself, prejudging Soomar's thoughts. She would have been equally as uncomfortable knowing that Soomar still regarded her as ugly and wholly undesirable in the way she was thinking. Soomar didn't help her uneasiness when he asked if she thought that he was the best hunter and the most skilled tracker.

She almost choked when she answered, "You are."

"And would An-na listen to Soomar?"

"Of course, Anna would listen." What choice did she have? She braced herself.

"Many changes since you come. Woman sit at fire with men; women speak at fire, sometimes too much; women and children eat with hunters; children go to others' fires; you hunt when no women hunt; Ran-ford cook, and now Joshway cook. Many changes; not Masaki way."

"Well, Joshway cooks because Sarahguy needs his help. She had a hard time carrying the baby and still is not very strong. If Janus was sick, would you help her?"

"What about other things?"

God, Soomar, Anna said to herself, you don't see the half of it. What about the changes of language? What about the words of French and Spanish and German the children have picked up in the songs? What about Widel's bows? What about some of the women wanting white children?

She thought back to when the three of them had worried about changing the Masaki culture. What about the children's games?

None of that did she mention. All of it was a fact of Masaki life now; for good or evil, she did not know. Her only defense was simple. "It is the way of the forest."

"That is what Wasmaggi said."

"You don't believe it?"

"I'm confused."

"Do you dislike it when Janus and Jappah and Jonquilla eat with you?"

"It is most pleasing. But it is not the way."

"Do you turn children away when they come to your fire?"

"No. Love children; sometimes play with them. Afterward say is not right."

"If Janus comes to you and says, 'Soomar, let us make love,' what do you do? Do you say, 'No, only a hunter may say when love will be made.'?"

Soomar studied the ground before answering. "No. Like be asked."

"Soomar, the village is really a family, a few families in one larger family. We have to take care of each other because every one is so important. We are on a long journey. You and I are strong; we will get to where Wasmaggi says we are going. But Tonto and Pollyque and Lucknew and Wasmaggi are not strong. We must help them. You know that. So Joshway cooks for Sarahguy because he has to. We all take care of the children because we have to. We have to take care of each other. Widel is a terrible hunter by your standards, so I help him hunt sometimes. The little children go to your fire because they love you and know you will protect them, and they go to Joqua's fire and to Moremew's for the same reason.

"And that's the reason the women go to the village fire. We are part of the Masaki family; we want to help protect it just as much as you do."

152

Anna stopped talking. She was sermonizing, but she had touched the cords that would relieve Soomar's doubts. He was satisfied for now, and later, when incomprehensible disaster struck, he would know with absolute certainty the truth of Anna's words.

"Ferraz, you seem to have made an impression of Jorge here. He hasn't told me a goddamn thing. I've known him for a long time, and he isn't given to impulsive actions, so I have to listen to him even when he isn't saying anything. But I warn you, I don't like to waste my time with two-bit schemes."

"Herr Wittenberg, I'm not going to waste your time."

"Then get on with it."

"I would like to do it with just the two of us."

"For Christ's sake, Ferraz. That's what Jorge told me." He nodded to Jachal. "Take a walk, Jorge."

When Jachal could be heard walking down the iron steps of the walkway that led from Wittenberg's third floor office on the waterfront, Ferraz began. He told Wittenberg about the SPI and about the "training schools," about his arrest and imprisonment, and something about his small-time activities along the waterfront. He described Projecto RADAM and his studies of the maps and reports, and he concluded by estimating that he could provide over a hundred young women.

Wittenberg listened patiently. "Have you left anything out?"

"I don't think so, nothing of importance, anyway."

"You didn't mention Alfredo Herrera."

"I met with him."

"He was dealing in Indian women."

"I know."

"And he was high up in FUNAI. I suppose he would have had all the information you have."

"If he wanted it."

"He had quite a substantial operation here. Someone finished it off one night. I might add that I suffered losses that night, too. Many of my best men were killed and some of the docks and equipment were mine. Do you have any ideas about it?"

Ferraz shook his head and pleaded ignorance.

"Yes. Well, Doktor, we'll see. But I'm not sure you've promised me much of a return. What do you figure a hundred women are worth?"

"Well trained? At least ten thousand each."

"A million dollars, and I suppose you'll want to split it. So I get half a million."

"Less some expenses."

"Yes, there always are expenses. What would my expenses be?"

"Taking the women when they are ready, providing them clothing, shipping them wherever you want to ship them."

"And what would your expenses be?"

"Organizing the procuradores, outfitting them, training the women. Food, equipment, whatever."

"It wouldn't seem to leave you much profit."

"Well, there are other benefits: skins, some male workers, Indian goods. They would help pay the expenses."

"Indian males aren't worth the trouble."

"A few are."

"And when could I expect the first women?"

"Nine months from when we begin."

"Why so long, if you think you know where to begin?"

"Because you want first class women. It takes months to train a first class whore." Ferraz began to describe just what the training involved, but Wittenberg was not interested.

"I'll give you ten months, Ferraz, and I'll expect ten perfect whores for which I'll pay you five perfect thousand dollars each. Fifty thousand dollars. Then we'll see what happens after that."

"You understand that there will be a limited supply, that once the supply is used up, there won't be any more."

"You've made that clear."

"So I want a commitment for the whole number."

"You what?"

"I want your commitment for a hundred women. If the first ten are satisfactory, I want to know the rest will be taken."

"Well, I can't offer that. If the first ten are good, I'll take another ten. And if they prove serviceable, another ten, until we get to one hundred. Only a fool would agree to purchase unknown goods sight unseen."

"And I want twenty-five thousand of those perfect dollars of yours up front."

"You certainly are in a demanding mood, Doktor."

"I'll have a lot of beginning expenses."

"Any other demands?"

"No, just those two."

"I'll have the money delivered to you. I warn you, Ferraz, if you fail to deliver this time, there will be no beating. You'll live to wish you never heard of me. Understand? Now, I've a couple of suggestions of my own. First, I want to make it clear we are not partners in any way. You will supply goods that I'll examine, and if they meet my quality, I'll buy them for the stated price.

"Second, when you go into the sertáo, my man Newcastle will go with you. Third...."

"No! I'll not take Newcastle. He is a man of senseless violence. The kind of brutality he demonstrates will make the whole plan unworkable. Send whoever else you want. I suppose you must do that, but not Newcastle."

"It will be Newcastle or there will be no deal."

When Ferraz left, Wittenberg opened a side door in his office and spoke to a man sitting in a wheelchair. "What did you make of it?"

Herman Lippstadt rolled his chair into the office. "The money isn't worth it," he told Wittenberg.

"No, but he might bring us other things, too."

"Maybe; I doubt it, but I approve. Actually, I began a list where such women would bring us more than money. It could be a good investment to supply some women. He's right about Newcastle, Hans. I don't think you should have forced that on him."

"Who else? We need Jorge here, and certainly we need someone to protect our interests."

155

In an earlier time, Lippstadt would have gone. When he and Wittenberg and Jachal first landed in Manaus, they had worked as their own tropas de resgates or slave hunters. Lippstadt had taken an arrow in his back during an Indian fight, and it had left him with partial paralysis. He could walk short distances with the aid of crutches but found it easier and more convenient to use the wheelchair.

The amazing thing about his disability was that it had not made him outwardly bitter against the Indians; he had come to respect their courage and bravery, arrows and spears against guns. But he wished he could continue the fight, prove his own superiority, the superiority of the branco over the brown.

Only when he slept with an Indian prostitute did his brutality surface. He would ravage her, tearing her open with his gigantic penis, delighting in her screams and finding his satisfaction in her blood. Only when blood flowed from between her legs could he achieve an orgasm.

Such sadism required many Indian women, and quite apart from all their other activities and investments, Lippstadt had his own small army of procuradores which spent its entire time finding Indian women for him.

Wittenberg tolerated this behavior, but now he felt he must make the situation clear. "None of these women are for us, Herman. They're no good when you get through with them. We have to deliver undamaged goods."

"Yes, Hans, I know. You know that business comes first."

Wittenberg accepted the response, although he knew no such thing. If there was trouble about the women, he would deal with it when and if it arose.

As if to prove that he had assumed the role of the chief hunter, Soomar called for the villagers to get moving. He chastised those who were slowly finishing their morning meal or who were delinquent in having their meager belongings ready for the trail. Already the manteau of leadership was resting heavily on his shoulders. He was anxious to make the journey, to go to a place where only Wasmaggi had been. The strange, frightening noises the forest had made and Anna and Widel's reactions of horror to those noises pushed him forward toward a place of safety.

He had no doubt but that they were embarked on an arduous journey. His mind was heavy with his responsibility for the old ones. He would not, and he had the medicine woman's full support, allow the elders to separate themselves from the villagers.

The initial days of walking, Widel noted, were directly east. The Masakis were far beyond their hunting range. There were no trails; if ever there had been trails, they long since had become overgrown.

It was impossible for the villagers to stay together and to keep the pace Soomar set. The village was spread out in several lines, one or two hunters and their families making their own way through the dense, tangled undergrowth. Occasionally a hunter would disappear, to reappear later with food which, as was the custom, was shared equally.

As always, the hunters led the way, followed by their wives and children. Joshway and Sarahguy had included Mansella and her son in their group. Oneson was getting on, Anna noted, and in a couple of years would undergo his trial. Mansella had raised him since birth with little help. Her husband had been drowned soon after Mansella became pregnant. Walkin, her nephew, had watched out for her, but when he married Desuit and Yanna, Mansella seemed to be on her own. Thus it was no surprise to Anna that on the trail Joshway had been to Mansella's bed, and Anna predicted that Joshway would take Mansella as his second wife.

If asked, Anna would have to disapprove the marriage; she hoped she was not asked. Perhaps she should offer Mansella some of the no-birth medicine, just in case, because if a child resulted from Joshway's and Mansella's activities, it would be allowed to die.

"Isn't she a little old for him?" Widel asked.

"Family, Widel. Family. No one has come along. She's had a hard ten years, but I've never heard her complain. Sarahguy will welcome it; she's not well. Joshway will adapt to it."

For the most part, Penny was carried in a hammock slung over Anna's shoulders and back. Unless children were able to keep up on their own, they were carried, often creating an exceptionally heavy burden for the mother. If hunting and food gathering was successful, mothers would more than triple the weight of their child with the loads they carried.

It was a rare hunter who carried a cumbersome load. First, he had his arsenal to carry: blow guns, darts, bow and arrows, spears. Second, he had to be on guard against attacking jungle beasts and ready to spring into action at a second's notice. And third, it was not the custom. On the long treks, the women were beasts of burden.

Widel was the one exception. Besides his weapons and the tools to make them, he carried many of Anna's precious medicines. The one thing neither of them carried in any great amount was food; that came from the hunters as Widel's deserved share.

TWELVE

It was amazing how silently the people moved through the forest. There was very little conversation; the effort of penetrating the nearly impenetrable forest left little energy for idle chatter. And there were no sounds from the children. They seemed to know instinctively that silence was demanded. They had only to utter the tiniest of whimpers to have their needs met, toilet and food being the most pressing.

Once, Anna and Widel had discussed the children's silence. Anna had reported on Blue's silence when he was dragged away by a jaguar. It's something in the genes, she said. Widel had argued that it was somehow learned, passed on from child to child rather than from parent to child. Very doubtful, Anna had replied, yet observing her own baby, she was changing her mind. Maybe it was learned. Penny did not cry. Instinctively, she seemed to know when quietness was necessary. How could she learn that, Anna asked? It isn't in our genes, Widel offered.

If Penny wished to feed, her carrier could be drawn around so she faced her food source and Anna could nurse her as she walked. It was not the most comfortable arrangement, putting additional strain on the mother's back, but it could be tolerated for a time.

Masaki children might nurse until they are four or five. Long after they are capable of eating solid foods, the children seek out their mother's breasts. And they are welcomed just as long as they suck. When Widel expressed wonderment, Anna told him that the practice was born of necessity. In times of severe food shortages, the mother would eat what food there was. Her milk would sustain the children. Sometimes, she had been told, a mother's milk would feed a whole family for short periods if water and food were not available.

"We're really cows, I guess," noting her own milk laden breasts.

Widel felt a tinge of guilt. The breasts that had stood out so firm and erect, the breasts he had admired so greatly, now hung swollen and sagged under their own weight. He still was aroused by the sight and thought of them, but he felt remorse and worried that he had done Anna some bodily harm. He frowned, and Anna asked him what was wrong.

"Just a man's thought," he offered as excuse.

"About me?"

"About what I've done to you."

"Done or are going to do?" Anna teased.

The families had converged on a tiny clearing. Some daylight remained, but Soomar said they would camp and rest. He pointed to the south, indicating the direction Wasmaggi had laid out for the rest of the journey. The past twenty-one days had been hard; the next ten or more would be twice as hard, Wasmaggi told them.

Now Soomar wanted Anna to examine every member of the village. There were lots of scratches and bruises. Particularly, he wanted Anna to examine the old ones. So far they had managed. Their loads had been shared by others and they had not had to clear any trails, but Soomar wanted no surprises and certainly he did not want any sickness.

"I suggest," Anna told Soomar, "that shelters be erected for the aged ones and that nice, comfortable beds be prepared. I'll give them something to make them sleep soundly. And while you hunters are making shelter, get someone to kill a few macaws. A good meal and a sound sleep will keep us going."

She asked those villagers with complaints to line up beside the fire. When only a handful responded, Anna spoke to Soomar. "It's not time for proving courage. Everyone should be examined, including you. You're first. Then you can make the others get in line."

"Soomar no...." One look from Anna and he stood at the front of the line.

As tired as he was, Wasmaggi would not take Anna's medicine until he had given Soomar instructions. At first light and for every day thereafter, a pair of hunters should push ahead. They were looking for a particularly large swamp in a land of large swamps. Wasmaggi drew a crude sketch in the dirt. He hoped his memory would not fail him.

"Should come to one, two, three swamps. High land between each, so walk will be easy. Third swamp will come. Will take three days walk around. Walk fast. Three days. If less, wrong swamp; if more, wrong swamp. When think found, Wasmaggi will know for sure. Make no marks on trees. No marks on trail. Secret place no secret if hunters leave marks. Only marks must be in mind."

Walkin and Joqua would leave at first light.

Around their fire, Widel reflected on Wasmaggi's directions. "Sounds like he was describing a moat. In the middle of one of those swamps there must be an island. I hope there is a lot of overhead cover. Just in case an airplane comes looking."

"Thanks a lot, husband. You've spoiled the mood. Back on the trail, you had my interest. Now you've get me worried. I won't be able to think of anything else except airplanes."

"Ever since the first one, they're never out of my mind. We have to learn to live with that, take what we can while we can." As Widel talked, he lifted the sleeping Penny from Anna's lap and placed her in her hammock.

"I looked at you today and felt guilty for making you a mother."

"What a weird thing to say. You wish you hadn't?"

"No. That's not what I wish at all. It just that...well, look what I've done to you."

"For God's sake, Widel. What do you think you have done to me?"

"What you said."

"What did I say, for heaven's sake."

"That you're a cow."

"Oh, Widel, you poor slob. You heard me complain about my breasts sagging and feeding our child, didn't you? God, Widel, that's just woman's talk. It doesn't mean anything. I wouldn't trade what has happened for anything in the world. You know that."

"But...."

"But they aren't as nice and round as they used to be? Is that it? I hated my breasts when I was a kid. No, that's not true. I liked them and I liked what they could do to guys like you. But I hated what you guys said about them, and sometimes I wished I was smaller."

"I never said anything. Not one word did I ever say."

"Yes, that's true. You didn't have to. I knew what you were thinking."

"And what was I thinking?"

"I'm not going to say because you know."

"That I wanted to hold them, rub them, kiss them? You wanted me to say it, didn't you?"

"Something like that. But now they don't stand out straight like they did when you first ogled them, and now you're disappointed."

"I never ogled them, and I've never been disappointed."

"You did too ogle them."

"Never."

"Like you're not ogling them now."

"I'm not ogling. I'm just looking."

"So I see. Perhaps you'd like a closer look."

Ferraz had put together his bandeira. Besides his own trusted men, Rangel, Eduardo, Eneas, Rogelio, and Simón, he had the two who had worked for Herrera, Czura and Pavón, and of necessity and much against his will and better judgment, Red Newcastle.

There had been an argument immediately. Ferraz's plan was to travel up the Negro River to Tauapeçaçú, complete the supplying of the party there, purchase a barge and barge north up the Apuahú River as far as the craft could go. Then they would travel the sertáo on foot.

Newcastle was opposed to trekking on foot. All Indians, he said, lived on the rivers. Boats were the only sensible mode of travel.

162

"These are undiscovered Indians we look for," Ferraz tried to explain. "First, the sounds of motors will send them fleeing into the jungle. They'll scatter so far we'll never even see one. Second, they don't live on the major rivers. They live on little streams and water byways. Boats will be useless. Our only chance for success is hiking."

Ferraz spread out the maps he had prepared and the maps released by Projecto RADAM. "See?" he asked. "Here are the possible networks of trails. There's an old camp there, and another one there. No rivers. Look, only tiny streams."

Newcastle didn't acknowledge the evidence. Sullenly, he remarked that gunboats would capture anything. In the end, of course, he was forced to accept Ferraz's approach. He had his orders from Wittenberg and Lippstadt not to interfere.

Offhandedly and apropos of nothing, Anna remarked to Wasmaggi that even with Mike and Fraylie off looking for another Masaki village, their own village numbered more persons than ever before. Since the whites had arrived, only Connie, Hagga, and Tomaz had died, and their places have been taken by Desuit and Yanna and their children and by Xingu's and Sarahguy's and her own baby.

"You give us more than one," offered Wasmaggi, "when you and Con-nie save Armot." He thought back to the very first day when Anna had dragged Armot from the river and Connie had breathed new life into the child. "Forest gave Masaki gift; forest gave Masaki new life when you appear. An-na life of Masaki."

She was uncomfortable whenever Wasmaggi spoke that way. It was as if he saw in the future some dire times for the tribe and saw her as the Masaki's salvation. He would or could not say what he saw in the future, and Anna had come to believe what Widel had claimed so often, that some of the Indians, especially Wasmaggi, had presentiments or premonitions that were remarkably accurate. It had been that way with Tomaz, too, although neither Widel nor Anna had discovered that power among the younger Masaki.

Everyone wanted to give the old ones a hand or an arm. At one point, Lucknew hollered out at one well-meaning hunter. "Let go, stupid one! There are more hands than vines!" She grunted and groaned along for a few minutes. "You cause more trouble than whole forest."

As the village rested in a tiny clearing on the thirteenth day on the southerly route, Walkin and Joqua rushed up. Yes, they believed they had found the swamp; no, they had not found the entrance leading to the swamp; they had not tried to find it because they had found footprints!

Four sets of footprints, to be exact, two women and two that might be children. Of the latter, they weren't sure. They had followed the prints for a short way, but not knowing what they were getting into, they backtracked the prints for a longer distance.

Whoever belonged to the footprints were in obvious hunger. They were eating roots raw; they had cracked open a turtle and had eaten it raw. Their trail seemed to lead from nowhere; it was aimless at every point.

Since there were only Masakis in the forest, the hunters decided immediately that the four must be lost, perhaps separated from a hunting party or from their own village. Soomar would go with Walkin and Joqua and find out who the strangers were.

Someone suggested that if the group of strangers was women and children, perhaps it would be prudent to take along a woman and a child. Soomar agreed. Mansella and Oneson would go in place of Joqua, then they would look like a family hunting party, not a raiding party.

In the meantime, the rest of the campers were to remain where they were and prepare to protect the group from whatever unseen enemies might be afoot.

Widel found this last suggestion highly unusual. If, as the Masakis believed, they were the sole inhabitants of the forest, who could be their enemies? His thoughts were drawn back to the day Sampson and his men attacked the village and how swiftly his own people had reacted with a well thought out defense and counterattack. It was as if they had practiced the procedure many times. He remembered the stealth and cunning both approaching Sampson's village and meeting the threats of nighttime attack and the ambush. It had to be more than instinct.

Four weeks and who knew how many miles away from their familiar hunting grounds and in a part of the forest never seen before, the Masakis find footprints at a swamp's edge. A people who never spoke of war and who had no word for war were out posting guards, hunters seeking the most advantageous sites. It was broad daylight when they started their cooking fires. Toward nightfall, all of the hunters had wandered away from the fires, and those who had gone earlier returned. And later, when the fires were allowed to burn low, only Tonto, Wasmaggi, and Widel remained with the women and children.

With daylight, a few hunters returned, ate and left. They would make a sweep of the entire perimeter, looking for evidence of unseen foes.

Nothing was found, for the Indians confirming their earlier judgment that whoever was wandering was lost.

It took two days for Soomar and Walkin to find the strangers. If they had been walking carelessly and aimlessly when Walkin and Joqua came upon their tracks, now they walked with uncanny skill, aware of being followed.

Soomar and Walkin were as good as any in the forest, and Mansella was as capable as most hunters. She was, after all, Tomaz's daughter and Soomar's sister. If the little party had a weakness, it might have been Oneson, but he was nearing the time of his trial and had been instructed by Mansella and Walkin.

During all his boyhood years, he had mirrored Walkin's actions. He was doing that now, step by step, motion by motion. He made no movement unless that movement had been made by Walkin; even his breathing was in unison with Walkin's.

Something had spooked the four ahead. Was it the howler monkeys? Their continuous ruckus hadn't seemed to change. Birds? So carefully had Soomar and the others moved that the birds had not seemed to notice. Yet the group ahead knew. Suddenly there was no trail, no footprints, no bruised or twisted leaves, no bent twigs. For all intents and purposes, that group had vanished into thin air.

Soomar called a halt. He had to find the answer to two questions: what was betraying them and how could the strangers vanish without leaving some sign somewhere?

The three adults conferred in barely audible whispers. Soomar was a little shaken when he realized he was seeking the input of a woman. Then he smiled, thinking of Anna.

Oneson listened, but he knew he would be reprimanded severely if he spoke, so he allowed his attention to wander. He made a little place for himself in the brush and stretched out.

He watched a group of black spider monkeys playing in the trees overhead. Unlike the howlers, the spider monkeys make very little noise unless they are scared or disturbed, and then they chirp, often being mistaken for insects or birds. And unlike other monkeys, if the spider monkey is frightened, it will dash away silently with lightning speed, jumping and swinging from tree to tree until it has gained a safe distance.

Oneson watched the group of six that played overhead. He saw another group, three this time, in another tree. And then, suddenly, both groups disappeared. At first he wanted to call out.

Instead, he touched his mother's arm. Mansella brushed away the boy's hand. He started to speak, and Mansella gave him the kind of look that only an impatient mother can give. He turned to Walkin and pointed up into the trees. There was nothing there.

"Not now, Oneson," Walkin whispered.

"Know," Oneson said.

Soomar looked at him angrily; Mansella raised her hand, her final signal for silence.

"Wait." Walkin interrupted the visual hushing. "Let boy speak. Maybe boy see what man miss."

Oneson spoke with the clarity of centuries in the forest. "Spider monkey here; spider monkey go." He had said it all in six boyish words. While the adults were studying the ground, overhead the spider monkeys were giving away secrets.

166

Monkeys, no less than other creatures, are creatures of habit. When they are upset for whatever reason, they flee; when the reason has passed, the overwhelming odds are that they will return to the spot recently vacated. If one watches scampering monkeys, does not disturb them himself, then they will return to the spot under which was the someone or something that had disturbed them.

Whoever was leading on Soomar's group had used the spider monkey as a warning system. But the system works both ways. Followers can watch the monkeys, too, and thanks to Oneson, Soomar and Walkin soon found their strangers.

But finding and holding proved to be two different tasks. They were, as guessed, two women and two children six or seven years of age. All four were visibly undernourished. From all appearances they were Masaki, and except for being badly in need of food, they appeared to be in reasonably good health.

Mansella and Oneson hid in the brush as Soomar and Walkin confronted the women. The women had fashioned inferior spears which they held at the ready, and when Soomar spoke to them, they brandished their spears as unmistakable threats. They understood Soomar well enough, but they made no reply. The children looked bewildered, and while they were not frightened by Soomar and Walkin, they did not give the appearance of welcoming them. At best, their reaction was an ambivalent confusion.

It was a stand off. Neither man wanted to approach the hostile women, and it was obvious the women wished the men had not appeared.

Only when Mansella and Oneson stepped into view did the women react; they dropped their spears, knelt on the ground, and cried, a wailing that Mansella had not heard since she herself was told of her husband's drowning. Whatever their agony, it seemed to her the two women had come to the end of their rope. She went to them to comfort them, and as she kneeled and reached out to put her arm around each, her mind reacted to the shortness of the women's hair.

These women were Solmar and Beck, the woman from Sampson's village who had attacked Widel, who had killed their

167

babies or had let them die, whose heads had been shaved, who had been banished to the forest, and who had been promised reentry into the Masakis' society only when their hair grew back to its initial length.

All this came to Mansella in the briefest of moments, but she was confused. Each woman had a child. Their children hadn't been killed; they must have been hidden away in the forest the night the woman came and attacked Ranford. The men had passed judgment on two innocent women whose only crime, beyond the unexplainable attack on Ranford, was to have hidden their children and to have refused to reveal that fact.

To be banished for hiding one's child.... Instead of wrapping the women in her arms, Mansella stood up and struck Soomar as hard as she could. Her anger was insatiable. Walkin had all he could do to wrestle her to the ground.

Soomar was stunned. Not only was there no explanation for Mansella's attack, Mansella had performed an unforgivable offense. Only the fact that she was his sister prevented Soomar from striking back, that and the presence of Oneson who had taken up one of the women's spears and stood between his mother and his uncle.

Mansella screamed out her story. Soomar appeared ready to burst. Finally he screamed. "Woman, I know who they are. Our father and Walkin and Soomar and all the hunters sent them into the forest. We were on the trail from Sampson's village when they left us with their babies. Look... at...the...children! They are twice as old as these women's babies would be. Look!"

It was true. The children Solmar and Beck had with them were five or six years older than their babies would have been. And when Mansella looked at the women again, they had regained their composure, a look of hate covering their faces. Mansella burst into tears.

Everlasting credit goes to those who unexpectedly do the right thing. Soomar stepped to Oneson, placed a hand on the boy's shoulder, took the ragged spear from him and broke it with one blow of his fist, and then hugged the boy. "You are a brave boy to protect your mother so," he said.

Then he reached down and drew Mansella to her feet. He held her face between his rough palms, and tears flowed from his eyes. He kissed his sister on the forehead, not because it was the natural thing to do but because he had seen the whites do it to comfort those who needed comforting. "I love you even when you are wrong. We say no more because Soomar does not understand women."

T H I R T E E N

They spent three days herding Beck and Solmar back toward the temporary camp. The two women fought every step of the way and for the most part literally were dragged through the forest. The two children, the female, Laiti, and the male, Awhawk, simply followed, quietly shepherded by Mansella and Oneson.

Laiti and Awhawk were without will or direction, lost in the depth of confusion and despair. They did what they were told to do by whoever told them, and if they were not told to do something, they did nothing. They had to be told to eat, to rest, even to attend to their toilet functions.

The ever-struggling women and the children who could not walk without a direct order slowed the party to a crawl.

Just after the third day's sunrise, Walkin whispered to Soomar. "Being followed."

"Soomar know."

"Four hunters maybe."

"That what Soomar think."

"Cannot move with speed."

"No. Must keep moving. If bad hunters, find out soon enough."

"Four against two bad."

"If all else, must help Mansella and Oneson escape. But soon have help. Tonto will have sent out guides to meet us. We been gone much time. But now wish even Ran-ford was here."

There was no more conversation. In the forest made more hostile by the unseen presence of unknown others, listening was the most important sense. Sight lines were necessarily short, especially if a man or a women wanted it so. Sounds were the only reliable warnings.

It was uncanny how the hunters could distinguish between their own sounds and the sounds of the women and children with them and the sounds of those who followed.

After a time, Soomar called a halt in a tiny clearings lit by a thin shaft of sunlight. "We wait," he announced. "Others come. Make no secret."

He turned to Mansella, whispering something that could not be heard. She nodded. In a louder voice he commanded her to build a fire. Similarly, he whispered to Oneson, then loudly ordered him to help his mother. To the two women prisoners he said nothing, nor did he speak to the two children.

The fire Mansella and Oneson managed was uncharacteristically large and smoky, just as Soomar had ordered. The smoke rose slowly in ugly billows, hanging in numerous layers over the forest floor. The smoke itself did not move far, but its odor radiated for a considerable distance. With luck, it would serve as a signal.

Soomar and Walkin took the best positions possible. If attacked, the most they could provide Mansella and Oneson was a few yards of advantage into the undergrowth. Should a battle ensue, it would have to do. Soomar and Walkin knew that Mansella would not run. She would stand and fight, her one purpose in a losing cause to give Oneson a chance to escape. She hoped he would take it. She would give her life for his.

Soomar and Walkin could hear the movement of the four unknown hunters and shifted positions to conform to those movements. The waiting went on almost to mid afternoon. To Soomar and Walkin, the waiting was precious time. Each minute of waiting could mean that help was a minute closer.

Nothing happened. Soomar remarked to Walkin that perhaps their unseen guests waited for reinforcements of their own. Or, he added, perhaps they could not afford to lose a single man, even though surely they would win the fight.

"Perhaps it is time to find out," Walkin said.

"Soomar agree." He motioned to Mansella.

Mansella stood up, careful to keep a substantial tree to her back. "Mansella," she shouted loudly, "have fire but no food to

171

feed hungry family. Mansella invite peaceful hunters to fire, even if have no food to share."

Her words were as non-threatening an invitation to a confrontation as she could make them. What happened next was up to the stalkers.

The four hunters had taken positions around Soomar's group. They were cautious in the extreme, not because of fear, not because they were waiting for reinforcements, not because they lacked will and motivation, but because, after a year and a half of futile searching by hunters from their village, they had found the children. Nothing would hasten their attack; nothing would threaten their success; after so long a search, time was irrelevant.

When Trulk and his searching party, Vecan, Bleer and Walcome, had cut the trail of Solmar and Beck and the children, they had tasted the first fruit of success. Then, when they cut a second fresh trail, they became both confused and apprehensive. Had the women joined up with a larger force?

Trulk and his companions had missed the actual meeting of Soomar's "family" and Beck and Solmar by a whole day, having picked up the final trail only as Soomar and Walkin had begun to drag the two women through the forest. It was this sight, with all its sounds of fury, that caused the hunters to follow rather than attack. Something was askew in the whole scene. The one right thing was that the children, Laiti and Awhawk, were being treated kindly.

More than a year and a half ago, food began to disappear from their village, dried fish and roasted monkey meat mostly. For a while the thievery was assigned to the cunning of a jaguar. That a jaguar could enter the village undetected was unnerving. Guards were posted, nets were set, the jaguar hunter worked night and day but to no avail. No jaguar was caught, much less seen, nor were there any signs of jaguars in the village vicinity, no paw prints, no spoor, no howling or whistling. Still, the thefts continued for several weeks, two or three nights a week. The amount of food stolen never was great, but in a land where there is never much food, even a small amount was a lot.

When it became clear that no jaguar was to blame, suspicions arose among the villagers, an awkward situation since outright stealing was unknown. Like all Masaki, the village had no word for stealing and no clear concept of theft.

As with so many mysteries, it's a little thing that leads to a solution. In this case it was the Masakis' habit of keeping tabs on each other. One dark night, someone noticed that two more Masakis entered the village than had left it to attend to their nightly needs and that later two people went into the forest who did not return. It took a night of thought for that observation to sink in, almost a whole day for the meaning of the thought to surface as an articulated thought. When it was announced at the evening campfire, it was greeted with disbelief; there were no other people, therefore how could others enter and leave the village?

Of course there were other people, and among the villagers Trulk and a handful of the oldest hunters knew that. Always there had been talk about other Masaki villages, although most had come to believe that that's what it was: talk.

The oldest hunters did not sleep that night; they spent the hours whispering among themselves. At first light they were on the paths leading in and out of the village. They had completely overlooked the most obvious clue, footprints, because until last night it had not occurred to them that there could be prints made by what they called *others*.

Human footprints, like fingerprints, are distinctively personnel if transferred carefully with ink onto a clean piece of paper. In the mud and rotting vegetation of the forest floor, footprints take on a sameness. They are either large or small or smaller; they are made by someone of largeness, that is, of weight, or someone lighter. Children's footprints can be picked out readily enough, but picking out an individual child's or a woman's or a man's prints proved impossible. So much for primitive detective work.

Widel would have known that something unique would have been done, that somehow or other the Masaki would invent the very method needed to determine the facts.

And the hunters did. Just before dark, the hunters spoke to each family. No one for whatever reason was to leave the village that night, not even to answer a call of nature. Under cover of darkness, all available entrances to the village were swept smooth. Any movement in or out of the village would be recorded on the smoothed pathways.

For the next three mornings, all accesses to the village were as smooth as an undisturbed puddle. And there were no thefts.

On the fourth morning there were two sets of tracks, and again food had disappeared. Did the tracks enter and leave the village, or did the tracks leave and then reenter the village?

There was no doubt the tracks were made by women. But which women? Beyond the smoothed out areas there were no usable clues. Although the hunters searched with all the skill of centuries, it was impossible to track one or two individual women in and around the village.

Then, as mysteriously as the stealing had begun, it ended. Weeks went by with no incidents of missing food, and gradually the village relaxed, finally lowered its guard completely.

Then one night two children disappeared from under their own shelters, from within feet of their sleeping parents, Laiti from one household, Awhawk from another.

Their disappearance went unnoticed until the sun had risen fully. While the children never would have left the village, it was possible they had wandered to other houses. Since neither set of parents was aware that another child was missing, they did not become unduly alarmed. But when the breakfast fires were refreshed and food was prepared and the children did not return to their homes, two pairs of parents began to hunt for their offsprings. No one had seen them, but very quickly it became obvious that the two children were missing not only from their homes but from the village itself.

Early departed hunters were recalled from the forest. An emergency meeting was held. Masakis think first of jaguars, but again, no evidence of tiger activity was found. The second thought was of the others' footprints, and searching and tracking parties were formed immediately. Every able-bodied person in the village was pressed into service, covering wider and wider circles around the village. Possible clues were found here and there, but some were so far apart as to be impossible to link to others.

Gradually, over a length of time and because of the thoroughness of the search, it was possible to piece together what had been going on for so long and what was undoubtedly the fate of the children. Well hidden trails and hiding places were discovered, one, two, three days from the village. Tiny piles of garbage were discovered, and hidden toilet troughs. Wads of kapok, traced with stains, were found hidden in the most unlikely places, evidence that women had been near the village for several months. It was no blind leap of logic to guess that at least two women had kidnapped the two children. Why or for what purpose, no one could guess.

For weeks the search for the children occupied the exclusive attention of the entire village. After several weeks, it became necessary to provide for the village. Women went back to the gardens and to their gathering; men went out to hunt. But always a small group of hunters searched, the hunters taking turns.

And for a year and a half the search continued. Always the group numbered six hunters, and always as they searched they hunted, and when they had hunted successfully enough to provide something for the village, two of the hunters would return to the village with the meat and two different hunters would join the four left in the field.

The hunters roamed vast areas of forest where none had set foot before, making secret and well hidden marks throughout the forest. Time after time they had been close, often without knowing it, but always they had been too late or too baffled by the false trails left by the women.

Until a few days ago when the four closed in on the swamp and found the meandering trail of two women and two children searching for food. In such areas it was impossible to tell whether a trail was an hour old or a week old, but it was a positive trail. With the women and children obviously in poor condition, it would be only a matter of time before the search ended. Successfully, the hunters hoped.

Trulk was a small man even by Masaki standards, shorter by several inches than the average Masaki male and so thin as to be scrawny. His size was accentuated by his age and by the volcano of gray hair that spilled over his head. He was ancient, with all the wrinkles that accompanied age. Yet he was as spry as a child and as alert as a cat. He was a force of power. He carried the jaguar hunter's spear. And now he made a decision.

Stepping from his cover in the forest, he revealed himself to Mansella. "I have hunters who will provide food," he said, "in exchange for the use of your fire." He ignored completely Soomar and Walkin, the two woman and the two children.

"All Masakis are welcome," Soomar said, "you and your hunters."

Trulk continued to ignore Soomar. To Mansella he added, "To be invited to a woman's fire pleases an old man."

Mansella looked at Soomar. He shook his head affirmatively. Mansella looked back to Trulk. "You have been a long time approaching."

"We have been a long time searching."

"For what do you search?"

"Two children. And the women who took them."

At no time did Trulk so much as glance at any one other than Mansella. He studied her carefully, not only looking at her but seemingly into her, into her mind and into her heart.

"You will know the children when you have found them?"

"We will know, and they will know us."

"Have you found them?"

Trulk did not respond to that question. Instead he asked, "Which is your man?"

"I have no man. My husband was drowned before my son was wet with birth."

"Is one of these your son?"

"Yes." Mansella nodded toward Oneson.

"Then these women belong to these men, and these are their children?"

176

"No. These men have wives and children in our village. But these women we know."

"And are these their children?"

"No."

"Then," said Trulk, "perhaps these are our children."

For reasons she could not explain then or later, Mansella became abnormally protective of the children. In a moment of inspiration, she decided she would like to have them, and in that very moment Trulk read her thoughts. She started to say that they were her children, but Trulk cut her off.

"Woman, we will take the children. Perhaps if they had no mother, no father, you would be their mother. It is not to be."

He lifted his hand slightly and his three companions edged out of the brush, spears at the ready. "It would be useless to fight us. We have had a long journey over much time for this moment."

It was, of course, hopeless. Soomar wondered why Mansella had taken such an obviously false track, but before he could explore the thought, there was a flurry of activity behind him. He turned in time to see Lurch holding one of the searchers two feet off the ground, and by the time he turned back to Trulk, his own villagers had completely disarmed and disabled the four strange hunters.

When it was over, Tonto walked into the midst of the group and addressed Trulk. "I am Tonto. I am Masaki. Who you?"

"I am Trulk. I am Masaki."

Tonto moved closer, studying Trulk. In the ancient folds of skin, Tonto thought he saw the reds and blues that had marked Tomaz and Wasmaggi and the jaguar-hunters. "Are you jaguar-hunter?" he asked.

"Once. Long ago. Before jaguar-hunters kill mother and father."

Tonto took Trulk by the arm and guided him into the brush. "Tell Tonto about Masaki. Tell as Tonto remember or surely you and others die."

Trulk talked. He told about the jaguar-hunters, about the others and the drums, about things Tonto never had heard, about witchcraft and magic. And Tonto told things, too, about which Trulk never had heard, about white people and white babies and Sampson and

177

murder. Almost to the setting of the sun they exchanged knowledge and experience, and when at last they walked back to the tiny clearing, Tonto approached the searching hunters and placed his hand on each man's shoulder.

"We are Masaki," he said. "We are brothers."

He turned to Hakma. "Can we reach the camp?"

Hakma nodded and led the way in the darkness.

Solmar and Beck were tied to trees. Their struggles bordered on the superhuman, and it took many hands to complete the binding of the pair to their crucifixion plants.

The look of fear on the women's faces was beyond anything Widel or Anna ever had witnessed or imagined in their worst nightmares. The women seemed to scream, yet their screaming was so highly pitched as to be inaudible. Their mouths were open; one could look into their mouths and see the palates vibrating. One sensed the sound of their cry rather than heard it. All hatred, all anger, all bravado was forsaken, replaced by fear, fear born of the knowledge of what was to happen to them.

The hunters took no delight in the women's distress; the hunters were acting out their ancient, origin-forgotten roles.

All night long the hunters stood guard. Only the children slept in the crude palm shelters erected as temporary cover on the trail. In the morning, the hunters would be judge, jury and executioner combined in ways determined centuries before.

As with so much that took place within the tribe, everything seemed to happen without expressed command, even without evidence of conscious thought.

As daylight slithered down through the trees, Masaki activity slowed to a snail's pace. Even the tiny wisps of smoke from the cooking fires lingered near the glowing embers, reluctant to drift upward. The children ate in slow motion. Women moved in slow motion. The usual morning chatter was missing. It was as if no one wanted the day to proceed, as if the logical sequence of punishment could be postponed.

Once the children had eaten, they were escorted into the forest by the younger women. They would not witness the execution of Solmar and Beck.

Soomar's hunters stood aside and lined the small clearing. What would happen was in the hands of Trulk's hunters.

Anna understood what was happening; she was powerless to stop it. With the older women, she cowered at the edge of the clearing, staring without focusing on the green backdrop.

The two women had committed unforgivable crimes: probably murdering their own babies and kidnapping two innocent children. Yet, if Anna was repulsed by the very thought of killing the women, she could not prevent their execution any more than she could think of an alternative punishment. But she didn't have to watch.

Anna and Widel had assumed, although neither had spoken of it, that the women would be speared to death or else shot with arrows or poisoned darts.

The minutes dragged on. Still, Anna did not look at the women. Sometime in the prolonged silence, she sensed that the execution had taken place without her being aware of it, and after further continued silence, she dared to look at the women. They were not dead. Rather, they were staring wide-eyed and open-mouthed as two hunters approached. Each hunter carried a bone knife.

Standing in front of the women, Trulk and Bleer lifted each woman's left breast, pulled it forward, and with the knives cut a deep arc across the top of the breast so deep that the breasts were left hanging only by the skin on the under side.

The hunters showed no emotion as they stepped back and were replaced by Vecan and Walcome. The second pair of hunters reached for and pulled forward the women's right breasts, made identical deep cuts, and stepped back.

Nothing during her life with the Masaki had prepared Anna for this brutality, and as the two women stared at their nearly severed breasts, Anna let out a shriek of anguish and a command.

"God," she cried, stretching out the word, beginning it with a low, guttural sound and drawing it upward in pitch. "Oh, God, Widel! Widel! Kill them!"

Widel was as shaken by the cruelty as was Anna, but at first he misinterpreted her demand. His first reaction was that Anna had become one of the executioners, but when he looked at her, he realized she was pleading for the only humane action left to them, to end the women's lives as swiftly as possible.

Widel was ensnared in his own state of confusion. He sensed Anna's distress, sensed her final solution to the horror being played out in front of them, but could not grasp a cogent concept of what he should do. As he tried to come to grips with his own possible participation, he watched Soomar cut the women free from their death trees.

Their arms and hands unrestricted, the women lifted their breasts and tried to reattach them and to stem the flow of blood. Widel was amazed, considering how severely the women had been slashed open, at how little blood actually flood from their gapping wounds.

As he watched the women pitifully attempting the impossible, the women from his own village began shoving the two toward the forest, and it dawned on him that here was the ultimate expulsion. The women had committed the most heinous crimes against the most precious of Masaki possessions, children.

If the most obvious outward sign of a man's maleness is his penis, then the most obvious outward sign of a women's nature is her breasts. They alone are the source of a child's first nourishment; they alone are the symbolic link between the forest which sustains the Masaki and the mothers who sustain the Masaki. The two women had given up all rights to motherhood, real or symbolic, and the severing of the breasts was both the punishment and the symbolic withdrawal of the women's eternal connection to the forest's life.

Cruel as it was, Widel could find the symbolism even as he was repulsed by the action. What he could not begin to rationalize, and what he knew added to Anna's distress, was the sending of the mortally wounded women into the forest. They would die soon enough from the wounds, and once the shock of the injuries began to wear off, they would be in excruciating pain. If they did not die quickly, they would draw flies and mosquitoes and a thousand other insects, and if the insects didn't suck the life out of the women, the hordes of insects literally might drive the women insane. And always there was the jaguar. The strong scent of blood wafting through the forest would draw the jaguar to the women.

Perhaps that was the reason for the expulsion, not only that the women had lost the outward sign of their femaleness, but that the forest's creatures would slowly and painfully eat out the life of two women who had violated both the Masaki and the forest itself.

He watched as the women were pushed into the undergrowth, and he wondered if there was a limit to how far he could let himself be dehumanized by the brutality which the expulsion of the women seemed to represent.

He came to no conscious conclusion until Anna yelled again. "Widel, do something!"

Without thinking, Widel fitted an arrow to his bowstring, pulled the bowstring back as far as it would go, aimed, and shot the condemned Solmar through her left chest. The woman staggered backward, caught herself, slumped to her knees, and died falling to the ground.

Widel was slow in preparing a second arrow. When Beck realized what had happened, she turned to face Widel. "Ran-ford!" she shouted.

Widel studied her. The woman dropped her hands, her breasts hanging, revealing the gigantic wounds. Her look pleaded with him.

Widel fixed the second arrow, aimed, and fired. The woman anticipated the blow and leaned forward to receive it. As the arrow struck her, she smiled and nodded to Widel. Whatever she was, whatever she had done, for whatever reasons, she could do them and speak of them no more.

Widel knew that he had killed as skillfully and as quickly as was possible. He did not look at the women or at the Masaki. He turned and went to Anna. He wanted to say something about being sorry, sorry for the women, sorry for Anna, sorry for himself, sorry, especially, for the Masaki, but he didn't say anything; he simply wrapped Anna in his arms and let her cry.

For a time, Widel wondered about the Masakis' reaction to his behavior, worried that at the least they would be angry because he had interfered and had prevented them from their intended expulsion of the women or that the Masaki would be so angry as to make some move against him.

It seemed, however, that the hunters and the women were amazingly contrite, that Widel's action had broken a kind of spell. The Masakis said and did nothing, not even the hunters from the kidnapped children's village. Widel and Anna were not ignored, but neither was any fuss made over them or because of them. Soomar and Lurch carried the women's bodies into the forest, and when they returned, they handed Widel two arrows.

The rescued children's guardians wanted the children examined, and as if nothing untoward had happened, the children were given over to Anna's care. Anna was in a state of emotional bewilderment if not of shock and went through her duties mechanically and unfeeling. She felt she had to do something, that she would burst if somehow she could not release her pent up feelings.

The younger of the two children, Laiti, was reluctant to have Anna touch her. Anna failed to reassure the eight year old child, and Laiti, uncharacteristically for Masaki children, began to cry. Lucknew and Pollyque joined Anna's efforts with equally negative results.

It was Sayhoo who managed to comfort Laiti. "An-na is our medicine woman; she good woman even if she look different." Sayhoo took the child's hand and reached out to Anna. "An-na wise. Not always say what want to hear, but An-na know what is in heart and what is right."

Ever since Anna had forbidden Sayhoo's marriage to Fraylie, Sayhoo had stayed apart from Anna and had avoided her. Now Sayhoo looked directly into Anna's eyes. "Know that Sayhoo must have children; learn how important children are."

Sayhoo was the catalyst. Anna rested her head on her knees and cried. Among the Masaki, crying is not unfamiliar, but it is unusual, especially uncontrolled and uninhibited sobbing. Sayhoo went to Anna and put her arms around Anna's shoulder. She felt the need to offer what comfort she could. She began crying, too.

Laiti watched the medicine woman and the young women. The entire ordeal, from being spirited away from her village, from running blind through the forest, from being pulled and shoved by Solmar and Beck, from being hungry and thirsty and dirty, to being rescued, to the execution of the women, was rolled into one episode of fright and relief, and Laiti, spurred on by the two weeping women in front of her, burst into tears of her own.

When Anna heard the child crying, she reached out and drew her to Sayhoo and herself. The others watched. Then Xingu went to the little group, tears streaming down her cheeks, and tried to embrace the three females. When Sarahguy also joined the group, she was followed almost immediately by all of the women. It was a sight no hunter had ever witnessed.

Yet, no hunter interfered or offered rebuke. Later, some of them would admit that they, too, had wanted to cry and to join the women. It was not manly; they kicked at leaves and pieces of the forest floor.

Few of the women could articulate the reason for crying. Perhaps they were relieving their tensions; perhaps they were expressing empathy; perhaps it was a symbolic gesture of unity. Whatever the reason, and none would speak of it in public, there was the awareness that at the core of all feelings was a sense of motherhood and of children.

No hunter could quite grasp that feeling. They could say they knew it, could even claim to understand it, but none could feel it the way a woman felt it.

In time the crying stopped. There was no self-consciousness about having cried.

Throughout, Widel had worried that the hunters would eventually get around to questioning his killing of the two women. When they did not, he brought up the question with Tonto. "What would have happened to the women?" he asked.

"They would have died."

"I could not see them tortured."

"It no matter. What Ran-ford did forest would have done."

"You were going to send them into the forest?"

183

"Yes. Women send to forest; hunters follow and kill. Is same."

Widel was looking for some kind of absolution from the entire brutal event; what he got was mild approval, not only from Tonto but from Soomar and Lurch when they returned his arrows.

At the height of the woman's crying spell, the male child, Awhawk, was presented to Widel. Awhawk could not have been more than eight, and he was visibly frightened, but he managed to retain the stoic composure bred into him and reinforced by his education. Just why he was presented to Widel, Widel could not fathom, but he did the one thing that seemed appropriate. He bent down, scooped up the boy and hugged him.

Fathers are affectionate with their sons; hunters are affectionate with all children, but it is uncommon after a boy is six or seven for any male to pick him up and hug him. At the moment, Widel was thinking not of the Masaki cultural habits but of his own childhood when he was hurt or afraid or bewildered and how badly he had wished to be hugged and soothed and comforted.

Awhawk wanted to pull away, and at the same time, he wanted to be surrounded by arms which protected and calmed him. After a brief struggle, he let himself go, burying his head against Widel's neck. Widel could feel the moisture from Awhawk's silent tears. He stroked the boy's head and shoulders and in his best Masaki voice reassured the youngster that he was safe and among good people.

When all the crying and stumbling conversations had died down, Widel carried the boy to Anna. "The medicine woman," he said, "wishes to see a brave hunter. She will be proud to look at Awhawk."

Trulk and his hunters were charmed, had they known that word, first by Mansella, then by Anna, then by Sayhoo, and finally by Widel. Everyone had such a genuine interest in the children that Trulk felt he had to speak to Mansella. "If we had not found, would have been happy for children to have had Mansella for mother. Much love here. The children's parents will be told."

Awhawk did more examining than did Anna. He studied her skin and hair, but what fascinated him the most were her blue eyes. He had said nothing to Widel and now he said nothing to Anna.

When he did speak, it was to Laiti. "Our mothers will not believe us," he said, and that was the end of it.

Like children everywhere, Awhawk and Laiti had viewed a difference, had examined it, had found it acceptable and good, and had taken it for themselves. Within hours, Widel and Anna were drawn into the children's universe. The children found the two white adults and their white child neither remarkable nor unusual, just different. They already knew that the forest had much to show them.

The events of the day were not so easily forgotten by the whites. Outwardly, for the most part, Anna was what she had been always, the strong, secure medicine women. Inwardly she was in turmoil. The brutal events of the executions had shaken her. She had come to accept the harshness of the forest, the dangers of the forest, the threats of the forest. She had seen violence in the Masakis, but always it had been provoked by threats or else, such as what had gone on with Sampson and his village, had had some kind of explanation. She could not account for the bestiality of the woman's executions; that revealed a side of the Masaki she had not known existed.

"Would you have these people behave differently from other humans?" asked Widel. "These are primitive people, Anna. They are not civilized in the sense we think of civilization. Maybe we have come to think of them as idyllic, of this place as some kind of Garden of Eden, when the fact is, it's no garden; in some ways, these people are pretty much like most people."

"Why didn't they just kill them? Why did they have to butcher them alive?"

"Why did the Romans crucify? Why did Americans gut Indian women? Why did Germans make lamp shades out of human skin? Why do humans act inhumanly? I don't know, Anna. Probably because we're not fully human, because there is some of the ancient beast in us still."

"But...."

"Why the Masaki?"

"Yes. Why the Masaki? Why, when there has been so much love, so much goodness, so much happiness did they have to go and do that to those women? Why couldn't they have just...killed them like...."

"Like any civilized people would have done? Is that what you're trying to say?"

"No. No. You're twisting my words. Oh, shit, Widel, I don't know what I'm saying. All I know is, I feel sick, sick to my stomach, sick in the head. We're not supposed to act that way."

"I know, but we do. We humans are always finding ways to remind ourselves that we are far from perfect. What surprises me, I think, is how seldom the Masaki have reverted to the level of the beast. Of course, they don't know anybody but themselves. Well, maybe the others. Maybe they'd act differently if outsiders appeared in any number, just as they did when Wasmaggi and Tonto were young."

"I don't think I can forget this day, Widel."

"I don't think I will, either, but I'm going to try."

F O U R T E E N

The next morning, after what was another restless night for everyone, Trulk, Vecan, Walcome, and Bleer, with Awhawk and Laiti, prepared to return to their village. Anna wanted them to linger a few days, complete her village's trek to the summer camp where, along the way, she could feed the children and nourish them back to more normal and healthy lives.

But she understood the desire to return to their village as soon as possible. The children had been missing for a year and a half. Distraught parents would be frantic, always fearing the worst. She wished she could be in that village when the children trooped in.

Before the small party departed, Sayhoo asked if she could speak to Anna.

"Sayhoo never has to ask," Anna replied. "What does Sayhoo wish to say?"

"I like go with hunters and children. Can cook and care for children."

"Sayhoo, these hunters all have wives and children of their own."

"An-na not understand. Sayhoo not talk with hunters, but Sayhoo listen. Maybe Mike and Fraylie are now of their village. Would like to find ...Mike." She held her head low and whispered the last few words, "Mike, not Fraylie."

"Then Anna will speak with the hunters. If what you say is true, we will talk more. Sayhoo knows I have to say you are not to marry Fraylie."

"Sayhoo know."

"Does Sayhoo know that your love for Fraylie and his love for you breaks Anna's heart, that I would...."

"Sayhoo knows."

Anna said nothing about her last conversation with Mike and his declaration that no woman could match the white women he could not have and about his declared intention to be unwed forever.

Anna had taken Mike somewhat less than seriously, considering some of what he said to be male theatrics. She felt sure that Mike would find another Masaki village and there find a wife.

Surely Sayhoo could find no one better than Mike, if she did find him. Anna was not totally convinced that Mike was the ultimate target. Should Sayhoo find Fraylie, well, let nature take its course. Should Sayhoo go, she would be beyond Anna's influence. Anna decided not to mention anything about first cousins.

Anna asked the only question remaining. "How say Saymore and Spiker?"

"Sayhoo has not spoken to her parents."

"Then you must. Now."

"If they agree?"

"I'll speak to the hunters now."

It was possible that Mike and Fraylie had found the other village, and Anna was as interested in learning of their welfare as she was hopeful for a forest romance between Sayhoo and Mike, as unlikely as it seemed.

No, the hunters told her, Mike and Fraylie were not in their village, but some time ago a hunting party had met two Masakis, a young hunter who carried the jaguar spear and a younger boy. The younger man had asked about the hunters' village, something about looking for someone. That was all. In full daylight they had slipped away even though the hunting party had watched them carefully and with much suspicion.

Anna explained briefly about the two. She seemed certain they were Mike and Fraylie. No conclusion was reached, and when she added that Sayhoo wanted to find Mike, and she established the notion of romance, the hunters agreed to take Sayhoo to their village.

There were two conditions, however. The first was an easy promise for Anna to make; she agreed to visit the village before returning to her own. The second condition was more complicated.

188

If Sayhoo did not find Mike and marry him, then she would agree to marry one of their village. Sayhoo would have until the season of the jaguar mating to find or be found by Mike.

Anna wished that Connie was here. Connie would know exactly how long it would be before the jaguars began their yearly frenzy. Anna felt that she had to bargain in Sayhoo's behalf. She offered a compromise. "To the end of the jaguar's dance," she said, gaining a couple of weeks. "And," she added, "when Anna comes, she may reclaim Sayhoo for her own village."

The addendum cast some doubt on the agreement, but in the end, the hunters agreed. At best, as Anna calculated it, Sayhoo had three months during which to find Mike or chose a husband or Anna would reclaim her. When Anna explained it all to Sayhoo and her parents, she was careful to explain that Sayhoo was going to a village where there were more women than men. If Sayhoo had a reaction, she kept it to herself.

The barge grounded in the shallows, the eighth time that day that the men had to flop overboard, wade in the low water and thigh deep muck and push and haul the huge wooden platform into deeper water.

It also was the eighth time that day that Ferraz and Newcastle argued. "Jesus Christ," Newcastle began, "why didn't you provide some rubber boats with outboards instead of this stupid abomination?"

To which Ferraz merely sighed.

"Tell me again the asshole idea you got in mind."

When Ferraz failed to answer, Newcastle let out a burst of fire from his AK-47. That always got Ferraz riled, and it certainly got everyone's attention.

There was no question that any kind of light boat would have gained scores of miles in much less time and with considerably less effort. But the barge and its poorly powered converted lifeboat tug were as necessary to the success of this venture as were the men. The sacrifice of a week was nothing nor were the extra inconveniences when compared to the rewards.

Once in place, a shelter that would look very much like an Indian's home would be erected on the barge. Here the captured girls and young women would be brought and here their education would begin, and when Ferraz was satisfied that he had made substantial beginnings, that education would continue on the barge as it made its slow journey toward Manaus.

Ferraz was too old to lead search and attack parties through the virgin Amazonian rain forest. That's why he had Rangel, Eduardo and Rogelio, Simón and Eneas. And he had Czura and Pavón. And Red Newcastle.

He had made a mistake with Czura and Pavón, he decided. They were lazy, shirked their duties, and worst of all, gave every indication that they could not be depended on if crunch came to crunch. Newcastle was an entirely different matter. He was part of the bandeira because Wittenberg had forced him on Ferraz. He was, Ferraz concluded, totally unstable, a menace to everything and everyone. *The Mad Branco* was how Rangel referred to Newcastle.

Within a few days of leaving Manaus, it was obvious that Newcastle had never been in the sertáo. Newcastle might have been at home in South Africa, although Ferraz doubted that, but South Africa and the Amazon were as unalike as any two places on earth. South Africa was more like western Ireland than it was like the Amazon.

Already Newcastle had used up almost half of the ammunition provided for the bandeirantes. He shot at alligators which posed no threat, at snakes which were harmless, at vines he thought were snakes, at logs. Sometimes he shot at imaginary Indians. He was, Ferraz concluded further, violent, unstable and a coward. What gave Newcastle power were his weapons and his penchant for brutality.

That posed a particular problem for the tropas de resgate. Ferraz made no bones about the hunt for females. Success with the females depended entirely on care, calm and consideration. It would be horrible enough to snatch the females from their villages, killing the males. Every ounce of brutality in the execution of the task would translate into a ton of resistance - and even a pound of resistance from the females would translate into failure.

Ferraz and one of the others, he hadn't decided who, must come on as saviors. The two groups would never meet within sight of the female Indians. One group would perform the deeds necessary to procure the women; Ferraz would rescue, calm, comfort, and train the women, first on the barge and later in a secure house in the cidaae flutuante.

The barge was so important. It was the physical ambiance that bridged the leap from forest to civilization. Ferraz smiled at the brilliance of the image: from a palm hut in the forest to a palm hut on the river; from a palm hut floating placidly down the waterway to a floating house on the Amazon; from a floating house on the Amazon to a ship's cabin sailing the oceans; from a ship's cabin to a whore's suite. Brilliant.

Anna was despondent and listless. The butchering of Beck and Solmar had taken something out of her life. She was unresponsive to Widel's attempts to cheer her up. She performed her necessary duties but more as ritual and mechanically than with any feeling. Even her care of Penny was robot-like. She spoke only when spoken to, did not join the villagers around the evening fire, sang none of the songs, and cried frightfully when new songs were made up about Solmar and Beck and the stealing of Laiti and Awhawk from their village.

Late one afternoon, Marci and Jonquilla approached. Other than Sayhoo, they were the only females within the village even remotely near marrying age.

"We would talk with the medicine woman," Jonquilla said, "if she will let us."

"Anna would be happy for Jonquilla and Marci to join her fire." The fact was, Anna was neither happy nor displeased; she really didn't care.

The girls sat, and Anna waited for the conversation to begin. Neither girl had ever been much of a conversationalist, so Anna knew something important was on their minds.

Marci began without any preliminary small talk whatsoever. "An-na knows no husband for Marci in village."

Anna did know. Except for Mike, what Marci said was true.

"And An-na know no husband for Jonquilla."

Again, except for Mike, that was true. The only other male among the villagers of suitable age was Fraylie, and he was a cousin of both girls. Even the younger Manway was not suitable. He was, after all, Marci's brother and third cousin to Jonquilla. If worse came to worst, Anna might approve of a Manway/Jonquilla match, but she would have to think hard about it. He was too young anyway, and all of the other male children were even younger.

"We know," Jonquilla continued, "An-na promise go other village. We know maybe many men there. When An-na go, want An-na arrange marriage."

"No, not arrange," shouted Marci. "Want An-na take Marci and Jonquilla with her and we see if husband can be found."

Anna remained silent. Wasmaggi had never said anything about being a marriage broker. Hackway and Westman as Marci's parents and Janus and Soomar as Jonquilla's parents might seek out potential husbands, might even achieve an arrangement, but, while the girls still were part of their parents' household, no one had the right to interfere, and that included the medicine woman.

Among all the duties Wasmaggi had laid out for her, it was clear that parents made the arrangements. And if a marriage between children of separate villages was arranged, there were numerous details upon which all parents had to agree, not the least being to which village the newly married couple would belong. That bargaining would involve the medicine woman and her counterpart.

But instead of declining to participate or agreeing to take the girls with her, Anna burst out, "Why, in God's name, would you want to get married?"

"Why...to have children," Jonquilla said meekly.

Wasmaggi came to Anna's fire shortly after the two girls left. Characteristically, he walked to the fire, announced his presence, "Wasmaggi here," sat down without invitation, stared at the whites, and asked to hold Penny. He played with her for a few minutes, little childish ticking games which Penny always enjoyed. Then from out of his hair he withdrew two tiny feathers, one bright yellow, the other a majestic purple, and presented them to Penny. She stumbled off to show them around the camp.

Wasmaggi watched Penny and laughed at her happy laughter. When he turned back to the couple, he looked directly at Anna. "Little child know only love and happiness; adult know more." He paused for a moment, then said, "We suffer because we alive; no other reason. Forest says grow up, and when we do, know other side of being child, of being happy. Wasmaggi not know, but think other side of sun very dark." He stood. "Masaki on light side of sun, no matter what An-na and Ran-ford think. Sometimes wonder if they agree." And he walked away.

After a minute or two, Anna asked, "What was that all about?"

"He was trying to reassure us about the nature of the Masaki and telling us to grow up."

"Grow up? What the hell...."

"To accept the bad with the good, to accept the pain with the pleasure. I'm putting words into his mouth, but I think he just told us what he knows, what we know, that we have within ourselves the savage. He wouldn't recognize the word, but honestly, I think he recognized that the Masaki sank to a bestial level in butchering Solmar and Beck and he wants us to know that such a level is not normal.

"Anna, I know the hunters. What was done is not normal; it was a hideous response to a hideous crime, an ancient, irrational response to a crime against every Masaki living or dead.

"I don't know about you, but should someone take Penny away from us, I would kill them if I could. And if I spent a long time looking for my daughter, I know that every day I would imagine the most vile punishment possible. For every second I suffered, for every second Penny suffered, I would extract eternities of punishment."

Anna had a hard time saying it, "So would I," but she did, and when she did, she began to understand. She did not approve, but she was gaining in wisdom, not only about the Masakis but about herself.

"I remember once," she told Widel, "that someone said or wrote that being human was mostly the struggle to control our savage nature. I think because I see hunters and not warriors here, I've come to believe these primitive people have conquered their savagery. They haven't, and as you reminded me before, neither has the so-called enlightened world."

"Nor we, as we just admitted."

"But we have to try, don't we, Widel?"

"In some ways, Anna, I would say our lives depend on it. Funny, they may not know it, but that might have been the most important lesson the Masakis learned from the jaguar-hunters."

"Widel, find Penny, please. I must talk with Marci and Jonquilla."

There is a saying that the forest changes you, or if it doesn't change you, it kills you. In uncounted ways, the forest had changed Anna, just as it had changed Widel and Connie. Anna wondered if she could change enough not to be killed by the forest.

F I F T E E N

Soomar, Tonto and Wasmaggi met with the hunters, wanting desperately to put the matter of Beck and Solmar behind them. It was best, they agreed, to push everyone to the limit and to reach the swamp as quickly as possible. It took three days.

Finding the entrance to the land bridge which led to the massive island in the middle of the swamp took even longer. There were no clear directions; at best it was the vague recollection of an old and sometimes vague memory. Wasmaggi knew what to look for; he couldn't remember where to look.

One of the small details forgotten by Wasmaggi was that the entrance to the land bridge did not exist on the mainland side of the swamp. One had to enter the swamp first before finding the narrow, underwater strip of solid footing that led to the island.

And before one could enter the swamp itself, one had a half day's journey through the densest, meanest jungle the forest had to offer. Searching, the hunters were torn by briars and thorns the likes of which they had never seen. The forest mocked them; the prettiest plants had the most hostile weapons.

Anna was so busy stitching and dressing the hunters' wounds that she had to enlist the help of Wasmaggi and Widel. Worst of all the wounds were those on the hunters' feet. Even as much as two feet down in the muck, a hunter might step on thorns from the same plants that pierced his arms and legs.

For five days the search went on, and when the entrance was found, only Wasmaggi and Tonto could be considered healthy.

Joshway and Moremew had stumbled onto the strip of solid underwater earth by sheer accident. Joshway became trapped in the muck, and when Moremew went to his rescue, he crossed a tiny, narrow ridge of solid ground a foot or more below the water's surface.

Once Joshway was freed from the goo, the two probed their way along the spit, and after a considerable struggle, stepped up out of the water onto a small savannah plain. Surrounding the plain was a ring of towering trees at least a quarter of a mile in depth. The island seemed to offer all the amenities one could want.

Soomar called the village together, but it was Wasmaggi who spoke. He praised Moremew and Joshway, confirmed what little they had seen, and then, in his most mysterious manner, told the Masaki they could enter the swamp and reach the island only in small groups.

"Must," he told them, "forever keep entrance secret. No trails, no signs; not even forest must know Masaki here."

In groups of two and threes and fours, the Masakis entered the swamp at various locations. As torturous as the going was, they were careful to leave no signs of their passing. Grunting and groaning could be heard over a long line as women and children struggled to move against pure jungle. Deep within the swamp they converged on the coveted underwater bridge and on it they reached the island.

Tonto stood on the mainland with Widel and a handful of hunters and waited until all human noise had ceased. "Now much work," he told them. "Must wipe out trails, and where cannot, must make many false trails far away."

When Widel wanted to know why, Tonto answered only, "In time; in time."

Widel assumed they would spend a couple of hours; in fact they spent two full days. All evidence of their having been near the swamp was erased and new trails with obvious signs were created to totally confuse anyone who might be looking. Tonto went so far as to have Widel leave darts stuck high in the trees and once had him shoot with an arrow a monkey that could not possibly fall through the branches to the ground. Only then was Tonto satisfied, and only when he was satisfied did he lead Widel and the hunters into the swamp.

Ferraz immediately put his men to work building a replica of an Indian house, complete with an open canopy. He unpacked authentic hammocks. The men built sleeping platforms. When they were finished, no Indian would have found fault with the house. Ferraz knew his Indian crafts well. He supervised the cutting of every branch, every palm leaf, and he personally slit every stem of every leaf that went into the roof and walls of the structure.

Even Newcastle was impressed, or at least he said he was. "Well, patrão, it looks real," but the way he called Ferraz boss, with just a hint of sarcasm, put an edge on his approval. Ferraz only nodded.

"We will not use this house. This is for our Indian ladies only. Rangel has found us a campsite up the river on the other side. There is a shallow that will make crossing easy."

The Brazilians, all experienced in the forest, took the announcement in stride, but once again Newcastle balked. "Why do we have to keep walking in the goddamn water? Make the friggin' camp on this side."

"Mr. Newcastle, probably there are no Indians right here. But if there are, we are not going to give them any more to look at than is absolutely necessary. We will move to the other side of the river."

Someday, thought Ferraz, Newcastle will not back down. He will destroy us all. And at that moment Ferraz began to seriously consider the murder of Red Newcastle. It was an action he should have taken.

While Ferraz did not underestimate Newcastle's potential danger, he overestimated his own ability to use Newcastle and to control him. There was no doubt that Newcastle could be useful, if he kept his violence in check. There would be many fights with the Indians and Newcastle would be a good piece of fodder. Better that Newcastle be a target for some Indian's spear or arrow than one of his own men.

Once the camp was established, Ferraz spread out his maps. He had over marked the government's maps with information from other agencies, especially certain information from IBAMA, Brazil's environmental agency, CVRD, Companhia Vale do Rio Doce, Brazil's state mining company, and Electronorte. Both CVRD and Electronorte had, in secret documents, mentioned the probable existence of *Indian nations yet undiscovered.* With all the information, Ferraz was positive he had pinpointed those nations or tribes, although he was quick to point out that pinpointing meant only that the field had been narrowed down to a few hundred square miles.

Even so, he told his men, the search was not as hopeless as it appeared on the surface. Projecto RADAM had provided more than enough information with its maps and aerial photographs to narrow the search areas to a relatively few square miles.

Ferraz marked their present location on his master map. Previously he had marked the location of one Indian camp that had been discovered and the several trails leading from it.

He explained briefly for Newcastle's benefit the Indians' use of summer camps. "We will find this camp," he said, "and from there, in eight or ten days, we will find a village. Even if the Indians are not in the village, we will have an easy time finding the other camps."

Newcastle already knew the answer but he wanted to hear Ferraz say it. "How far away is that camp?" pointing to a spot on the map.

"About sixty miles, I guess," Ferraz answered casually.

Newcastle exploded. "And you expect me to crawl sixty miles through that jungle?"

"That's about the size of it, Mr. Newcastle. Either that or stay here. Do whatever Wittenberg and Lippstadt pay you to do. I don't much care." Turning to the others, "We will leave first thing in the morning."

"Wait a minute, Ferraz. How long is this going to take?"

"I don't know. No one has ever been there before. Three weeks; maybe less; maybe more. Less if we all work together."

"You got to be shittin'."

"A stroll, Mr. Newcastle, and at the end of it a pot of gold. Now, if you're coming, you'd better get your gear ready."

"Wait just one fuckin' minute. Let me see the map again. You got villages all over the place. Why this one? Why not that one?"

198

"Actually, Mr. Newcastle, it doesn't matter. But since there will be more than one trip, we'll take the nearest first."

"How many villages from here?"

"If you mean starting from here, I count four or five."

"And how many pigs in each village?"

"Suitable ladies? Not more than ten; more likely six or seven. Based on past experience, that is. Maybe by the time we get back to Manaus, five."

"That's twenty trips."

"Your math is good. Is there a point to this?"

"I want to go to that village." Newcastle put his finger on the map. "It's closer and it looks larger."

"Well, it is closer on the map, but I determine it more difficult to reach."

"That one, Ferraz."

It took three weeks plus one day, and as it turned out, the camp was not the one indicated on the map. Newcastle's chosen camp, so clear in the aerial photographs, was impossible to reach. Uncounted miles of swamp blocked all passages to that camp. Even Ferraz's best men gave up finding a route through the endless surface waters, so Ferraz was forced to consider alternative goals and plotted a route away from the swamp but which intersected other trails.

Newcastle provided the only humor during the long, unsuccessful trek. No one, Indian or Brazilian, thinks of moving through the forest in a straight line. One glides, sidestepping five or ten times the distance made forward. One takes the path of least resistance, avoiding as much as possible the vines and thorn bushes that form impenetrable walls within the forest. If one must take fifty or a hundred steps to the left or to the right to take a dozen steps forward, well, that's the intelligent way.

Not Newcastle. From the beginning, he sought to overpower the forest. His machete flashed left and right in what little sunlight stabbed through the forest canopy. His was a straight line, albeit slow and extremely tiring. Every day Newcastle swung his blade, and every day the Brazilians smirked, and when Newcastle viewed

199

the smirks, he became enraged, threatening Simón or Eneas first and then Eduardo or Rogelio. The only reason he didn't threaten Rangel was because that skillful bandeirante was always far ahead. And Czura and Pavón were always far behind. Ferraz had his hands full just keeping those two moving on the trail.

In the late afternoon of the day they found a trail obviously made by humans; an exhausted Newcastle stretched out beside the fire, hogging the space of two or three others.

Simón asked him to move his feet. "If the branco didn't try to cut down every tree, he wouldn't be so tired."

Newcastle jumped to his feet. "Why you little coffee colored bastard!" Newcastle reached for his machete. He took a full, vicious swing with the forest blade, narrowly missing Simón's chest. "I'm going to cut off your balls," he yelled, and he moved toward the frightened man.

"Newcastle!" Ferraz unholstered his handgun. "I'm an excellent shot. Put down the machete."

Newcastle paused, glanced at the men around the fire, and calculated the weapons that had been raised and leveled against him. He backed away. "I'll finish this one day."

Ferraz did not order his men to break camp the next morning; instead, he sent Eduardo and Simón to explore in one direction and Rogelio and Eneas in another. The group had been too long in the unbroken forest; they needed a rest. But more, they needed to refocus on the purpose of all the work and hardship. He knew that neither pair would go far; he didn't expect them to, but he had to separate the men if only to protect them from one another.

He sent Rangel with Czura and Pavón in search of game. Food, he knew, was about to become an acute problem. He hoped the men would find a small 'gator. He particularly liked the back meat diced and fried.

And he had to meet the other problem head on: Newcastle. "It is not good that we fight among ourselves," he began. "There is no need for it. The sertáo will get us soon enough if we let it."

Newcastle made no response. Ferraz knew it was hopeless, but he made a second effort. "These are good bandeirantes; they know what they are doing. They would teach you if you would let them. They...."

"They will regret laughing at me. They can't teach me anything unless they can teach me to fly. Before it is over, I'll teach them."

"Newcastle...."

"Hear me, Ferraz. Keep them clear of me. If one of them so much as looks at me, he is dead meat. Do I make myself clear?"

"It is possible, Newcastle, that before this bandeira is over you will need them."

"A threat?"

"No. A statement of fact. When we find the Indians, they are not going to be the easy conquest you seem to envision. They will fight in ways you have not known before."

"With sticks and stones, for Christ's sake?"

"Not stones; there are no stones here. With sticks, yes; spears and arrows and darts. And, Newcastle, with a cunning you will not believe. You will not see them even if you have eyes in the back of your head. They will stand next to you, and you will not see them. You will need others to see for you. Don't make the mistake of making enemies of those who might save you."

"Ah, bull shit, Ferraz."

Rangel's discovery of an active trail was the brightest day in over a fortnight. Not only did the sun shine down on Ferraz and the others without interference from the canopy, but at long last a positive goal had been reached. The only shadow cast on the trail was Newcastle's. "Well, patrão, which way, left or right?"

After a moment's hesitation, Ferraz declared, "East."

For weeks Mike and Fraylie aimlessly wandered the forest. They had long since forgotten the original reasons for leaving their village, Fraylie to meet his final test as hunter and to find another Masaki village and, perhaps, a wife, and Mike to avoid what had become his overwhelming physical passion for Anna. Fraylie was escaping and searching at the same time; Mike was escaping, with no goals other than to remove himself from the source of pains and frustrations he could not understand and which he barely recognized.

Mike was young, but he was an accomplished hunter. He had begged to be the jaguar hunter when Connie died, had been refused by Tomaz, but when Tomaz died and there was no one to take up the colored spear, Mike had begged again, and this time the hunters accepted him, more to keep him out of their hair than anything, some suggested.

His elevation was tinged with sensual overtones, sexual, perhaps. Connie had represented an ideal woman, the jaguar hunter and the mother of his children all wrapped up in a subliminal presence beyond his reach. When Connie died, Mike withdrew from social contact for a time, his dreams and nightmares all mixed up in his head. And when he came to realize the finality of Connie's death, he focused similar fantasies on Anna. Escape was his only remedy.

The younger Fraylie had far less forest experience than Mike, but he was becoming his companion's equal. Circumstances forced that accomplishment. Mike was a good teacher, and because they had been traveling for over seven weeks in forest areas totally unknown to them, it was necessary that they lived off the land. Mike let Fraylie do most of the hunting and much of the tracking. Fraylie had a motivation that was hard to resist. He had a compelling desire to marry and have a family. Since he was forbidden to marry Sayhoo, he had to find another Masaki village and, he dearly hoped, someone he could love. Anna had promised that he would.

The two youths lived agreeably well. They hunted successfully and had, except once, met no untoward emergencies. And that emergency arose because of inexperienced unpreparedness, the meeting of other Masaki hunters from another, unknown village. The meeting had terrified the youths, and they ran from it as they might have run from attacking snakes. Nothing had happened and the meeting was reduced in importance, although the resolve they made soon after only to approach an established village remained.

And so, too, did the memory of their carelessness. Never again would they be so preoccupied or so inattentive as to be face to face with anything or anyone not of their choosing.

One day they talked about home, wondering if the villagers had ever reached a new summer camp, realizing they had no idea where Wasmaggi's new camp was, wondering how the people were, asking if they were being missed and who would miss them.

So engrossed were they, they stumbled into a small bog. There was no damage done, but again they were careless and, worst, blind to their surroundings. In truth of fact, the two young hunters were experiencing a totally now emotion; they were homesick. They had no word for the feeling, but quite spontaneously, they decided to return to their village.

And it was at that point they faced another fact. They were hopelessly lost. If in all these weeks they had been moving in a certain general direction, they might have reversed direction and sooner or later found a familiar landmark. Their travel had been aimless, meandering without regard for anything other than movement. Their only ally was the sun.

They spent a whole day camped in a small clearing in earnest, serious discussion about which direction to take. They had, they decided, traveled south or southwest. They would, then, go at an angle toward the rising sun, and by keeping the sun on their right chests, they hoped to be on the proper line.

Now their goal was sure. Whatever they had sought before was forgotten in the headlong dash for home.

To the north, a group of Brazilians and an Irishman were walking due east on a trail well defined from centuries of use. East, Ferraz had reasoned, was the most promising direction if only because it aimed deeper into the sertáo. And, he knew from experience, such a wide trail as they had discovered meant no more than a day or two before they reached some kind of encampment. If the trail led to a summer camp, it would be a simple matter to reverse direction and follow the trail to a village. If the trail led to a village, then....

He called a halt. "Rangel," he spoke softly, "find us a camp site," by which he meant one that was well off the trail and well out of sight and sound. It was time to lay out the carefully considered logistics of attack and capture.

Again he went over the value of young females; they must be undamaged. He outlined the process by which the girls would be separated from the village and herded toward the hut on the barge.

"I cannot be seen," he said, "otherwise I cannot *save* the females from the likes of you. Nor can...." He wavered, still pondering the selection of the one other man who would assist in the education of the females.

He never considered Newcastle, and Czura and Pavón were useless. They would use the women, and they lacked motivation and discipline. Rangel was the obvious choice, but he was too necessary for survival in the forest. Eduardo and Rogelio were excellent procuradores, having demonstrated their skill with Indian women long ago, but they were needed in the actual raid and killing of the Indians. Eneas was the logical choice.

But when Ferraz opened his mouth to name the man who would assist him in training the females, he said "Simón." At the last instant he named Simón because he would be one less irritant to Newcastle.

Ferraz and Simón would not participate in the attack on the village or in the capture of the women. A half day from the floating barge, they would rescue the females, take them to the floating house, and befriend them, thus beginning the special training of the special whores which Wittenberg and Lippstadt would deal around the world.

The men accepted their roles in silence. They knew what was expected of them, what they had to do, and the rewards. If the first venture was successful, the Brazilians were resigned to spending eight or ten months in the forest, searching out and raping every village they could find. And once they began delivering the females to Ferraz, what would it matter if one or a few were lost? Patience, and reward.

Simón was pleased with his assignment. It was unexpected. He would have to bathe regularly, he told the others, and keep himself fit. "What a way to die," he joked. "I must keep my weapon in good condition."

Ferraz divided the men into teams: Rangel with Czura, Eduardo with Pavón, Rogelio and Eneas with Newcastle. There were no objections. Once the village was found, it was to be surrounded. At first light, when all the Indians were in their houses, the attack would begin.

Rangel would throw a firebomb into the center of the village. Like all good protectors, the hunters would dash out of their houses, leaving the women and children inside. It would be an easy matter to pick off the males before they could react or escape into the brush.

The most successful attack would be the immediate elimination of all hunters, followed by the rounding up of all females and children. Anyone not fitting the profile of the young women needed were to be killed on the spot. There was to be no delay in herding the chosen females to the river barge.

"They will go quietly," Ferraz reassured the men. "They will be in such a state of shock they will do whatever they are told."

Newcastle spoke for the first time. "Ferraz, there is one thing. I've saved a letter from my bosses. It says that after the women, I can have anything in any village that I want. Here, read it." He withdrew from his pocket a soggy piece of paper.

Ferraz studied the paper. "It is not signed," he said, "and it's so vague it could mean anything. But there won't be much worth taking. These people don't have anything of value. What the hell, anything you can carry is okay with me."

"I'm not thinking of articles. I want the men."

"Are you crazy? You're out of your mind. What good are they?"

"They are worth a lot to the right parties."

"Jesus, Newcastle. Even if you can capture them, how are you going to keep them? How are you going to get them out of the forest?"

"That's my worry."

"Do you know these people can't be turned into slaves? They'll just sit down and die on you, even if you beat them senseless. They are useless."

"I have special ways, my friend. Now, I'm telling you. I want six of the best men from that village."

"The best men will have died trying to fight us."

"Six men."

"Your heart is set on it?"

"You're betting your life it is."

"All right. Two conditions. First, if any man is alive after we take the village, he's yours. I warn you, though. Either he will die on you, or if he lives, you will never be safe."

"Bull shit."

"Second, if you insist on taking a man or men, you will have to make your way to Manaus on your own, on your own trail, on your own two feet. I can't risk the complications your slaves might present to my women."

"Ferraz, I'll be glad to leave you."

Mike and Fraylie studied the strange tracks. They went in two directions, those headed toward the setting sun being the freshest. Nothing like them ever had been seen in the forest. Mike and Fraylie were mystified completely. Were they looking at the prints of unknown creatures, unknown animals?

What the hunters saw, of course, were the shod feet of the tropas de resgate. Never having seen boot marks before, the two studied them with great care and considerable fear, speculated about them, and came to no conclusion whatsoever.

What made the mystery so much deeper were other mysteries within the mystery. Nine pairs of the strange prints headed east. Toward a village, perhaps. Those prints were two or three days old. Two pairs of prints the same age headed west. Then today, only hours earlier, three other pairs of the strange prints also headed west.

What made the last set of prints so unusual were the seven pairs of Masaki feet that walked in a single file. Or at least Mike thought they were Masaki feet.

What creatures had made the strange prints? Why would Masakis have anything to do with creatures? And what had happened to the other sets of prints? Had those creatures disappeared? What creatures?

206

Fear and homesickness aside, never must the forest harbor a mystery. The very lives of the Masakis depended on knowing what the forest knew. Whatever made the strange prints on the forest floor had to be seen, be understood and be accommodated. To do otherwise was to be in ignorance, and to be in ignorance was to be in danger.

With little discussion, the hunters decided to follow the tracks going toward the setting sun. If Masakis were with the unknown creatures, much might be explained. Mike and Fraylie did not walk the trail, keeping to the forest, each on either side and well out of sight of anything or anyone. Sounds would tell them all they needed to know until they could gain an advantageous sighting place.

The two hunters kept in touch by mimicking the forest sounds. They hurried but not so carelessly as to make any sounds of their own, and thus it was several hours before they heard the noises in front of them.

Mike crossed the trail, leaving no sign of his passing. No words would be spoken, hand signals only, as the two silently crept forward.

When they could see, they were plunged into deeper mystery. In the center of a small clearing were seven men, not one of whom the hunters knew or ever had seen. They looked like Masaki. But what startled and unnerved the two young men was that the seven were bound, their hands tied behind them, short lengths of rope binding one man's neck to the next.

And around them stood three others. What they were was impossible to say. They were covered from head to foot with strange skin. The only things that remotely resembled anything familiar were their hands and faces.

Mike felt his heart beat faster. He thought he caught a glimpse of something or someone he knew. He pointed to one of the others.

"Ran-ford!" he said out loud, the sound ringing clear through the forest.

Immediately, the loudest noises he ever had heard pounded through the forest, and simultaneously he could hear the snapping of branches above him and he could see great scars being torn in the tree trunks.

207

Mike and Fraylie turned and ran as fast as they could. There were no explanations. Not even the most farfetched imaginative explanation could do justice to what they had just seen and experienced. Only when they exhausted themselves completely did they stop running. Fraylie was sick and threw up on the forest floor; Mike was stone cold and stood shivering uncontrollably in the one hundred degree heat.

Back in the clearing, Newcastle shouted at Pavón and Czura, "Go get them, you cowardly bastards."

Neither man moved. They knew relatively few words of English, but what they had heard shouted from the forest was certainly an English word.

"That cuts it," said Newcastle. "You two are less than useless. You couldn't even stand up to the old bags in the village."

Newcastle might have gone after the unseen speaker, but he was without any sense of the origin of the sound. All he knew was that a name had been spoken, clearly spoken, and by someone close by. He sensed the potential danger and was powerless to erase it.

Mike and Fraylie were afraid to light the smallest of fires. The sense of doom was all pervasive, hanging tightly above their heads, suffocating them in their own fearful anguish.

Strange what thoughts one has, and stranger still what simple thought can turn a disastrous situation around. When Fraylie spoke for the first time after seeing the band of men in the clearing, he said quietly, "Mike must tell hunters Fraylie fail test."

"Mike run, too."

"But not Mike's test." When Mike did not reply, Fraylie announced, "Fraylie go now. Fraylie must be alone in the forest."

Mike watched the youngster take a few steps intro the underbrush.

"Wait," he called softly. "What is test?"

Fraylie turned. "Courage."

"And what else?"

"To be a Masaki for all Masaki."

"Have you failed test?"

"I am coward."

"Perhaps we ran today to help the Masaki tomorrow."

"Twice I run. Neither time have I helped the Masaki."

"There is still time."

Village, pride, family, fear of miserable failure, disappointment with themselves, tribe? Senselessness, stupidity, youthful ignorance? Who would know what stiffened the two young hunters' hearts. Certainly not fearlessness newly found. They were frightened almost beyond their ability to make one foot go in front of the other, and yet they gingerly retraced their steps back toward the clearing.

One thing Mike had to know. Was the white man Ranford or Ranford's image? And he never had seen Masakis bound together. He had no word for the sight, yet he sensed humiliation and degradation and had a powerful sense of the Masakis' ultimate fate. Not that he could articulate it, but again he sensed loss and death.

The band was not in the clearing the next day. Newcastle had convinced himself that his display of firepower had frightened off whoever had been hidden in the brush.

It was mid afternoon before the hunters caught up to the creatures and their prisoners. Worry had tempered their speed.

When they did find the band, they were stricken again by the scene. Newcastle had told Ferraz that he had special ways of dealing with the recalcitrant Indians. The Indians, aware that their destiny was imprisonment and death, had sat down on the trail. Die they might, but they would not walk willingly to their deaths. If death awaited them, it would have to come to them here.

Newcastle was aware of the Indians' attitude, and he was prepared to change it. He had Czura and Pavón lift a man to his feet. With one hand, Newcastle reached for the man's penis; with the other, he made a slicing blow with his machete, severing the man's maleness from his body.

Even Pavón and Czura were stunned by the brutality of the act. They dropped the Indian, themselves cowering before Newcastle.

"The next one," ordered Newcastle.

When the Brazilians hesitated, Newcastle took a swipe at Czura, cutting his shirt. The Brazilians reached for the Indian next in line.

209

When he was standing, Newcastle took his blade and severed the cord that held the Indian to the first man. He took his AK-47 and fired a burst into the first man. The man's chest burst, his flesh and blood spattering the other Indians. Newcastle reached down, grabbed the dead man's testicles, and deftly sliced open the sack, and one at a time he produced the elongated objects within. These he held in front of the Indians, squeezing them until the juices squirted between his fingers.

The lesson was successful. The remaining six Indians began to walk the trail, obedient to every command and gesture, even those they did not understand.

Pavón and Czura lingered behind. When Newcastle turned to reinforce the lesson, to tell them how easy it was to train Indians, the words never came from his lips. Pavón was sprawled face down on the trail, a single unadorned seven foot spear of polished branch sticking in his back. Czura was standing over him, speechless in fear, unable to move, unable to breathe.

Newcastle fired his assault weapon systematically, covering an arc of about two hundred and seventy degrees and no more than twelve inches above the ground. Twenty, thirty, fifty rounds went spinning through the forest, saturation firing done with skill and deadly purpose.

Then Newcastle turned and killed the lead Indian.

In the underbrush, Mike found the shallowest of hollows and hugged the ground as closely as he could. When the firing stopped, he moved his spears to the right to get Fraylie's attention. When Fraylie did not move, Mike crawled to him.

Fraylie had a small hole in the top of his head and a larger one at the base of his skull. Mike felt the tears welling up in his eyes. "You passed the test; Fraylie is a great hunter," he whispered to the silent body. "Be one with forest."

Mike touched his friend on the shoulder, wiped tears from his eyes, gathered up Fraylie's remaining spear, and retreated into the trees.

Mike followed Newcastle and the others for two days, making no move against them. On the third day Czura squatted by the side of the trail. Mike watched in amazement as the creature shed his lower skin. In the midst of his bowel movement, the man grunted, looking back between his legs to view the success of his efforts. When he looked up, an Indian stood directly in front of him. Before he could utter a sound, he felt the point of a spear enter his throat, felt it exit through the back of his neck. He also felt his bowels evacuate as they never had before.

The Indian did not remove the spear. Czura could not breathe. The spear blocked his air passage, had in fact severed some of the cord leading to his brain. Czura had no ability to move, and yet he felt no pain. Even the lack of air was painless. Silently, he thought a Hail Mary. His last conscious thought was wondering what Hell would be like.

Quickly, Mike stepped back into the forest. He had two purposes left. One was to free the Indians; the other was to know the white man. He could not get Ranford's image out of his mind. What if Wasmaggi had been wrong? What if the forest had given the white man as something evil, not as something good?

If white was evil, then Connie and Anna were evil. Not those two. Not Penny.

Even as he was wrestling with such thoughts, he moved through the forest so as to be in front of the white man, and he watched when Newcastle found Czura sitting in his own dung with a spear sticking through his neck. Newcastle reacted by killing two more Indians. He didn't shoot them; he gutted them. He sliced their stomachs downward and then across with his machete and let their guts spill out.

Now Mike was faced with a choice. He couldn't seem to get close enough to the white man to kill him, and if he could, it was obvious the white man would kill the remaining Indians first. Killing the white man was necessary, but so was saving three Masakis.

In the end, Mike choose to try to save three Indians. Perhaps, he reasoned, the white man would still be available. In the morning he would see what he could do; now he must withdraw, find food, and sleep.

Sometime in the night, Newcastle beat Mike to the draw. When Mike found the small group, Newcastle was nowhere in sight. Without approaching, Mike could tell that the three Indians had been murdered. Flies and a few birds were already winging around the men's bodies. Newcastle had slit their throats. He would be waiting somewhere in the dark shadows of the forest, waiting for Mike. Then he would kill Mike as surely as he had killed the Indians.

Mike moved away as silently as he could. Nothing of the forest could have moved with more stealth. Let the white man wait, Mike said to himself. There is time. As fast as he could, he moved back along the trail. The Indians had come from somewhere, a village perhaps. Mike had a sudden compulsion to find it and to find other Masakis.

The swampland, as people started calling it, was plush, so Widel thought, and the small savannah field in its center was a pleasant environment after so many years under the forest canopy.

That was not the Masakis' reaction. One by one, as they took their last step out of the swamp and onto the island, they looked upon the sight with profound trepidation. Without the protection of the canopy, the vastness of the open sky was a threat; the strength of the unfiltered sun blinded them; they had a hard time focusing on objects at the opposite end of the savannah. When they moved, it was to the protection of the trees ringing the field.

The island itself was oval in shape, seven or eight football fields in length, Widel would guess, and maybe two football fields at its widest. The savannah followed the general shape of the island, two hundred yards long and about sixty yards wide. Yards and football fields meant something to Widel and Anna only, of course; they would not even try to interpret their estimates for the Masakis.

Beyond the grassy area was a surrounding forest some two hundred and fifty yards deep. It was almost as if someone had dredged up the island and had created a swampy moat at least a half mile wide. No attacking force in any number could possibly reach the island. Individuals might, but they would not be much of a threat. Additionally, the island stood five or six feet above the swamp water, and if Wasmaggi could be believed, there was only the one underwater bridge to the island over which everyone had to pass in single file.

When the first of the villagers congregated under the trees near the entrance, a few wove temporary shelters for the children. When Wasmaggi told them it might be a day or two before Tonto and the hunters completed hiding their trail and that everyone should relax, there were a thousand questions. Wasmaggi said only that all hunters should examine the swampland and get to know it.

And when, two days later, Tonto, Widel and the others reached the island, Tonto being satisfied no one could track the Masakis to this place, Wasmaggi called the villagers together, under the trees Widel noted, and addressed them.

"You have many questions. I'm the one who knows. In time Wasmaggi will answer you. But first we go to that end." He pointed to the far end of the island. "Once Masaki live here. Wasmaggi's parents born here. All Masakis born here."

"So?" Anna whispered to Widel.

"So what? Don't know." Widel shrugged his shoulders.

Wasmaggi said no more, walking away and leading the Masakis to their temporary home sites.

Everyone seemed to notice a difference in the place. There were kinds of monkeys never seen before, flowers brand new to everyone, a hundred shades of jade and emerald not remembered from the familiar forest.

"Wasmaggi said," Widel observed, "that it would take three full days to walk around the swamp. It wouldn't take but an hour to walk around this island. That would make the swamp quite large. Look at the differences in monkeys and plants. The swamp must be a natural barrier separating the species."

"Yeah, and I've never seen so many shades of green."

"Reminds me of Connie."

"How so?" Anna asked, holding her breath.

"You know, how her blond hair used to pick up and capture the viridescence of the forest colors. Her hair absorbed the colors, the yellow-green of the palm, the black-green of some of the ferns. That's how she could melt into the forest so quickly and naturally."

That was all. Widel rambled on about the Masaki's symbiotic partnership with the forest, doing what life required as hunters-gatherers-planters. If he had remorseful thoughts about Connie, he did not voice them. He seemed, in fact, to have found a place for her memory and contained her there. For the moment, anyway, he was more interested in and more aware of their new home.

"Strange," he told Anna, "that I think of this as a new home when it's only supposed to be a summer camp."

"I think it's the Masakis' final stand. I can't shake that feeling, Widel. Not since the airplanes came. I think Wasmaggi has planned it this way. I really do."

"Oh, Anna, the planes were an anomaly, a coincidence."

"I hope you're right, but I don't think so."

"If you're right, why did Wasmaggi delay so long after the plane noises to bring us here. He was in no hurry."

"I don't know. We'll just have to wait and see."

If there had been a village on the swampland, there were no traces of it. And Widel looked. As far as he could tell, it was a virgin landscape. There were no clearings, no stumps where a tree might have been cut or burned, no evidence of any kind that a group of people had inhabited the island. He spent so much time looking that he was delinquent in preparing a shelter for his family.

"We're going to sleep in the open again, Widel?"

"Sorry. I get preoccupied with all the questions I have and time slips away. I'll rig up something for the night."

Forced to it over the years, Widel was reasonably successful as a house builder. "Remember once," he asked Anna, "that I asked you and Connie what kind of house you wanted and that Connie had pointed out one of the most elaborate? Well, I ask you again. What do you want? This time I can do it, with your help, of course."

"Let's just start with a simple shelter, then tomorrow you and Penny can build something larger."

214

"Penny and I?"

"Well, Wasmaggi is taking me on a little tour. Different medicines, you know. That kind of tour."

"So, in our hour of need, you're taking off? Just like that?"

"Just like that. And, Widel, don't make Penny do all the heavy work."

It didn't take long to construct a shelter: find a couple of saplings, cut some vines, gather a number of fan palm fronds, and hook the leaves over the vines. A more adequate shelter, using a couple of more saplings and more vines and a lot more fronds, would take on the appearance of a Masaki house. Enough fronds and the house would be protection from the hardest rain, if there was time enough left to build the sleeping platforms that elevated them above the ground.

But adequate sleeping platforms would take longer to build than would the house. They would be built tomorrow or the next day.

The extra daylight afforded by the open savannah allowed Widel time to erect the bare necessity. Anna teased him. It was amazing how few were their wants and how simple were their tastes and that neither of them even thought to ask for more.

The campfire that night was under the trees and well back from the edge of the grassy expanse. Was this because of habit or because the Masaki didn't want to be exposed? Exposed to whom? Widel wondered about that, and he wondered if he was beginning to become as paranoid as was Anna. Perhaps some of his questions would be answered tonight.

Especially, he had had one question lingering just below the surface, one he couldn't quite grasp. Now it lunged to the front of his mind. Was Wasmaggi the only one who know about this place? How did he explain to Trulk the purpose of moving a whole village so far from home? Did Trulk know this place? And would Trulk bring his village here? And if he did, why would he? What was going on?

All the Masakis were at the bursting point. They had asked Wasmaggi a hundred questions and each had received the same answer: in time. It was time. Who knew what would happen if Wasmaggi prolonged the suspense.

SIXTEEN

"This is first home of the Masaki," he began. "Wasmaggi born here when made medicine man."

That simple statement cleared up one of Widel's questions. When Wasmaggi spoke of being born here, he meant figuratively, not physically.

"Long time should have brought An-na here, but so many things lost to Masaki. Now bring whole village, because this place of safety. When Wasmaggi young medicine man, medicine men need place of safety. Not all Masaki liked medicine men like Wasmaggi. Masaki fight. Much bad. Were bad medicine men. All bad medicine men gone now. Here Wasmaggi and others take Masaki and make fight with our cousins. Here medicine men make power."

Civil war? Revolution? What was Wasmaggi talking about? Shamans, witch doctors? More questions than answers.

"Now ask why village here. Once when here, Wasmaggi see two evils, more creatures like the others and Masakis who kill Masaki. Both I've told you. Tonto and his wives have seen the others; all of you have seen the jaguar-hunters. Now Wasmaggi see more evils, see creatures, see time when maybe no Masakis.

"Wasmaggi old like Hagga and Tomaz; time to die; I'm the one who knows; everything I know, I tell An-na. She will be the one who knows. Listen to her. Seek her mind. When Masaki leave here, Wasmaggi will not be with you. An-na will."

Protests were useless, and the Masakis seemed to know that. They affirmed their affection and trust for Anna when Soomar told Wasmaggi that Anna was the medicine women. But they were reluctant to acknowledge Wasmaggi's announced intention to die.

217

It would happen sometime; they knew that, but sometime was so far in the future it might not happen at all.

In a roundabout way, Mansella asked for everyone. "We not wish the forest to take Wasmaggi, but the forest decide. How long will Masaki stay in this place?"

"I've much to teach you. I've much to teach An-na. You will not leave until teaching complete."

To forestall more questions about Wasmaggi's final walk into the forest, Tonto stood. "I've learned much this past time, and I've much to learn. Perhaps the forest will talk to Tonto, too, and to Lucknew and Pollyque. But here we live for a time, and Wasmaggi wishes me to teach you."

Tonto spoke about hunting and how the swampland could not stand to be hunted for long. All hunting would be done off island, and that meant all hunters were responsible for leaving no tracks or other evidence of people. Hunters would learn to be scouts and would learn every inch of the land surrounding the island. And they would become swamp hunters, knowing every inch of the underwater bottom. Wasmaggi had assured him that the swamp would provide many fish, but new ways of fishing had to be tried and learned.

"We're preparing for a siege," Widel told Anna. "For some reason, that damn intuition again, they think we're going to be attacked. Has Wasmaggi said anything to you?"

"Nothing, only that I've much to learn, whatever he means by that."

Tonto went on to tell the women that Wasmaggi would lay out the garden plots, under the trees Widel noted again, and that no one was to use the center field for any activity. "We are the people of the forest; we don't live in the grass. In time you will use of the grass, but not now."

Widel spoke up. "Tonto, will other Masakis be coming here?"

"No. Why should they?"

"What did you tell Trulk about the whole village walking through the forest. Surely he knows we are here."

"He does not know about the island."

"But our tracks will lead him to the swamps. Won't he guess?"

"Maybe, but is not Masaki to watch for."

"Does his medicine man know about this island?"

"Maybe, too," Wasmaggi said, "but maybe not pass on knowledge if dead. Trulk never been here; swamp too far beyond range. Why Ran-ford ask?"

"Because you seem to expect trouble, and if there's trouble enough to move a whole village, then maybe that trouble is seen by other medicine man."

"No trouble, but want every hunter know where safe place is if come trouble. You bring family here; you bring village here if trouble. Can keep trouble away once here."

"Be prepared," Widel said as he sat down. "For what?"

"Now Wasmaggi answer all questions."

Wasmaggi repeated much of what he had told the Masakis earlier. Masaki history seemed not to exist before the others arrived and pillaged the tribe. Yet, as Wasmaggi probed his own mind, there seemed to exist a prehistory, a rambling oral history about which Wasmaggi was not clear but which hinted at head hunting and cannibalism, neither phrase or word did he use, what he called *the darker depths.*

"That's a strange choice of words," remarked Anna. "Are those his words or words he picked up from us?"

In references to those darker depths, he described the medicine men who claimed to be the intermediaries between the people and the forest and how those shamans, again not his word, had used the jaguar-men as enforcers. Wasmaggi had a vague sense of the Masaki transition from hunting and root gathering and grub collecting to hunting and cultivation.

Widel considered his own sense of the Masaki people. They were simple and free, but they were not simpletons or innocents; they led complex lives, hopelessly complex because they were prisoners of their own isolation. They were doomed primitives who one day would be extinct, himself included.

Now Widel knew the source of Anna's depression. The Masaki way of life was fragile. They didn't see it, but they lived on the edge of extinction, had lived on that edge for a long time. Widel recalled a statement one of his Brazilian contacts had made a long time ago, something to the effect that *the Amazon is not ours until every Indian has been replaced by a Brazilian.*

"Remember," Wasmaggi was saying, "the forest is forever."

"Is it?" Anna sighed. "I wonder."

She had been listening to Wasmaggi only partially aware of everything he was saying. She indulged herself in her own interpretations and speculations. She remembered that the Aztecs had recorded the destruction of the world three times: once by flood, and before that by fire, and once by the world being devoured by a jaguar. The Masaki's world had come close to being devoured by the jaguar-men.

Again, Wasmaggi was speaking of the swampland as a safe place.

"Why this sudden interest in a secure hiding place?" Anna asked Widel.

Security is a human myth. Everything is in movement; nothing is static, not even the Masaki Indians who seem to have evolved their culture less and to have invented less than any prehistoric civilization anywhere in the world. The entire cosmos is in perpetual motion, and to attempt to stand pat is to challenge the very nature of nature. And yet that is what the Amazon Indians have done for thousands of years. Their security may be in not changing, but they cannot prevent the changes happening elsewhere. Lives are in motion because the universe is in motion. That may not be apparent in the middle of a seemingly unchanging wilderness, but it is true nonetheless. Security against outside influence is a fallacy, and when the world outside moves in, security is an illusion.

Wasmaggi, of course, was not taking about outside influences and cultural clashes. He might wonder about the potential existence of other people, but he was not consciously speaking about the possibility of confronting them. He was not proposing something real, now or in the future. He was completing the final chapter of his teaching duty, and for reasons he could never articulate, he had decided to include the whole village. That was his reason, that and his intuitive fear.

While Soomar was considered the lead hunter, it was Tonto who was the older generation's most skilled, and it was Tonto, with Wasmaggi's impulsive encouragement, who also had lessons to teach.

No Masaki other than Tonto and Wasmaggi at the time of the others ever had been trained in warfare. There was no word for war. The closest word was a rather vague concept, one that joined the word for struggle with the word for unnecessary or meaningless and ending the word with a suffix meaning bad or harmful to one's self. No Masaki had been trained in the art of a harmful, meaningless struggle, yet as proven, all Masaki could and would kill if the killing was judged necessary.

All that Widel and Anna had witnessed was defensive warfare. Now Tonto wanted to teach the Masaki hunters how to go on the offensive. "Is what Tomaz should have told," Tonto said by way of explanation. "Never need, but must know."

"Another be prepared," Widel added.

Widel was astounded when Tonto told him he was to teach arrow making to the women, not just the palm core kind, a skill they already possessed, but the serious, killing arrows for the long bows and for Widel's strange curved bow. Widel also was to organize the children in feather collecting and resin collecting and was to teach the gluing of the feathers to the arrows to the children.

"Serious business," Widel said.

"Staying alive is Ran-ford's business," Tonto replied.

Wasmaggi's continued training of the medicine woman began with a practical lesson: how to make lime. The swamp provided an unending supply of clam and snail shells, unlike the stream at home. Burning the shells produced the lime. The trick was to cook the shells without turning them into black charcoal.

Next, Wasmaggi introduced Anna to a new coca bush, a low growing, thick shrub with glossy green leaves about the width of her thumb. When the leaves were sun dried, they shrunk in half and lost their color.

221

Then, with the leaves ground into powder and the lime ground into powder, the two were mixed. A highly concentrated cocaine was the result.

Wasmaggi stressed the medical use of the medicine. In tiny amounts and made into tea, it could refresh the mind and spirit and soothe thirst, hunger, itching, and fatigue. It could be eaten, and it could be burned as incense. It was dangerous, Wasmaggi warned again, to burn it in a closed hut. The result could be devastating. Anna thought back to Wasmaggi's own drug trip and to her mental pictures of Chinese opium dens.

In the midst of one of his medical lessons, Wasmaggi announced, "Much serious. Now will show An-na what will please the Masakis. Show An-na how to make *quena* and *antara*."

The quena is a reed flute similar to a recorder. The simplest has two notes, the most complex, six notes. The antara is a pan-pipe, six single note reed flutes tied together.

"An-na learn to make and play so Masaki taki."

"Taki?"

"Taki. Dance. An-na learn quena and antara, and Masaki taki, not to drum only but to music of forest."

Mike delayed only long enough to revisit Fraylie's resting place. He brushed away the flies that already were eating the corpse, a fruitless gesture, just as he knew moving Fraylie to a more comfortable site would be. It was the forest's way; let the forest take back the lifeless body of the hunter, he said to himself. And as he was saying his farewell, he gathered up the few possessions he and Fraylie had between them: a small hammock each, a blow gun and a small quiver of darts, two bows and some arrows. As few as the possessions were, Mike could not carry them conveniently. He stuck one of Fraylie's spears in the ground beside the body, thought better of it, broke the spear in two and laid it across Fraylie's chest.

Why, he asked himself, had they not used the arrows against the creatures? Without ego and with no sense of false pride, he decided it was because they lacked experience. Fraylie had learned the final lesson; Mike would not repeat the mistake.

But now he must put distance between himself and the white man with red hair and search out the nearest village to warn it of the great danger, the deadly danger he could not comprehend.

Mike could not travel as fast as he knew he must. His desire for swiftness was negated by the need to remain alert to danger. Only now and then, after careful listening, did he use the pathway that seemed to lead to a village. Most of the time, he kept to the forest.

When he came to a junction, he was surprised and startled to read the signs. More creature footprints, and more Indian footprints, this time not made by adult hunters but by women and children. Was there another party on a different trail being murdered by the creatures? Were there other white men?

Since all recent footprints led away from a campsite, Mike chanced the risk of meeting more creatures. He ran along the widening trail, his one mission to warn whoever lived there.

Even before he entered the village itself, he knew; nothing could have prepared him for the sight. Masakis bodies were everywhere, grotesque caricatures of what once had been human beings, bodies ripped of their limbs, bodies without heads, gutted babies and old women, hunters without stomachs, all strewn about in random disregard for the life of the people. Ravens, eagles, hawks were ripping the flesh from the bones. Mike wondered why the birds first went for the eyes; empty sockets stared blindly into space. A million insects crept or crawled over the dead, and probably inside them, too.

Rage overwhelmed him, then pity, then sorrow, and sorrow dominated. He had seen the ravaged Sampson's village; now he saw another village, and in his mind he saw the Masaki becoming fewer and weaker and eventually disappearing.

He was not a hunter when he went to Sampson's village, and the hunters had done the nasty work of burning the village and the bodies. Now he was the only hunter, and even if he had carried his message of danger too late, he was responsible for burning this village and its inhabitants.

It was almost more than he could manage to touch the first body. The hunter had three large holes in his chest and one gigantic hole in his back. What could have done this? Who could have done this?

He slowly dragged one body after another to the center of the village, laid the bodies on the mats of palm leaves he had taken from the houses, covered the bodies with more mats, and started a second pile. He noted the absence of young girls and women. Had the creatures taken them away? To kill them somewhere else?

He set the bier on fire in a number of places, but he could not watch. He had not counted the bodies. Forty anyway, he guessed, counting the babies and little children. The village must have been considerably larger than his own when he added the females that must have been part of it. He didn't want to think about it, and he didn't want to think about the fact that not one of the Indians had died with his spear in his hand. Whatever had happened had happened so suddenly and so swiftly not a single hunter had been able to defend himself or the village.

Somewhere close by there had to be a stream. He would wash there, camp some distance away, and plan what to do next.

When he found the stream, he did not stop. He moved upstream, away from a beach similar to his own. When he thought he was as safe as he could be, he washed himself and drank, and then found a particularly good hiding place for the night. Once there, he broke into tears, uncontrollable and pitiful. In part, he cried for his loneliness; in part he cried for the loss of Fraylie; mostly he cried for the deaths of so many Masakis.

The loss was beyond all understanding, and most frightening of all, he was the only one alive to know of it and to have witnessed the result. How could the forest allow this to happen?

What sleep Mike managed to get was little more than a series of nightmares filled with creatures led by a white man murdering and torturing Masakis. In his nightmares he was attacked by Ranford and tormented by Connie and Anna who in turn brought the jaguars to feast on the villagers, and what the jaguars didn't want they threw to the alligators and the birds, all of the forest animals tearing the Masakis apart limb by limb, piece by piece, all fighting over the eyes, the eyes that looked into his eyes and begged for revenge.

"You will have it," he said to the empty forest, his duty clear. He had to get to his own people and warn them about the whites. He had to get to his own people and kill the whites. He had to find his own people before it was too late to save them.

He did not eat. He drank again from the stream, wondering if the whites had poisoned it and guessed they hadn't because he was still alive. He retraced his steps of yesterday, and took one last look at the village, an action he regretted immediately. The burning had not been completely successful.

As he studied the remains, he had to decide. Should be complete the grizzly work or should he hurry on to find his own village people? He found the question profoundly deep and stressful. He should hurry, before it was too late. He should honor the Masaki by finishing here.

Hurry, warn the people, his inner voice said. Take care of those who cannot take care of themselves, he heard Tomaz say. The whites are evil, his inner voice warned. The whites are a gift from the forest, he heard Hagga say. Go now, his inner voice said. Do what is right, Wasmaggi said.

"Finish the job, son, then help an old man." That voice was not within; that voice was out there somewhere in the forest. Mike spun around, on guard, afraid.

"It was the creatures, young jaguar hunter, who did this. Now finish what I cannot do. Then come and help me. I'm wounded."

So artfully had the old hunter concealed himself among the forest's growth that Mike could not locate him. "Step out where I can see you," he commanded.

"I cannot move. It took me two days to hide where I am. Look. Turn to your right. That's it. See? I make the leaves move."

"And why can't you come out and face me?"

"I've no legs."

Trap or true? Mike had no way of knowing.

The old man saw his doubt. "If I meant to kill you, I could have done it yesterday or now."

"Are you a Masaki?"

"I am a Masaki, soon to be a dead Masaki. Sooner if you not help me."

Mike saw the moving leaves, stared intently at them, and only then did he see the second oldest man he had ever seen, Wasmaggi being the oldest.

"I am Trulk," the man said. "Once the jaguar hunter. You are a jaguar hunter. What do they call you?"

"I am Mike."

"Yes, Mike, on way to another Masaki village with Fraylie in search of wives."

"What...how...do you know that?"

"I've met your village. Where is Fraylie?"

The exchange of information and knowledge was done sparingly as Mike tended to Trulk's wounds. It was not quite true that Trulk had no legs, but it was true that he had no useful legs, bullets having shattered both legs just below the knee caps.

"I wish An-na was here," Mike said, forgetting for a moment that she was an evil one. "I mean, I wish Wasmaggi was here."

"Your An-na has the power of healing."

"She has bad powers."

"I saw only good."

"But she is white; all over she is white."

"And now white is evil?"

"I'm sure of it. I saw a white man kill your people."

"Yes, I've thought on it, too. We will think together. Now, Trulk in much pain. Would talk to forest before you came. Now must talk with you. You have much to do besides help useless old man."

In a moment of inspiration, Mike asked if the medicine man's house still stood.

"Yes, there at the end of that row," Trulk said, pointing. "What good does that do us? Do you know anything about medicine? Are you a healer?"

"No, but I used to help An-na when she gathered the leaves and roots. I know some of the medicines."

226

Ferraz's pistoleiros, in their rapid search for valuables, had noted the medicine man's medicines only long enough to destroy the pots and bamboo containers. Not knowing what was in them, they smashed everything in sight. Mike had a difficult time sorting out what might be useful. What he wanted especially were coca teas or manioc liquids, either of which would reduce Trulk's suffering.

Trulk started talking as soon as Mike returned. "At least you know the coca leaves. I hope you know the curare, for when I'm through talking, you will help me meet the forest."

Mike started to protest, then realized Trulk was helpless. Not even Wasmaggi's medicine, or Anna's, could do anything for the old jaguar hunter. It was amazing he had lived this long.

"Mike bears the scars of the jaguar and carries the jaguar hunter's spear. Hunters must have faith in Mike. Now Mike bears inner scars. You must wear them with bravery. No one will know they are there; cannot see them, but means Mike now must battle with self. For all Mike has seen, is not prepared for what Trulk now must tell.

"These people you not know, but one you know has been taken with the other young women by the creatures, the female you call Sayhoo. She come with Trulk here to find husband. Maybe that husband one of my village, maybe she think Fraylie here, maybe, so An-na say, she think Mike here. No matter now, only you here and she gone."

That one whom he had known his whole life was among the captured women came as a direct blow to Mike's innards. He felt faint. It was one thing to have to deal with people he had never seen; to deal now with someone who had shared his village as part of his family of Masakis was the cruelest of duties.

"I must go to her," he said. "I'll try to save the women."

"No. No. That is why Trulk must talk. Alone, you cannot defeat the creatures. Even if you kill one or two, the others will kill the women as they killed the hunters. You must find help. You must find your own village."

227

"But how? Mike is lost with only sun and vague memory to guide. Where is my village? Fraylie and I were on our way to find it."

"Listen to Trulk. Remember all I say."

Between his raspy gasping for breath, Trulk carefully described the route he and his hunters had taken home from their last meeting with Tonto and the others of Mike's village. He thought, he said, that Tonto and Wasmaggi were leading their people to the great swamps. Once or twice his medicine man had hinted that the swamps were the ancient home of the Masakis. Mike had to find the swamps, but from there on, he was on his own.

"Trulk have special reason for wanting Mike to find people. One you burn with others is Awhawk. One who was taken by the creatures was Laiti. Awhawk died bravely. Laiti should have the right to live free."

Some long ignored words of Anna's popped into Mike's head. "Free means not being trampled on and told what to do by someone who would control you. Not being a slave."

"Trulk not know word."

"An-na's word."

Mike repeated every direction and memorized every sign just as Trulk told him.

"Long way, Mike. You must go now."

"Hard to leave you."

"Is hard for me to tell you go. But I watch you go, and then I'll go to be one with the forest."

As Ferraz had promised, once the tropas de resgate or procuradores had dragged the kicking and screaming young women out of the brush, they were as docile as lambs. But Rangel was disappointed. There were fewer young women than Ferraz had anticipated. That's why Rangel had dragged Laiti along. Perhaps some foreign stud would like a fresh child. If not, well, there were other rewards besides money.

One young woman occupied most of his attention, not that physically she was different, but she had an attitude or a presence or an awareness, he didn't know which. It was in the way she carried herself with a certain surety. She looked at the procuradores in a way that forecast trouble. If she wasn't money on the hoof, Rangel would have given her to the men to enjoy and then would have killed her. He didn't like mysteries, and he didn't like Indians who seemed to know more than he did about what was going to happen.

Sayhoo was anything but sure of herself. However, she had one advantage over the other Indians. She had already seen and experienced what the forest could do. Not that that diminished the shock, revulsion and fear generated by the procuradores, and she was as frightened as any other Masaki, but somehow it allowed her to achieve a sense of futility without caving in, a paradox perhaps best explained by Sayhoo's ability to wait without protest for the next startling development. Rangel and the others were not quite the shock to her they were to the other women. And while the procuradores were not white, they reminded her of Ranford. Sayhoo made no other connection at the time.

Close up, she could see that her captors were man-like. She wondered if these were the *others* Wasmaggi had told about and decided they were not. What these men wore was not skin but a covering of some mysterious kind they put on and took off as circumstances required.

They chewed on pieces of vine and blew smoke out of their mouths and noses. They smelled foul. They performed their body functions without regard for the forest. They built fires three and four times larger than necessary. That was one of the peculiarities of the others, Sayhoo remembered.

But for her it was one thought at a time, and now the thought was to survive long enough for help to arrive and rescue them. If on the one hand she had given her being to fate, on the other hand she was determined to do everything possible for help to find her.

The first instance came immediately upon being tied to her new women friends. Sayhoo had to wet the ground. When she made that need clear, she was untied from the others and allowed to squat beside the trail. No one had ever watched her eliminate her body waste. Her captors took great delight in the act and failed to notice the many marks Sayhoo made on the ground. She wanted all the women and young girls do the same thing. It would slow the group up and it would leave an easily read trail.

Ferraz and Simón had an easy time backtracking the trail to the spot where they originally had emerged from the forest. Ferraz wanted to camp and rest. "I'm too old for this, Simón. I should have known that from the beginning."

"There's no hurry, Paulo. It'll take the others much longer. We've time for rest."

"Do you think you can find us some meat?"

"The only meat I've seen is monkey."

"Jesus, I hate that stuff. You'd think there would be something better."

"It's a matter of hunger, I guess."

"Never could understand the Indians' diet. Even when I was younger, I never could stomach grubs and snakes and monkeys. Alligator meat I like, but we haven't even seen an alligator."

"We haven't seen much of anything except trees."

"Well, Simón, light a fire, please. We have much to talk about." Simón was not the best choice, but once having made it, Ferraz was determined to make it work.

"First thing, Simón, you'll take a bath every day. And you'll shave. And we'll have to cut your hair. Indians don't take kindly to much hair, and they are clean to a fault. They all get washed in the morning, and many of them wash again at night. We can't offend their sense of cleanliness.

"Second, you may wear some clothes; pants will be enough. Probably these Indians don't wear clothes, or if they do, it will be the tiniest little thing covering their crotch. The young Indian girls will not even have that. And they will be bare chested.

"Now, I know you will have a hard time with naked young women. I did at first; it's natural for a man. But this is one time when natural isn't going to help us. I hope I don't have to save the women from you, too. Remember, we're training young ladies of

230

pleasure. And wipe that silly grin off your face. You'll have plenty of opportunity to hump the girls later. First things first."

Ferraz spoke at length about the task at hand: winning the confidence of the women, teaching them self-pleasure, rewarding them, teaching them how to give pleasure, rewarding them. The only pain an Indian woman was to feel was the lack of reward for having failed one of the steps Ferraz outlined.

"It's really very simple, Simón. We are going to attack Rangel and Newcastle, chase them off, herd the women away to safety, and comfort them. We are going to hold them in our arms as if they were children and give them meaningless trinkets of beads and cloth.

"The holding is very important. You can hold two women at the same time. And when you hold them, you'll cup their breasts and manipulate the breasts very, very gently. It's not something Indian males do, and it's a new experience for the women, and if you're gentle enough in the holding and squeezing, they'll like it, even respond to it. But that's all you'll do. Understand?

"Then, depending on how each responds, in a day or two you'll take an individual woman and give her more gifts and caress her, and the more she lets you, the more gifts she receives, until finally, and here you have to be the judge, she lets you play between her legs. You must not show emotion. Only the woman is to show and demonstrate emotion. Your time will come, but not yet."

"God, Ferraz, does this work?"

"It works, my friend. And it will be the hardest work you ever did, no pun intended."

"When...."

"Your time will come when the woman comes to you and in front of you gives herself pleasure. Then, only then, will you teach her to give you pleasure. She gives herself pleasure, you give her pleasure, she gives you pleasure. Once she does that, she's ready. And I dare say you'll be ready."

"Christ, Ferraz. What if I can't wait?"

"Then I'll have to save the woman from you. And, Simón, I will. But I beg you, don't let it come to that. In the first place, I'm too old to perform as I used to. As a matter of experience, you'll

231

beg me one day to excuse you from practice. You'll beg for mercy because you'll think your balls are busted and your little tool will fall off."

Michael "Red" Newcastle was alone, shivering in the brush, waiting for an Indian to attack. Newcastle had waited two days in his palm bush cover. He hadn't left it even to empty his bladder. Now, in spite of his best efforts, he needed to empty his bowels. He wondered why that was; he had not eaten or had a drink of water for two days.

Perhaps he had killed the Indian with a lucky shot, then remembered that after finding the body of his stupid companion, he hadn't fired a shot. Out there somewhere was an Indian ready to kill him. Every noise he heard could be that Indian. He still could see the spears in Pavón's and Czura's bodies, the silent weapons that killed so suddenly. He was afraid.

Not only that, he was lost. While the others were still rounding up the women and young girls, he and Czura and Pavón had captured the males, or at least those who had surrendered meekly, and had started down a trail. Not *the* trail, he admitted, just a trail which led he didn't know where. If he had taken the correct trail, Rangel and Eneas, Eduardo and Rogelio would have passed with their female captives.

He would have to go back up the trail, past the dead Indians, past his comrades, past more dead Indians, and into the village. Then he would have to find the proper trail and catch up with the others.

"And those bastards will tease the living shit out of me."

The more he thought about the remarks and jeering, the madder he got, and that madness made him move. "I'll kill them all," he said.

Newcastle looked at neither body. He saw them, but he did not look. He took rifles and sidearms from Pavón and Czura, but he didn't look at them. He should have taken their canteens and the bits of food they carried in their pockets, but he wasn't thinking. He thought only the thoughts of the thug: guns, plenty of guns. He took no ammunition.

He smelled the village long before he entered it, the smoldering, distinctively pungent odor of burned flesh. It was a smell he knew.

Just before he stepped into the village itself, there on the trail, stuck at an angle in the center of the trail, was a jaguar hunter's spear, its many colors and feather decorations a warning. Newcastle did not know it was Trulk's spear. Newcastle did not know Trulk or any other Masaki hunter he had helped gun down. And Newcastle did not know the spear was Trulk's futile attempt to reach a final resting place in the forest.

Trulk had thrown the spear and had tried to reach it. If he was successful, he would throw the spear again, and again he would try to reach it. And if he could throw the spear enough times and reach it enough times, he would be away from the village and in the forest. There he could die at peace in the only world he knew. He had thrown the spear once; he had not reached it.

The spear sent Newcastle into a frenzy of unabridged fear. He fired his AK-47 in repeated bursts, making a complete circle. He saw Indians in every shadow, thought he saw spears in every tree limb, knew he saw a hundred thousand eyes staring at him in every leaf. He slumped to the ground, waiting for the death blow that never came, and when down on his knees, he looked into the unseeing eyes of Trulk. He fell over the edge of sanity. He pumped shot after shot into the old jaguar hunter's body and blew it into a thousand pieces of dead flesh and bone.

"I got you, you prick," he yelled in triumph. "I got you before you got me."

Trulk did not reply.

Mike raced toward the rising sun, following the secret marks Trulk had described. On the fifth day, he came to the edge of a swamp. Somewhere along the edge of one of the many swamps, he would find the meeting place where Soomar and his "family" group had first met Solmar and Beck and the two stolen children.

From there he could follow the signs, first to where Trulk's hunters had confronted Soomar and Mansella, and then to where Trulk and Tonto had exchanged talk, and then to the campsite where Mike's villagers had waited.

After that, Mike was on his own. Trulk had no idea where Wasmaggi was leading the villagers. All Trulk and his hunters wanted were the children. He had not tarried beyond the execution of the two women, Anna's examination of Laiti and Awhawk and the hurried agreement concerning Sayhoo.

Mike was in distress as he searched the swamp edges. From first light to last light he looked for signs. He tried to recall every detail of Trulk's directions. At the end of the second day, he was exhausted, not from the physical needs of the hunt but from the mental. The stress was overbearing.

Food and rest, he decided, were urgently needed, and he allowed his mind to play with the choice between monkey meat or bird meat. That diversion itself was therapeutic. Lighting his fire helped. He had not had a fire for several nights. And stalking the bird directed his attention elsewhere. When he ate in the darkness and contemplated a full night's rest, he was certain that with the new sun he would be successful.

Mike slept the sleep of the exhausted, only now and then awakening to unrelated bits and pieces of nightmares. For the first night in a long time, he did not dream of his own death.

In the early light, he retraced his steps to where he first had encountered the swamp. He had missed something there. He had been looking on the ground and at eye level. Now he looked higher, up where a hunter might reach. And then he saw them, two tiny marks he would have missed had not Trulk told him about the signs. In less than half a day he reached the temporary campsite and saw for himself the remains of the executed women.

The trail of the villagers leading southward was easy to follow. What had taken the villagers three days, he covered in half a day, and by nightfall he was on the edge of another swamp. There the trail ended.

For half of the next day he followed a trail only to have it peter out and then disappear altogether. He retraced the trail and followed another, with similar results. Then a third trail. All false, all carefully done, all leading either to dead ends or to areas of water where tracking was impossible. Another day wasted, he told himself.

The next morning he began a careful search of the swamp's edge. It was possible his villagers had entered the swamp, but nowhere did he find a single clue that supported that conclusion. Finally, in desperation, he entered the swamp itself. Every step he took was punishment. He withdrew and tried other locations of entry. Each time was the same. The swamp was impassable. He returned to the last place of positive signs and set up his camp. He would have to think.

What would Tomaz have done? What would Tonto do, and Soomar, and Connie? White Connie, what would she have done? Despite his anxiety that whiteness might be evil, he thought of Connie, the jaguar hunter, and he knew what she would have done. She would have gotten flat on her belly and would have examined every inch of the swamp edge from a worm's point of view.

Mike waited for most of the early morning shadows to disappear, then he measured out a section of swamp edge. He got down on his hands and knees and saw things he never would have seen while standing. If that was so, he reasoned, then crawling on his belly would reveal more.

So intent was he on his examination, he was totally unprepared for the hand that clutched his hair and jerked him off the ground.

"Too much look," a voice said, a spear thrust tight against his middle.

"Kill now?" a second voice asked.

"See what got first."

Mike was spun around, a hand clutching his throat. He could hardly breathe. His feet dangled in the air.

"Westman, look what have here," a grinning Lurch said. "Little lost jaguar hunter."

"We throw him back to swamp," Westman laughed. "Not worth keep."

"Put me down," Mike managed to squawk.

Lurch did, and then embraced him. "Glad see Mike."

Westman joined the reunion hug. "Mike welcome. Where son of Hakma?" Westman asked.

"Look behind you," said Mike, and when the two hunters turned, Mike grabbed Westman's spear and held it to Lurch's heart. "You just learn lesson from jaguar hunter," he said, handing back the spear. "Never take eyes off enemy."

Mike told a little of what had befallen him and about the Masaki village. "Must get to people."

The joy of Mike's return was short lived; his news was devastating, especially to Saymore and Spiker, Sayhoo's parents, and to Wasmaggi, her grandfather. There were tears throughout the village.

Tonto gathered the hunters. An outwardly placid man, he was enraged by Mike's descriptions of the Masaki village, of the slaughter of Masaki hunters and the abduction of the young women. And he was worried; his own village's child was among them.

He quizzed Mike thoroughly. Three separate sets of tracks: two creatures only in one set that had not gone to the village; a set of three creature tracks that left the village with the bound Masaki hunters; and a set of four creature tracks that left on another trail with the women. Undoubtedly Sayhoo was among the women; he had not carried her to the death fire.

Yes, all the hunters were dead. No, he had not followed the tracks with the women. Why? Because Trulk had said to get help, that one hunter alone could not rescue the women; the women would be killed before Mike could kill the four creatures. No, he did not know if the three parties had joined up or if they intended to. Yes, Trulk surely would be dead by now. He was a man of remarkable courage. And finally, Mike counted on his fingers. Ten, twelve days at least.

And, finally, yes, Fraylie had passed his test. He died at the hands of the forest which had put two holes in his head, one small

236

one in the top of his head, a larger one at the base of his skull. But not before Fraylie had killed one of the creatures.

And one more thing. He was afraid to say it. With the creatures, or maybe he was one of the creatures, was a white man.

Widel let out an "Oh, shit. It finally has happened."

"That how Fraylie came be dead. White man kill all Masaki men."

The hunters looked at Widel, waiting for an explanation, hoping for an explanation, and when he said nothing more, the hunters questioned Mike further.

"Look like Ran-ford. That all Mike know." Turning to Widel, Mike said, "White man evil; white man much evil; forest give Masaki much evil."

S E V E N T E E N

There was much for the hunters to discuss and to decide at the community fire. Every hunter, woman and child showed the strain. What Mike had brought to them was beyond belief; his descriptions of death and torture were unbearable; and his conclusions went deep into the Masakis' hearts. They did believe; they did suffer; they did think.

First, Mike had to repeat every detail of what he saw and experienced, and he was made to recall every facet of Fraylie's test, including his death caused by the mysterious holes in his head.

And Mike had to recount every word of his conversation with Trulk. To Wasmaggi and Tonto, that conversation seemed to hold the key to their decisions. Exactly what did Trulk say about the creatures and about the white man - and about Anna and Widel?

Mike's charges against the whites were not taken lightly, and his speculation that the creatures and the whites were different forms of the same beast was considered carefully.

Widel took no part in the talk. He brooded quietly. Anna sat with the women, and she offered nothing, her face a mask behind which she had her own private and disturbing thoughts. Anna and Widel knew very well the creatures were men; that a white man was among them was not a surprise. What surprised Anna was that non Indian Brazilians were not considered white, but she confessed she knew no Brazilians and so couldn't say what color or hue they might be.

Wasmaggi repeated Trulk's generous words about Anna. "I've told you I'm the one who knows, so I tell you this. There may be more white people in the forest than we have known. Maybe not all are good people. We have known bad people of our color, Sampson,

238

Solmar, Beck, who have killed babies and a whole village. Knowing them, would you say that all Masaki are bad? I believe in An-na and Ran-ford, just as our brother Tomaz believed in the other white woman, the jaguar hunter. Not usual speak name of dead, but Tomaz and Hagga, they loved Con-nie and An-na, and know you respect Ran-ford. We put our lives in them many times. They never disappoint. So Mike wrong when say all white evil"

Tonto spoke directly to Mike. "Must settle one thing first. Ran-ford your friend since first day. Con-nie, An-na, they treat Mike as man, not boy. They love Mike, yet Mike sees them as bad people. Tonto not know why. With Wasmaggi, say our whites best of Masaki."

It was difficult to know Mike's feelings. The shock of seeing a white man mutilate Masaki hunters by castration was not easily overcome. His hopeless love for the white women helped him find an excuse for hating them, making it somewhat easier to accept the fact that he never could have one as his wife. And seeing what a white man could do added a sense of betrayal, not withstanding the fact he had witnessed the result of his own people's ability to murder and destroy. At times of great stress, one notices the differences, in this case color, when the difference never meant anything in normal times. Color was the only variable Mike could find to help explain the tragedies he had witnessed.

Mike made no reply. Tonto turned to Widel. "What Ran-ford know?"

Widel wanted to tell the Masaki again that there were as many people in the world as they were trees, that those people came in black and white and yellow and red and brown, that people lived in villages covering far more land than the Masakis' entire hunting range. He wanted to, but he didn't. How would he begin to describe the outside world? And how could he possibly explain now when earlier he a had failed that he came to the Masaki not from the forest but from that alien world, the one they could not begin to imagine.

"Ranford knows there might be other white men," he conceded. "The forest is full of surprises. To the Masakis I say that Anna and

I, and Connie when she was with us, love the Masaki, are proud to be Masaki and would do the Masaki no harm. But I understand how Mike must feel."

He waited a few seconds, considering what he should say next, "This I tell you from my heart. If there is doubt, if the hunters or the women or even the children believe Anna and Penny and I are lying or are a threat, we will leave the Masaki and go to live in the forest alone. I don't know any other way to prove what I say except to say we will leave you if you wish us to. It is up to you."

Widel did not wait for a response and walked toward his tiny shelter. From her place among the women, Anna got up with Penny and took her place beside Widel.

"This is a terrible day for the Masakis," she said.

"Worse," Widel answered. "It may well mark the end of the Masakis."

"And of us?" Anna asked.

"As a family? No. We can live our lives in the forest. I've no doubt about that. As Masakis? I don't know. It all depends on whether what Mike has told them carries over to us or whether they can separate us from that bastard with the red hair."

"This might not be the right time to bring it up, but what about Penny? We live in the forest. That's okay for you and me. But what about Penny? What does she do? Sooner or later she's alone."

"You're right, Anna. It isn't time, just one more complication we're not ready to face. Not that I haven't thought about it. God knows I have. If everything had been normal, one day we would be faced with Penny's marriage to one of the hunters, to say nothing of what goes on before marriage. Probably we'd have taken it all in stride. Now I don't know. I just don't know."

Anna and Widel and Penny sat beside their cooking fire like accused criminals waiting for a jury's verdict. Not since the early days had they felt so isolated, the only difference being that now they possessed the knowledge and skills necessary to live successfully in the forest. The possibility of expulsion, nonetheless, was very real, and the potential for execution was not ruled out entirely by either Widel or Anna.

Time dragged on. It seemed the hunters had a lot to say to each other, about what, Anna and Widel could only guess. Apart from the hunters, the women were engaged in their own animated conversation. The whites watched from a distance, knowing their destiny was in the hands of a people who couldn't possibly know the consequences of what they debated and wouldn't have understood had they known.

After what seemed an eternity of waiting, four women left their group. Tonto's granddaughters, Contulla and Cutilla, headed toward Anna and Widel. Mansella and Xingu went to the men.

When the twins reached Anna's fire, Cutilla asked if they might sit and talk. They were invited to do so, and Widel volunteered to leave.

"No. Ran-ford stay," Cutilla said. "Women have fight."

"No fight. Argument," Contulla interrupted, "over who will speak to An-na and Ran-ford."

"And you two lost?" Widel said sarcastically.

The twins ignored the open hostility.

"Does Ran-ford think bad of us because we would speak for all women?" Cutilla asked. "We know how Ran-ford feel; we have husbands not of this village. Sometimes hard for them, too, in beginning."

"I'm sorry, ladies. It's just that so much is happening. Forgive my bad manners."

"Is forgotten already," Contulla replied. "Women want An-na and Ran-ford know you are Masaki. If you leave, all women say they leave with you and live in your family."

There was more, and there were some tears shed, tears of solidarity and commitment.

When Mansella and Xingu approached the men, they were much less civil and observed none of the customary manners.

Mansella voiced the women's decision. "If An-na and Ran-ford are to leave, the women and children will leave with them," she said as directly as she knew how.

"How you could even consider this matter is mystery," Xingu added, "because each of you knows medicine woman and weapon maker are Masaki, better Masaki than you. You shame us by your talk."

Turning to her husband, Xingu continued. "Joqua, our two children live because of An-na. If you were a man, you would stand here with me and say if An-na go, you go."

"Woman," Joqua said, "you prove only that women are...." He wanted to say stupid or some other word that would put Xingu in her place, but images entered his head and raced through his mind. His daughter was named for the two white women, and for good reason. Walkin's stepsons and Joshway's daughter were named as they were because of the whites. Sarahguy had her baby because of the medicine woman's care and that child had lived because of the medicine women. Two children had been saved from death by the white women. The white man made the best weapons the Masakis had ever had, and he fought with courage and skill. "You prove only that women are in agreement with the men," Joqua said.

Mike, Wasmaggi, and Widel sat off by themselves. Widel described a world and a world of men and women neither Indian could hope to comprehend. What gave Widel credibility was Wasmaggi's agreement that what Widel was saying might be true. "I have felt that; I believe that could be true; I imagined that," or similar words were spoken by Wasmaggi. Only when Widel tried to describe the outside material world did Wasmaggi express disbelief, his doubt voiced because he had absolutely nothing in his experience as a frame of reference.

"All this Mike must see," Mike said toward morning.

"Some of this Mike has seen and did not know what it was."

"What did Mike see and not know?"

"A piece of metal, a glass jar, a needle, a razor, a spear blade, a metal bowl, a fire maker. Those are common things out there."

The hunters prepared quickly and resolutely. They would attempt to rescue Sayhoo and the other Masaki women, including the child Laiti. Only two questions remained: who would be in the rescue party and who would lead.

242

Without question, Spiker, Sayhoo's father, would be in the group. And Westman, Walkin, and Mike. Hakma and Moremew would not be. They were considered too old, and the aged group included Tonto and Wasmaggi. Joshway was needed by Sarahguy. Widel would go, and Soomar, Joqua, Lurch, and Amstay.

And Anna and Mansella. When the women's names were proposed, the hunters put up a tremendous howl. Never had women been on a mission of this kind. It was unheard of.

About Anna's inclusion, Wasmaggi had the last word. "Much danger; much possibility of need for medicine woman. Wasmaggi cannot go; Anna must, else some Masakis die."

And once that was settled, Anna spoke for Mansella. "Anna will need help. The hunters will fight, Anna and Mansella will take care of their wounds, maybe women's wounds. The women will want the medicine woman, and the medicine woman wants Mansella."

"Soomar agree."

Thus it was settled. Soomar, Mike, Widel, Spiker, Westman, Walkin, Lurch, Amstay, Joqua, and the two women would leave.

It was a large party, and it was agreed before hand that Mike, Lurch and Amstay would track and kill the white who had killed Fraylie and the Masaki hunters.

Mike would lead the hunters to the demolished Masaki village. He knew Trulk's signs and had been over the trail. And once in the village, he would help save a lot of time because he knew the trails the two groups of others had taken.

What seemed a large party at first glance was really very small. Three hunters would seek out the white man. Somewhere down a trail, two others had separated from the main group. They had to be tracked and found, perhaps by three more hunters. That left three hunters and the two women to find those who had captured the women. The simple math didn't add up. Lurch would go with Mike, and only two hunters would be assigned to the two unknowns. Even so, that left only five hunters and the women to deal with the four others. It would have to be enough.

Red Newcastle left behind the destruction he had helped cause. He had no idea which of several trails to take, and his initial choice proved to be a wrong one. He ended up on a little beach from which he could see no other exit. He drank from the warm water and refilled his canteen, ever watchful. He returned to the village. Another trail led to a small garden and another dead end. A fourth trail, chosen only out of desperation, appeared to be the correct one if for no other reason than that it continued on for some distance. He committed himself to the trail, the trail on which Rangel and the others were leading the captured women.

Newcastle moved slowly. Every bush was a threat, behind every tree lurked an enemy, every forest noise was someone or something intending to harm him. He was armed to the teeth, but at least he had learned that shooting at every potential threat was useless. As far as he knew, except for the old Indian, he had killed no one.

When the trail narrowed, a short way into his second day, he proved again just how ignorant he was. He fought the jungle. If a limb stuck out over the trail, rather than duck under it or go around it, he chopped it off. If a new growth had emerged on the trail, instead of stepping over it, he cut it off. Not only were his machete efforts a waste of energy, he was leaving a trail a blind monkey could follow.

On the third night, his ignorance nearly cost him his life. He had built his customary large fire, and because it was so smoky, he had moved upwind out of the smoke and sat some distance away from the overheating fire. As he sat in the darkness isolated from the fire, a jaguar moved upwind. To Newcastle who faced the fire, there was much light. He could see everything in front of him; he could not see more than a few inches into the shadow he cast on the forest. Newcastle was a perfect target for the cat.

The jaguar made no noise as it crept toward Newcastle. But give Newcastle credit; he smelled the jaguar's musky odor just before the tiger pounced. Thinking he was smelling a human enemy, Newcastle turned and fired. The jaguar was hit, but with its primitive, animal reasoning, continued to advance, now not searching for food but searching out an enemy. Between its growling and hobbling,

Newcastle knew where it was, and round after round of AK-47 fire found and killed the beast.

There was no more noise, but the smell lingered. All night long, Newcastle smelled the jaguar, sat with his back to the fire, his guns propped on his knees, and waited. Only after the sun was high in the sky did he dare to look at what he had killed. He didn't touch it.

The next night was no better. Newcastle saw a paca, the giant rate of the Amazon, and what little sleep he he had was filled with nightmares of attacking Indians, jaguars and rats, all eating his flesh as he looked on hopelessly.

It had been four, five, he didn't know how many days, since he had eaten. He had intended to live off the land, not knowing what the land had to offer or whether he could find anything to kill and eat. Some claim the paca to be the best meat in the world, but Newcastle hadn't seen the rodent in that light. Monkeys and birds stayed away from the human making so much noise, and what roots and fruits might have been available were never seen.

Newcastle was starving, and in his weakened physical condition he was bordering on insanity. He would leave the trail, shoot into the brush thinking it was a deer or a cow and then eat the leaves, telling himself how good was fresh meat. He wished he had eaten one of the Indians. Long pig, he called them, remembering an old story.

Just before dark, he could see bats making early forays into the jungle. Somewhere there is a vampire, he said, and he made little crosses to hang around his neck. He even took two rifles and made one big cross which he thrust in front of himself. He tried to whistle, believing the devil didn't like whistling. He shot at imaginary Indians, jaguars, rats, vampires, man-sized bats, and devils until his AK-47 failed to fire. He had used up all of the ammunition, blaming Ferraz.

He fixed his attention on Ferraz. Ferraz and Simón would be sitting comfortably on the barge, waiting for a string of whores-to-be. That lazy prick, he vowed, I'll kill him, too. Then I'll eat one of the young women. He ran along the trail, his machete swinging back and forth, every swipe a dead enemy.

Rangel and Eduardo, Rogelio and Eneas were making slow time. The women not only held back, they made extraordinary demands for toilet stops.

It became so obnoxious that at one point Eneas claimed, "I'm sick of watching them pissin' birds." The name *pissin' birds* stuck. What had been fun and full of lustful ideas, watching a woman empty her bladder and bowels, became a bother, then a disgust, and finally a source of irritation.

Rogelio suggested the women do their business on the fly, as it were. Horses, among other animals, might manage it, but generally humans cannot. Eduardo pointed that out. "Ain't no such thing as a flyin' shit," he offered. "I tried it a few times. Can't be done."

There were other testimonials affirming that practical matter and thus the general agreement that even if it slowed them down, the women's needs had to be tolerated.

"For the money we're gettin', ain't worth it," Rogelio said. "I'm for sticking a twig up their ass and lettin' 'em explode." He was serious, but the others took it as a joke.

"I see a couple I'd like to stick my twig up."

"Maybe we could ass screw one, make as example of her."

"Least we ought to screw one. Wouldn't take me long. Do it while the others are shittin'."

Gradually the talk evolved from the women's toilet needs to the men's desires.

"There's twelve of them, four of us. That makes three pieces each."

"I'll even take the little one."

"That's because you got a little prick."

"Must be nice, though. Your woman told me it was."

"Which woman was that."

Rangel hadn't taken part in the banter and let it continue as long as it didn't threaten to get out of hand. He would protect the women as best he could, but if the other three got it in their minds to rape the women, there would be little he could do. Maybe the talk was a creative outlet; he hoped that talking was better than a confrontation. "I wonder," he said, "if Simón and Paulo will be able to train this group?"

"Tell me again what I'm goin' to get out of this."

"Twenty, thirty thousand American dollars, Rogelio, if we do our job and if Paulo does his and Lippstadt and Wittenberg like what they get. Maybe less, but twenty thousand won't be bad."

"And maybe next time," Eneas added, "we won't have that horse's ass Newcastle. Or Czura and Pavón. They're out of it anyway. Once they went off with Newcastle, I think Paulo will consider them out."

"Shit on them anyway."

"I think we can agree that if Newcastle ever comes with us again, he will stay in the jungle forever."

The trail became indistinct the next day and then petered out altogether.

"Obviously, we've come to the limit of this tribe's hunting range," Rangel told the others. "Now we're on our own."

He got out his maps and photographs and spread them on the ground. "This is the trail we took out of the village, and this is the trail Newcastle took. His trail is much shorter. You can see that it points way downstream of where we have to be, but he has a tremendous hike through the jungle. If we've guessed right, we're about here. From now on it's all unmarked. Looks like virgin jungle, although a few Indians could be living there and would never show up or make enough of an impression to show up. If we'd come the way Ferraz wanted to, we'd have a trail back, but we don't, so we have to work."

It was agreed that two men would make a trail, followed by the women, and that two men would bring up the rear. The men would change places every couple of hours and each day the pairings would be different so that no one man or pair of men would end up doing most of the work.

None of the women, of course, spoke Portuguese. They didn't have to. For the most part whatever the men said about them was understood, if not the exact meaning then at least the intent.

The women spoke very little among themselves. Conversation was not allowed and physical punishment was given those who spoke more than a few words. Gradually, the women developed a means of communication. A couple of words, silence, a couple of more words, a statement in the form of a question to one of the men, a gesture, a nod of the head, all conveyed a unity and an understanding, not the least of which was that given the opportunity for a single woman to escape, that woman would be Laiti. Even Sayhoo, barely more than a child herself, knew the promise of the Masaki was in Laiti.

Had Laiti been much younger, the questions might have been different. Then the questions would have been, could Laiti survive in the forest, did she have any chance of finding other Masakis, would she know enough to be able to get back to her own village and then to the swamp?

Just as gradually as learning to communicate successfully without being punished, Sayhoo instructed Laiti in the trails leading, not to the swamp but to the last meeting place between Trulk and Tonto, the place where Laiti and Awhawk left Sayhoo's villagers and where Sayhoo left.

From there, Laiti was on her own. "Three days, Wasmaggi said, to swamp, and in middle of swamp is island," Sayhoo told the child. "Sayhoo not go there, so Sayhoo not know what tell. Can Laiti build fire? Good. Best Sayhoo say is build big fire. Every night build big, smoking fire. Let hunters find you. Will work. Then go to An-na or Wasmaggi. They know what best for Laiti."

When one of the women asked about Sayhoo's hunters finding them, Sayhoo had to admit that unless the hunters knew, they would not even know they should be looking. Her village had gone to the swamp to be shown a safe hiding place.

"But," she added by way of assurance, "Sayhoo see many strange things done by forest. Sayhoo believe forest has told about this, that my father and many hunters come to rescue us and kill these creatures who make us like slaves. No slaves, An-na said. I believe no slaves."

Sayhoo had spoken too long and too loudly. For that she got a slap on her face and a yank on her rope halter. When she fell to the ground, she received a kick in the back.

"I'd cut the tits right off you if we weren't so close. You cause trouble. I can see it in your eyes. So I'm telling you, one more speech and my men will have you, and then I'll slice you from that mouth to that mouth." Rangel ran his gun barrel from between Sayhoo's legs up to her chin.

Sayhoo understood not a word, but the meaning was clear. Shut up or get raped. The word rape was not in her vocabulary. She had no word that came close, but she knew what was being said. She sat quietly and cried, Rangel thinking she had understood.

Apart from the beating and kicking which she could take with stoic resolve, her uncharacteristic tears were not for herself but were for Fraylie and for the love they had made together. She would not give herself to another Masaki in spite of what she had told Anna. To be forced to take one of the creatures was too much. She would die first, and in the ways of the Masaki, she began to prepare her own death.

First, one dies in her own mind. There is no tomorrow, only the last day with its final, falling sun. The mind is cleared of every thought except the thought of not being. As the light fades, even that thought is dimmed, and one floats above her own body, views her body from afar, sees the forest begin to absorb it back into itself, sees the forest use the body for its own purposes, all purposes giving life to new life and nourishing the very life of the forest itself. One sees the flesh fall away until only the bones are left, and when one sees the bones begin to disappear, death is near, death is at hand, death has come.

The other women watched Sayhoo, knowing she was dying, knowing they, too, would die, not at the hands of the creatures but in their own way and in a time of their own choosing. The women began to sing a death song.

"What's going on? For Christ's sake, shut up," Rangel yelled.

One of the women shook Sayhoo. "Not time," she whispered. "Must get Laiti free."

249

When Rangel kicked the woman, the women stopped their singing and watched as Rangel bent over Sayhoo, yanking her to her feet. "Are you sick?" he asked. When he let her go, she slumped back to the ground.

"Eduardo, Eneas. Cut her away from the others. If she's sick, I'll kill her. Tie her to a tree. Let the little girl take care of her. Rogelio, cut the baby one free. Watch out she doesn't run away. We'll camp here for the night."

Sayhoo hovered between wanting to die and dying. The woman's whispered words had restored Sayhoo's sense of reality. Her life would not be complete unless the child escaped. Yes, she was sick; the other women should be suffering a mild illness, too. Anything to slow the steady progress to wherever they were headed. "Tell the women, Laiti. Two, three days here. We can squeeze out a couple of days. Who knows what will happen."

In those places where the trail was easy, Widel could not keep up. He managed when the trail was narrow and everyone had to slow down, but when the trail was open and uncongested, he fell hopelessly behind. Not only was his leg a bothersome burden, he was carrying a heavy load of bows and arrows, spears and blowguns, darts and who knows what all. More out of frustration than sympathy, Amstay took on Widel's load of weapons.

"Ran-ford take one blowgun for support; Amstay take rest."

That, and with Lurch's help, made the half-walk, half-run easier, but in truth, Widel was a semi-cripple when it came to making fast time. More than once he had to lean on Lurch.

"Lurch not mind, Ran-ford. Lurch carry if like."

Widel did not like but thanked the hunter.

When Mike reached the wider trail that led into the village, even Lurch left Widel behind. The devastation had to be seen and studied, as gruesome as it was. Once in the village, the men stood transfixed. Mike's fire had not done its work entirely, and it was possible to count a number of bodies.

Trulk's jaguar hunter's spear still stood, and when Mike went to it, he discovered what remained of Trulk's shattered body. Mike wanted to take Trulk's remains into the forest. That was what the old man would have wanted, he said. Soomar had other ideas.

"We no time. Show trail women take. Show trail of dead hunters."

Mike pointed out the trail, and the hunters gathered around to study it. Rain had washed out the tracks.

Anna and Mansella hung back, hardly looking at Mike's fire. "Mike said Trulk told him one of the children was Awhawk," Anna said softly.

"Yes. I've wept for him. Is bad when don't know who dead are, worse when you know, even worse when one is a child, more worse when child might have been own."

"I was told you would have taken the children into your house if no one came for them."

"Is true, so now like losing one of own child." Mansella let tears roll down her face.

Anna put her arm on Mansella's shoulder. "Come. We will leave this place. The hunters will lead us."

There was a minor discussion going on when Anna and Mansella approached the men. Who would lead the rescue party the rest of the way?

"Hunters, while you think, Anna has something to say. I've not studied the bodies, but Anna can tell you this. The creatures have weapons you have never known. They kill at long distance, far longer than your best arrows. They don't go into you so sometimes Anna can remove them. They go through you, leaving holes that cannot be fixed.

"Whoever leads you, when we find the creatures, must be a hunter of cunning, sly enough to fool the jaguar, daring enough to touch the others, wily enough to fool even his own hunters. I don't know who that should be, only that every life depends on that hunter."

No hunter volunteered. Each examined his own qualifications and found something lacking.

After a long silence, Widel spoke up. "I know one hunter who might be as Anna has said. I would trust Mike to be our leader."

"He's too young," one said.

"Lack experience," another said.

"Not proven," said a third.

"I know the arguments," Widel responded to the negatives expressed. "I' ve considered them. Mike is a good hunter, trained by Tonto, one of the best. He went on the mission to Sampson's village. He was the one who offered to go into the village with me when others were afraid. He is our jaguar hunter. He fought the jaguar, has the scars to prove it, and won. He has met and killed a creature. He carries in his heart the approval of Trulk whose village has been ravaged. And Mike knows first hand the weapons of which Anna has spoken. I say no more, but if you think about it, I'm certain I speak of a good leader."

Again there was a long silence.

Mansella broke it. "If I were a hunter, I would choose Mike."

Soomar turned to his sister. "Woman, you speak like a women, but I agree. Ran-ford is right. Mike should be our leader."

"And to prove that Mansella is more than your lowly sister and only a woman, she has found tracks. While you great hunters talk, Mansella study. Four men Mike said took women away. Mansella see five creature prints."

Mike rushed to where Mansella was pointing. "That print of white man. He joining others. Now we go."

Mike never accepted the appointment; he simply acted as he had observed Tomaz and Soomar and other leaders act. Once given the authority, he gave no orders, just announced what was going to happen.

He sent Westman and Amstay on ahead. He knew they were many days behind. By finding a recent campfire, he knew they could tell how many days, and if Westman and Amstay could find readable signs, they would know how rapidly the women were traveling, how they were coping and if they were able to slow their march to a crawl.

Westman and Amstay ran ahead. They could expend much energy, knowing that tomorrow they would be relieved by two other hunters. Not all hunters would be exhausted at the same time. It would be stupid to meet the enemy physically and mental tired.

Always there must be fresh hunters leading the way, reading the signs, calculating the distances and time.

Widel tried to get Lurch to tell him how the Masakis knew how to do all this, never knowing other people, never having been at war, never having had to rescue so many. Lurch was no help whatsoever. He just knew.

Amstay and Westman were late returning. They had much to tell. First, they were many days behind. The signs were so old it was hard to tell. Second, the women were dragging their feet, making slow progress. Eleven women and one child. That would be the one called Laiti, said Mike. Mansella gasped, happy that the child was alive, fearful that she had been captured. Third, the white man was alone. He was several days behind the others. His trail was very strange to follow.

The next day Soomar and Walkin took the lead. It did not take them long to leave the main body far behind. When they returned, they reported finding many signs left by the women. The hunters guessed they were at least six days behind the white man and probably four more days behind the women. Ten days.

Mike and Lurch went out on the third day, found the dead jaguar, and at the end of their shift, decided that they had gained a whole day, maybe two, on the women.

When Mike reported, he spoke clearly about one matter. "I've seen the white man kill. I spend only short time with Trulk. Him dead. I burn so many Masaki. It my wish, for Trulk, too, that Mike kill the white man. I'll take Ran-ford with me. Then he will see other side of white."

Widel did not have to see to know what evil was possible. He would help Mike kill, that was already determined, because that one white man had betrayed everything that Widel and Anna, and Connie, had come to love and be. It was not that another white man had found the Masaki; that potential always had existed. It was that the white man came as evil itself, not out of curiosity, not in friendship, but in the darkest spirit of death and destruction and exploitation. The white man represented the worst of white civilization. He should have been stillborn, and if Widel had his way, the man would regret the day his mother gave him life.

Four days later, the women still faking their illness, Newcastle stumbled into camp. His greeting was typical.

"No guards, I find. Anyone could have walked into this dung heap and killed you all." Looking around, he saw Sayhoo tied to a tree. "And I see that you have saved the best one for me."

Rangel and the others were silent. They had no guards, had not thought guards were necessary. Guards against who or what? Yet some response to Newcastle's arrival had to be made.

"Where are your slaves, Newcastle?"

"Bastards died on me. After I helped them along," he added for effect.

"And Czura and Pavón?"

"Stupid assholes got themselves killed. Some Indian you missed, I suppose. But I got him, got him good. What have you got to eat?"

When told that monkey was the only menu, Newcastle made a face. "I'll try some," he said. "Got any cachaça, that stupid white rum of yours? Bring it over by the girl. I'll eat while I look at her tits. Then I'll screw her, show you how it's done."

"She's sick, Newcastle."

"What's she got?"

"Don't know, but we're not taking any chances. I don't want to catch some tropical disease."

Five days later, Spiker and Joqua came onto that camp. The fires were old, but the signs told many things: the camp had been used for more than one night and the white man had joined the main group. Now there were five who must die. And the hunters were still at least six days behind.

"If only we knew this forest," Mike said, "we could get in front. Then know what must be done."

"My guess is," Widel offered, "that they are headed toward a big river. Probably they have a boat waiting for them there."

"What boat?" Walkin asked.

"Canoe. Oh, shit. You don't even know what a canoe is. Raft. Do you know what a raft is?" The universal puzzlement was obvious. "Remember when we had to get rid of Sampson's men? We tied some trees together and put some bodies on it and set it down the stream. That was a raft. A boat is a big raft, sometimes with a house on it. It can go very fast. Once on the raft, we never will find the women."

Mike looked at Anna. "Is so? Or does Ran-ford tell us something to make us think funny in head?"

"It is so, Mike. Truth has been spoken. The whites in their journey have seen such a thing."

Mike thought about what had been said. Other hunters would have dismissed the notion of a big river and a big raft, dealing with the reality only when confronted by it. Mike had been close to and nurtured by the whites for so long that he had begun to learn the meaning of action and consequence, of planning ahead and planning for the unforeseen. His primitive intuition had told him there was plenty of time to catch the enemy, and when they had been reached, there was plenty of time to plot an attack. Now, he recognized that time might not be available; that time was precious, that he had to take certain steps now before it was too late.

But what steps? He turned to Widel. "Does Ran-ford have idea?"

"Does Mike remember when on the walk from Sampson's village that Mike carried messages back and forth to our hunters? I suggest you send some hunters on ahead. They will not stop until they have gotten far ahead of the women. Then they can measure the enemy. If there is something the rest of us should know, one becomes the message carrier. With hunters in front and hunters behind, you will have the enemy blocked in. Arrange signals, do what you do best in the forest, keep the women in sight. I'm sorry I'm so slow. I'll try to keep up."

Splitting his force always had been an option. Everything Widel said made sense. It was time to establish visual contact. Soomar, Spiker, Westman, and Lurch would go on ahead. And Anna, Soomar insisted, although he was not sure why he insisted.

"Why Anna?" Widel asked.

"Because she fastest runner."

That was true.

"Amstay next fastest. He stay with you. Maybe he need run to us."

Anna gave over the care of her medicines to Mansella, selecting only a few for her own possible use. Widel selected his best spear for her.

The four hunters repacked their tiny hammocks, and while doing so debated their weapons. A bow and many arrows, spears, and for two of them, a blowgun instead of a second spear. Widel provided his best arrows and enough freshly tipped darts to bring down an army.

"Remember," Mike warned. "No fight. Must have all others together or else even one will kill women."

"And," Widel added. "No rescue of just one woman. If one woman is freed, the creatures will know we are here and will kill the other women."

There was nothing more to be said. As the four hunters and Anna stepped into the forest, Anna turned and said, "I love you, Widel." She did not wait for his response.

Mike, Walkin, Amstay, and Joqua wasted little time reorganizing their loads. Widel accepted the offers of sharing because, he said, he had to help Mansella carry the medicine woman's medicines and equipment.

As they were about to set out, Widel had an unnerving thought.

"Mike, wait. You said there were two other creatures, two who never went to the village, who broke off and went their separate way. We have not accounted for them. What if they lie in wait just in case we come along?"

Mike had forgotten about the other two. They could be a threat. "Hope someone remember what Mike forget. Too late now. Just hope, that all. Now we go."

"I suppose they'll join the others," Widel offered by way of absolution. "Or maybe they are waiting on the raft."

"You know raft is there?"

"No, I don't know for sure. I feel it, that's all. I feel it and I fear what it means, that if the women are taken on the raft, we'll have lost them." He didn't add *forever.*

"You keep this up, Paulo, and I won't have any profit from this whore hunt."

"Oh, you'll have your rewards. Believe me, laying the women will make you forget what you've lost to me."

"How much longer?"

"You keep asking. A day less than yesterday. Another four days, then we'll head out, and if all goes well, we'll meet your students, after we save them from the likes of Rangel."

"What will those bandeirantes do?"

"Trade for some sex and some canoes, follow us down river for a way, make their way to Manaus. They'll be sitting in the cidaae flutuante before we get there, waiting for their money."

"Yeah, speaking of money, deal. My luck's gotta change before too long."

EIGHTEEN

It took all their energy to keep Spiker from rushing the procuradores, and in the end it was Anna who managed it. She simply engulfed Spiker in a bear hug until he quieted down.

"Spiker," she whispered, "she's fine, at least physically, as far as I can see. You can't do her any good right now. All you're going to do is get her and yourself killed." Anna led Spiker away from his daughter and deeper into the forest. Once out of hearing, she made him sit down. "Think for a minute about Saymore. Do you want me to go back and tell her that her husband's foolish actions cost the life of her husband and her daughter? She'll say you should have stayed in the swamp, that you were too old to be a successful hunter because you couldn't think straight. She'll blame you. Yes, she will, but she'll blame herself more, for letting you go, and she'll die loving her daughter and hating you and hating herself."

"She not believe you."

"Perhaps. But Westman would know, and Westman would tell Hackway, and her sister would tell her. Would she not listen to her sister?"

"She would listen."

"And when Walkin tells his mother, would Saymore not listen to Magwa, her sister who already has lost her son Fraylie?"

"She would listen."

"Does Spiker listen to Anna now, or does he agree with Anna just to get the woman to shut up?"

"Spiker listens. Anna makes shame of Spiker."

"Oh, no, Spiker. There is no shame in wanting to save your child, no shame in wanting to save the women. I'm not ashamed of

258

Spiker; I only want to remind Spiker that there is a time to act and a time not to do anything that would spoil the success of our attack."

The hunters listened. They couldn't help overhearing. One by one they touched Spiker on the shoulder, and then each touched Anna.

"Is settled," Soomar announced. "Now Soomar have say. Long time past, Soomar not like whites because they do things different than Masaki. Con-nie and An-na hunt; An-na talk much at hunters' fire; my father think forest most like Con-nie; so much change.

"My own sister, Mansella, change. Secret from me, but our father teach Mansella to hunt and track. My brothers, this hunter say whites are Masaki and An-na great medicine woman. Women would even leave hunters to go with An-na. Must be good woman.

"Long time change mind. An-na is good woman, strong leader, powerful medicine woman. I want An-na because she is best Masaki we have. I say she lead us on this fight."

"No. No! I don't know anything about fighting. I'm not a killer; I'm a healer. Please. Don't ask me to do this."

Spiker stood in front of Anna. "It has been decided. Hunters do killing. Anna tell hunters what to do." Each of the hunters confirmed the decision.

"Oh, please, don't make me do this."

"We ready to do as An-na says."

There was no turning back. Soomar had seen to that. Was he testing her or putting her in a position in which she only could fail? Would he do that, knowing that their lives and the lives of the women were at stake?

"Why does the chief hunter now give a lowly woman a hunter's job?"

"Because I have the beliefs of my father and Wasmaggi and Hagga in the skill of the woman. I've witnessed your tenderness, so I know you will think of us when you put us in danger; I've seen your firmness, so I know you will not fail us when you are most needed; I've seen your love for the children, so I know you will think of them when their fathers go into battle."

"But you don't think a women should do a man's job."

259

"That has not changed. What has changed is Soomar. You are the best leader for us. Soomar not, Mike not, Ran-ford not. When is over, An-na have so many babies she not have time for man's job."

"What if I fail?"

"You will not. Soomar sees into eyes and sees already you are making plans. You don't believe in fail."

"But what if...?"

"Who will tell? We be dead because we no fail until last one is dead."

"Then it will be as you ask. Send someone to get Mike and the rest. We will need everyone here."

"If the bandeirantes or procuradores or whatever they are called keep moving as they are," Anna told the hunters, "we cannot attack in the daylight. Having men both in front and in back of the women means that some of the women will be killed. We are going to attack at night. I've decided that.

"But one thing worries me. The white man is always in the middle of the women. Even on the march, he uses them as a shield, protecting himself. At night he sleeps among them, always using them for protection. We must find a way to isolate him.

"Until Mike and the others get here, we will keep our distance, maintaining just enough contact to be sure we know where they are and that they don't change direction on us, although they're going in a straight line, so Widel probably is right."

Mike's group had nothing to report and no new decisions had been made. Soomar reported Anna's selection as leader and why. Only Widel protested, and then not very strongly. It was abundantly apparent that the choice was both popular and wise, although Widel would have liked to discuss the wise part. But he agreed, having looked at Anna's face and seen the determination there. Come hell or high water, she would be the true Amazon he always knew she was, and now she was leading a society in which women were considered almost a lower species.

After observing the captives and their captors, Anna announced her plan. "Four men sit around the fire at night. Killing them is easy. It is the white man who is hard to reach. I listen to his talk. He may talk in a language Widel and I know. Widel and I will take care of the white man when the time comes. Now, we will...."

"No. We agree. Mike must kill white man."

Walkin stood and confronted Mike. "Mike be quiet. I should kill white man. It was he who killed my brother."

"Stop it, both of you. I've decided. If you don't like my decision, find another leader. Only Widel and I can understand the white man. If he was dead, that wouldn't matter. But he's not dead yet, and it might matter. I didn't want to be your leader; I'll do whatever another leader tells me to do; just make up your minds. If I'm leader, then it's my way."

For his part, Walkin had tried to divert Mike's displeasure. He had no intention of leading and was less concerned over the actual act of revenge than he was that the whole attack be successful. Saving the women and saving Sayhoo was one part of that success. Killing the others without being killed was the other part. He knew that for the two parts to be jointly successful required a leader with a plan. He supported Anna.

"Mike will kill the white with or without you." He considered the subject closed.

"My plan is simple," Anna told Widel. "You and I get close to the white man and you will kill him. I'll carry your arrows, I'll feed you arrows, and with your skill with the bow, the white man is dead. And while we're doing that, the hunters kill the others. Many arrows, many spears, all over. Simple. Do you find any fault with what I propose, something I've missed?"

"Seems simple enough. Used to work in the western movies."

"That's what worries me. It's too simple. Those men are sitting targets. It's almost as though they dared us to attack."

"They don't have any idea we're here, Anna. They think they killed all the Indians. Who would they think to watch for?"

"I don't know. Anyway, when it's dark, I want to get close, hear what they're saying."

"You've learned to speak Portuguese?"

261

"No. But I think I can tell what's on their minds just by hearing them. Are they nervous? Are they impatient? That sort of thing."

"I'll go with you."

"No. I'm taking Soomar. You said he was the best in the dark."

"He is that. Uncanny."

Two of the hunters eased through the forest on a path parallel to the captors and the women, and from time to time, one or the other reported back to Anna's party which likewise maintained a distant parallel course. When the captors and the women stopped to make their evening camp, Anna spoke to the hunters.

"When it is dark, Soomar and I are going to get close to the others. When we return, perhaps tonight will be the night to attack. The others always stop before the light fails. Perhaps you can use the light to hunt birds. We need to eat, too."

With Lurch, Amstay, and Walkin out hunting, Anna familiarized Mansella with the medicines and especially the knives.

"The wounded will be taken in order. God, I hope there are no wounded, but if there are, the youngest women will be treated first, then the other women, then the hunters. But if one hunter is terribly hurt, then he must come first. You will have to decide, Mansella. Knives, kapok, medicine, in that order."

"What about the others?"

"If the hunters do their job, there will be no others to consider. And, Widel, tip the arrows in the cassava. Should any other get away, he will die."

Then she turned to Spiker. "I've a special task for you. I'm guessing that if any other does get away, he will head in the direction they're going. If we decide to attack tonight, I want you to go ahead of the others and stretch a vine across the most likely trail, about this high off the ground." Anna stretched one hand about a foot above the other. "Anyone running will trip over the vine."

"But I want to attack."

"So you will. Mike will arrange all the signals. You will attack from your position. Everyone will have a position surrounding the others.

262

"And, Mike, you will position the hunters, making sure that everyone knows his target. Assign specific targets to each hunter. Can't have the hunters all attacking the same other. And, Mike, make the signals easy."

Anna had spoken slowly and deliberately, making sure each one knew what was expected of them.

"One last thing. When the attack begins, Mansella will light a fire. You are to bring the women to the fire. If you are wounded and cannot continue to fight, you are to come to the fire. Remember, the others cannot see in the dark, but their weapons can. Keep the trees between you and the others."

Everything had been said for now. Anna and Soomar melded into the forest.

"An-na has done well," Soomar whispered.

"Now, Soomar, you must lead. Anna does not know the night forest."

The others had two roaring fires, one for themselves and one for Newcastle and the women. If Newcastle had learned a lesson, it was that in the hostile forest one sits obliquely to the fire, never presenting his full back to the darkness beyond. And Newcastle had positioned the women well. They formed a wall around him. He was going to be a hard target to hit without risking the women.

The other four men were easy targets. They sat facing the fire, and while they could look beyond each other, their shadows and the shadows of the forest blended into pitch darkness only a few feet away. A hunter's spear could touch a man without the man being aware of the hunter's presence.

Anna and Soomar studied every inch of seeable landscape, and Anna listened to the talk. When Soomar had led Anna out of hearing, she told him that nothing in their speech indicated anything but satisfaction. She was convinced there was no trap. She reported the same to Mansella and the hunters. "The only concern," she said, "is the white man. We will not attack tonight. I must think more. Tomorrow night we will attack. By then I'll have a plan."

263

The next morning, three separate groups of people walked three separate but parallel pathways through the forest. The only noise came from the others who led the captive women. The larger party of Anna, Mike, Mansella, and the hunters strolled easily. They had no difficulty keeping pace. Two of the hunters also ambled quietly along with the prisoner party. They kept apart but stayed within hearing, occasionally looking to be sure no one had left the group they followed. It was almost too easy, and they had to remind themselves repeatedly that they were on a hunt of the most serious kind.

Lurch and Walkin peered through the underbrush just as the others were taking a break. The white man stood alone. He was an easy target; if he exercised extreme caution at night, in the daylight sometimes he was careless.

Walkin rush to deliver that news. Perhaps Anna would change the plan. And while Walkin was with the main group, Amstay went to be with Lurch.

"I cannot risk it," Anna said. "At night the women have only to take a couple of steps and they are in darkness. Remember, they are tied together. They must all go in single file. In the daylight they are easy targets. At night, less so."

That day, Ferraz and Simón also begun their forest hike. They would tramp into the forest for two days and wait for Rangel and his men.

"Aren't we doing this blind, Paulo? How do you know where Rangel is?"

"Don't exactly. He'll be following the same maps and aerials that we have. If he keeps a straight line, we'll meet him. Anyway, we have our old signals arranged. His gunshots will lead us to him."

"Tell me again how this works."

"We're going to walk for two days, then camp. We may have to wait a couple of days, but when Rangel gets to where I expect him to be, he will camp. Then he will fire shots. One, two, three, pause, four. The fourth shot tells us everything is satisfactory. We follow the sound. Thirty six minutes later there will be a single shot. Twenty seven minutes later there will be two shots. It's all worked out."

"How will he know we've heard him?"

"He won't. That's why everything is timed so carefully. But just before we attack and save the women, I blow on this whistle. It's a bird call. Rangel will know we have found him and will wait for morning. Then, while they're eating, we burst in, shoot them up, and race off with the women. Once I've got the women moving, you'll fire some shots, then catch up to me to tell me you've killed all the bad guys."

"And the women will be grateful?"

"Will they ever. We'll have two nights on the trail and the third night we'll be on the barge, snug in our little thatched house. Rangel will be on his way, and you and I will begin the education of a bunch of whores-to-be. A couple of days, then we'll start downstream, and by the time we get to Manaus, you'll be begging me not to make you screw another Indian woman."

"I can't believe that part of it."

"You'll be dried up and worn to a tiny nub. Once the Indian women get the idea, they're insatiable. First, they'll love you for saving them; then they'll love you just for the sake of loving."

Rangel called a halt in a small clearing, got out his maps and compass, and after studying the maps and photographs, determined he was where he was supposed to be. He announced camp and had the men build the usual fires.

"Eduardo, fire the shots," he commanded.

With the first shot, the women captives wailed pitifully, sure their time for death had come. Deep in the woods, Anna clutched Mansella's arm. Nearby, Soomar and Joqua stiffened, fearful of what was happening. But when the two hunters crawled forward for a closer look, except for the wailing women, nothing had changed. No woman appeared to be hurt, and all of the others remained standing.

"Perhaps only is signal," Soomar suggested, hoping that was true, daring to believe it.

He and Joqua slipped away and returned to the main party. They reported their observation.

"It must be a signal," Widel said. "Clearly it was a pattern."

Minutes later a single shot was heard. And sometime later, two shots were heard.

"I'm convinced now. We are hearing signals. But for whom?"

"That means there are others, then." Anna wasn't sure what that meant, only that it complicated the attack, maybe even canceled it. She called Mike. "You said there were two others."

"Yes, two who did not go to the village."

"Could there have been more than two?"

"Saw only tracks of two. Did not follow. Who knows how many might wait in forest."

"I don't want to do this, but we must know if there are others here, too. Soomar, can you send the hunters out? That way," Anna said, pointing in the general direction of their travels.

There were no more shots. Lurch went to check on the captors and the women and returned, reporting that everything seemed to be as before. Hours later the hunters returned, reporting no sighting of creatures or others.

"Then," Anna said, "it is tonight. Spiker, you know what to do. Mike, take the hunters and position them. Mansella, when you hear the first shouts or the drums, light the fire. Widel and I will try to take care of the white man. Watch the white man. He is to be killed first. His killing will be the signal to attack. If Widel cannot kill him, then kill the rest anyway and hope for the best."

As he moved slowly toward the others' fire, Mike paused just long enough to say, "The white man is mine."

Sliding through the forest, making as little noise as possible, Anna put her hand on Widel's arm. "God, I hope Mike doesn't do anything stupid," she whispered.

Then she uttered what Widel considered the most stupid suggestion of all. "I'm going to get close enough to warn the women."

"You're what?" Widel was incredulous. "No you're not."

"But how will they know what to do?"

"Believe me; they will."

"But...."

"Christ, Anna. No buts. The women will behave as they have been taught. Your stupidity might cost us everything."

It would be stupid, Anna thought, if I got caught. How can I warn them?

It took a long time for Widel to find a good position. He tried several before finding one that provided a clear shot. No branches or leaves could be in the way to deflect his arrows. One arrow, he thought, holding a second arrow in the fingers of his left hand in such a way as to be ready immediately after the first arrow was let loose. Anna held two more arrows at the ready, just out of reach of Widel's right hand. He had only to open his first two fingers and Anna would slip an arrow between them.

Widel had his bow half pulled. From where he sprawled, the white man was shielded by a woman. The man would have to sit up before Widel could shoot. Widel waited, and the hunters waited. Nothing would happen until Widel shot at the white man at least once.

Minutes stretched into an hour, and one hour lengthened into the second hour. The camp slept, the white man behind his human barrier. Someone take a pee, Widel prayed. Please, someone make some kind of movement that will cause the white man to move.

Two hours. One of the women moved just enough to put some wood on the fire. No one else moved.

Three hours and still no movement. It had been so quiet for so long that monkeys had moved into the trees, chattering quietly, seeking to absorb some of the heat from the fires. One of the monkeys must have dropped its excrement on one of the women. She sat up and yelled a string of foul words into the tree tops, pointing at the offending monkey.

Newcastle sat up, pistol in hand. He looked up, and as he did, out of the corner of his eye, in a shadow barely illuminated by the fire, he thought he caught the tiniest glimpse of a white man aiming an arrow.

Widel had drawn back the bowstring and was taking aim. Just before letting the arrow fly, he heard Mike.

"Ran-ford, he is mine!"

Newcastle sent off one shot and spun around to face the charging Indian. Widel's arrow hit the white man's left upper arm.

Mike had his spear ready to throw. Newcastle raised his pistol and fired at Mike. Widel sent another arrow into Newcastle's back. Then another.

But Newcastle did not fall. He kept firing at Mike.

There were other shots. Mike's bizarre behavior momentarily distracted the other hunters and warned the creatures. Their shots were ineffective, serving only to draw the hunters onto them. But Mike's actions gave the creatures the time necessary to fire and thus to reduce the scene to one of mass confusion, in the midst of which Newcastle slipped away, as badly wounded as he was.

Spiker had set his trip line as ordered and had joined the attack. Newcastle had not taken that expected route, had in fact quietly disappeared into the jungle night. Taking a quick assessment and finding only Mike wounded, Soomar organized the hunters, and fanning out, they searched in the blackness for the one man wanted more than all others.

Spiker became a casualty. He tripped over the very vine he had strung. The result was a broken ankle. Lurch became a casualty when he ran into the broken branch of a tree. Thinking it a spear, he defended himself. His injury was three severed fingers.

As soon as the fight began, Anna was beside the women, cutting their bonds, directing them toward Mansella. She searched for Sayhoo. She was not with the women.

Widel lay on the ground. Newcastle's one shot in his direction had struck Widel in his groin. He was in intense pain, but he uttered no word or cry.

In the excitement Anna had to ignore Widel. He had done his job; he was on his own.

Lurch's hand was useless. He moved back into the firelight to look. The last three fingers of his left hand were missing. As he studied the stumps, he saw Mike crawling between the two fires. Lurch went to him and bent down. Two holes were seeping fluid where bullets had entered his shoulder and chest

"Lurch carry Mike," the big Masaki said. "You not good hunter yet; too much to learn."

When he got to Mansella's fire, only Mansella was there.

"Where An-na and women?" Lurch asked.

"Not know. Should be here by now. Did the fight go well?"

"The white man get away. Carry Ran-ford's arrows, but get away. Only Mike hurt."

Only after Lurch put Mike down and had made him comfortable did Mansella see Lurch's hand. "What happen?" she asked.

"Not know. Think somebody try to spear Lurch, but only tree. Then feel hand; fingers gone."

The fingers had been sliced off by Newcastle's machete. In the dark, he slashed at everything that made a noise. When Lurch struck back at the tree limb he thought was a spear, Newcastle had swung at Lurch's noise. Luckily, Lurch was leaning away from Newcastle, not even knowing he was there; otherwise Lurch would be dead.

"An-na fix."

"If she alive."

"An-na will live," Mansella said calmly. "Has to."

And on cue, Anna walked into the firelight, followed by eleven women of varying ages, from Laiti to the oldest.

"Oh, Lurch. What happened?" Anna cried. "Let me see your hand."

"Is nothing. Mike needs you."

"Oh, Mike, you poor, stupid bastard," she said, seeing him for the first time. "What kind of trouble have you gotten yourself into?" She examined him closer. "Shoulder, no problem. Chest? We'll have to see. Anywhere else?"

Anna kept up a chatter, more to reassure herself than Mike. "Mansella, check the women. Any hurt? I didn't have time to look. Laiti okay? Lurch, bring your hand over here. Nice clean cuts. Some kind of knife, I suppose. Hurt? Like hell it doesn't. Mansella, the big pot. No, the next one. Take a big pinch and add some water. Make Lurch drink.

"Two women have holes in their legs? Bring them over here. Let me see. That one's going to be fine. Two nice holes. The other

269

one's going to need some help. Put her beside Mike. Build up the fire, you. And you, get out of my light.

"Shit, don't try to say anything, Mike. Hold your hand up, Lurch. Higher. That's it. Mansella, the little pot. Take the powder and put some on Lurch's fingers. Let's see. Just the tip of the little finger. Right at the joint of the ring finger. Half of the middle finger. Some kapok, please."

All the while Anna studied Mike's chest wound. "Anyone here know medicine?" she asked. "I could use some help."

Laiti came and stood beside Anna. "They afraid to speak. In dark not know color; in fire see you white."

"Laiti is not afraid?"

"Laiti remember An-na."

"Then, Laiti, do any of these women know medicine?"

"One does. She daughter of medicine man."

"Then will she help me?"

"She afraid."

"Mansella, see what you and Laiti can do with the medicine man's daughter. I've got to cut Mike open. It can't wait until daylight, and Widel's not here to help me."

Turning to Lurch, she said, "Put your hand down, Lurch. I'm going to need your help. Someone has to hold Mike."

Anna went to her medicines. "God, we don't have much water. I need more. Can you get back to the others, Lurch. They had water in canteens, round jars, shaped like.... As many as you can find. Hurry."

Spiker crawled in just as Lurch was leaving.

"Oh, Spiker. Another one. What happened?"

"Caught in own trap." And Spiker described the whole trip. "As An-na say, stupid."

"A great hunter you are, Spiker. When we get back, we'll all laugh at your trap; probably laugh at you. Think you can stand the pain?"

"Not as much pain as catch self."

"Good man." Anna did some twisting and pulling. "Mansella, that hammock with the feathers and powdered clay in the bamboo

270

case. Dig a little hole in the ground and pour everything in. Then start mixing with the water. Nice thick paste. You're going to be fine, Spiker. Feels like a decent kind of break."

Turning to the women, she said. "Come on, one of you. Help me with the kapok. A nice, thin, little layer of kapok for one of the hunters who saved your life."

No one stepped forward. "Laiti, will you help me?

The child seemed to know what to do.

"We have saved the wrong women, An-na," Mansella said sarcastically. "These women are useless. We should have left them to the creatures. They owe you their lives and they act like cowards."

"A little child shall lead them," Anna said. "Perhaps they forget their manners." Anna finished with Spiker's cast. "It will take a while to harden. Then in five, six weeks, Spiker will be running again. In a few weeks, we'll make you a proper walking cast. For now you will have to hop."

"Like a mouse?" Laiti asked.

"Like a mouse with two left feet."

Laiti laughed.

Lurch returned, carrying Widel.

"Oh, you poor slob, Widel. Got in the way again?"

"Jesus, Anna. Don't. I'm in real pain."

"Let's see. Oh, Christ, Widel. What a place to get hit."

"It's bad, huh?"

"Worse than bad. You might not be able to...you know...for weeks."

"It didn't...."

"Shoot off your whatever? No. But you are going to be sore."

"Anna. I didn't do my job. I hit him. The first arrow should have been enough, but I missed. Even with Mike running around crazy, I should not have missed."

"It's okay, Widel. It wasn't your fault. Things got out of hand at the last moment."

"Is he dead?"

"No. I don't know. You got him two more times. I saw that. But he's gone. In the forest somewhere. With Sayhoo."

271

"With Sayhoo. Hurry, Anna. Fix me up. I've got work to do. I can't leave it unfinished."

"You're out of it, Widel. For now, at least."

"For God's sake, Anna. I'm a Masaki."

"A wounded one, I'm afraid. Even when I get the bullet out, you won't be able to walk. Others will do it."

Widel complained and begged, but he knew he was unable to go on. He looked at Mike. "Goddamn it. Why couldn't you have done your part?"

Mike looked over at Widel. "Did not trust white man."

"You don't know the half of it, Mike. Maybe if you live, you'll learn."

Anna had Mansella mix a number of liquids. That one is for the woman. Will make her sleepy until I can get to her. Give some more of that to Lurch and a little to Spiker and Widel. The other one is for Mike. Drink it all, Mike."

Anna sat back. "Laiti, do you know what happened to Sayhoo?"

"White man take her when run away."

Anna thought about that for a bit, then asked, "Spiker, Lurch, can you call the hunters back?"

"Can try," answered Spiker, "but will not know where they are. Will have to wait for light before follow marks back."

"Of course. Can you call them to stop following the white man? If he has Sayhoo, perhaps it is too dangerous to follow him in the dark. He will be using Sayhoo for protection, might kill her if the hunters get too close"

Spiker and Lurch took turns mimicking the forest noises. There were a few returned, although apparently not all the hunters received the message.

"Now we attend to Mike. Laiti, you go with the women. Man...."

"Laiti know what is to happen. Laiti help. Have helped before."

"Okay, child. But if you want to leave, then go." Turning to Mansella, Anna explained what she was gong to do. "I'll cut here. Very carefully. I've never done this before, so I must go slowly, not do any more damage than has been done already. You will hold the flesh away while I probe for the weapon in Mike's chest."

272

"Will Mike be all right?"

"I hope so. He will if I can remember what Wasmaggi taught me."

Anna stuck a tiny, long probe into the hole made by Newcastle's bullet. The blade did not reach deep enough. She felt under the armpit and traced her fingers out toward the nipple. Somewhere deep inside, having gone through the chest bone, was a piece of metal. As Anna felt and traced the path her knife would take, she described for Mansella what she was doing.

"I hope you don't mind my talking, Mansella," she said. "Talking it out helps me remember what I'm supposed to do and just how I'm supposed to do it."

Anna made a slice in the flesh. "Use the kapok, soak up the blood. Lurch, I know your hand's in pain, but can you and Spiker hold Mike. Can't have him moving."

She was about to make a second incision when a hand pulled hers back. "Tannee show how," a soft voice offered. "Tannee know how."

Anna looked from the woman to Laiti. Laiti shook her head affirmatively. "You are a woman of medicine?"

"My father was medicine man. I did what his old hands could not."

"I'll be glad for your help."

"Tannee cut." She took the knife and drew a shallow incision under the armpit. "Very good knife. Very sharp. You keep good knife. Good sign." Tannee deepened the incision. "See. Must cut here. Not much blood. Anna got needles?"

Tannee got as close to Mike as she could, the better to see where she was cutting. When she had opened Mike's wound as far as she dared, she took one of Anna's needles, a long, carefully shaped quill, sharpened by sanding to a very fine point and polished with painstaking care.

"Tannee use needles to look. Tell, please, what Tannee looking for."

Anna described, without real first hand knowledge, what she thought a bullet might look like.

Mike took the pain as his deserved retribution, not for messing up Widel's shot but for being unable to spear and kill the white man. That and the manioc juice dulled his senses. And a good thing they did. Lurch and Spiker had little trouble holding Mike still.

"Here is your piece of weapon." Tannee had a needle embedded deeply. "Much bone in way."

The two women worked carefully in the feeble, dancing light of the fire. Amstay and Joqua came in from the blackness. They had no news. Spiker answered some night noises. They told nothing except the hunters were out there. The message had been passed on.

While Tannee cut, Anna removed shattered pieces of bone. The largest and most dangerous pieces were behind the breast plate. Could they be removed?

After what seemed an eternity, the bullet was revealed and removed. Anna pointed to her medicines, and Mansella placed them beside the prone Mike.

"Does Tannee know how to get at other bone pieces?" Anna asked.

"Tannee not know. Father would say leave, see if cause trouble."

"Yes, we'll have to. Maybe when we get to Wasmaggi, he'll know what should be done. All right, Mansella, we'll close him up. Thread a needle, please."

Threading the needles was difficult. Several women had a go at it. When that was accomplished, Anna sutured with her finest stitchery.

She moved on to the wounded women and quickly treated one for her wounds. In the fleshy part of her upper leg lodged another bullet.

"Want to go at this, Tannee? I have another patient, my stupid husband."

The women laughed.

"Widel, my dear target, you are one lucky husband. Another couple of inches and I'd be married to a very strange man. The bullet passed through the flesh, right next to your...well, you know...the sac. I'll medicate the holes. I think you'll be okay. But I can imagine a lot of pain for the next couple of days."

With that completed, Anna spread out next to the fire and went to sleep, a treasured skill she had learned from Wasmaggi. She had done the best she could under inadequate light. Her only worry was Mike, not that he might die but because his personality had changed so dramatically and because he had come to distrust, even hate, all white people. As she drifted off, she wondered if she was now Mike's enemy.

Nearly a full day's march through virgin forest, two men had heard the signal shots. All was well. Then in the middle of the night they heard the other shootings. It was a bad sign. They extinguished their fire and sat uneasily in the darkness. That the men had fought was the only possible explanation. Ferraz wondered if anything was left of the women; Simón wondered if Newcastle would kill him next.

Newcastle had grabbed Sayhoo on his way into the darkness. Actually, his first impulse had been to kill her, but his machete had missed her and had sliced through the vine binding her to the next women. When she refused to follow, he struck her with the flat of the blade, knocking her unconscious. She was unconscious when Lurch almost touched Newcastle.

Newcastle had not gone far; he disappeared easily into the shadows. The hunters had assumed he would run as far as he could, and so they had overran him by a considerable distance. Rather than being in front of the hunters, he and Sayhoo were behind them.

He had jerked the arrow out of his arm and had felt the blood flowing toward his elbow. He could not reach the two arrows in his back. Neither seemed to cause much pain, and he wondered why. When the girl recovered consciousness, he would make her remove the arrows.

Widel's arrows had not penetrated deeply. Newcastle wore a thick leather vest and a series of leather belts and slings that held his ammunition and machete and sidearms. Both of Widel's arrows had struck that protective coating, otherwise they would have gone deeper. But they were deep enough to deliver the cassava based poison with which they had been tipped. Newcastle would die, if not from the arrow in his arm, then from the arrows in his back.

He became confused. His body began to stiffen. He was very tired. When Sayhoo regained consciousness, he held her tightly, feeling her breasts pressed against his chest.

"My darling," he said, "I should have had you before this."

"No man have me," Sayhoo answered defiantly.

"Why you little bitch. You speak my language."

"Enough."

"Then you little whore, you know I'm going to kill you."

"Sayhoo knows."

"And do you know who shot me?"

"Ran-ford shot you. You will die soon."

"Ranford? What is Ranford? I heard that name once before."

"Ran-ford is our weapon maker."

"Son-of-a-bitch. A white man?"

"Like you."

"I'll kill him."

"Others have tried. He is much wounded, but he lives."

"Not for long. Now, take the arrows out of my back."

"Take them out yourself."

Newcastle reached back and struck Sayhoo with his fist, sending her flying against a tree trunk. He reached for his machete.

"I'm going to enjoy ripping you apart, right from your tits to your...."

Newcastle stopped. Behind him there was a sound of rustling leaves and the sound of someone scraping the ground. A cloud of flies could be seen approaching the white man and the Indian girl, and diving into the cloud and almost to the ground were hundreds of ant birds. Newcastle was about to witness one of the most frightening phenomenon in the South American jungle, the legionnaire mass raid of the army ants, two hundred thousand, five hundred thousand, seven hundred thousand worker ants forming a column fifty feet across and five feet high and sweeping all life before it, snakes, spiders, lizards, mice, and whatever else happened to be in the way.

276

The poison on Widel's arrows was taking effect. Newcastle wanted to run. He couldn't. He seemed rooted to one spot directly in front of the advancing army. He begged Sayhoo to help him. She laughed.

"They not move fast, white man. You can walk away."

But Newcastle couldn't. He fell to his knees. The poison was doing its work. "Help me or I'll kill you."

Sayhoo had moved behind the tree trunk. "Kill them, white man. If you can."

Newcastle turned slowly toward Sayhoo. As he raised his pistol, the first of the ants crawled over his boots and under his pant legs. He didn't have the strength left to swat at them, and in a few minutes he was so completely covered that Sayhoo could no longer see him, only an elongated mound of ants on the forest floor. She turned and walked away.

"This is nuts, Paulo. Something went wrong."
"And we've got to find out what."
"You think Newcastle killed everybody?"
"He's crazy enough to do it."
"And stole the women?"
"Maybe. Keep moving."

One by one, the hunters returned. They had not found the white man and they had not found Sayhoo.

"Soomar, I will not return without Sayhoo. I'm no longer interested in the white man. He will die, if not today, then tomorrow. I saw Widel's arrows strike the man. Nothing can save him, not the best medicine woman in the world. Our only concern now is the daughter of Spiker. I did my job; now I'm turning it over to you. Organize the hunters and find Sayhoo. We need to rest here for a while anyway before we can move Mike"

Not counting Widel, the eight hunters had been reduced to five, the other three having been wounded. In an emergency, Lurch could have gone out, but Anna insisted he stay behind.

277

Soomar led Westman, Walkin, Amstay, and Joqua back to the white's campsite. They would begin there, follow every track, and search until they found Sayhoo. Alive, they hoped.

"Here where white man was," Soomar told the hunters. "There where Ran-ford was," pointing to the underbrush. "Here where Mike ran toward white man. And here all tracks of women."

The five hunters spread out. Soon they had Newcastle's tracks. "Where Sayhoo's tracks?"

It took the hunters a while to figure out that the white man had carried Sayhoo.

"Here they hide," Amstay pointed out. "Not go far; in dark we go too far."

"Ah, no!" It was Westman. He had found one of Lurch's fingers. "Should save; make white man eat it."

"Throw it away," Westman said. "No tell Lurch find."

The tracks led deeper into the forest. There was no talking now.

The *Eciton burchelli* had done their job. The thick columns of retreating ants revealed the skeletal remains of someone or something. It was too large to be Sayhoo, too large to be a monkey, and the ants had cleaned the bones so thoroughly it was impossible to tell how long the body had been there. There was some evidence, none of it familiar to the Masakis, that might have settled one question: a machete, two pistols, and a couple of handfuls of cartridges. Everything stayed as it was found.

When Amstay found the tracks of a female, the hunters' spirits were lifted. Sayhoo must have escaped. For a short distance, the female made no effort to cover her tracks. Then for some reason, the tracks disappeared and all signs were absent.

"Good Masaki," said Soomar. "Make work much hard."

Sayhoo began working her way toward the setting sun, but when she thought about it, she reversed direction. That change of course confused her trackers. They missed her turn and continued on for some while before determining what must have happened. Backtracking their own trail was easy. They had made no effort to hide it, but finding where the forest wise female had backed around on them was very difficult.

278

The light was fading. Should they continue, return to camp, start out again in the morning?

"An-na be angry if we return without Sayhoo," Soomar told the hunters. "We look until dark, then make camp."

NINETEEN

Ferraz and Simón were not that careless. They proceeded very slowly and very quietly, with great caution. By nightfall, they, too, were looking, not for a single girl but for a campsite filled with women. And because navigation in the forest is not precise, they found Anna's camp and the women, or at least they could hear the women chattering. Ferraz could understand a few words that amazed him. The women were not frightened or cowering; they were speaking of killing and rescue.

Ferraz moved closer. He had to know what was going on, why there were only women's voices, why the women weren't whimpering and crying.

His earlier years in the forest served him well. He knew how to use the shadows and the underbrush. What he saw simultaneously excited him and frightened him. He couldn't remember whether he saw the tall white woman first or whether he saw the white man first. He noticed the Indian women, but his eyes were riveted to the two whites, and the more intently he fixated on Anna, the faster his heart beat. He saw one Indian male and failed to see two others stretched out on the far side of the fire. He withdrew, not knowing what to make of what he had seen.

He and Simón went a great distance away. Only then did Ferraz tell about what he had seen. "A naked white woman. Holy shit. I've never seen anything like her. And a white man. And a big Indian. And a dozen women, all young and all exactly what we want."

"But who are they?"

"I've no idea. No Newcastle, no Rangel, no Eduardo or Rogelio or Eneas. The white man and the Indian swiped them. Probably their guns we heard. Ambush. Take the women. Someone beat us to the idea."

"But naked? What white man or woman runs around in the jungle naked?"

"I don't know. Right now, I don't care. Those women belong to us, and we're going to have them. I'm excited, thinking about the white one."

"And just how are we going to do it? Maybe we should just let it be, admit failure, go home and work out our dues for Lippstadt and Wittenberg."

"Bull, Simón, bull shit we will. Two against three. We can kill the men easy, before they know what hit them."

"In the dark?"

"Just before daylight, when they least expect it."

"What about the women? Won't they fight?"

"For what? We're rescuing them, just as we planned."

"Yeah, I guess so."

Spiker called Lurch. "Did Lurch hear anything?"

"No. Did Spiker?"

"Might. Don't know. Maybe hear things because worry."

"Tell An-na?"

"No. Tell Ran-ford. Bring Spiker spear."

"Then Spiker sure of noise?"

"Not sure but not take more risk. Spiker stupid enough."

Lurch went off, holding his injured hand up by his shoulder. He approached Widel. "Lurch glad not hurt other hand," he said by way of greeting.

"I'm glad I didn't lose more," Widel offered, chuckling.

"Lurch glad because may need hand."

Widel didn't catch the seriousness of Lurch's conversation. "And I'm glad I didn't lose everything."

"Ran-ford not think why Lurch glad for good hand."

Thinking it was polite conversation, Widel asked, "And why is that?"

"Because Spiker hear noises."

"Christ! People noises?"

"Yes. If true, must be ready."

"Damn right we'll be ready."

Anna heard Widel's last sentence. "Ready for what, Widel? Lurch?"

"Spiker thinks he heard the noises of unwelcome visitors."

"Oh, geez. What else can happen?"

"Could be the white man."

"I'll spread the word."

Anna spoke first with Mansella, warning her and seeking her advice.

"Tomaz," Mansella said, "would spread everyone out, make less target. Then, because all hunters are wounded, would tell women must fight to save selves. Men will die; women will disappear."

"Would you run away, leaving your husband to die?"

"Mansella would not run. Mansella will fight."

"That's the girl. You and I will fight with the men. I know the bow, and I know the spear."

"Mansella good with spear; good as Soomar."

"I know you are. As brave, too. What about the women?"

"Some lost husbands. Will not run. Give them weapons."

"The younger ones. We must let them get away."

"Mansella think none will go, not even Laiti. They saw village destroyed, mothers and fathers and brothers and babies killed. Not even Laiti will leave."

"Then come. We will talk with them."

There were no dissenters. If the site was attacked, every women would become a warrior, even Laiti.

"Laiti will have new mother," the child said. "I choose Mansella for mother because know she will take me. Laiti will stand by Mansella and do as she does."

"Forgive me for not asking sooner, Laiti. Where is your mother?"

"She die with father, when others kill village."

"I'm sorry, Laiti. Truly sorry. Mansella will love you."

Mansella spread the women around the campsite, and as many as could be were given spears. Others were given blowguns to use as swinging sticks. Anna took one of Widel's bows and a handful of arrows.

"It could be a false alarm," Widel said.

"Then we will have had a good exercise."

"But if Spiker says he might have heard something, I'm inclined to believe him. He's made one mistake; he's not likely to make a second."

"If someone is out there waiting to launch an attack, when do you think it will come?"

"I've talked with Lurch and Spiker. We agree the best time to attack is just before it gets light. That last little bit of darkness seems to be the blackest, and then they can mop up in the daylight."

"Can we call the other hunters?"

"Asked that, too. Spiker says we will put them in danger. They'll come rushing in in the dark, and who knows who will get killed. Maybe kill each other. Lurch and Spiker will let them know what is happening sometime tonight, when the monkeys get jabbering. Our concern is to hold out until just before dawn."

Lurch sat down with Anna and Widel. "Will let fire die to almost no see. Can move Mike?"

"No. But he will not move. I'll give him medicine that will see to that. How's your hand?"

"Very hurt, like Anna say. Maybe not matter if Lurch die. If Lurch live, then let Anna help pain. Now pain keeps Lurch awake as should be."

There was no telling if there was an enemy force waiting to attack and if there was, how many men there were. Unlike the Masaki attack on the unsuspecting captors when the enemy fired almost aimless and fruitlessly, those who might attack would be purposeful and have the advantage of choosing targets in advance. The Masakis knew the first targets would be the males. Some would be killed. The women would have to do their fighting immediately, at the first sign of attack, otherwise the entire group would be wiped out.

Spiker and Lurch made their monkey calls. They sounded so much like what was happening naturally that Anna wondered if the hunters could hear and distinguish the sounds. It took a long time for Spiker to report success.

"Suppose hunters will move in dark anyway," he said. "Spiker would, Lurch would, so Soomar and hunters will."

"Now we get to work," Lurch said.

Lurch and Mansella spread the women out and had them lie flat on the ground, those with weapons keeping them close to their bodies to hide them from attacking eyes. No one would think that the women were armed and were willing and capable of fighting.

Spiker had piled up some of the forest debris where he had been, hoping the pile would appear to be a sleeping man. He than slithered off into the shadows, taking two spears with him. Lurch did the same, hiding in a different location.

Widel lay facing the direction from which the sounds had come, a bow and a fist full of arrows at arm's length, one arrow already fitted to the bowstring.

Anna sat by the fading fire, next to Mike. They were as ready as they could be, sitting ducks waiting to be slaughtered.

If the enemy approached from the original direction, the first warning would come from Spiker or Lurch. If there was enough warning and if the attackers made noise, Widel might have a chance at one or two of the enemy, a long change with very slim odds.

Spiker and Lurch had directed Widel's attention to a narrow firing range. Having considered the forest carefully, they selected the spot most likely to be used as the entrance to the campsite. Lurch and Spiker were on either side, the first line of defense. If an enemy broke through, Widel was to shot his arrows until he ran out of them, and if he hit one of the hunters, well, that was the risk they assumed.

Anna was the last to get down. She had been willing to offer herself as a target, a generous if over dramatized offer which she hoped would be rejected. She had no wish to die. She had no wish for anyone to die. When she thought of her daughter, Penny, she had a great wish to live, and so she did what the others did, spread out flat and hoped the forest and the forest gods looked favorable upon all Masaki.

The fire had almost gone out. Here and there a women stirred, griping her weapon tighter in anticipation of the coming onslaught. Then a particular monkey call, followed by another. And off in the distance another, and then a second. The hunters had returned just as Spiker and Lurch signaled the coming of the others. Only two, the signals said.

Spiker and Lurch let the two pass. Now they were behind them, even if they could not see them. For Spiker, the crawling was particularly painful, his leg protesting. He let out an involuntary sigh. One of the others turned and fired in his direction.

Widel let loose a barrage of arrows, aiming at the flash of light. Four, five arrows left his bow. A creature charged into the tiny clearing, firing at every form he saw. He was met with a hail of spears, several of which found their mark. A second man staggered into the opening, two arrows and a spear pointing out of his belly.

The second man slumped to his knees. Anna stood and approached him.

"Who are...you?" he asked.

"I am Anna, medicine women of the Masaki. Who are you?"

"Your...admirer. Did...you organize...this?"

"I had help."

"My...men?"

"Dead. All except the white one. But he will be dead soon. He carries the same poison arrows as you do."

"Against the guns?"

"Because you killed so many of us."

"But...you're white."

"I am a Masaki."

"Gone...Indian."

"Whatever."

"Others will...come, you know."

"I know. Too bad you came. I suppose you came for the women."

"If...I'd known you...were here, I'd have come...just...to look at you."

"You've seen me. Now you will die. Was it worth it?"

285

"To...have seen...the Amazon woman? Yes. But who...would believe me?"

Anna nodded and turned her back on Paulo Ferraz. Lurch reached down and yanked his spear our of the man's back. Widel hopped up and withdrew his arrows.

"Don't want to waste these, old man. Takes too long to make them."

"You...bastard. Think...hurt me...more?"

"I wish I could," Widel answered. "You and yours have turned me into a killer, a savage, and I wish I could hurt you so much your kind would never step into this forest."

"Fu...."

Ferraz died with his ultimate profanity incomplete. His companion had died minutes before, not even knowing he had been struck by the spears of the very women he was going to educate.

"Where Spiker?" Lurch asked.

Anna gasped at the answer. Soomar and the hunters came out of the forest. Soomar had Spiker in his arms.

"Put him down carefully. Mansella, get my medicines."

"No need for medicine, An-na. Spiker dead."

"No. He can't be. I won't let him." Even as she protested, she knew she was too late. A neat hole entered Spiker's throat and exited his neck.

Tears ran down Anna's cheeks. "Who else? Oh, goddamn it, who else?"

Widel put his arm around Anna's waist. "Mike has gone, too. Shot in the head, just the way he said Fraylie was killed."

"Two of the women," Mansella added, hugging Anna. "Tannee and the youngest one."

"Not Laiti!" Anna shouted. "God, not Laiti."

"Laiti died in my arms. My child is dead." Mansella wept uncontrollably.

"Oh, what a waste. What a waste. Spiker, Mike, two we came to save. Sayhoo probably."

T W E N T Y

Anna used Widel and the two wounded women as an excuse to delay any travel. She hated to stay where death was, but even more, she hated the inevitable return to the village of murder because there the women would revisit the destruction and death they had been forced to witness and then made to leave behind. They would relive the hideous horror that had swept down on them and which had taken their husbands, parents, brothers, sisters.

She discussed with Soomar the possibility of finding another route, one that would bypass the village, but Soomar said the women would not take it, as terrible as was what they would see. They had to see, or else even worst images would be in their minds forever, and they had to know the finality of death, otherwise they might not be able to make new lives for themselves somewhere else. Anna marveled at the Indian's insights and at the depth of his empathy.

The search for Sayhoo continued. Occasionally, the hunters found evidence of a female's tracks, but the tracks always petered out. Someone was skilled in hiding her tracks and evading discovery. Whether they were Sayhoo's tracks, the hunters did not know.

. "How long can Sayhoo stay alive?" Anna Asked Soomar.

"If not hurt, long time. Very long time if careful. Eat grubs, snakes, lizards, bee honey, berries. Knows how to find water. Can make fire. Will make spear."

"But the dangers. Sayhoo is young."

"Sayhoo old enough to survive. No danger except jaguar."

"And loneliness."

"Yes. Being alone greatest hurt."

"What would happen if you sent the hunters out in every direction for two day's walk. Then have them signal for Sayhoo?"

"Don't know."

"Well, could you try it? Six hunters could cover a lot more ground that way."

"Not leave women without protection."

"Come on, Soomar. You know the women can take care of themselves. We've proven that over and over. Widel will be here. He can't go far yet. We'll be fine."

"Will talk with hunters."

It was simple enough. Six hunters would radiate out from the camp in six different directions, signals given all along the way. Sayhoo was bound to hear one of them. Two days out, two days back. That was all Anna asked. If the effort failed, she would leave, and Soomar could lead the group to the village and then to the swamp.

Sayhoo knew Newcastle was dead, and yet she had a terrifying urge to escape him. Everything she had witnessed was a blinding nightmare, urging her to run as fast and as far as she could. She knew her running was irrational, that she ought to find her own hunters, and yet her only rational act was to make false trails and to double back on her own trail so as to confuse whatever demon followed her. Whenever possible she made no tracks at all.

She had headed west at first, then had the presence of mind to head east. Eventually, she hoped to reach the swamp, but she was going to do it in the most roundabout way possible. In the process, she became hopelessly lost, her one bearing the direction of the rising sun. Even with that, she did not try to maintain a straight line. That would be too easy for whoever followed. She did not know if someone was following. Better safe than to find out.

Sayhoo was not an expert in the ways of the forest. Her skills were barely adequate for a long life in the forest. She knew the basic things she had to know, but she lacked the pragmatic experience of having done many of them. She could make the bow and stick with which to make a fire; she could fashion a crude spear; she could find water; she knew the roots and fruits which would sustain her; she could construct an adequate shelter for protection from the rain. But she had never hunted, and she had never been alone.

Spiker and Saymore always had been there to guide her, and Wasmaggi. Always grandfather Wasmaggi had been there to listen and to talk. And Anna. She had not involved Anna deeply enough in her life. She had shut Anna out after Anna had refused to approve of her marriage with Fraylie. Perhaps now it was too late, recognizing what a friend the medicine woman could be.

Sayhoo was a woman. She had made love with Fraylie as a woman. She had gone to a strange village as a women to find a husband. She was capable, she told herself, of living like a woman.

So why was she crying? Why was she feeling so sorry for herself? Why did she continue to think of death? Death was for the old and infirm, not for young, strong, independent women. But she cried anyway and thought the forest creatures cried with her.

And she thought the forest creatures were speaking to her. "Be strong," they said; "be brave. Sayhoo, you are one of us; we are one with you. Listen to us; we will help you. Come to us; we will protect you."

"Yes. Yes. I am one with the forest," Sayhoo said, and she made the voices of the howler monkeys and of the parrots, chirped like the wrens, and sang the songs of the crickets.

And the animals yelled, "Sayhoo, I'm here."

And she yelled back, "Sayhoo here."

And the voice said, "Sayhoo, is Lurch."

And Sayhoo dissolved into the arms of the hunter.

Lurch could not find the words. "An-na will explain all," he told her, hiding the terrible news of death and despair. For the first time, Lurch thanked his missing fingers. Sayhoo's concern for him postponed his tellings, and Sayhoo's recital of her trials and escape filled the time getting to the temporary camp.

Spiker and Mike had been carried into the forest along with Laiti and Tannee. At what should have been a moment of joyful reunion, Sayhoo had no idea of the price paid for her and the other women's rescue until Anna took Sayhoo by the arm and led her away from the others.

Anna wondered where to begin. With Fraylie, with Spiker, with Mike? "Sayhoo," Anna began, gently leading Sayhoo away from the camp. "We have cried together. Now we will cry together again. The forest has taken...."

The tears streamed down Anna's face. Never had she had to break such agonizing news. A father, a lover, a friend. Gone. Killed by the white man and his evil companions. A child, another woman, both killed by the same evil creatures.

It was more than Sayhoo could comprehend. She sat mute, not wanting to believe Anna's words, not understanding that almost everything she loved had gone, deaf to the words that ripped away her youth and made her so old so suddenly. She looked at Anna in disbelief, saw Anna's own distress, and fainted.

"Mansella, the gray pot, and some water," Anna yelled.

When Sayhoo regained consciousness, she looked at Mansella, also in tears. She turned back to Anna. "Sayhoo cannot breath."

"Drink this, Sayhoo." Then Anna drew Sayhoo close. "It is okay to cry, Sayhoo. You have much to cry about. Anna will hold you and cry with you. And Mansella, she will hold us, too, and she will cry."

Between sobs, Sayhoo asked, "And who will tell my mother?"

"We will tell her together. I'll be with you whenever you need me."

In time, one by one, the hunters approached, each touching Sayhoo on the shoulder, each speaking a word of comfort. Lurch, Amstay, Joqua, Westman, Walkin, Soomar, and Widel came to support the young child-woman. And then the former women captives came, sharing their grief and taking Sayhoo's as their own, adding her misery to theirs, for they, too, had lost their loved ones only weeks before.

It was a somber and grief stricken group that retraced its steps through the forest. Widel hobbled in considerable pain, but he did not complain. So little pain, he said, compared to the women. But he did ask a practical question.

"Has the medicine woman thought about so many women in our village? How will we accommodate eleven young women? There aren't enough men as it is?"

"I haven't thought about it. Thanks for adding one more problem."

"I didn't mean...."

"No. I'm sorry. Excuse my sarcasm. It's just that I never thought so many things would fall on me. All I ever wanted was to learn the medicines, treat people and be a woman for you."

"You were a woman the day I first saw you."

"Oh, hell. You only saw someone you could sleep with."

"I've confessed that. Damned if I haven't. But you were. Young, that's for sure. But you had character and courage. You saved me. I've said that a thousand times. Your spirit or whatever you want to call it saved me, and that was what Wasmaggi saw. He was right, you know. I see you all troubled. I wish I could just hold you and have all the troubles go away, but I can't. Thank God you have a grace that touches these people. It must be a special feeling, knowing that you have their love and respect."

"Oh, Widel. Nice words. How long have you been rehearsing them?"

"Just now. I'm getting smart later than sooner. I realize that each of us has a place and a function. Even the children have a function. In many ways, they are the reason for our being, and when you come right down to it, you are our mother."

"Come on, Widel, that's crap."

"No, hear me out. Before you, Wasmaggi in some ways was everybody's father. That's one of the roles of the medicine person. It comes with the job. You, and by you I mean the medicine man or woman, are the binding link. Believe me, you may find the role burdensome sometimes, but I think it's awesome."

Widel had touched the right chord. His praise meant a lot, and Anna recognized the respect with which the Masakis regarded her. In many ways, she felt as though she was mothering the Masakis.

Her spirit revived, she walked a way with Mansella. It was the first time they were to speak directly about the fighting.

"Thank you, Mansella, for your help. It was terrible losing Spiker and Mike, and Laiti and Tannee. There will be much crying."

"I've cried before, for my husband, for my father. I cry for Laiti. I would have loved her like my own."

"I know. I might have taken Tannee for my assistant. She had a touch for the knife and for the medicines."

"Could have been worse," Mansella said reflectively, "but is hard to imagine. Could it have been worse, An-na?"

"I thought it would be. I really thought everyone would be killed. I imagined the worst. And then when we couldn't find Sayhoo, I added one more to the list of the dead."

"You will add to your list soon enough."

"Why do you say that, Mansella?"

"All these women. They will want An-na to know their mothers and fathers, their husbands, their brothers and sisters."

"But that's expecting a lot, isn't it?" Anna asked, thinking about the thirty or forty families affected.

"Is duty. An-na rescue; now An-na increases our village."

"Yes, I see. I wanted to talk with you about that."

"Mansella listen."

"Not listen. Mansella, tell me what we are going to do with so many women in a village that doesn't have enough men now."

"Tell An-na what know and what Mansella feel?"

"Please."

"When Mansella give husband to forest, some hunters offer take Mansella as wife. Maybe good idea, but Mansella have two brothers, Hakma and Soomar, and father, Tomaz, who had no wife. So Mansella say no."

"There wasn't anyone you liked well enough?"

"Not say. Ones I like no ask."

"Okay, I won't ask which."

"But that one way. Hunters take new wife."

"That's one way, you say, so there must be another way."

"Maybe."

"Well, tell me."

"Tannee say she knew another Masaki village."

"Good Lord, where?"

"Only know direction."

"Come on, woman. Point."

Mansella pointed toward the northwest. "Her father took her there once when she was small. Wanted arrange marriage."

"And?"

"That village not believe they Masaki. Not let in. Made to go home."

"That was very strange. The only people in the world didn't believe a man and his daughter were Masaki."

"More strange."

"There's more?"

"Yes. Let Sayhoo tell it."

Anna called to Sayhoo, asking her to walk along with her and Mansella. "Mansella says you know something strange about these Masakis."

"When we dragged away from village, not allowed talk. But Sayhoo talk anyway. Work out way to talk. Learn not very much, but learn not one women have child. Some more old than me married long time; no children. More hunters than women; still no children. Ask why. No one know. Way of forest, they say. Wasmaggi and An-na's way, I say, because Sayhoo know An-na have no-baby medicine. Maybe women take."

"But there were babies in the village. We saw their remains."

"Sayhoo told only certain women have child, not these women."

It was strange. All of the captive females, from nine or ten year old Laiti to those in their late teens, were or soon would be prime child-bearing women. Were those who were married forbidden to have children?

But accidents happen. Women would become pregnant; it was inevitable - and natural. An individual woman might be barren, but for a group to be would require outside manipulation. The medicine man was the only logical answer.

Anna asked the next logical question. "Sayhoo, when you were in the village, did you receive any medicine from the medicine man?"

"No."

293

"From anyone?"

"No again."

"Did you associate with these women?"

"Sayhoo see them, talk to some of them. They polite to Sayhoo, include her in conversation. Sometimes we play games together. All friends."

"Where did you live?"

"With Trulk."

"As his wife?"

"As his daughter, if An-na mean what Sayhoo think."

"I'm sorry my question came out as it did. I was thinking out loud and shouldn't have. I know better."

"An-na wonder why no children?"

"Yes, Sayhoo, Anna wonders why. Here's a village with many men. Trulk and his hunters think you might find a husband in their village. If there had been too many women, he would have said so and not taken you with him. Something is very strange, very strange."

"It's natural evolution, Anna," Widel explained. "One group splits into five and they evolve their own customs. Who knows why. They just become different. And maybe you're looking for your answer in the wrong place. Maybe it's not the women who can't have babies, or some of the women anyway, but the men. Maybe their medicine man discovered a male pill or something."

"That's contrary to...."

"To our cultural habits, where the woman takes the pill?"

"But...."

"We know three villages, Sampson's, Trulk's, and our own. Each is male dominated. Who's to say the men in this village didn't decide who would be daddies and who wouldn't be."

"That's something I can understand. But I thought you men never wanted to give up your procreative powers, you know, the macho thing of planting your seed for future generations."

"Then again, maybe the men didn't give their seed sowing ability away; maybe it was taken from them."

294

The thought of a fourth village and the unexplained failure of the women to bear children occupied Anna's attention on the long walk. At one point she invited Lurch to walk with her.

"You came to Wasmaggi's village looking for a wife. Did you come from Sampson's village or Trulk's village?"

"No. Lurch come from own village."

"Where is that village?"

"Lurch not sure, only remember direction."

"And which direction was that?"

"With the sun on Lurch's left shoulder."

"You mean when you left your village and headed out?"

"Yes."

"And Amstay. Where was his village?"

"He came from there," and Lurch pointed to the northwest.

Of the five Masaki villages, three were known to Anna, and now she had the general direction of the fourth and fifth villages. In her mind she began to plan for a meeting of the medicine men or women. Once the tribe had broken up because of the others, the creatures. Perhaps because of the creatures, it was time to meet again and to consider the alternatives. People from two villages knew now that the creatures were men in different forms. People from three villages knew there were white people besides An-na and Widel. Everybody knew that the others were closing in. And if the Masakis did not know the threat, Anna and Widel did. The slaughter of one village was only the beginning. There would be more bandeiras and more bandeirantes and more brancos. The cangaceiros and procuradores and tropas de resgate would rape and kill in increasing number until the Masaki were no more. The Masaki world was shrinking. One day it would shrink to zero.

The Masaki could fight and die, or they could run and hide and then die, or they could try to hide and in the end either die or be sent to a reservation where they would die, or they could be assimilated, one more poor, uneducated, disease prone, tiny population worth about the value of a gnat.

Knowing no other alternatives, Anna began to outline the Masaki's survival. They would hide, and while hiding, she and Widel would prepare the Indians for their introduction into the civilized world.

"Preposterous. Stupid. Impossible. I don't want to," Widel said.

"Why not? What other alternative is there?"

"Let them, us, die a natural death. That's the other side of evolution, you know, that species become extinct because...."

"Because they could not adapt. We can help them adapt."

"To more of what they've already seen? Kept on reservations like zoo animals? No thanks."

"But it doesn't have to be that way."

"No, but it will. Why would you think these Indians will fare any better than the North American Indians or the Australian aborigines? They won't, you know. They can't, because they won't fit in, because they have no civilized skills, and because there simply is too much prejudice for them to have a chance."

"What about Penny?"

"Yeah. What about her? Oh, she has a chance, if we teach her proper English and start her math lessons and feed her on western history. Her chance is her color and then only if we get her to a place where she can grow up in our culture."

"Our culture? I thought we were Masaki."

"You know what I mean. The Masaki culture is a dead end. You and I might not live to see the end, but Penny will. We have some serious thinking to do about that."

If Anna was going to think then and there, it proved impossible. They were walking on the wider trail to the village, and Soomar fell back to ask her what they should do.

Anna suggested they stop. She would address the women.

"Masaki women, if I could, I would have Soomar lead us around your village so that you did not have to set eyes upon your houses and the dead people you knew and loved. It is a sight no one should have to see. But I know you need to look and will look, no matter what I say. When we first came to your village, there was no time to burn it and no one was able to take the dead into the forest.

"You women will go on alone from here. Those of my village will follow. When you have had enough of looking, Mansella and I will be on the far side. Come to us. We will cry with you and have medicine for your pain. The hunters will burn the village, and together we will go to meet the rest of our people."

The women move forward, shuffling their feet, not wanting to go but compelled to. They didn't want to view the remains but they had to be certain that the village was gone. Only then could they move on to whatever uncertain future welcomed them, if it welcomed them. Besides the fear of what they were about to see, the women suffered dreadful doubts about any future of any kind.

"Soomar, it's important you find the medicine man's house. I have to study it, study his medicines, maybe replenish some of my own."

The medicine man's supply of barks and herbs and leaves had been damaged beyond saving. Nonetheless, Anna went through everything with great care. She could identify almost everything, and as she literally cleaned the house, she spoke the names of the medicines out loud, refreshing her own memory and going through a kind of memory check.

She finished by the time the hunters were ready to burn the house. She noted the respect with which the men disassembled the house and carried it to the gigantic fire in the village center. Instead of simply pulling over the corner posts, the hunters struggled to uproot them, and when they did, from two corners, buried deep in the ground, emerged two containers the like of which Anna never had seen. She showed them to Widel.

"Clay pots, with heavy glazing. Not Masaki. The Masaki don't know anything about glazing pottery. And look at the designs. Carefully painted. Works of art, I would say. But whose and what the paintings represent, I don't know."

"Look at how closely the covers fit."

Widel tried to open one of the large jars. "Won't budge. Don't want to break it."

"Here. Let me help. I'll hold the jar; you try the cover."

"Wait. Look. It's sealed with resin."

Anna took one of her knives and carefully worked it around the crack. Once the seal was broken, the cover came off without undue force.

"I'll be damn," Widel exclaimed. "Look at the clay figures."

"Pretty damn indecent, I'd say."

"Well, they're both well endowed."

"And then some."

Two carved figures in bright white filled the clay jars. The male figure sported a penis that came up to his chin, or at least it appeared to be his penis, although it also could have been an alligator's tail, and the female figure had breasts nearly as big as the entire figure. Such art forms are not unknown, but what made the female figure unusual was what protruded from her vulva, the tail of an alligator.

"It's sick, Widel."

"It is gross. I wonder where in hell they came from."

"Anything else in the jars?"

"Some kind of powder."

Anna smelled the content but couldn't identify it. She asked Widel, "Do you think there's a connection between the figures and the fact that certain couples couldn't have children?"

"I've no idea. Maybe it has something to do with the powder."

"And how come the figures are white?"

"Again, no idea. Once, you had Wasmaggi going on about some Incan words. Nothing came of that, but perhaps he can shed some light on these things."

"Connie studied the Incas because she was more interested in that stuff than I was. She never mentioned anything like this."

"Anna, my knowledge sums up as total ignorance. One thing I do know, no Inca ever painted or carved a head like these, nice and round and so European looking."

When Amstay came to tell Anna the women had completed their farewells and had bid goodbye to the village, Anna packed the two large jars in with her medicines and went to comfort the women.

298

On the way, she asked Amstay about his former village, particularly, had the village ever had any contact with outsiders.

"Amstay not know, but medicine man used to talk about other Masakis coming to see medicine man. Is that what An-na want to know?"

"Did you ever see anyone who was not of your village?"

"No, not until see Cutilla and Contulla and Lurch. Then Tilla and Moremew. They first people Amstay ever see not of my village."

Anna thanked Amstay, and she thanked Mansella when she reached her. "I'm sorry," Anna said. "I got involved in the medicine man's medicine. How are the women?"

"I gave them drink as you said. They very sad, very much sad. Think time now go."

"Yes, it's time for all of us to leave this part of the forest. I won't ever want to come back here."

Mansella took Anna by the arm. "One thing for you to know. Sayhoo says maybe the women will make their own village."

"Let's hope that is just a normal reaction to losing Fraylie and Mike and Spiker. Right now I can understand that the women feel unwanted and unprotected. There are no men for them."

"Mansella might join them."

"I make no judgment. I think the feeling will disappear in time, but if it doesn't, let's face what happens when it happens. Right now we have people waiting for us." Then, almost as an afterthought, Anna asked, "Would you like to find the other Masaki villages?"

"An-na no tell?"

"Whatever you say will be to me only. I promise."

"Mansella grow old. Were not for Oneson, perhaps be like Hagga was, mean and unkind."

"But you're not old. You're still a young women."

"Then An-na understand. Mansella want husband, want to be in hammock with own man while...." She did not finish her statement.

"Mansella, one way or another, we will find the other villages."

"Then Sayhoo and I will wait for a time, but not long. An-na hear? Not long."

"Anna hears you."

TWENTY-ONE

A half day from the swamp, the rescue party and the women were met by Moremew and Joshway, hunters sent out to ensure the secrecy of the swamp.

Withholding their joy and their desire to welcome the returning Masakis, Moremew and Joshway first tended to the business of hiding tracks and of creating false trails. That duty was adhered to with religious diligence.

The homecoming was bittersweet. The village mourned the loss of its hunters and yet was thankful for the return of those who had accomplished the rescue of so many women.

Saymore was devastated. That Sayhoo had been a captive and had been delivered safely gladdened Saymore's heart; that Spiker had died at the hands of the tropas de resgate drove her into despair, and she swayed between those two emotions for days. Only when Anna insisted that Saymore take her medicine did the wife and mother begin to calm down, and even then she hung to Anna and Wasmaggi for comfort.

Tonto and Pollyque and Lucknew were distraught. Tonto took Mike's death stoically; his wives less so. After all, Mike had been like one of their own children. They had raised him and taught him. Losing him was like losing a son, a loss deeply felt.

No one ever suggested that Mike's death was his own ego fault. He was portrayed as brave and courageous. If he had acted unwisely, the hunters forgave him. What good would that part of the story do anyone?

The sadness of the two losses delayed a proper welcome for the eleven women, although they were not neglected. The women were pestered for their story, even the saddest parts, and asked a thousand questions about their village and its life. Hakma, Tonto, and Joshway were pressed into making several shelters for the women, Tonto more supervisor than worker. The children were put to work helping.

In one way or another, everyone became involved in the welfare of and the assimilation of the women into the village, no one more than Penny, not that she did very much physically, but because of her color. The white child became the object of intense interest. Widel and Anna had been a part of the terrible trouble, their roles had seemed almost natural if not understood, but a white child? That was something different, and it had to be touched and spoken to and listened to.

And the women gave Wasmaggi an entirely new audience. He had a hundred questions and a thousand observations. Yes, no, we did, we didn't, on and on for two days, experiences, habits, customs traded back and forth, shared, and sometimes causing amusement or dismay.

At the end of the third day Wasmaggi sat at Anna's fire. He offered no greeting and did not wait for an invitation to speak.

"Wasmaggi can see on your faces you have something to share."

"What makes the old man think so?" Widel asked, holding back a grin.

"White people cannot hide thoughts from Wasmaggi. I see on faces you have something need to tell."

"Someday," Anna said. "Someday I'm going to have a secret and you will not know it."

Anna related the rescue and the events leading to it, especially the destruction of the village, and concluded with the finding of the strange jars and their contents. For the moment, she left out her and Widel's speculations about the Masaki's future. There would be time for that later.

When Widel produced the jars, Wasmaggi was unable to identify them, and when Widel withdrew the sexual figures, Wasmaggi, other than commenting on the obvious sexual appearances, could not relate to them.

"Never have seen such," he said in all seriousness.

Anna watched his face closely for any sign of recognition, either of the jars or of the figures. She was certain he spoke the truth. When she told of the powdery substance in the jars, Wasmaggi examined it carefully, smelling and tasting.

"Don't know what is," he admitted.

Again Anna looked for any sign of recognition. There was none. The old medicine man was as mystified as were Anna and Widel.

"We thought," Widel began to introduce his speculations, "the color of the figures might mean something. And the shape of the faces."

"Wasmaggi not know."

"You've never seen anything like these?"

"No. Would remember."

"Wasmaggi, look carefully at the faces," Widel said. "Have you ever seen faces like those?" Wasmaggi studied the faces again, turning the figures around and around in his hands. "They are faces like yours."

"They seem to be, don't they. I wonder if that means the medicine man, if not the entire village, had contact with whites at some time in the past."

Once more Wasmaggi thought deeply and long. "Not think so, not for village. The women not see white people until see you and man who killed so many." Then he added, "But Wasmaggi will ask again in different way. Very strange. You have more for Wasmaggi?"

Anna went on to tell about the childless women and the fact that only certain women had babies, and she repeated Widel's speculation that maybe only certain men had the ability to procreate, that power having been taken away from other men.

Wasmaggi thought about that, too, for a long time before speaking. "An-na knows all of my medicines. I've no medicine for men like you say. Not know such thing."

"Do you have a medicine," Widel asked, "that eliminates a man's urge to...well, you know...make love?"

"An-na have that in cassava and in coca. Someday might have to give to Ran-ford." Wasmaggi smiled. "But not right question.

What you want is, can give man something so he make love but not baby."

"Exactly. Something that would kill the sperm or prevent a male from manufacturing it."

Wasmaggi was lost. The concept of sperm was not known to him, and Widel thought better of trying to explain. Probably Wasmaggi wouldn't have believed him anyway, that in a male's semen were thousands of living, active spermatozoa just looking for a woman's egg. Widel backed up.

"The man plants a seed in a woman. Do you have a medicine that makes the seed inactive?"

Wasmaggi tried to digest that thought. "No. Can make a man not plant seed; cannot make a man whose seed will never grow."

"But some of these women were married to such men."

"Maybe," Anna said, "you're jumping to conclusions for which there is no evidence. Change the subject for a minute. Wasmaggi, after the creatures, did you ever visit another village?"

"Yes. Wasmaggi go to Sampson's village."

"Lurch and Amstay came here from two other villages. Did you ever go to their villages? Do you know where their former villages are? Or any other village besides Sampson's?"

"Went to Sampson's village because of jaguar-hunters; never go to other villages. When creatures make Masaki separate, each village on own. Sometimes hunters go to another village, never Wasmaggi. Always keep other villages in mind. Too bad all hunters who went other villages now dead. No one from our village been to others for long time."

"Do you think," Anna asked in all seriousness, "that maybe it's time for the medicine men and women who are left to get together?"

"That one reason Wasmaggi bring you here. In his dreams, Wasmaggi see what has happened. Time to plan for life of Masaki."

The evening fire began as a somber meeting of morbid people. Soomar explained the connection between Fraylie's death and the slaughter of a Masaki village and the capture of its young women. He told of the rescue party's entrance into the village, of the partially

303

burned bodies done originally and hastily by Mike, of following the trail of the women, and of the final rescue. He did not mention that the final attack had been planned by Anna or that Mike's actions had resulted in his own death, maybe in Spiker's.

Widel told of the actual attack and was specific about the murderous white man called Newcastle, and he told of the attack upon the wounded and the women by the two others and how Spiker and Mike, Laiti and Tannee were killed.

And Lurch told about his loss of three fingers and about finding Sayhoo deep in the forest.

The tellings in the traditional Masaki way drew each of the hearers into the events, made them a part of everything that had happened, and seemed to ease much of the pain and anguish of those who had lost so much.

The last to speak was Sayhoo. She told of going to the village with Trulk and the hunters, living in Trulk's house, wondering if she would see Fraylie and Mike or if she would meet someone who would be her husband.

When she told of the morning of destruction, she repeated every sound, every voice, every action she could remember. She did not know the names of each hunter who fell or of each older woman killed or of each child murdered. It did not matter. Later, the women would recite the names. It was enough that Sayhoo told their story of bravery in the face of certain death.

Then she told of the journey, the women bound by the neck, their hands tied tightly together, their feet hobbled, and even how they managed to leave signs for those who followed.

She told of the plan the women hoped to make that would allow Laiti to escape, and she told of her own escape from the white man carrying Widel's arrows and about the army ants and her running. Finally, she told about being found by Lurch.

"Many things happened to Sayhoo," she concluded. "Sayhoo decided to die because Sayhoo knew the white man would use her. I was prepared to die, wanted to die when one of the women told me I could not because Laiti was not free. I came back from dead to help the child. It seemed important to me. When it was over, the fighting, the running, I was a child again and An-na helped me. For a little while, she was my mother. She helped me know my father had gone to the forest, never to return to me. She helped me when I had to tell my own mother that my father was dead, her husband was dead. An-na is my mother's mother, too. She is all our mothers."

The silence that followed did not indicate disagreement; it was more the silence of awe before a person of great stature and of great importance. The Masakis looked and with their eyes drank in the full measure of their medicine woman and gave thanks to the forest for the gift. Anna sat and twitched uncomfortably; Wasmaggi and Widel beamed with delight

Xingu and Sarahguy both stood, each wanting to be the first to ask Anna to speak, arguing who would have the honor, and while they argued and caused a considerable commotion which in turn caused a great deal of laughter, Saymore went to Anna and embraced her.

"Please, Saymore."

"Saymore would speak." She held Anna by the hand. "What my daughter has said is true. An-na is our mother. All my life I watch Wasmaggi be father to the Masaki; sometimes I jealous. My father give more, I think, to others than to me. It was not true; it was a child's view. When An-na become medicine woman, I see her give to Masaki, and at last I know how special my father is because I see how special An-na is.

"But not what want say. Want say time for mourning over. We who have given back to forest will be sad for a time, but we will go on. Village should not be sad because we are. Time to be Masaki and to care for those who live and say to those women who come with Sayhoo, we welcome you. Know that An-na will love you as she loves us. Saymore finished now."

In their shelter that night, Anna asked what they were going to do. She had in mind the extra women, her plans for preparing the Masaki for the future, her concern for Penny's future.

"Well, tomorrow, I'm going to play with Penny. Contulla and Cutilla gave her great care and spoiled her, so I'm going to spoil her some more. Tonight, I'm going to make love to a goddess before the Masaki spoil you."

"My God, Widel, you're wounded. You can't...."

"Maybe not, but at least let me hold you and tell you how much I love you, and maybe I'll get well."

"It's those little figurines, isn't it?"

"It's you. It's always been you."

"We'll wake up Penny."

"So what? She'll take a look, say it's natural, and go back to sleep."

"It is natural, isn't it."

While hunters hunted and women baked bread from the manioc and cassava roots; while Widel played with Penny and the other small children, Coanna, Threesome, Twoman, and Love; while the older children, Oneson, Blue, Barkah, Armot, Jappah, and Jonquilla received instruction from Tonto; Wasmaggi and Anna talked with the rescued women.

Now, after death and destruction, uncomprehended fear and immense sadness, the women worried about what would become of them and how they could fit into a village whose families were so rigidly established. The women saw no future as wives, and while several had been widowed recently, all expressed hope about marriage and family.

"If Wasmaggi was not so old," he said, "would take all of you for wife and you would know what a Masaki hunter could do."

The women giggled. One named Kalo responded. "Would Wasmaggi have talked so big when young? When man get older his brags get bigger."

There was more giggling, and Wasmaggi confessed that maybe he had exaggerated just a little. "Half of you, and that truth." And the women laughed when he added, "Truth as Wasmaggi like to remember."

He had put the women at ease. Now it was time for more serious talk. "Wasmaggi and An-na see that not enough men here. And we hear talk about women having own village, even taking Mansella and Sayhoo who have not found husbands here. We cry when think some of you lost husbands; we cry when think some have not yet found husband. An-na thinks should find other villages. Yours gone; Sampson's gone; two others are somewhere, or were once."

"One question we have is whether you know the other villages or whether some of your hunters might have visited the other villages," Anna said. "Tannee said once, when she was small, she went to another village."

"My husband went to same village twice," the one called Maltra said, "before we were married, to look for a wife. I was just little girl. When he came back without wife, I said to him, why not me? He made me feel bad when he said I just little child. That how I remember. But he never go again, and soon we are married, and I never little girl again."

"Did he say anything about the other village? About the people? Anything at all that you remember?"

"Only he not like, not true Masaki village."

"Why was that?"

"Not remember."

"Not true. Maltra not want remember." Sistal put her hand on top of Maltra's. "Maltra was little girl when married, nine years, ten years. Some women were jealous. How did little girl get Halcoli, a big hunter, a strong hunter, too big for little girl? First nights we hear Maltra cry of pain. Some glad. Say little girl not know how big big hunter get. But her pain was worse when our village attacked by other village. Masakis come to take all women, just like others come. Big fight. One grab Maltra and carry her off. Halcoli in rage. He fight five, six men. Kill them and find Maltra struggling with man who took her. More fight. Halcoli hurt bad, but save Maltra, but never does Halcoli able make love. His male part cut off by huge knife."

Sistal drew Maltra close, holding her tightly. "Since that night, Maltra remember nothing for long time. She grow fat with baby, but baby die. All time Halcoli take care of Maltra; she take care him. Much love."

"What happened to Halcoli?"

"Him die when others come."

"You're sure the first attackers were Masaki?"

"Yes." Sistal looked around for confirmation. Some of the women nodded in agreement.

Anna looked directly into Maltra's eyes. "I'm so sorry. I didn't know."

"I think Halcoli only went to that village once," Sistal added. "The other time he went away was to find another village. He not find."

"What makes you think that?" Wasmaggi asked.

"I'm Halcoli's sister."

Questions, confusion. A huge knife. Masakis attacking Masakis to take the women. Anna went to her shelter and returned with the glazed jars. "Does anyone know what these are?" she asked.

There was no apparent recognition; all the women claimed ignorance, and Anna had no reason to doubt them. But when Anna removed the white figure of the male, the women drew back.

"What is this? What does it mean?"

No one answered, although it was obvious that all had seen it before. Maltra tried to distance herself from the circle of women. Anna asked her what she was afraid of.

"An-na no make...." She burst into uncontrollable tears.

Milken, who appeared to be the oldest of the women, positioned herself between Maltra and Anna; a look of hatred and revulsion covered her face. "We thought never have to see Lackee again. Lackee much evil. An-na much evil. An-na fool us."

"Who is Lackee?" Wasmaggi asked.

"Who is Lackee? All Masaki know Lackee. You fool us with talk of welcome and kindness, but we not fools. That Lackee," Milken said, pointing to the grotesque male figurine. "Who has Lackee has right to us. Is Masaki way."

"Never will you touch us. We kill An-na before let touch us." The woman called Costill stood up and moved toward Anna, threatening to strike her.

As old as Wasmaggi was, as frail as he appeared, he jumped up and held the women, commanding the others to sit where they

308

were.

"An-na does not know Lackee. She found these in the house of your medicine man, this strange man and an even stranger woman. She has no evil toward you; she only asks what the figures are and what they mean."

It came out, a revolting tale of a white man who came to the village a long time ago, when Maltra was a small child. He had the figurines, and because the male figure looked like the man, he convinced the village that he, his special whiteness created by the forest, was someone special, and his unique status meant that he slept with each and every young woman until he was satisfied she was ready for marriage. He even convinced the medicine man.

His appetite was insatiable, and he found few young women ready for marriage. He performed ceremonies before the evening fire and had intercourse with one or two women by the fire as the village looked on. Two hunters dared challenge him one night, and somehow he killed each. After that there were no doubters until the white man took Tannee.

By then he had revealed the female figure. All women should look like this, he said, with big breasts that stick out, women capable of taking an alligator between their legs.

The night he took Tannee, her father, Milo the medicine man, struck the white man. The man did not kill Milo immediately. Instead, he took a knife and stuck it between Tannee's legs and deep into her. She bled for many weeks. Then the man said he would kill Milo, but before he could, the hunters killed him.

Everyone thought Milo had destroyed the figures and in time the village returned to normal, except that Milo convinced the village it was a good idea for women to be prepared for marriage and that he would prepare them, which he did in his house. All of the women present had been prepared by Milo.

Wasmaggi either was a little slow or just couldn't believe what he was hearing. "How did Milo prepare the women?"

"He slept with us," Kalo said.

"One day," Milken told more, "we ask Tannee why her father have to do that. She say he sick in head. And one day someone ask if Tannee know father's medicines and Tannee say yes. And one day Milo dead. And one day Tannee become medicine women. She always talk about father as medicine man but he gone to forest and Tannee medicine woman."

"My God, Wasmaggi. Can you believe all this?"

"Not want to; not want to."

"First, we've got to destroy the figurines. In front of the women. Wipe out the whole idea. Now, Wasmaggi. Do it now. And the jars. No, wait. Ask about the jars."

Wasmaggi tore into the figures with relish. He was disgusted, not by the figures themselves but by what they represented and by the hurt they had caused. When he had reduced the figures to little particles, he threw them on Anna's fire. The women watched silently until every shred of carving had been burned.

Only then did Wasmaggi ask about the jars. No one remembered having seen them, but it was suggested that when the white man first came to the village, he came to trade. Maybe the jars were something he offered Milo.

Whatever they were, shortly after displaying them and having the women examine them, Wasmaggi threw them on the fire. Within seconds there were two loud flashes and a wide scattering of pottery and fire sparks. Widel came running toward the group.

"Now I know what the powder is; too late, I guess. It's gun powder. Lucky you didn't blow someone up." In all the excitement, no one thought to ask what gun powder was. It was just as well. There were enough questions to last a long time.

"It's an unbelievable story, Widel," Anna said later. "Just unbelievable, that a white man could come into a village and publicly rape the women and have their approval."

"What was the man's name?"

"Lackee, I guess. The women didn't make a distinction between the figure and the man."

"My guess is his name was 'Lucky' something or other. Sounds like the kind of name a degenerate would have. What about the female figure?"

310

"The women said he carved it, but I doubt that. Probably he had both figures."

"Tannee might have helped kill her own father. She was the medicine woman, and I didn't know it."

"Raped by her own father, and by Lucky who mutilated her. Probably she was so badly injured, she never could have children."

"Probably she never let a man near her."

"Can't blame her."

"And that's why our being white was mostly a non-event. Most of the women had seen a white man."

"Well, we're lucky they didn't try to kill us."

"Actually, I wonder why they didn't."

Just before the evening fire, Wasmaggi appeared again, his face twisted in questions and doubt. "Ran-ford, An-na, Wasmaggi not think well of idea of going to other villages. Too much strange. Too much danger. Cannot send Lurch and Amstay and their sons to bad villages."

"That thought has been in my mind, too, Wasmaggi. When Widel and Connie and I came to your village, and you told about four other villages, we thought all of them would be the same. Then there was Sampson's village; then Trulk's village; then a village that attacked Trulk's village. Is this village the only sane village?"

"Tonight, An-na should listen. When Wasmaggi speak, An-na listen."

The mood of the hunters assembled for the fire was surprisingly jovial. Had the village women known the reason, it might have been a more subdued group of hunters, but what the women didn't know was just as well. In their talk at least, the hunters had been dividing up the new women members of the village, playing the game of "who" and "what if" and generally teasing one another, especially Walkin and Widel. Of his generation, only Walkin had two wives, a fact he sometimes paraded before the others, declaring it was a man's duty to have many wives - if he was a man. It was all in fun when there was no possibility of multiple marriages for the other hunters.

Toward Widel was directed the potential for a non-white wife, and the hunters teased Widel, saying that in his house the wife ruled and that Widel couldn't have another wife even if he wanted one. Widel played the game, when it was a game, by declaring that Anna would accept another wife with happiness. His thoughts always were on Connie, never on anyone else.

Now, for all the hunters, while they joked and teased and speculated, there was the very real need to deal with the fact of a surplus of females, all of whom were or were nearing marrying age. The hunters handled the issue as a joke played on them by the forest, never considering the consequences.

Wasmaggi, standing by the fire, had, in his mind, considered as many of the consequences as he could accommodate. He was not in a playful mood when he addressed the village.

"The jaguar hunters we have known are dead, Tomaz, Connie, Mike, Trulk, and soon the jaguars will be dead. And when the jaguar dies, the forest will die, and when the forest dies, the Masaki will die. I've seen it. For a long time I've seen it. I've kept my seeing from you."

It was a somber note, too somber for some.

"Let An-na speak. She will say pleasant things," someone said.

"Anna will speak when her turn comes. Tonight I'll speak first because I'm the oldest. I'll say words you don't wish to hear, words you don't know, words which will forever change the Masaki.

"Forever we believe we are the only people in the world; now we know is not so. Spiker and Mike were killed by other people; Soomar and Westman and Lurch and Walkin and Amstay and Joqua have seen other people; Kalo and Milken and the women who have come to us have seen other white people; Mike told us of others who were men, the others I once thought were different creatures.

"We thought our world was very large. Once I walked to the end of the world, and still the world went on. I walked more, and still there was more world. I believe Ran-ford and An-na when they say the world is so many times bigger than I thought.

"Masaki, the world of the Masaki is very small, more than enough for us, many times more than enough, but it grows smaller because others would have it and use it and not care about us. We are the people, chosen by the forest. Those who come are not the chosen people, but An-na says they number more than the monkeys and birds put together.

"I've thought on this a long time, before the whites came to us, and now I know I should have told you before. I thought there was time. There is no more time."

It was a long speech. When he finished, he sat down, his back to the fire, his eyes glazed with tears. His worst fears had come true. Over the past few weeks his world and his people had become very small and very fragile, and he worried that he might live to see the end of both.

"You brought us here to tell us this?" Hakma was angry. "You brought your daughter here to tell her the Masaki are dead?"

Very slowly, Wasmaggi turned around. "I brought my daughter and her husband here because this is a place of safety. Out there, to a white man and the others, she and you have lost a son; I've lost a grandson. You have lost a brother and Saymore a husband and Sayhoo a father. Lucknew and Pollyque have lost one who was like a son, and Tonto, too. I' ve lost a son-in-law. These women have lost husbands and fathers, mothers and brothers and sisters. Yes, I tell you this. Be angry. I'm angry. If anger can bring back those the forest has taken, I'll shout my anger until I die."

"Hakma sorry. Hakma too angry to think straight. Let An-na speak."

Wasmaggi motioned, and Anna stood before the Masaki.

"Soon," she began, "Manway and Jappah and Oneson and Blue and Barkah and Jappah and Armot, so many fine, young men, will be hunters and Marci and Jonquilla will be women ready for marriage, just as Sayhoo is now and as are Maltra and Costill and the other women who have joined our village. And one day Love and Threesome and Twoman and Coanna and Penny will join them, and the village will live on.

"When Fraylie was killed, and Mike and Spiker, and when Trulk's village was destroyed and almost everybody was killed, we knew the forest had changed. So we must change.

"Ranford and Connie and I came from that world outside this one. The forest did not give us birth; the forest gave us rebirth, because once we were of that other world. We had to live in your world before we became Masaki.

"I'll tell you something of that world if you will listen. I know you will not believe me, but I ask you to listen. Masaki...."

In one evening by the fire, Anna tried as simply as she could to tell the Masaki something of the world which surrounded them: many people of many colors, villages so large one cannot see from one end to the other, animals never imagined by the Masaki, tools for every kind of work, gardens that stretched from village to village, rivers one could not see across.

There was laughter. Anna was telling a joke.

"What color were the men who captured you?"

"One white; the rest brown."

"What color were the men who killed Tannee?"

"White and brown."

"What color was Lucky?"

"White."

"What did their knives look like?"

"Long, wide, sharp."

"Were they made from something like this pot?"

"Yes."

"Did they have long drums?"

"Yes."

"What did they do with the long drums?"

"They killed people."

Some of the people believed; some of the people doubted; some of the people disbelieved.

"It is your right not to believe Anna," she said. "I would not believe either. But what I tell you is true, whether you believe me or not. I've always told you the truth. But if there is anyone to say

314

otherwise, let him or her speak and Anna will sit down." No one spoke; no one had cause to speak.

"Then, whether you believe what I say or not, you must believe Wasmaggi. He tells the truth because long ago, in his memory, he knows even the Masaki came here from the world out there."

Wasmaggi fumbled with his words. "It is true, what An-na says. We came to the forest and the forest became our mother. I don't know why. I don't know where we came from. Our mothers and fathers brought us here long time past, so much past I forget.

"At first we afraid, afraid of the forest, afraid of the jaguar, afraid of the alligator. But we brought the guena and the antara and our hunters played the music we brought and the forest liked our music. We made the drums and our people takied to the music. We had the chavin on our side, and pachacamiac, and ...." Wasmaggi talked on.

Widel whispered to Anna. "What's a chavin?"

"The cat god of the Incas, I think. The jaguar."

"And pachacamiac?"

"That's the word from before that he remembers. Some kind of creator god or, maybe, earth god. I don't know. I can't remember."

"And takied?"

"That I remember. A taki is a dance."

Whether the Indians of South America arrived via the Bering Strait from Asia, or from Europe by way of Greenland, or from the South Sea Islands or from Africa via drifting rafts, or whether they are the lost tribes of Israel (and setting aside theories of human origination and evolution in South America as the least likely explanation of the Indians' habitation of the continent), anthropologists and historians cannot find the beginnings of South America's Indian civilizations and cultures.

The beginnings as well as the endings of the so-called "lost" civilizations of Central America, the Mayans, Aztecs, and Toltecs, are still clouded in mystery. So, too, the Inca civilization of Peru and Chile. Were these migrating people(s), stopping every now and

315

then for a few hundred years to reorganize? Were they separate waves of migration by unrelated people(s)?

The Inca, at least, sent its people deep into the rain forest. Why? For settlements, for trade goods, for slaves and sacrificial maidens? Who knows. But the great mystery is known, if not the answer, and the mystery is this: The Mayan-Aztec-Toltec-Incan prehistory civilizations were unmatched anywhere in the world for their achievements in astronomical calculation, writing, weaving, road and aqueduct building, architecture, temple and home building - and the Amazon Indians both as a whole and as individual tribes seem to have evolved their cultures less and to have invented and innovated less than almost any primitive people on earth.

Were the rain forest Indians in South America before the Mayans, Aztecs, and Toltecs? And before the Incas established their vast holdings? How, then, did certain Inca words and vague Incan concepts come to the Masaki? The only logical explanation is by some kind of contact, whether fleeing invading people or by trade and other social intercourse.

But the Masaki had no knowledge or memory of either. Until recently, in Wasmaggi's youth, the only people on earth, the Masaki, did not know any other people existed, not until the creatures appeared, and the creatures were not considered people, men, but some kind of aberration created by the forest, the same explanation used to explain the whites, *made by the forest.*

None of this speculation helped. If anything, it further isolated the Masaki and made more dramatic the Masaki's situation. They were not beyond reach, had not been beyond reach for a long time. Only other men seeking other dreams in other areas of the Amazon had slowed the inevitable discovery of the Masaki. But now the agents of IBAMA, Electronorte, CVRD, and FUNAI, taking over for SPI, and hundreds, thousands of bandeirantes, cangaceiros, and tropas de resgate acting on their own were entering the sertáo. Some, the engineers and planners for Electronorte, were working on plans for damming the Trombetas River; others, the Ferrazs and the Newcastles, were looking to loot and rape the land before it was flooded. Efforts would be made to remove indigenous people, but if they could not be found or moved, then, well, they were expendable. After all, there were so few of them.

No specifics were known to Widel and Anna; they knew only that outsiders had come and more would follow. What to do, that was the biggest question.

Wasmaggi had finished talking. He was looking at Anna. What did he expect? What was she supposed to say? She hadn't been listening.

"Repeat that again, Wasmaggi. I'm not sure I understood."

He had asked Anna to listen, and she hadn't. Wasmaggi was exasperated. "You have a plan for the Masaki."

I don't have a plan, for God's sake; I don't know what to do; why would these people do anything I say, she asked herself? She looked at the Masakis and saw nothing but bewilderment and fear. Oh, shit, she thought; oh, the shit of living hell, and I'm in it up to my mouth. Jesus, I wish Connie was here.

Out loud, she said, "Masaki, if you understand anything that has been said, please hold up your hand. Just lift it up if you have any idea what has been told to you."

Amazingly, a number of hands were raised; not surprisingly, the hands belonged either to the women from Trulk's village or to those who had participated in the rescue. They had seen enough to recognize the danger even if they did not understand it.

But there were two other hands raised, Xingu's and Sarahguy's. God bless my friends, Anna said to herself; the blind leads the blind.

One of the women stood up. "May a woman speak? I am Noisle, one of those shamed by Lackee, not fit for marriage, and when Lackee gone, shamed by Milo and not fit for marriage. And when Milo gone, no hunter would even look at me. Who wants woman who has had alligator, they said? Who wants Noisle because she can sleep with any man she chooses?

"I not choose to sleep with any man, only one, my husband. But I have no husband, never had a husband because no one would have me. I know that Lackee said I was no good; wanted me for self. Even Milo who I trusted only wanted use me. When Milo no more, no one wanted me. I had but one friend, Tannee. No man look at her either. We used and damaged. Now she gone; Noisle alone. But maybe not alone. Think maybe An-na might be friend. Don't know, hard to understand, cannot dream of such things as she says are true, but Noisle believe her. If friend, then An-na tell friend the truth. That all Noisle need know. Why you doubt your friend?"

A welcome ally, thought Anna, but my God, what a way to have lived. "I thank Noisle; I thank a friend."

Mansella stood. "I've seen a white man kill my own; I've seen my own try to kill others of my own. The forest plays with us. The forest tests us. I'll go where An-na leads."

The faith of many Masakis in Anna's leadership was heartwarming and sincere, and ill deserved, Anna said. "I don't know where to lead the Masaki. Please. Understand that I don't know where I could lead you that would be safe forever. Wasmaggi has led us here. For the moment, it is as safe as any place."

"And here," Wasmaggi said, "we can learn to live as people among other people."

"*As people among other people*. What an amazing man," Widel said later. "He's a dreamer. I still believe he knows far more about the world than he lets on."

"I've come to believe," Anna replied, "he knew we were coming; he was waiting for us. He didn't know whether we would come as branco bandeirantes or as friends, but he knew the outside world would come one day and one day he would have to lead his people to a safe place. Only he didn't realize there is no safe place once civilization begins to move in."

"So he changed his tactic. Hide, and while in hiding, learn how to live. If that is true, he is the most remarkable man ever."

"The American Indians, the red savages or whatever they were called, did the same thing. Chief Joseph, Black Elk, Sitting Bull, Sequoia were wise men even though our ancestors saw them as ignorant, primitive people. God, Widel, how I've come to resent the word primitive, right up there with pagan."

"So what are you, we, going to do?"

"I don't know. I just don't know."

318

When Anna walked to her cooking fire the next morning, Wasmaggi was sitting there, waiting for conversation.

"We talk," he said.

"You'll have to wait. I can't talk before.... Damn it, Wasmaggi. At least let me take care of a few things." Anna walked into the forest ringing the island.

When she returned, she asked if Wasmaggi had eaten. He had not. Anna produced a small amount of cassava bread.

"Widel has gone with the hunters. Hunting takes more time now that we have so many extra women to feed and because the hunters have to be careful not to leave tracks and signs."

"We come to point."

"Okay. What's on your mind?"

"Wasmaggi want to see those things you talk about, big villages, big gardens, big rivers, many people. Know An-na tell truth. Know An-na has seen that of which she tells."

"You believe me?"

"Wasmaggi believe because Wasmaggi see once."

"Yeah, with your coca leaves."

"Not with leaves; with eyes."

"You mean you've really seen other people?"

"Wasmaggi never tell anyone before."

"Tell me, for God's sake."

Before the time of the others, Wasmaggi said, there had been rumors of other people in the forest. When the whole Masaki tribe gathered one time before the others came, a group of young males from the various villages decided to check out the rumors. None of the youths were yet hunters, so it was more a game than a serious endeavor. There were twelve or fifteen boys all eager to prove their skills and their manhood, and so they worked their way deep into the forest toward the rising sun.

They spent a night in the forest, and on the second day they continued their walk, then spent another night in the forest. They knew their parents would be worried and angry, but a couple of boys dared the other youths to keep going, calling those who didn't

319

want to continue cowards and babies and women. Wasmaggi, younger than most, was one who would have turned around, but when his courage was challenged, he kept going.

Several days later, the boys heard sounds they had never heard. A great roaring and much talk and loud crashes came to their ears. A monster, they thought, and many wanted to run away. Two of the boys crept forward, daring the others to follow. They came to a huge clearing.

A monster was uprooting trees and creatures of some kind were cutting off the limbs with knives that made earsplitting sounds. Creatures were running all around, shouting unfamiliar words. The monster would grab another tree and pull it out of the ground, and smoke came out of it and noise such as they never had heard.

Some of the creatures were cutting at a gigantic tree, and there was a lot of yelling, and the tree fell over dead. One of the creatures was caught under the tree and the other creatures attacked the tree and took the creature, and another monster came and dug a big hole and the creature was put into it and the monster buried him, and then the other creatures went back to killing the trees.

The boys watched for a long time. Some female creatures came and made a noise with a thing and all the creatures went into a big shelter.

After a while the female creatures came out and the other creatures ran after them and some fell to the ground and the creatures got on top of the females and there was a lot of yelling and laughing. Until dark, the boys watched, and then a creature came from somewhere, the *patrão*, he was called. Wasmaggi remembered that word. And he rolled a big pot out of the shelter and yelled *cachaça* (Brazilian white rum), and the creatures drank from the big pot.

Later, the patrão yelled a few times and the creatures wore bright lights on their heads (parongas, kerosene headlamps) and went back to killing trees. In the dark, one of the creatures ran for the forest. A long drum spoke and the man fell to the ground.

At that point the boys withdrew, not knowing what they had seen. The next morning they began the long walk back toward the temporary camp. Along the way, they pledged that they never would tell anyone about what they had seen. It would be a secret.

Two days from the camp, they were met by an angry party of hunters sent to find them. They never did tell what they had seen, not even at the next gathering of the tribe, the gathering upon which the creatures descended with such destruction and death. Never until now.

"So, all these years you and the other boys knew about other people and never told."

"That is true."

"It must have made quite an impression on you. How did you manage to keep it secret?"

"Wasmaggi only one from this village. Who would believe?"

"But the other boys? They had a secret and someone to share it with. It must have leaked out somewhere."

"No. Secret is to death. No Masaki would tell. Is honor."

"Now you tell. Have you broken your honor?"

"Have. But An-na must know. Maybe help?"

"Maybe."

"And because Wasmaggi want see other people, the ones An-na say are good. Wasmaggi believe An-na. Masaki must meet good people from other tribes."

"It's a long way. A very long way. You would have to wear clothing."

"What that?"

"Oh. We are a long way. Clothing is like another skin, one that would cover you so no one would see your.... Anna would have to wear clothing that covered her...female parts, from neck to knees."

"That very stupid."

"But other people always cover themselves. Don't want anyone to see real skin - and don't want to see the real skin of other people."

"Can make from grass, then, as An-na say."

"No. Must make from cloth."

"Not know cloth."

"What a long way we have to go. Such a long way."

Anna repeated Wasmaggi's revelation for Widel, including his remarkable memory for the words cachaça and patrão, and when she concluded, she said, "I think I can sooner send a Masaki to Mars or Venus than I can send these people to any outpost of civilization. And with greater success. There's only one place on earth where I think they would fit in, and that's with the aborigines of Australia, and I'm not even sure about that."

"Then you've given up about teaching them the modern world?"

"I don't know where to start. Or if I should start. I thought the idea about walking out of the forest with a whole bunch of Indians who could speak a few words of English, who wore clothes, who jumped from thousands of years of isolation into a world of electricity and automobiles and machines without batting an eyelash was really cool."

"And it can't be done?"

"Oh, it could be done - if the Masaki were guaranteed a few hundred square miles of forest, and if no one invaded the land, and if the meeting with other people was allowed to happen gradually and naturally, and if no one came to convert them into something they aren't, and if civilized people saw them for what they are, innocent and happy, and if there was time. Too many ifs. Too many exploiters. Too little protection."

"What would happen if we took, if we could, just one family to civilization? They could come back and help in the transition, a Masaki family of two worlds, as it were."

"Okay, Widel. Let's suppose a family agreed. And let's suppose we knew the direction to take. We walk, and then we walk some more. And then we come to the outskirts of a town. What then? First, we need clothing. Can you imagine what would happen if you walked into a store?

"You'd be arrested. So instead of that, you steal some clothes. Arrested anyway. Suppose you could talk your way out of jail and somebody gave you clothes. What do you do for food? You walk around with your bows and arrows and spears. There goes a dog. Might be something to eat. Do you kill it? Jail again. Somebody says something to you in Portuguese. Can you answer them? You speak English. Nobody else does. You're naked and you've killed a dog.

"Then I walk in, tits hanging out, bare assed, holding the hand of a naked child and followed by a man and a woman also armed and also naked and with a child or two. What I see is not pretty. What I see is disaster. I'm not going."

"What if we could find a mission?"

"What if? Think about it. Even if we did and even if the priests or ministers or whatever were sympathetic, we're gone a year, two years maybe. Think the world will stand still while we experiment?"

"Then?"

"That's the hell of it. You and I could walk out, leave the Masaki behind. A white family might stand a chance, especially when that family has a small child. I'm not ready to do that."

"So we stay and hide and fight when we have to."

"That's the conclusion I've reached."

"And Penny?"

"She takes her chances. Life is not fair. I understand that. I also understand that life is what we make it and that we can even out the odds if we can keep our sense of values and have courage. I'm going to take my chances with the Masakis because that's what I am, a Masaki."

"Then it's settled, Anna. No more talk of giving up. I hoped that's what you'd say, that for better or worse we'd work out our lives here with the Masaki. So tell them. Tell them that we are the people of the forest and that we will always be the people of the forest, no matter what happens."

"We will tell them tonight at the fire."

"And...."

"And what?"

"You can tell them that never have I loved you more than right now."

"Widel...."

"I'm not leading up to anything, Anna. Honest. Not what you think, anyway."

TWENTY-TWO

Wasmaggi's face registered disappointment when Anna spoke to the Masakis gathered at the fire. He really thought he might get to see some of the things about which Anna had spoken only yesterday. As old as he was, he was not too old to anticipate new experiences, a complete contradiction when one realized he had not changed or thought to change throughout his entire life.

One a scale of one to ten, his innovative processes scored a zero or at least were closer to zero than to one. He imagined but did nothing with his thoughts.

Widel wondered if Wasmaggi could. Could Wasmaggi invent something? Not likely. Even when he was given the glass bottle on the first day, he could not imagine a use for it, and so he gave it away. His one moment of inspiration, perhaps a man has but one such moment in a whole lifetime, was to make Anna the medicine woman. And that was inspired, Widel thought.

Wasmaggi had seen other men, had seen machinery, had spent a whole day watching other men work, yet he kept it a secret until it became a non-event and he dismissed the experience as never happening.

He thought there might be other people, but that was speculation, not tied to any conscious awareness, not even related to the people he had watched working!

And Wasmaggi was not alone. It was the nature of the primitive man and woman. Anna hated the word primitive, but that was the proper word. But, and here a thought of wonder, Wasmaggi had insights about his own people, and about the whites, that would have done social scientists proud. Wasmaggi knew his people. He was more than their physician; he was father and friend, comforter

324

and confessor all rolled up in one person. He was the Masaki memory and the Masaki mind and he was totally, utterly unprepared for and incapable of being a functioning member of modern civilization.

And there was about Wasmaggi an innocent purity that in its own setting made him remarkable. He was the kindest, gentlest, most loving man Widel ever had known. To live in his shadow was to live with God.

What a stupid analogy, Widel said to himself, and yet he said it again and believed it.

Anna was finishing her words. "We will play the drums softly. We will be afraid, but we will have courage. We will not make war, but we will fight to save our lands and our people."

"I think that bastard tried to screw us again, Hans. Ferraz should have been back long before this, or at least Newcastle should have brought us word."

"Unless there's been trouble or Ferraz couldn't find any women. We'll either get our money back or kill him." Wittenberg was angry.

"It was a stupid investment."

"You liked it at the time."

"What I liked was the idea of having all those fresh whores Ferraz promised."

"Not one of which you could have, Hermann."

"I know. But the idea was tasty. A hundred Indian women, every one of them used to being undressed. Hans, I already promised some of them to a few of our better clients."

"Well, you may have to unpromise. There's still time, though. And I did agree that we'd wait ten months for the first delivery."

"Well, I like to keep track of my investments. At least we should know that Ferraz is going to be able to deliver. Isn't that why you sent Newcastle, to protect our investment?"

"Hermann, I don't know why I sent Newcastle. You were right; it wasn't a good idea. The whole idea was lousy."

"I think we should send Jorge to find out what's going on. Wouldn't take him but a day in the helicopter to fly up river and at least find the barge we gave Ferraz."

Hans Wittenberg and Hermann Lippstadt agreed. Jorge Jachal would do a little scouting; checking on their investment, the two Germans said, hoping it was still viable. Their investment was small enough. Pin money. The greater investment was in a man they didn't trust; the money was irrelevant; Paulo Ferraz was not.

Unlike Newcastle, Jachal was educated and at ease in any society. That he had arranged the disappearance of hundreds if not thousands of disgruntled Argentineans during the trouble years of the Peróns made him desirable for the former Nazis' clandestine work.

Following the sketchy map drawn by Ferraz, Jachal's pilot retraced the water route taken by Ferraz. That was the easy part. The hard part was spotting the barge with its palm hut tied to the river bank somewhere under the overhanging canopy.

"You've only got five or six minutes more, Jorge," the pilot said, "before we have to go back for fuel. Even if you find the barge, there's no place to land."

Although they flew over the barge twice, they did not see it, thanks to the skill of the architect who had planned the whole bandeira. Jachal went back to Wittenberg and Lippstadt and reported his failure.

"Go back tomorrow, Jorge, and take a helicopter with pontoons. Find that barge. And find Ferraz." Almost as an afterthought, Wittenberg asked, "Do you think the Indians could have got him?"

"I doubt it. All the villages are small, few hunters. Ferraz had enough firepower to take on an army. And the men he took with him are all experienced cangaceiros. They know the sertáo, and they know how to deal with the Indians."

"Well, find the barge. Let's see if that tells us anything."

The barge was found the next day, artfully concealed, its Indian shelter beautifully constructed. There was no question in Jachal's mind that Paulo Ferraz had every intention of using the barge and of following through with his idea. But where were Ferraz and the women? Already the shelter was beginning to look time worn and bug infested, although apparently no one ever had used it.

Jachal reported again. "Ferraz and Newcastle are still out there in the jungle. I might be able to round up some bandeirantes and cangaceiros and go look for Ferraz, although by now their trail will be colder than snow."

"Could you spot them from the air?" asked Lippstadt.

"Might, but it's not likely. All you see is the canopy. Millions of people could hide in the jungle, don't even have to hide, and you'd never see them. Even the Indian villages don't appear, most of them being under the trees. There are some clearings, nothing large enough to land in. Some tribes clear the land of the trees, but not where Ferraz said he was going."

"Well," said Lippstadt, "I hate to leave ends dangling, and sure as hell I don't want anyone to get the idea that they're dealing with a bunch of weak frauleins when they do business with us. I think we should send Jorge into the jungle."

"Let's give it another week. In the meantime, we send someone to watch the barge, just in case Ferraz shows up. Whoever we send can contact us by radio. I wish we had given Newcastle a radio. Too late now, I guess. Let's just hope we hear from somebody. What say, Hermann? One more week?"

"One more week. Then we'll let Jorge go after the prick."

While Lippstadt and Wittenberg waited, others went after the riches of the rain forest, which is to say the riches provided by alligator skins and jaguar hides and wild parrots and other much sought after birds. Most men would not go deeply into the forest. For all intents and by all perceptions, it was a very dark territory, a living green hell of death and mystery. No one went alone; few went in pairs; most went in parties of some size, eight, ten, a dozen men. They hunted the shores of the rivers, and when they had eliminated the alligator and jaguar population, reluctantly they went deeper into the jungle.

Four days into the sertáo, one such bandeira found the remains of Rangel's group, and a little farther on they found two more bodies, those of Ferraz and Simón. There was not enough left to identify any man. The animals, birds and insects had done their part in recycling the bodies. But there was enough left to make identification likely. An initial etched on a machete blade; a name carved into a pistol handle; brass belt buckles and shirt buttons, a few pots and pans, all hastily gathered up by the retreating expedition. The arrows were plain enough; they had prevailed against the guns.

The word got around quickly. Six men had been killed by the Indians, and when the word reached Wittenberg and Lippstadt, they had Jachal check it out. There was Ferraz's special Argentino pistol, a machete with Rogelio's name scratched on the blade, Eneas's flashy belt buckle with his initials cast is script.

"Newcastle among the bodies?" Wittenberg asked.

"Don't know. No one was able to identify the remains. The jungle acts fast when fresh meat is left around. No AK-47 though."

"So he could still be alive?"

"Could be, along with a couple of others. They might have split up."

"Or got killed somewhere else."

"Or that. What do you want me to do?"

Lippstadt and Wittenberg looked at each other. There was nothing to be done. Finally Lippstadt asked, "Do you know the men who found the bodies?"

"No, not really. Seen a couple of them. They're just common bandeirantes, mostly animal hunters. They go into an area and clean it out and move on. Don't know where they sell their goods; maybe ultimately to us through one of our procuradores."

"Well," said Wittenberg, "I don't want to get into it. We can kiss our money goodbye; piss Ferraz goodbye. Maybe someday Newcastle will show up." Suddenly changing the subject, Wittenberg asked, "Jorge, what would it take to have our own men hunting the jaguar?"

"More than it's worth; far more than it's worth. What do you pay for a skin, a few hundred centavos? You couldn't buy a man's ammunition and food for that amount. Herr Lippstadt can tell you you'd be deep in red ink if you had to outfit your own hunters."

"He's right, Hans. We would lose a bundle of money if we went private in the animal business. The system we have works fine just the way it is."

"Yes. I'm just looking for something to take the edge off our loss."

"Then be thankful it's not more. Myself, I was rather looking forward to one of the leftover ladies."

"Is that all you can think of?"

"That and money, and the money is so I can have that." Lippstadt laughed his characteristic cruel laugh. "Jorge, send me a fresh young lady tonight."

"We don't have any fresh young women."

"Then go and find one, someone from up on the hill. Two. One for Hans. I'll pay. I'll even pay for one for you."

Jachal went out, shaking his head. Lippstadt knew Jachal would fail. Jachal would bring back a fat old pig who could take on the entire cidaae flutuante. Lippstadt would tear her anyway. "I was so counting on Ferraz," he said to Wittenberg.

Not only did the word get around, but the word grew: those found had been killed by a large tribe of fierce and savage warriors; must have been at least a hundred of them to have so clearly defeated the armed bandeira. They murdered the men just for the fun of it.

For all intents and purposes, for a time the exaggerated word closed the western approaches to the lands of the Masaki. The many workers for Electronorte, guards and cooks, surveyors and engineers, common laborers and camp followers, effectively blocked the northern approach to the Masaki lands. An eastern access was too impractical. An approach from the south was filled with so many impassable swamps as to be impossible.

The net effect of the story of murdering Indians and of the swamps and of intense government activity and sanctions meant no one entered the immediate Masaki territory for an extended period of time.

The Masakis had been given a reprieve.

Wasmaggi taught the music of the drums; Anna and some of the women learned to play the guena and the antara; the people takied. Life became placid and carefree.

The women from Trulk's village found a brazilwood tree and made dyes of reds and purples. The children colored their faces, and their parents laughed, and soon the parents were splashing themselves with red. Anna let her hair grow, and a few women followed suit. There was time for games and lovemaking. On one of the hunting excursions, someone found sara plants and brought back the kernels, and a crop of corn was planted in the garden. The swamp island was not Eden, but it was close.

Or would have been had not two small groups within the larger village been unhappy. They did not allow a consensus to be formed on all matters. They went along with most decisions, but on two they did not agree.

A few of the older Masaki were ready to go back to their traditional home. Hakma and Magwa, Soomar and Janus, and Moremew and Tilla. They were not outwardly vocal, but they were not content to stay in the swamp.

The second group was comprised mostly of the women from Trulk's village with Sayhoo and Mansella, those without husbands.

The first group only wanted to go home, to return to their real home. The second group wanted to find mates. Both groups appealed to Anna for assistance and guidance.

One day Hakma, Soomar, and Moremew approached Anna's fire. Could they sit? They were made welcome. Anna is a great medicine woman, you are great hunters and other formalities were exchanged. Serious business was at hand.

"I've been chosen to speak," Moremew said, "because I knew Con-nie best."

That statement by itself gave witness to the seriousness of what was to come. To speak the name of the dead was as close to being a taboo as any behavior the Masakis' exhibited.

"Connie spoke often of your courage and skills."

"Then An-na will listen?"

"Anna will listen carefully."

Moremew poured out a well rehearsed litany of feelings: the wish to be on familiar ground, homesickness, the sense of being lost in the forest, the hope for long lives with their wives in the old village of their birth.

"Anna understands. Sometimes Anna has those feelings herself."

That Anna could relate to them lifted a great weight. The hunters had feared that she would not know what they felt.

"Would Anna return with us?"

"Moremew, Hakma, Soomar," she addressed each one personally and directly, "I have desired to return to our village and to our stream and to the familiar trails, and to the fire beside which I was married, and to the village where my child was born.

"But Anna must be the medicine women for all Masaki. Wasmaggi might be the medicine man again, but he becomes old and cannot be expected to live forever. He cannot make the trip back to our village, nor can Lucknew and Pollyque. What should I do about them? You know in your hearts I cannot leave them or the others who wish to stay here.

"And there is the danger of the creatures, the other people who so cruelly kill our people. Even if the old people could make the journey, what would happen to them if the others came and attacked us?

"I don't have a ready answer for myself. If most say stay here, I must stay here. But if you must go, then I say go. I would not keep you where you don't want to be. And if you go, go with Anna's love. I'll remember you always until I'm called by the forest."

Tears appeared in Anna's eyes and spilled down her cheeks. She reached out and touched each man's shoulder. "I'll miss you," she said.

Anna had wanted to say only that if the hunters had to go, then as far as she was concerned, they could go. But the way she expressed it bound the hunters even closer to her and to the larger village. They wanted to return to their ancient home; they could not and would not leave Anna.

When, a few days later, the women came to Anna's fire, she had been forewarned by Mansella. She was no better prepared than she had been for Moremew and the hunters, but the forthcoming request was no surprise.

331

Sayhoo spoke for the women. "Does An-na love Sayhoo?"

"Yes. Maybe Anna loves Sayhoo too much. I know what you feel. I, too, had similar feelings."

"But you had many hunters to chose."

"That is true, although I wanted only one."

"That is difference. You had someone. None of us have someone."

Anna noted that Mansella was not among the women. Perhaps she had worked out an arrangement with Sarahguy and Joshway. It would be a good thing if she had. Sarahguy needed someone to help; she had not been well since before Love was born. Joshway had not complained and had done the woman's work without complaint. And Mansella needed a man, just as Joshway needed a full time wife.

"Does An-na know how we feel?"

Anna looked off into space, revisiting her years of frustration and desire, her loneliness, her single encounter with Connie, dear Connie who lived with her own frustrations and with whom Anna shared the almost insatiable physical passions for Widel. Yes, Anna knew. To have paraded in front of her week after week, month after month, year after year the object of her desire and not being able to have it. Yes, she knew.

"Does An-na know what it like to see husbands and wives making love, to hear their love sounds, to know their happiness?"

Yes, Anna knew that, too. A thousand time she had seen a women give a sign, a raised eye, a turned hip, a lifted breast, a nod of the head, and a thousand times she had seen that woman's husband's erection as he rushed to their love bed, and a thousand times she had heard the joyful sounds.

"Does An-na know what is like to see Ran-ford and An-na make ready for love and to know they are lovers?"

No, Anna had never known that other people saw and knew and heard. Her lovemaking with Widel was private. Even when Widel betrayed his desire, they had gone into their house and out of sight had enjoyed their mating. No, Anna never had realized that making love with Widel had been anything other than private.

332

"We cannot know such pleasure because there are not men to be our husbands. An-na knows that?"

"Anna knows that, and Anna worries for you. And Anna wishes it did not have to be."

"Sayhoo knows that An-na knows that Sayhoo made love with Fraylie. Sayhoo knows never could marry Fraylie, so Sayhoo knows must have other man for husband. Once Sayhoo said no other man. That angry Sayhoo talk."

"What would you have me do, Sayhoo. I can't just make a bunch of men. I wish I could."

"Some say let hunters take more wives. Let Ran-ford take more wife. Let...."

Oh, God, not Widel, Anna thought silently, the only possible solution staring her in the face. I couldn't bear it; another woman in Widel's bed? Taking my place? Where I should be? The son-of-a-bitch would enjoy it, too. He always has envied Walkin. God damn him; I'll bet this is his idea.

"No more talk about being in someone else's bed. I won't hear of it." Anna was angry. The very idea sickened her.

"Not even if hunter want?"

"What hunter? Who have you talked to?"

"What make An-na so mad? You think all women want Ran-ford? No woman want your husband."

"Why? What's wrong with Widel?"

"An-na, let Milken speak. Sayhoo tease. No man here for women. We all young; want young men; need young men. They no come here; we wish go find."

"That's...that's...impossible."

"You no give choice. Stay here, we never happy, be like old women who cannot hunt. So we depend on hunters who must feed own families. We see one way make everybody happy."

"And that is?"

"You give us medicine make all have baby, then we leave. Start own village. Have babies and babies grow and have wives and husbands and make more babies and we happy."

"I don't have a medicine that makes babies. Besides...."

"You have no-baby medicine, so you have baby medicine."

"It doesn't work that way."

"Milo said it does. He said medicine man has medicine to make babies."

"He was not telling the truth. He was using you. You all slept with the medicine man. Which of you had a baby?"

"He was preparing us."

"For what?"

"For marriage and for having babies."

"He was screwing you in more ways than one. Don't you understand? When you slept with him, you gave him pleasure. He gave you some medicine so you wouldn't have a baby, his baby. When he was finished with you, he let you go but he didn't stop the no-baby medicine. Then you get married, still no baby. Then you ask why no baby and he says you were not prepared enough and should sleep with him more. But some women have babies. Think about it; think hard. Who had the babies? Women who displeased Milo. He was finished with them. But he wasn't finished with you because you went to his bed willingly and performed well for him. Babies come only one way, and that is when a man plants his seed in you and starts a baby. Anna has no medicine for that. You need a man."

How she wished she hadn't said that last bit. That was the whole issue, the women's need for men, not only to provide for them and to protect them but to love them and to father their children.

A young woman with the name Blie said to Anna, "You speak with knowledge. I was with Lackee. I was with Milo. I had no baby. When I got married, still no baby. My husband made me go back to Milo. But no baby. I said to husband of shame. I gave him no child. He said tell me what Milo do and we will do it. I no have baby, and now I no have husband."

One by one, the women spoke. Almost all had been taken by Lackee; each had been used by Milo. Anna guessed that some of the women had been taking the no-baby medicine too long. Perhaps they never would have a child.

"I am Flower, a name given me by Lackee. My parents called me Smalsh. They died when I was a young girl and Lackee cared for me. I was his serva and his misty."

"How old were you?"

"I was eight when he made me his serva, ten when he said I could be his misty."

"I don't know the word serva."

"It is one who does what must be done."

"Would the word be servant?"

"Yes. I his serva."

"And I don't know the word misty."

Flower turned he head. "That when...when.... I cannot say."

"That's when he raped you."

"That's when he said I was his misty."

"Mistress. Is that the word?"

"Yes."

Only Sayhoo did not tell of disgusting mistreatment and abuse. How could these women have been so misused and still want husbands, Anna asked herself? Is the desire for children so ingrained that such women would risk everything to have one?

"An-na, we wish to leave this village," Sayhoo told the medicine woman. "There is nothing here for us. We would go and make our own village and cry our tears among ourselves. We thought perhaps An-na would know a better way. There is no better way."

That was the bitter truth, and it was going to be the truth for the young women of the village nearing marrying age, Jonquilla and Marci. Once again the obvious solution was to find a Masaki village and hope that it had a surplus of men.

"Before you do anything, let Anna think. There has to be a way to deal with this."

Aboriginals seem to have an endless amount of patience, and so the two disgruntled groups waited either for an answer to their concerns from Anna or for the forest to inspire an insight. By now the entire population was aware and involved. But awareness did not always mean sympathetic understanding and being involved often meant discussion if not outright argument.

It was during such an argument that Walkin and Westman returned to the island with upsetting news. Other people were in the forest not too far from the swamp.

A council was called. How many people, what were they doing, what color were they, how close were they? Westman and Walkin could not answer many of the questions.

A party should be sent to kill the intruders, an idea to which Widel objected strenuously. He proposed an alternative. Two hunters would go out. He would be one of them. If anyone knew anything about the others, it was Widel. Normally, the second hunter would be the jaguar hunter, the most expert tracker and the most experienced in observation. But there was no jaguar hunter, and there was no volunteer.

It wasn't that the hunters were afraid; it was because of Widel's deformed leg and limp. In spite of his valued participation in dealing with Sampson's treacherous men and his daring attack on the white man, some hunters still thought his forest skills had not been honed sharply enough.

"I'll go with Ran-ford," Mansella said, "if the hunters are afraid. I'm not afraid. My father taught me, and now I teach Oneson. Ran-ford is a hunter."

There were objections, Anna's included, and all were dismissed. There was no question about Mansella's forest skills. There were no questions about Widel's skills. But there were questions about Widel's ability to move silently and unseen so as to be close enough to observe the strangers without being detected and killed.

Anna's objection, oddly enough, had nothing to do with Widel and Mansella. She had been on too many journeys with men, and Connie had been on many more, to object to that. She objected because Widel did not seem to have the instantaneous instinct to kill. He had to think about it, and thinking would mean indecision, and indecision could mean death.

In the end, of course, Anna agreed, and with the whole village in attendance, she watched Widel and Mansella enter the swamp water. At the last minute Soomar and Walkin also stepped into the water and followed Mansella and Widel.

Twenty men were in the forest. From a distance is was hard to tell what they were doing. They weren't hunting. A dozen men had rifles and acted like guards. The other six had many strange devices and orange and white and yellow banners attached to long spears.

Widel knew what was happening. The outsiders were surveying the land. Widel couldn't know, but what he saw was one of the scores of surveying parties sent into the sertáo by IBAMA to make rough onsite maps of the vast area that eventually would be flooded by Electronorte. The surveyors were no threat, and their guards were present because of Indians and wild animals. Unless threatened, the guards had no interest in either Indian or animal.

To Widel, surveying meant but one thing: development, people in gigantic numbers. He did not know that in time the land on which he stood would be covered with water.

The surveyors moved about freely, spending little time in any one place. When they approached the edge of the swamp, one of them climbed a trees and with binoculars viewed the large area. A lot of shouting occurred and on the ground a lot of writing took place. Widel assumed the shouting largely was heights and distance and that on the ground, using simple trig functions, the measurements were translated into map lines.

Suddenly it possessed his mind. Smoke from the cooking fires! He directed Walkin to rush to the island. Put out all fires. Hide in the woods. Make no sound. As Walkin rushed off, Widel explained to Soomar and Mansella. "Must not see our fires. Must not know anyone is in the swamp."

Walkin returned; behind him were the hunters, armed to the teeth, ready for battle.

"No attack," Widel told them. "Even if we kill all of them, others will be sent to find them. We will start a war we cannot live to finish."

When night came, the hunters ringed the surveyors' camp. The surveyors were gathered by their fire, a small one, noted Widel, deciding that the men in front of him had some forest experienced and would be much more aware of unordinary noises in the dark. Someone's foot slipped on the dew soaked ground underfoot. The noise was slight. The surveyor's talking continued; the guards had quietly shifted the position of their weapons. They gave no other outward sign acknowledging the noise. It could have been a natural one, but they had heard it, and they were alert.

Each hunter would spend the night on guard. Tomorrow they would gather and Widel would tell them what he had knew, which was, he reluctantly acknowledged, exactly nothing.

For several days, pairs of hunters kept watch over the surveyors, and as Widel had said they would, the intruders left the forest on their own accord.

That creatures, men, in such numbers could approach the swamp with ease upset everyone, none more than Anna. "They just walked in," she shouted at Widel. "Just like that!" Then she asked the question on everyone's mind. "How far away are their villages?" She felt her chest contract; the Masakis were being squeezed. She had trouble breathing.

In his ignorance, Widel misunderstood the purpose of the survey. He deemed it a new highway, and he compounded his mistake by suggesting that the highway would be too close to the swamp for comfort and that the Masaki should consider moving far away.

Move they would. Widel had said they should. Soomar verbalized the hope that they would move back to their original home.

What the Masakis also did not know was that the experienced IBAMA guards had long since discovered Indian signs, not many, but enough to indicate an Indian presence. That information would be forwarded to FUNAI. The National Indian Federation dedicated to preserving Indian culture would send in its own people, and instead of passively mapping the area, the FUNAI men would aggressively search out the Indians and force their submission and relocation.

That would take some time. Funding and planning might take a couple of years, but it was as inevitable as was the flooding. It was during those intervening years that Ferraz had hoped his bandeiras could take the young Indian women.

338

But FUNAI was not the old Indian Protection Service, the SPI. Government money was available; Electronorte put up money; a dozen social activist agencies put up money; millions of reals from individual citizens flowed into the coffers of IBAMA and FUNAI to save the animals and certain plants and the Indians. Greenpeace, the Sierra Club, the Walden Society, even the Save the Whale organization sent both money and workers. A dozen religious organizations sent missionaries to Christianize the Indians before the government civilized them. There was a mad rush to save everything, most of it well meaning.

And some of it was outrageous contradiction. While scientists rushed to save the world's largest population of undiscovered flora and fauna, the government of Brazil allowed the burning of twenty to thirty million acres of virgin rain forest each year, an area four to five times the size of Vermont. And while the CVRD, Companhia Vale do Rio Doce, and thousands of independent prospectors painted and tainted the Amazon river system, in the world's greatest rainfall area governments, national and local, searched for clean drinking water. But the largest contradiction was with Indian tribes and their homelands. Subdue the jungle; replace every Indian. It was Gospel truth in a land of religious devotion.

TWENTY-THREE

No one knew how it started or who struck the first blow. The only fact known for sure was that the trail was littered with the bodies of Masakis being led back to their home village.

The Masakis had divided into two groups. Anna was in the first group, led by Soomar. There had been no conscious division of the tribe, only that the first group would leave a day earlier than the second, giving the first group time to prepare the village site and to erect a few temporary shelters. The second group would contain the older Masakis and was expected to move much slower. Only the hunters were divided more or less equally. Widel, with Penny, found himself in the second group. His arrows almost guaranteed fresh meat. The second group was led by Joqua, and for some reason known only to themselves, also contained the women from Trulk's village.

Three weeks away from the swamp, Joqua's group was making a temporary evening camp when Oneson came down the trail, yelling at the top of his lungs. "Big fight; many dead," he yelled before collapsing. "Many dead," he repeated, writhing on the ground

Even as Wasmaggi tended to him, the questions came fast, competing with each other for the young man's attention. "Who's dead?" "Where did it happen?" "Who did the killing?" "What about....?"

Wasmaggi pushed everyone away. "Give Oneson time." Then he whispered into the boy's ear, "Where is your mother?"

"I think she's dead," the boy answered. He shook compulsively. Wasmaggi gave him a drink.

Widel raced down the trail, his cries of fright and anguish heard by everyone.

340

"How far away?" Wasmaggi asked.

"Two days."

Joqua turned to send hunters. Lurch, Joshway and Amstay had followed Widel. Sayhoo spoke to Blue, Armot and Barkah. Without asking permission or bidding anyone goodbye, they, too, dashed along the trail. They hadn't gone far when Sayhoo stopped. "Blue, I didn't ask about my mother, or An-na."

Blue sped back to Oneson. One look and he knew. The medicine woman was dead. But he asked Contulla anyway.

"It is as Oneson has said. An-na is dead."

Blue retraced the trail, his eyes clouded with tears. His whole life had evolved because of Anna. So had Mansella's, and Barkah's, and Armot's. He screamed out his own anguish: "An-na is dead!" Sayhoo clutched at her breast, stumbling, nearly falling down, caught herself, and without saying a word, ran on.

Lurch, Amstay and Joshway did not stop for the night. They navigated the trail in the darkness, following what little they could see in the moonlight, pushing and dragging Widel with them. Who would be alive?

Sayhoo and the boys made so many mistakes in the darkness that Sayhoo had to stop for the night. "An-na said it is proper to cry sometimes. I'm crying. You don't have to listen; I will not listen if the hunters cry."

They did, like babies. They cried and hugged one another and wondered what they would do without Anna.

"I live because of An-na," Armot told the tiny group. "I'll kill those who killed An-na." It was a pledge taken also by Blue and Barkah.

"You don't take the pledge?" Armot asked Sayhoo.

"I take the pledge, but not as a hunter. I'll find my own way."

The toll was heavy. Soomar, Westman and Hakma were dead. Only Walkin was alive, barely so. Saymore was alive, but Hackway, Magwa, Janus, and Mansella were dead. And Anna. None of the children had survived. Marci, Manway, Jappah, and Jonquilla had been slaughtered.

The hunters touched nothing, but they began to read the battle's story. They found the places where the pistoleiros and cangaceiros had hidden. They counted twenty pairs of feet and only eleven bodies.

They would begin the hunt as soon as the second group arrived. No bandeirante would leave the forest alive.

They looked at Anna, her body positioned to shield Mansella and Saymore. They studied the hunters' positions. Badly wounded, they had charged the enemy, dying to save the lives of family and friends. Even the children had fought and had been felled without mercy.

Was this the outside world?

Widel was inconsolable. He lifted Anna's body from on top of Saymore and Mansella and cradled her as he might a tiny child. Once, he had begged Connie's forgiveness for her death; now, he begged Anna's forgiveness. "We never had a chance to say goodbye," he said to her lifeless body. "I should have told you I love you at least one more time." He buries his face in her hair, unconsciously noting the Indian haircut. "My Amazon," he whispered, "my life."

When Sayhoo and the young boys arrived, Joshway gave them specific orders. They were to touch nothing and no one except Walkin and Saymore, and for them they were to do what they could to keep them alive. They were not to move them no matter what happened until Wasmaggi treated them. While they waited, they were to hide themselves in the forest in case the others came back. "Don't try to fight them," Joshway warned. "If they come back, we will be right behind them."

Joshway, Amstay and Lurch went into the forest, three against nine, to avenge the death of the Masakis. The war had begun.

Once on the scene, Joqua and Moremew went in search of the killers, too. The village had been reduced to five hunters, not including Widel, and they were hunting nine others who had murdered without cause almost half an Indian village.

The loss of the Indians would never make the news media; the loss of the killers would, if people knew about it, make the headline news. Another contradiction.

Widel didn't cry, not outwardly anyway. He sent Armot back up the trail to ask Tonto to hold everyone else back, especially Penny. He did not want her to see the five holes in Anna's back. Then he sent the other boys away.

He tried to send Sayhoo away as well. She would not go. "I have Saymore and Walkin to care for. They need me. And Sayhoo help you with An-na."

"Your mother, how badly is she hurt?" Widel went to Saymore. She had died a few minutes earlier, like the others, unattended and alone.

Widel wrapped his arms around the young woman. "I'm sorry," he said.

"Sayhoo is sorry, too. Ran-ford will forgive my tears?"

"There is nothing to forgive. We will cry together. We have suffered many loses. Don't be ashamed to cry." Widel embraced the child-woman, and the ground received their tears. "The earth accepts our tears," Widel said, "easier than it accepts those we loved."

Walkin was badly wounded, but a hasty examination by Widel was not adequate.

"Sayhoo, go back to the other group. Have Desuit and Yanna come. Walkin will live, I think. No children. This is not for children."

"Ran-ford, I must...."

"Take your mother into the forest?"

"I must. Is my duty."

"Then find a place for her comfort. I'll carry her."

When Saymore rested under an oak tree, Sayhoo thanked Widel. "The woman thanks you. My mother and father thank you." She touched Saymore's shoulder and ran back toward the second group of villagers.

Widel took another look at Walkin. He had been shot in the neck, but the bullet had passed clean through just under his chin. Walkin had no trouble breathing, a good sign. "You'll have a sore throat," Widel said out loud. A bullet had fractured Walkin's left elbow. Another one was lodged in Walkin's left thigh. "Some work here for the medicine man," Widel again said out loud. "Has to be something else to keep you unconscious."

There was. A bullet hole about the diameter of Widel's thumb had entered Walkin's lower back and had gone straight through. "The spinal cord has been severed," Widel told the unconscious Walkin. "Don't know why you are alive."

Widel studied the handsome hunter. "If we traded places, I'd want you to do this for me." Widel placed his hand over Walkin's mouth and with the other hand pinched closed Walkin's nose. "I may rot in hell for this, my brother. One day you'll forgive me."

For the second time that day, Widel let the tears flow. Walkin made no resistance; he went calmly never knowing how he died or why. The why was the hardest part.

Widel looked again at the carnage. His family, his friends, his wife lay scattered and shattered before him, the spilled blood now dried, the insects doing their eternal work, the bodies stiffening under the protective canopy, the canopy that did not protect his love.

Widel looked down on Anna. He did not see the maimed body disfigured by the cruelest of men. He saw Anna as she first was, the Amazon women, the earth mother, the love of his life.

He picked her up and carried her into the forest and found a tiny area where the light shown down from above the canopy. He did not speak to her; his thoughts would be enough. "The two things I have loved the most, I've left in the forest," he said to no one within hearing. "No, that's not true, is it? I love Penny, too. If there is a God, I won't leave her in the forest."

He chipped away at the ground with his spear, broke it, went to get another. For hours he took his revenge on fate by digging in the ground. When he had carved out a shallow grave, he lined it with leaves and placed Anna's body beside it.

As he was beginning to lower Anna into the grave, he was conscious of a figure watching from the shadows. Widel stood up and faced a man he had never seen.

As incongruous as it sounds, Widel spoke to the man. "This is a private burial. Please go away. I would like to say goodbye to my wife alone."

"A fuckin' white man. I suppose you went with the white woman. Who the hell are you? Those Indians yours?"

"Since you speak English, yes, the woman you killed was my wife. And yes, the Indians are mine, my friends and my family."

"They killed some of my friends."

"You killed all of them."

"Yeah. Too bad they didn't give us the gold."

"What gold?"

"The gold all the Indians have."

Widel laughed. "You fool. These Indians don't have any gold. They barely have enough to keep themselves alive. What would they do with gold even if they had it?"

"Give it to some asshole like you."

"And which pocket would I keep it in?"

"You wife was quite a looker. We meant to fuck her, but then we had to shoot her. Pretty good with that spear of hers."

"Are you the one who killed her?"

"One of the ones, anyway."

Out of the corner of his eye, behind the man, Widel caught a movement. Someone had followed the man. Companion or Masaki hunter?

"What's a cripple like you doing in the jungle anyway?"

"I live here. Want to fight me for the privilege?"

"What?"

"What the hell. You've killed the only one I ever loved. Maybe I can kill you. Or you might kill me. Either way, I've nothing to lose. What say, my spear against your machete. Or are you afraid to fight someone face to face?"

"You can throw the spear. How about your spear against my gun."

"My spear is over there, beside my wife's grave."

"Get it."

Widel deliberately turned his back on the man. If he was to be shot, it might as well be in the back. Or maybe, just maybe, there was a friend there in the brush.

Very carefully, Widel reached for the spear, careful not to give the appearance of throwing it. "Any ground rules?" he asked when he faced the man again.

"Can you count to three, or are you as dumb as those poor bastards we killed?"

"Three it is. You count, just in case I've forgotten."

"One."

Widel watched the man's eyes.

"Two."

Anna's body was slipping into the grave, and for a split second it diverted the man's attention. Widel threw his spear with all the strength he possessed. Even as his arm went forward, he saw a second spear on its way and watched it strike the man's back.

Three never came. The man pitch forward. "You bastard," the name cried, "you didn't wait for three."

Sayhoo rushed out of the brush. "Game Con-nie teach us," she told the man. She withdrew her spear. "Now Sayhoo teach you game. Called make man cry."

She came around to face the man. He looked confused and very much afraid. Sayhoo drove her spear into the man's lower stomach. "Sorry," she said, "meant to hit penis. Sayhoo try again." The second time she drove the spear through the man's stomach. "Sorry again. Sayhoo need much practice."

She would have thrust a third time but Widel grabbed her arm. "It's enough, Sayhoo. We will let the man die thinking about living."

Widel reached down and took the man's guns and knives. "You'll wish I'd let her continue," he told the man. "There's nothing like dying in the jungle at night. Now, if you'll excuse me, I have to bury my wife. And so she doesn't have to see you, I'll drag you away. You won't mind; you'll forget all about it in your pain."

"Why did you come back?" Widel asked Sayhoo.

"Because I wanted to say goodbye to An-na."

"Well, I'm glad you did. How come you waited so long before throwing your spear?"

"Games, like Con-nie taught us. One, two, three. Only sometimes one would start before three. I knew man would. You started, too. Con-nie said not nice start before three."

"I think she'd make an exception today."

"Hope so. Sayhoo start on two."

Several weeks later, after the murdered Masakis had been placed in the forest by their loved ones, after the village had been reached and rebuilt, after days of sadness and lonely nights of tears, Wasmaggi invited Widel to his fire. "What you do, Ran-ford? This is your home; you are a Masaki. But you have no woman."

"No."

"I always tell you have another wife, one wife not enough. You say no, one wife is enough."

"That was the custom where I can from, before I came here"

"But you are Masaki, and you were going to have two wives."

"Yes, I was. Now both are dead."

"Now you have no one to love and no one to love you."

"I know."

"Ran-ford, you loved the ones too much."

Widel wondered whether Wasmaggi meant love or remembering. The Masaki word for each was the same. Either way, Wasmaggi was right. Widel loved or remember too much.

"We find you another wife. Many women would love you. There are women who want you. Even the hunters say, get Ran-ford wife. Some men say they share wives with you. So now hear me, Ran-ford.

"You came as gift to us, with An-na and Con-nie. We did not ask how you came. I did not ask where you were before you came. But we glad in our hearts you came. When Con-nie go back to forest, we mourn more than we ever mourn. She was everyone's sister. When Anna return to forest, we mourn even more. She was everyone's mother. We remember Con-nie and An-na. We glad, we happy, we sad."

Wasmaggi sat as straight as a ramrod. His own conversation was getting out of hand. Why had he mentioned the two girls? Widel had taken on the stature of a great man among the Masaki, but the girls had been the sun and the moon, and now, with Anna's passing,

347

they were gone, and just by mentioning them, Wasmaggi had placed himself in an emotional arena where he never had been and where, somehow, he knew he did not want to be. His shoulders slumped toward the fire, and he reached out to stir the ashes. He blamed his tears on the smoke, but whatever the cause, for the first time in his life he cried, not just tears but sobs.

"An-na brought us life," he said between sobs. "When we were sick, she made us well; when we were broken, she made us whole. She made Wasmaggi's medicine magic. Sometimes I did not feel well just to have An-na's touch. And when she had the baby, we held our breath for joy. An-na lives forever.

"And then she died. And you, Ran-ford, are alone. The Masakis have you, but you are alone, and what is left of us, we are alone, too."

Widel could feel the old medicine man reaching out, could feel the Masakis reaching out, and he was unsure of the reason.

Were these primitive people, how Anna hated that word, reaching out because he needed them, or were they reaching out because they were dependent on him?

Oh, my god, he thought, I've lost the only people who could give meaning to my life, and they lay this on me? Shit, I'm hurting so bad I could pack it in. If it weren't for Penny, I could do it. What do they want? Christ, what more do they want from me? I've given them everything I ever had. No. They can't have Penny. She's the one thing I do have.

The long silence gave Wasmaggi time to compose himself. He wanted to get back to the original reason he started the conversation in the first place.

"Ran-ford, what do you do now?"

"I told you. Stay here."

"Ran-ford, these days since An-na die, we see in your eyes a far away look. We not see that look before, even when you first came to us. Even when Con-nie die, we not see that look. We never see that look until An-na die. Now we see that look and we wonder. Does Ran-ford prepare to leave us? Does Ran-ford want to leave us?"

"Wasmaggi, I don't want to leave. When Connie and Anna and I came here, we were frightened, scared almost to death. When we realized this was to be our home, we came to love the Masaki. We became Masaki. I have no other home."

"You say that is so, but even the children see in your eyes the far away."

Widel wondered if in truth the Masakis knew more about himself than he did. It troubled him, and it annoyed him that the Masakis sensed such thoughts even before he thought them.

Thinking of the girls, Widel recognized one source of his discomfort. Putting aside his own deep loss, he sensed he owed the girls something in death that he had not been able to give them while they were alive. He owed them a chance to be with their families, with their fathers and mothers, brothers and sisters, not in life, not even some remains to be buried according to their Christian custom, but at least a memory.

All these years, the families would have existed in doubt and fear. They would have pictured a plane crash, horrible death, or, if survival, starvation or illness or savage ravagement. All these years, they would have carried in their minds images of destruction and desolation, their child in the center of it. He owed Connie and Anna at least the effort of easing their families' pains. Somewhere in the deep recesses of their minds, Anna's parents and brothers harbored a tiny ray of hope that Anna would return. Somewhere in Connie's family's mind, the same, fragile, everlasting hope remained. Only Widel could extinguish the impossible and allow two families final closure.

"Wasmaggi, I've a duty to perform."

"It is expected, Ran-ford. What is your duty?"

"I must try to find the families of Anna and Connie. I must tell them what happened to their daughters. I must tell them of the greatness of the Masaki and of the Masaki family."

"Con-nie and An-na are dead. They will be remembered. You can do no more. They have gone back to the forest. That is the end."

"Wasmaggi, when one Masaki goes into the forest and does not return, we try to find him. Maybe he is lost and needs us to point the way. Maybe he is sick or injured and needs us to make him well. Maybe he is dead and needs us to know that his life has ended."

"Sometime we don't find him. Then we remember him, and when the sadness goes, we remember and are glad."

"But, Wasmaggi, always we go to look for him. Even if we cannot find him, we have gone."

"Did your people look for you? Did they find you? They did not find you, but now they remember and are glad. Their sorrow is finished; now they are only glad that you lived. You would make them sad again? For what? Con-nie and An-na are dead."

"I accept your wisdom, but in this I say I have a duty that tells me I must go. I know you don't understand what I feel; I'm not sure I understand, but it's something I must do or I'll mourn forever that I did not. I must go with the sad news, and when I've told it, I will come home."

"We could keep you here."

"Yes, but I would no longer be a Masaki. I would be a captive, and like any captive you would have to kill me or let me go. If I go now, I go as a Masaki. If you kill me, what will have been accomplished? All the Masaki will know they killed a brother."

"Never would we kill Ran-ford. We know if you go, you not return. Then we will search forever and never find you, and all Masakis will be sad forever. When Con-nie go, we know where she has gone; when An-na go, we know where she gone. If you go, we not know."

"Then you understand why I must tell those Anna and Connie have left behind."

Widel could feel the village embracing him. Wasmaggi had spoken the truth. If he went away and did not return, he would be missed and mourned, and the Masaki would never know what had happened to their one link with Anna and Connie. He had grave doubts, and chuckled maliciously at the malicious pun, making a joke on himself, wondering if he really could walk out of the rain forest. His duty might be the death of him.

The night was very quiet, and looking beyond the fire, Widel was surprised to see several Masaki standing or squatting in the

350

shadows. How long had they been silent participants in his conversation with Wasmaggi? He didn't know, but from their appearance he guessed they had been there for some time. Even as he looked at them, they remained in total silence, not moving or making any sign whatsoever.

"Wasmaggi, I'm very tired. We will talk more in the morning."

"No need. It has been settled, Ran-ford. We will follow your faraway look, help you do your duty. We will go with you, and when you have done what you must do, we will come home."

"Wasmaggi, what you say is impossible. We'll talk more about it in the morning. For now, good friend, good night."

Widel walked toward his own shelter. A dozen or fifteen Masakis stood in his way. He looked into the eyes of each of them. As he stepped forward, the group parted, but not before each member had reached out and touched him. Each touch was gentle and warm, each touch reestablished a bond of such depth that Widel was moved. His knees felt weak, and when children came and touched him, he embraced them vigorously, not only to steady himself but to reaffirm his bond with the tribe.

Stooping to enter his hut, a temporary structure of a few posts and a thatched roof, he looked toward the hammock where Penny slept. Every night since her birth, he had silently gone to her and gently had kissed her. Tonight she was not there.

"Penny here, Ran-ford." Sayhoo was on the floor, holding the child in her arms. "She cried for An-na. She sleep now."

"Sayhoo...."

"Don't say, Ran-ford. I go now."

"Sayhoo...." She tried to go around him. "Thank you, Sayhoo."

"Is nothing, only what An-na or Con-nie would do."

As she moved, her tight, firm breast brushed against Widel's arm. For a fleeting moment he thought of having her, a foul thought, Anna so recently in her grave. He said nothing.

"Ran-ford, when you return, Sayhoo will be here. Maybe you will see Sayhoo as a woman, one who would love you and take care of you and raise your child as her own. I loved An-na. I not take her place. Not try, but I could be someone else for you to love." She walked quickly toward the shelter erected for the women.

Widel called himself all the names he could think of and berated himself for even thinking about sex with Sayhoo. Less than two months and he was doing what he had always done, fantasizing and making an ass of himself.

He stooped and picked up the child. "You are my life now, Penny. I hope you will understand and forgive me for what I'm about to do."

He had decided to leave the child with the Masakis. It was the only realistic course. He could not take her; she was far too young for such an arduous undertaking. If he failed, if he died or was killed, there would be no one to take care of her. Here, with the Masaki, she would have someone to take care of her and here she would have a far better chance of living.

He would arrange for one of the families to adopt her before he left. She would be treated well and loved.

Widel could not sleep. All rivers lead somewhere, he said to himself, so I'll follow a river. I can find the surveyor's trail; that will lead to a river, I'm sure, and there will be other people, some who will help me.

He wondered if other people would be friendly, and he wondered if he might die of fright if friendly people were not found. He went to sleep covered with sweat, not from the heat but from worry and indecision.

TWENTY-FOUR

Morning came too early. Penny flopped out of her hammock and crawled onto her father's chest. She needed his attention. She knew her mother had gone away; that happened now and then; she asked few questions. But one of them caught Widel unaware. "Where is Sayhoo? She said she would sleep with me all night?"

Sarahguy and Love appeared early at Widel's cold fire. "I'll make fire for Ran-ford if he will do something for me."

"I'll do something for Sarahguy even if she does not make my fire."

She took Penny to her breast and fed both children. "Joshway need second wife," she said. "Perhaps Ran-ford know right one." It was the kind of question a woman might ask Anna; it was totally outside the customs for Sarahguy to discuss such a thing with Widel.

"I'm not Anna; you ask the wrong person."

"I ask a wise person."

"Well, I thank you for your kind words, but honestly, Sarahguy, I can't even keep my own family in order."

"Then you need a wife, one to help you."

"And I suppose you know just the one."

"I do, those who would love Penny and Threesome and Twoman and Oneson."

"What do the children have to do with it?"

"You could marry Desuit and Yanna and have a nice, big family."

"That's really why you came to my fire, isn't it?"

"No. I do need help deciding which wife for Joshway. If you help me, I think maybe you like help and will not leave us. Ran-ford, don't go. We are few now. We need you."

353

And so the day went. People in need sought Widel's advice. He was busy the entire day and into the early evening.

At the fire, Wasmaggi said there was a consensus to be taken. He had worked out many details in his mind but he needed Widel's and the other hunters' input and approval.

Actually the women had worked things out without consulting the hunters, and it was Tilla who informed Wasmaggi. The unmarried women had been divided up, all but one who had refused. Joqua and Joshway would take two additional wives; Moremew would take one. Lurch and Amstay would take three. Desuit and Yanna would move in with Lucknew and Pollyque, so Tonto would have four wives.

The one woman who had not agreed was Sayhoo, and the one hunter who had not been consulted was Widel. Would Widel take Sayhoo as the mother of his child? Widel noted that Tilla deliberately avoided the word wife.

Penny left Widel's lap and went to Sayhoo. "Are you going to be in my mother's bed?" Sayhoo looked at Widel when she asked Penny, "Would you let me?"

"I don't think my mother is coming back." Penny dissolved in tears.

Sayhoo tried to comfort the child, finally asking, "Could Sayhoo be your mother, then. Until she comes home?"

"I'll ask my father." Penny walked slowly to her father. "Can Sayhoo be my mother for a while?"

"Would you like that?" Widel was in tears. He looked at Sayhoo. She, too, was crying. "Mother is never coming home, Penny. She's gone away forever."

"I know, Father. Sayhoo told me. Mother has gone to meet the forest."

Widel wrapped his child in his arms and cried like a baby.

"Don't cry, Father," Penny whispered through her own tears. "Sayhoo will make it better."

Widel nodded his head.

* * *

"This is so awkward, Sayhoo. Let's be honest. Physically, I want you in my bed. In my heart, I hold Anna. You know that, I guess. Perhaps you will always hold Fraylie in your heart, so we're not starting out on very solid ground."

"I talk with Wasmaggi. He say same thing."

"But you're still willing to try it?"

"I remember Fraylie. Remembering is good, Wasmaggi said. You remember An-na. I understand. But Sayhoo and Ran-ford are here. Penny and Oneson need a father."

"What's Oneson got to do with it?"

"He comes with me. I've spoken to Wasmaggi. Besides father, he need mother. We can be both."

"And I suppose you'll want children?"

"We do what is natural. Forest take care of rest."

"There is one other thing, Sayhoo. I have a duty...."

"To find An-na's and Con-nie's mother and father?"

"Yes."

"Then one day we find them together."

"Sayhoo...."

"Tonight only talk. Sayhoo know must talk. Ran-ford will say when he is ready for Sayhoo. Sayhoo come when Ran-ford call."

Sayhoo walked a short distance in the dark, then returned. "Forget. Have no place to go. May Sayhoo sleep by your fire?"

"I would...rather.... It would honor me if Sayhoo would share my sleeping mat."

They walked into the shelter, Widel upsetting a couple of spears on which he had started working. Penny awoke. "Is that you, Father? Is Sayhoo with you?"

"Yes, Penny. Yes to both questions. Now go back to sleep."

Penny slid out of her hammock. "I'll sleep with you tonight. I don't want you to have bad dreams." She lay down in the middle of the sleep mat. "Good night," she said softly.

"Our daughter makes our choice for us," Sayhoo said.

"Our daughter does not know what we decided."

"What did we decide, Ran-ford?"

355

"We decided to be husband and wife."

"That's what I decided. Does Ran-ford decide the same?"

"I do. I believe in time we will come to love one another."

"I already love Ran-ford."

"I'll need your help. Did Wasmaggi tell you that?"

"He did. Now I will put Penny in her hammock and we will dream about each other." Sayhoo lifted the child and kissed her.

Widel sat on the mat. Sayhoo knelt in front of him, then bent her hips, her face close to his. "I would like to learn the kissing part," she told him. "First, if it pleases you. I have much to learn about the white man."

When Widel emerged from his shelter the next morning, his mind was in turmoil. He had satisfied his lust, using poor Sayhoo for that. He felt guilty. He felt he had betrayed Anna; he knew he had taken advantage of Sayhoo. "Too soon," he said out loud.

"Too soon for what?" Joqua asked.

Widel had not seen Joqua standing just beyond the cooking fire.

"What are you doing here so early, Joqua. Are we to hunt?"

"Joqua is ready, Ran-ford. Xingu and Armot and Coanna are ready."

Behind Joqua, in the still morning shadows that sometimes last forever, the village waited. Each hunter had his spears and bow and arrows, the family goods were packed into their small carrying hammocks, and each Masaki grinned with anticipation.

"What's going on, Joqua?"

"We ready help with your duty. We like meet white families of An-na and Con-nie."

Widel put his head in his hands. Then he laughed, the first good laugh he had had in months. "What a surprise that would be!" he shouted.

He studied the people. They were grinning.

"We make one big family soon," Wasmaggi said.

"Masaki, we don't go today. Someday we will go. I promise that, but for a little while I must be with my new wife. She will help

356

me decide when the time is right."

Once more, Widel released his tears. He went to each member of the village, hugged them and thanked them. He took an extra moment with the children. The older boys tried to back away, but in the end they endured the fuss and hugged Widel back.

When Sayhoo came out of the shelter with Penny, Widel went to them. He kissed Penny, holding her so tightly she gasped for breath. Then he embraced Sayhoo and patted her on the stomach.

"Masaki, I hope one day to plant new life here. Sayhoo will be my wife, and one day we will lead you out of this wilderness."

The Masakis cheered.

"We not go today for sure?" Joqua asked.

"Not today. I have to get to know my new wife."

The Masakis cheered again, their sound echoing far and deep into the forest. For now, there was no one else to hear. Soon there would be, but this happy moment was for the Masakis only. Widel looked up. Through the canopy, tiny, golden shafts of light rained down. The mist lingered just long enough for him to see its wonder. Off in the distance a jaguar whistled. It was that time again, time to plant the seeds of new life and to cherish the life one has.

Sayhoo looked at her husband-to-be. This morning he was different. Was he taller, did he stand straighter, were his eyes brighter?

She looked at Penny. Someday, she thought, I'll be the one to tell you about your mother. Ran-ford will not, not everything anyway. He will keep some of it in a secret place. She touched her stomach. I hope if a baby comes, he will be as beautiful as you.

The Masakis returned to their houses. There would be no burning today. Today there would be no hunting or work in the garden.

Today the Masaki would sit by their fires and be pleased that Widel was knowing his new wife. Today they would hear the sounds, and tonight new wives would know their new husbands.

It was natural.

Today, for a little while, the villagers would set aside their fears and doubts, one day of happiness, one day for family, the old family in remembrance, the new family in beginnings. It was not entirely natural; it was what must be. Above all else, family. The Masaki tribe must be one family. That was natural. The forest mother told them so.

TWENTY-FIVE

One night, after months of mental agony and spiritual anguish, Widel stood before the people. "Masaki," he began, "I have a story to tell. Many times I've tried to tell this story, and Anna before me, and Connie. Only Wasmaggi listened because he knew the truth. You know I tell you what is true, but you do not listen because what I say are words you do not understand. I ask you to be patient now; let me tell my story; listen to my words even if you don't understand them; hear me."

Seldom did the Masakis speak the names of the dead. For Widel to speak Anna and Connie's names so openly sent a shiver through the collective village. Yet by so speaking, he gave his presence before them a heightened importance. They listened carefully for that reason.

In their shelter that night, Sayhoo asked for no explanation. She wrestled with her fears and finally settled for being held tightly. A thousand questions raced through her mind but she gave voice to none, only a few tears betraying her doubt and bewilderment.

When Widel stroked her face, he felt the wetness and an involuntary shiver.

"Wife," he asked, "are you crying?"

"No. A Masaki woman doesn't cry."

"Then why the tears?"

"Because I wish to cry."

"And what would you cry about?"

"For the Masakis, for Penny, for our unborn child, for us, that we'll not always be together."

"Sayhoo, we'll be together until death do us part."

"I would cry for that, too."

"You don't trust me? I'll never leave you."

"Did An-na say that to you?"

"Yes."

"And she left you."

"She was killed."

"I cry for that, too."

"Sayhoo, do I know the forest?"

"You know the forest, Ran-ford."

"And do you know the forest?"

"I know the forest."

"Then you and I could live out our lives in the forest. No one would ever find us, just two people."

"What about Penny? What about our child?" With her questions, Sayhoo knew the people must stay together.

"Sayhoo, you and I will lead. Only I know the others; only I know the other world. You have all Masaki knowledge. We'll lead our people."

Widel pulled his wife close. A dozen times he whispered his love for her. A dozen times she verbalized no reply, each time tightening her hold on him, biting deeply into his shoulder.

The Masakis had multiple troubles. They posted sentinels along the three main trails leading to the village, but sentry duty withdrew a hunter from the hunting necessary to feed the village, and the village had many hungry mouths.

To relieve the need for meat and to provide armed sentries, the hunters pressed young Oneson and Armot into guard service. The Masaki future might be in the hands of two immature boys. It was a risk that had to be taken.

And there was a redistribution of the women from Trulk's village. Months before, temporary arrangements had been made. Some worked, some did not. It was decided by the women that all prior arrangements were void and that the whole process of division and family enlargement would begin anew. It also was decided that the women would work out the arrangements. The hunters would have no say. It was made plain that they would accept and like whatever their wives told them to accept.

But it was not that simple. In fact, it might have been the hardest thing any of the village wives had done, and it complicated the existing marriages almost beyond endurance.

Many of the women from Trulk's village had an insatiable desire for motherhood that would, at the least, mean being in the bed of their new husbands. Sarahguy welcomed the new wives. Her childbearing days should come to an end; Anna had told her that. Xingu knew that she, too, should have no more children, although she enjoyed the lovemaking. Lucknew and Pollyque, already long into their plural marriage, thought having another wife or two was a fine idea. But neither Contulla nor Contilla entertained any such thought.

Yet, if there were to be children, they would come from the seeds planted by Lurch and Amstay, Joqua and Joshway, and maybe old Moremew. And that added to the dilemma. Should the Masakis have more children? The village was divided. The young women said yes, Sayhoo among them. Most of the resident wives said no, although it was not clear whether they said no because of the extraordinary nature of their shrinking world or because they did not want to share their marriage beds. Surprisingly, most of the men also said no. They seriously doubted the wisdom of bringing children into a doomed world.

Oddly, Widel gave the village an excuse for living. He spoke of the children as the Masakis' most precious possession. There was no disagreement. Nor was there any disagreement when he said that to cease giving birth was to give up on life completely, to tell the forest the Masakis wished to be no more. To knowingly choose to die was to belie the forest's life. One might be killed by the jaguar or by the others, but to kill oneself or to deliberately allow one's people to die out was cowardice of the worst kind.

Thus the entire family structure of the Masaki village was dramatically and radically changed. Blie and Kalo moved into Lurch's house and became second wives after Contulla. The sisters-in-law, Maltra and Sistal, moved into Amstay and Cutilla's home and became second wives. Joshway and Sarahguy made room for Ohtray and Costill. Yuma and Smalsh became Joqua's second wives after Xingu. Desuit and Yanna and their children joined Moremew and Tilla. They informed Moremew they had had two husbands already, both of whom had died violently, and that they had decided they did not want to lose a third. Moremew would not have to marry them, although they might like to share his bed once in a while. Otherwise, they would help Tilla, perhaps be more like daughters.

Three women remained apart, more or less, Usula, Milken and Noisle.

Milken was the oldest of the women, trained as a hunter by her late father and brothers. When it became apparent she never would have children, her husband had allowed her to hunt with him. If Lucknew and Pollyque agreed, and if Tonto agreed, she would join their household, not as a wife but as their hunter.

Noisle startled everyone by announcing she wished to join no family. She would wait for Oneson to become a hunter. When Usula said the same about Armot, and when the two young women said they would live together until the boys were made hunters, a time overdue according to the women, a decision had to be reached. Neither Armot nor Oneson seemed to mind the women's suggestions, and everyone knew the boys would couple with the women with or without approval.

Moremew suggested that the boys, and he included Barkah, had passed their manhood tests already. They should be declared hunters, and it was agreed immediately. The ceremony would take place that night.

Had he thought it through, he would not have included Barkah. At most, Barkah was eleven years old. Maybe he was only ten. But it was too late to withdraw the name; it had been accepted.

Everything might have gone well if Barkah, proving how childish he was, had not demanded that as a hunter he deserved a wife, too. It was an awkward moment for everyone. A few would have laughed outright had the situation not been so serious; others would have said prove it; someone did wonder who would teach the boy a man's business. Amstay turned his back. To him, his son still was an innocent child. Cutilla stood in shock.

Widel saved the moment. "I'll talk with the boy," he said. Barkah followed Widel to his house. Widel never would reveal the conversation; everyone knew that, but they knew the conversation would be about two things: sex and family. The talk would be about a man's seed, about making love, about making babies; then it would be about taking care of one's wife, providing food, keeping a safe home.

When Widel and Barkah returned to the villagers, Barkah kept his eyes focused on the ground. Widel told the people, "Barkah and I have talked. We decide perhaps is too soon...."

He never finished. Smalsh, Lackee's "Flower," Lackee's servant and mistress, the tiny child abused and misused, shouted, "That's not fair. Barkah is brave; Barkah is hunter. I'll be Barkah's wife. If he will have me."

There was total silence. No one moved. A single thought went through the adults' minds. Here was a boy-child who undoubtedly had not touched a female since he left his mother's breast, who might have had an erection and wondered what to do with it, and a girl-child who had experienced years of rape and forced intercourse. The thought stopped there. It might work, the women agreed. Later, the women would wonder how it would be to teach an ignorant boy about love. The men wondered how it would be to be that student.

Finally, Tonto spoke. "What does Barkah say?"

"If I could, would speak with An-na. I speak with Ran-ford again."

Widel went and whispered into Barkah's ear. "Son, you must say something to Smalsh. At least thank her. Tell her you hesitate only because you are not sure what is best for her."

Barkah did as he was told, even though he looked only at the ground. "I thank Smalsh. Now I must consider what is best for her." That was easy enough. Then Barkah added, "I think Smalsh very pretty." And he ran toward Widel's house.

Oh, God, Widel thought, Anna would have handled this well. What would she have done? Instead of following the boy, he walked toward Smalsh.

"Do you wish to speak with me, too?" he asked.

"There's no need."

"Perhaps we should talk anyway." Widel took Smalsh's arm and gently steered her away from the assembled vilage.

"What made you offer to become Barkah's wife?"

"I felt sorry for him. People were making fun of him."

"Then you have no affection for him?"

"I do and I don't."

"Which is it?"

"I don't know. Could come to like him. Love him, maybe. I don't know him."

"He's just a boy, you know. He doesn't know much about love and marriage."

"I not know about either. Didn't An-na tell you about me? That Lackee had me three years before my first cycle, that Milo had me after that, that no man wanted me because they said I could take the alligator between my legs, that no one has ever loved me? Barkah might love me, and I would love him because he did. I think about that, too."

"You would teach him about love, then?"

"No. We would have to learn together."

Widel was impressed by the response. "What would you have me say to him?"

"That I know he will be great hunter. That I'll be his wife and that we'll learn to be a family."

"And if he is not yet...isn't able...can't.... Hell, what if he's still a boy in the, you know what I mean, the man part?"

"I'll wait. I think I'll not have to wait long."

Widel walked to his house where Barkah waited.

"What does Barkah wish to say?"

"I wish know if An-na would say marry Smalsh."

"I don't know what she would say. Probably she would say you are too young, that you don't know the first thing about making your own family. I say both of those things."

"What if Barkah said would marry anyway?"

364

"Than I'll wish you luck and hope it works out well."

"Am I brave, Ran-ford?"

"Yes, you are brave, and you have proven it."

"Am I a good hunter?"

"You are learning to be a good hunter. To be a good hunter takes years, but, yes, you will be a good hunter."

"Am I a man?"

"I don't know, Barkah. I guess when you're on that line between being a boy and being a man you have to ask yourself. Maybe being a man is in the mind, what you think about yourself, how you think about yourself. Do you think you are a man?"

"I think so."

"And what makes you think so?"

"I'm ready to leave my parents' house. I have thoughts about the women. I wish to have children."

"And?"

"There's more?"

"What do you feel about Smalsh?"

"She is pretty. I would...like to...hold her...."

"Is she prettier than all the others? Would you hold none of the others?"

"There are others I would hold. I would like to hold many."

"And do what?"

"Hold. Do what you and An-na did; what you and Sayhoo do, what my mother and father do."

"And what is that?"

"I.... I don't know exactly, but I see my father. I've seen you."

Widel was in over his head. He had no interest in Barkah's sensual thoughts or those of any other Masaki.

Widel wondered at Barkah's innocence. That wouldn't last long with Smalsh or any woman. A couple of minutes and he'd be well educated. In a way he knew was perverse, Widel envied him.

But what troubled Widel more was Barkah's lack of commitment to Smalsh. Apparently he liked all women just because they were women, although he hadn't fully discovered or defined his sex drive. Smalsh would commit herself to Barkah; Barkah was

365

not going to make a commitment to Smalsh or to any one woman. Was that his nature or his youthfulness? An interesting question.

Widel decided to bring the conversation to an end. "I believe Anna would say it's not time for you to marry, and I believe she would disapprove of your marriage to Smalsh at this time."

Barkah did not seem unduly upset. He asked only, "Will you tell her for me?"

As Sayhoo rapidly pushed and pulled the bow that twirled the stick that ignited the coals of her cooking fire, a shadow from the mist fell across her. She jumped up with a start, a look of great anguish smeared across her young face.

"I not mean scare you, mother-to-be. I should have made a noise." It was Wasmaggi.

"Even a noise would have scared me."

"Wasmaggi is sorry. We're all frightened these days."

"Is no matter. Say no more. Sayhoo jumps at every little thing. You've come to talk with Ran-ford?"

"With him, and with you."

"I'll call him."

"No, we'll talk first."

"And what will we talk about?"

"About a medicine woman. I once said you'd be the medicine woman. I've changed my mind."

Sayhoo winced, thought about protesting but waited for an explanation. She could feel her heart breaking. Once she would not have cared. Now, to be the medicine woman would make her Anna's equal, would give her a chance to take Anna's place, would increase her importance in Ranford's eyes. But she did not speak, knowing that the choice of a medicine man or woman was her grandfather's right. She bit her lower lip and waited.

"Don't be disappointed, Sayhoo. It's not that I don't think you will be a good medicine woman."

"Then what is it? What have I done to displease you?"

"You've done nothing wrong. It's what I should have done long ago. I must teach all woman the secrets of my medicine, all except the life and death medicines. Those I'll teach only to you."

"Why? Sayhoo doesn't understand."

"Wasmaggi is old. I have all secrets. An-na had all secrets. An-na was killed. Suppose Wasmaggi dies. Who would know secrets? No one. Think of Trulk's village. Milo had all secrets; Tannee had all secrets. Milo was killed; Tannee was killed. If that village had lived, who would have known the medicine? Who would have known the people?"

"And you think you'll die soon? And I'll be killed?"

"Who knows the mind of the forest? Yes, I'll die, though I hope to meet the parents of An-na and Con-nie. If I die, and you die...."

"There would be no one to take care of our people."

"Sayhoo understands then?"

"I understand. An-na said once that is hard to carry understanding. I'm beginning to know what she meant."

"One day, Sayhoo, you'll be a great Masaki woman, not because you are my granddaughter but because you are strong and will be wise. Ran-ford is wise man. He has learned his wisdom. Listen to him.

"But, Sayhoo, Ran-ford has a special sadness within him, a secret sadness, born when he was born. Sometimes you will think it's because of An-na and Con-nie, and you'll have to deal with their memories, but is deeper than that. Somewhere within, he doesn't know his full strength. He doesn't always believe in himself. In their ways, An-na and Con-nie made up for that. You cannot, I think. You must do better; you must draw Ran-ford's strength out, and when you do, each will feed the other."

"Wasmaggi says words I don't understand. Ran-ford is strong. Only his twisted leg prevents him from being the strongest."

"It's not that strength Wasmaggi speaks. Inside, in the heart, is a person's real strength."

"I still don't understand."

"Then we'll speak of it again as I teach you the life and death medicines and the meaning of holding such medicines in your hand." Wasmaggi kissed his granddaughter on the forehead. "Now I must speak to Ran-ford."

* * *

"Ran-ford, I listen. You've said those words before, but now I see in your eyes that the words about leaving the forest are real. The village wishes to meet the parents of the white Masakis; but also I think the village doesn't wish to leave the forest."

"Wasmaggi, if I could, the Masakis never would have to leave the forest. But look around. How many are we? Forty, counting the children? Thirty-nine, actually. I count the village every day."

Widel asked Wasmaggi to walk to the beach, and once there Widel counted out thirty-nine grains of sand and held them cupped in the palm of his hand. "See these bits of sand? They're our people. Now try to hold all the sand on the beach, or just try to count the grains between your feet. Look. I throw these grains into the others. You can't find them any more. They have been eaten up by the beach. As far as we can tell, they are no more, gone, overwhelmed and overcome by all the other grains of sand."

"But in the forest...."

"In the forest we could hide the grains of sand. We'll put some on the path to the village. Who will see them? Worse, unnoticed, they will be stepped on and ground into the dirt. One grain of sand."

"Is much for an old man."

"It's no easier for a young man. Wasmaggi, you have seen the others close up. You saw them as a boy, then you fought them as a young man. You know what they did to the Masakis once, what they did to Spiker and Mike and Fraylie, what they did to a whole village, what they did to our village. If good men don't come to us, we must go find the good men. To stay here invites bad men with their killing drums to murder us all."

"But to leave forest...." The thought overwhelmed the old man. Somewhere, he had thought, in some far away, remote area of the unending forest lived the parents of Anna and Connie. He would go with Ranford to find those parents, but he would never have to leave the forest. It would be an adventure, always under the canopy of the forest mother. If there were others, the Masakis would become like the jaguars, silent and unseen and....

368

"Ran-ford, we must return to the secret island," Wasmaggi announced suddenly, as though he had had a revelation of immense importance. "That is our only safe place now. There we'll decide our future and prepare for it."

Widel agreed. The island was much safer, if temporary. There was so much to teach, so much to tell, so much for the Masakis to absorb.

Wasmaggi did not reveal the full revelation which had struck him. He needed Tomaz now, Tomaz the jaguar-man, Tomaz the warrior.

When they parted, Wasmaggi went straight to his house. He prepared the special mixture of leaves and barks, roots and shells, and when he had mixed his concoction, he dragged his fire inside and increased its flames. Then, straining for the face of Tomaz, he spread the mixture of cassava and quina and coca and lime on the fire.

"I am the one who remembers," he said, "and I would remember Tomaz and the jaguar-men and those who would make the Masakis strong in the face of their enemies."

He cried aloud when Anna's images raced across his memory; wept quietly when he saw Connie's jaguar scars and relived the agony of her death; tried to hold the image of Tomaz, colored in the ways of the jaguar-men; reacted violently upon seeing Samson's face. None of the images lasted. His memory raced backward and deeper at ferocious speed. He saw the Masakis digging for roots and grubs; saw them hunting; saw them as dark shadows killing each other, the heads of their victims proudly displayed on the end of their spears; saw them eating the flesh of the conquered. He saw the medicine men before they were men of medicine, shamans who held the jaguar in one hand and man in the other, the intermediaries between the forest and man and the incomprehensible realm of the spirit. It was a world he had not visited since he was a young man, a world he had never wanted to visit again, an evil world of darkness and unspeakable horrors.

When he saw his wives, their skeletons reached out to grab him, their skulls twisted in grotesque laughter. He saw Anna and Connie reaching out from their unnatural graves, trying to suck him into the ground of their final resting places. He saw the others quartering the bodies of living Masakis. He saw the tallest trees falling and crushing the Masaki homes. He saw babies stomped and flattened by strange feet. And by some unseen hand, he was forced to witness the rape of the young, males and females at the hands of beasts he had never seen.

Wasmaggi drank a bit of coca tea from a tiny pot to refresh his mind and spirit, the tea that soothed his thirst, the tea that added strength to the cocaine mix he had thrown on the fire. And when the tea failed to refresh him and soothe his fatigue, he drank the manioc beer, nourishing, intoxicating, deadly.

Every fear he had ever known, every danger real or imagined, every cruel death was paraded before him. A thousand times he saw his own death - and his escape - and he wondered aloud why he was not dead. He saw himself as medicine man, and before that as shaman, and before that as magician, soothsayer, conjurer, and sorcerer. He had power and no power, he was a man of awe and mystery, and he was helpless.

And he saw the truth: the Masakis were on the edge of extinction and there was nothing they could do about it. The Masakis were prisoners of their own isolation.

Unless. Unless Wasmaggi could draw from the image of Tomaz the power to fight back, to become the jaguar-man. Tomaz would help him teach the people.

Three days later, Wasmaggi emerged from his house, painted in the reds and blues, the black and white of the jaguar-men. The villagers had heard his crying and his muttering, had smelled the smoke from his fire, and knew that the old medicine man was practicing an ancient rite, but only Moremew and Tilla had a vague idea of the real nature of the practice and only Tonto, Lucknew and Pollyque had any knowledge. So, when Wasmaggi emerged, Tonto was waiting for him.

"Wasmaggi has lost his senses?" the old man asked. "Wasmaggi is going to be the jaguar-hunter? Wasmaggi is going to walk the path of death?"

"Tonto, I have seen the next world. It is death for us all."

"There's always death. It's foolish to search for it."

"I did not look for death; I sought Tomaz. He would know how to fight death."

"He would know to fight death is useless. Did he not tell you that?"

Wasmaggi looked down at the ground. "I did not speak to him. I saw him; he did not look at me; I could not speak with him."

"Then why the colors? The jaguar-men were evil."

"The others are evil."

"Evil and evil not produce good. We have lived in good; let us die in good. To search out evil will kill us anyway. Your way dooms your granddaughter's child to evil; all the children will be as evil, and they will die whether the others come to us or not."

"I'll speak to the people."

"No! What you offer them is certain death."

"They have a right."

"A right to die? Yes, they have that right, but only to die as Masakis; they have no right to die as murderers. They have a right to die protecting the forest and each other, but the forest doesn't kill."

"Tonto, all my life I've believed that. Now I don't wish our people to die without fighting."

"And who would fight? Lurch, Amstay, Joqua, Joshway, Ranford? You're old; I'm old; Moremew old. Or would you have the women fight, or the children? Armot, Oneson, Barkah, Blue? Would you have them fight and die before they are old enough to know their own minds? Tomaz would not have told you that."

The two men argued, unaware that the entire village had been drawn to them and was listening. The remnant village was undecided. Certainly a half dozen hunters stood no chance against the others' killing drums. There was wisdom in hiding. But the hunters could seek out the others, ambush stragglers, hit and run when the time was right.

Barkah, Oneson and Armot, brave in their inexperience, were for that, but the newly ordained hunters did not speak. They seemed to know their words would not be considered, having neither experience nor proven skill.

Then Barkah shouted, "Will Blue join us?"

Blue bore the outward marks of the jaguar and inward the mark of having cheated death. Except for Oneson, who had been trained in the ways of the forest and of the hunter by Mansella and by his uncles, Soomar and Walkin, Blue's skills were superior to those of Armot and Barkah. He seldom spoke; when he did, it was to ask a question, never to proclaim an idea or an opinion. He was, therefore, easy to overlook.

On the day of the horrendous killings, he had said nothing, had simply slipped into the forest in search of the others. No one noticed his going; when the killings had been avenged, he simply melded back among the survivors. He had found no other; he had not killed an other; he said nothing about having tried.

He might have been made a hunter with the other boys if anyone had thought to include him. They had not. He did not object. He did not object when Oneson and Armot and Barkah had women willing to be their wives. If he had a thought about that or any other thought, no one knew enough to ask.

He had the same quiet, inscrutable demeanor as his father. When the whites first met Lurch they thought him slow-witted; he soon proved he was a wise hunter of unequaled skill. Blue was the very image of his father.

"Blue doesn't answer. Is he a coward?" Barkah laughed. "Or just dumb?"

Blue made no reply.

"See?" Tonto whispered to Wasmaggi. "It begins already. Now we fight among ourselves."

Contulla would have reached out for her son had Lurch not drawn her back. "We not interfer," he told her. "Blue has much strength. He will do what must be done."

372

Barkah advanced toward Blue. "I should teach my cousin how to fight. Does Blue know how to fight? Or would he be like the women?"

If the villagers had ever intended to bring the confrontation to an end, their intentions dissolved with Barkah's derogatory insinuation that the women were inferior. Time and time again they had proved they were not, and they resented the child's lowly opinion. Let the two boys fight and hope that Blue knocked Barkah silly.

Two spears were produced. Such fights were rare. Wasmaggi had to explain the rules. The object of the fight was to produce a wound, not to kill the opponent. A senseless killing would not be tolerated, and if the hunters judged one of the boys to have killed needlessly, the killer would have his head shaved and be expelled from the village. And, said Wasmaggi, the spear could not be thrown. To insure that the spears would be less lethal, Wasmaggi had the sharp points cut away.

Barkah advanced cautiously. He had made a foolish suggestion; he was not going to risk defeat by rushing in. He jabbed and swiped. Blue defended, blocking Barkah's thrusts. Back and forth the two boys went, Barkah the attacker, keeping pressure on Blue who parried each of Barkah's moves with a countermove of his own.

On one parry, Blue lifted Barkah's spear; as he did so, he drew his hands together and swung his spear at Barkah's knee, and when Barkah reacted to that blow by lowering his guard, Blue struck him with full force on the side of the head. Barkah slumped to the ground.

"Con-nie taught me," Blue said. "And much more if you wish know."

"You will be sorry for this," Barkah shouted, the ache in his head almost as painful as his lost pride.

"Oh, and Blue doesn't wish to join with you."

"You are the asshole of the anaconda."

"But my knee isn't all swelled up, and I don't have a headache."

"You will, some day."

As Wasmaggi tended to Barkah's aches and pains and as Cutilla and Amstay looked anxiously after their son, Widel joined them.

After asking about Barkah's condition, he said he wanted to be sure there were no lasting hard feelings because of the outcome of the fight. He hoped Barkah and Blue would remain friends.

"Blue has his own mind," he said. "He doesn't say much, like his father, but he is a loyal Masaki and, I think, will be a fine hunter. And a steadfast friend." Barkah heard none of Widel's words.

That night, Amstay and Contilla approached Widel and Sayhoo's fire.

"How is Barkah?" Widel asked, inviting the couple to sit.

Contilla answered. "Wasmaggi gave something to make sleep. Will be fine in morning. But something has happened to him. Ever since great killing, has been different boy."

"It's as though his mind has become twisted," added Amstay. The hunter paused, and his wife took hold of his elbow. "We come to you because.... You were.... An-na said once your mind was twisted, and later you untwisted it."

"We would know how to untwist our son's," pleaded Contilla.

Widel stared into his small fire. "Many times my mind was twisted; too many times," he said softly, thinking back to the beginning in the jungle. "Each time I was wrong. I was mad at myself because I couldn't function as a whole man; I misinterpreted what I saw; I misread Connie's and Anna's actions; I was angry because I couldn't understand what was going on around me. I blamed myself for failures that weren't mine."

Amstay and Contilla didn't understand very much of what Widel was saying, but they could feel his pain, evidencing the same remarkable intuition about so many things that Widel had come to admire about the Masakis, even if he did not understand them.

"Ran-ford doesn't have a twisted mind now."

"No, Amstay, I'm happy to say I don't, although there's a lot of things I don't understand."

"Can you help Barkah?"

"Amstay, Contilla, so many bad things have happened that Barkah can't keep them sorted out, can't even understand them. He would like to turn to you for understanding, but he can't because he thinks he's a man and men don't ask for understanding from their mothers. Or from their fathers, because as a man he is trying to be better than you. To talk with you, Amstay, would be to confess that he is not your equal. So he listens to himself, and what he hears is confusion. His only way to deal with that is to be bullheaded and demanding."

"Being beaten today by Blue has only made it worse." Contilla shook her head and reached for Amstay's hand.

"Yes. I'll talk with him tomorrow. That's all I can promise."

Wasmaggi was the first person Widel saw the next morning. He told the old medicine man of his talk with Amstay and Contilla and concluded by demanding that Wasmaggi remove the jaguar-man paint and stop acting like a fool, suggesting that Wasmaggi was making a bad situation worse with talk of killing others.

"It's what An-na would have said. I'll wash. Walk to the beach with me. We talk."

On the way, Widel spoke of Anna's wish to try the smoke, to have the visions. "I worried she would try it," he said, "and that she would be changed forever."

"Is well she did not. This Wasmaggi's second time," the old medicine man replied. "First time was not prepared. Made me old before my time. Saw horrors I never knew, and I saw the future. This time I also saw the past, and again it was a time of horror. I wasn't part of it, yet I was. Tomaz wasn't my friend; An-na wasn't my beloved medicine woman; Con-nie wasn't the woman of strength and skill; they — everyone — were agents of death. And when I saw the future, I saw nothing but death. I wanted to die and could not. I think that is now my burden. I would die before the Masakis die, and I cannot."

"Cannot or will not?"

"Perhaps they're the same. Once I said An-na was the future. An-na is dead. What future is there without her? Saw all Masaki dead. I was last, and I had to watch them die."

The pain of remembering shot through Widel's heart. He did not want to relive Anna's death, but he had to ask. "How did the Masakis die?"

"The forest fell on them, crushed them with its falling. I was the last Masaki, and I had to watch the forest die."

As Wasmaggi scrubbed away the red and blue, the white and black paint of the jaguar-men, he said to Widel, "Is strange. I not remember seeing you, or Sayhoo. I not see your Penny or your unborn child, yet I felt you there, watching, crying. I not see any of the village, and I wondered if because all dead and gone."

For a moment, Widel did not respond, wondering what the old man's hallucinations could mean, not believing in the delusionary visions yet not able to disbelieve either.

"It's time, Wasmaggi, to leave this beach, to leave this village. As you said, it's necessary to go to the island of safety. Only there, where we'll be less afraid, can we make sense of all that has happened, and only there can we prepare ourselves for the future."

"We'll go as warriors."

"We'll fight only if we must."

"And what about the old ones? What about Lucknew and Pollyque and Tilla, even Tonto and Moremew? How will the old ones manage?"

"If we have to, we'll carry them. The whole village, all of us. It will take time. Along the way we'll teach the children to be hunters." Then, almost as an afterthought, Widel added, "We've nothing to fear from the forest mother."

"My visions...."

"I think Wasmaggi will have other dreams."

"Wasmaggi is old fool, to think the smoke will reveal the truth."

"The smoke, my friend, reveals only what you already know. The smoke is bad. It makes you think only of the bad, only the worst fears which are in your mind."

Almost lightheartedly, Wasmaggi said, "Along the way I'll teach the women my medicines. But," more seriously, "the life and death medicines I teach only to Sayhoo."

If Widel's talk went well with Wasmaggi, his talk with Barkah was a disaster. The youngster would have nothing of reconciliation, nothing of friendship, nothing of village welfare. Was it ego or was it something deeper, darker, more sinister than a boy's hurt pride?

"I'll prove I'm a hunter, Ran-ford."

"I've no doubt that you will be, Barkah. You need prove nothing to anyone except that Barkah has wisdom."

"I know enough."

"It's not knowledge of which I speak. Wisdom is knowing how to use your knowledge. You misjudged Blue's skill; wisdom would be to admit you had. Wisdom would be making Blue your friend again. Wisdom would be knowing that one day you might need him. Wisdom would be learning what Blue knows and making that knowledge yours. Wisdom would be caring for the whole village, from the oldest, Wasmaggi, to the youngest, Coanna and Love, even my unborn child."

"Why? The village doesn't care for me."

"Son, you know that every hunter in this village would give his life for you; every women would sacrifice her life for you. It's the Masaki way. Even in your mistakes, you are loved. That is the whole of Masaki wisdom. Would you throw that away?"

"I would prove myself. If no others, I'll wear the jaguar-men's colors."

"And invite your own death?"

"Who would care?"

"I would care. If Anna was here, she would care. Connie would care. Your mother and father care. Everyone cares more than you realize."

"Hear me, Ran-ford. One day they'll all care because I will prove I am a great Masaki hunter."

That night Barkah slipped into Joqua and Xingu's house, slid past Armot and Coanna, stepped over Yuma, and stretched out beside Smalsh. His intentions were not clear, probably only to prove he could sneak past a hunter and into a hunter's home. Had he been more subtle and gentle, he might have awakened Smalsh quietly, and if nothing else, they might have enjoyed Barkah's stealth and daring. But now Smalsh was one of Joqua's wives, although Joqua knew one day she might leave his house for Barkah's. So, when Barkah placed his hand over Smalsh's mouth, she did what came naturally. She turned toward Barkah, not knowing who he was, and with great force sent her knee between Barkah's legs. At the same time she bit his hand as hard as she could. After years of being raped and abused, she knew what would hurt a man.

Barkah yelled out in pain, and Smalsh struck his nose.

Within seconds, Joqua had Barkah in a bear hug, and Armot had Barkah's legs.

Xingu hustled Coanna out of the house.

Any unusual night noise brought the entire village to full alert. Women with children disappeared into the forest darkness more quickly than their shadows. Lurch, Amstay, Joshway, and the boys, Oneson and Blue, reached for their spears. Remarkably, most of the women appeared with assorted weapons, ready to do battle with unseen forces because now every battle was one of life or death.

Joqua and Armot did not know who they had captured, only that whoever it was was an unwelcome intruder and thus dangerous.

Barkah's behavior presented the Masakis with a new dilemma. Smalsh was Joqua's wife. Although he had not touched her other than to put his hand over her mouth, the general opinion was that Barkah had intended to do more. Either he was going to rape her or, a theory that had some support, Smalsh and Barkah were going to engage in willing, mutual lovemaking.

Whether Barkah was going to rape another man's wife or whether Barkah and Smalsh's affection was mutual, either way Joqua had the final decision about Barkah's fate, a decision he was not prepared to make because there were but three choices: deny the event happened; demand Barkah's death, and his asking would be granted; or send Barkah into the forest alone, unarmed, head shaven.

Nothing was decided in the dark. With daylight would come the Masaki version of a trial, the hunters acting as judges and jury. Women would be excluded. Barkah was bound, and Oneson and Armot were assigned guard duty. They would not be needed in the morning.

Barkah was not fed; he was given only water. When tiny Love offered him water, Barkah took a sip and spit it in her face. "I don't take from babies," he cried.

When Cutilla took water, he turned his head. "I'm your mother," she wept.

"I have no mother. Get away from me, woman."

Cutilla went to her own mother. "Tilla," she sobbed bitterly, "It's more than I can bear." Her anguished sounds rang throughout the village.

Tilla wept, too. And when the grandmothers, Lucknew and Pollyque, joined the family, they also cried in unrelieved despair.

The only female family member missing was Contulla, not that she felt less pain. She feared risking her sister's hostility. Blue had beaten Barkah badly; perhaps Cutilla would blame Contulla and then blame Lurch, and then perhaps Lurch and Amstay would view each other as adversaries, and the family would be torn apart and with it the village. Better that Contulla stay apart, let things calm down a bit.

But, with Barkah's irrational behavior, things did not calm down. With all the crying and moaning and mourning, the situation was out of hand.

If not for Cutilla's sake, then for Tilla and Lucknew and Pollyque's, Contulla entered her sister's house. There was an immediate embrace, sister with sister, sisters with mother, sisters and mother with mothers and grandmothers. The agony was too great not to be shared; the sense of family too strong to be broken. Unity was more important than assigning faults; at this time in Masaki life, unity was the most important value.

That more than anything troubled Cutilla. Her son was destroying the unity of the village. His declaration of independence, his irrational behavior, threatened the fabric of Masaki life at the time when wholeness was most needed.

No one could explain Barkah's behavior. If there was an explanation, it would emerge from among the hunters.

Barkah's rebelliousness was soon dismissed. Widel convinced the hunters that was irrelevant to the main question. The question

379

was agreed upon by all: what was Barkah doing in Joqua's house with Smalsh?

Joqua was asked to retell the events of the so-called invasion. No, he did not know Barkah had entered the house, not until Barkah yelled in pain. No, he did not know what Barkah was trying to do. No, Barkah and Smalsh had not had sexual relations. Yes, Xingu and Sarahguy had examined Smalsh very carefully. No, he had not yet taken Smalsh to his bed. Yes, he had taken Yuma. Yes, Xingu was not pleased. He would wait a while before having Smalsh.

Wasmaggi broke in. "We ask more than need to know. Would ask Joqua one question. If Smalsh wished be Barkah's wife, would Joqua object?"

Joqua took a long time before answering. "Joqua would think maybe something wrong with Joqua that a wife would ask for such. But Joqua would agree. Bad have wife who dislikes in house. Bad have man without wife."

Tonto asked if anyone had talked with Smalsh. Did she have a part in the night's happening? No one knew. Joshway suggested they ask Smalsh to come to the fire. It was agreed, although Widel thought the quickness with which the agreement was achieved was due more to the hunters' voyeurism than their search for truth.

Wisely, the hunters chose Widel to ask the questions.

"Will Smalsh tell us what happened?"

"Smalsh was sleeping. Suddenly hand clamped on mouth. I not know who it was, just a man. I turned on my side, enough to swing knee. At same time bit hand. Man yelled. Only then did Smalsh know it was Barkah."

"Did you expect Barkah to come to you that night?"

"No."

"Did he try to do anything with you?"

"Only keep me from crying out."

"If you'd known it was Barkah, what would you have done?"

"Would have told to leave. Smalsh Joqua's wife."

"Have you been in Joqua's bed?"

"No."

"Will you?"

"When he tells me. He has not told me."

"Would you like to be Barkah's wife?"

"No."

"Why not?"

"He doesn't respect me. He is twisted in his head. He has no love for me."

"Don't you think he went in Joqua's house and to you because he wanted you?"

"I think he did what he did to prove how great a hunter he is and so could laugh at everybody."

When Smalsh was dismissed, Widel said, "I believe Smalsh has told the truth; Barkah was trying to prove how superior he is. He picked a poor target. Smalsh has much experience." And then he added for Joqua's benefit, "Perhaps you should invite Smalsh to your bed. I think you may have a loyal wife."

"Joqua will, when Xingu says I can. During her cycle. Xingu will not feel so bad then."

Amstay had not said a word throughout the proceedings. Now he spoke. "Barkah my son. A father not wish to say son is bad. But son is twisted in his head. Have spoken to Ran-ford about this." Amstay looked at Widel, and Widel nodded in agreement.

"Don't know what do. Not believe Barkah entered Joqua's house to make love with Smalsh. If that were so, even Amstay say punish." The hunter paused, trying to gain control of his emotions. "But something has happened. Barkah is beyond Cutilla's and my reach. We don't know what do. Barkah wrong. Amstay has told Joqua Barkah wrong. Barkah must be punished. But how, for what?"

For what? That was the immediate issue. The Masaki had no capital punishment for crimes other than murder, adultery and child abuse. For now, any thought of rape or attempted rape or mutual lovemaking was dismissed, and Smalsh was deemed innocent of any wrongdoing and publicly would be assured of that. Barkah's misdeeds were diminished in size, from one of the worst crimes to something lesser, entering one's house without permission, attacking a member of the household, violating privacy. Nothing was stolen; no one was hurt, except the criminal, and the hunters had several laughs about that; the household members were unnecessarily scared. In the life of the Masakis, it was a new crime. They had no name for it; they did not know how to deal with it or with the miscreant.

Perhaps Barkah himself could explain it.

As Widel waited for the hunters to bring Barkah to the fire, he wondered how a little boy could get into such a bind. What possessed him to be so outlandishly outspoken, to brag of accomplishments he had never even attempted, to downgrade the efforts of experienced and skilled hunters, to challenge the bravery of the women, and, finally, to flaunt the Masaki values? In more normal times, it would be two years before his manhood test was considered. Now he was a hunter because a few desperate men needed able bodies, any able body, to protect the village, not to seek out enemies and fight a war.

When Barkah was seated at the fire, Wasmaggi asked if any hunter would speak for Barkah. Widel was surprised to hear himself volunteer. "Amstay would wish to speak for his son, but he cannot. I'll speak for the boy, if he wishes."

Barkah nodded. He would have agreed to almost anything. He was hungry; he was in great pain for having been tied to a tree for so long; and he was scared, the last thing he wanted to admit. "Ranford will speak well for me," he said.

"Then I would speak with Barkah. Alone. So I can know what the boy would say."

"And how long will that take?" Joshway demanded.

"Until tomorrow. Barkah will sleep in my house tonight. I'll be responsible for him. He will not run away." Widel was sure of that.

Sayhoo was so opposed to the idea of having Barkah in her house that she and Penny spent the night with Lucknew, Pollyque and Tonto and Tonto's wife-in-waiting, Milken.

Tonto made light of the arrangement by telling everyone that when he was a young man having all those women in his bed would have been just a warm-up. Pollyque and Lucknew cackled at the joke.

"Don't worry," they assured Sayhoo, "Tonto always talk bigger than he is. Even two wives more than enough."

"Two wives? Should have had twenty. You two would have been last."

"You couldn't last. That was trouble," Lucknew giggled, pleased with her little joke.

"Always get plenty of sleep with Tonto," Pollyque added.

It was the affectionate banter and teasing of those totally comfortable and secure in their marriage. Even as they poked fun at him, Tonto hugged them and kissed his wives' foreheads.

There was no innocent cordiality between Widel and Barkah. The lack of mutual regard was not generational, had nothing to do with color, and had nothing to do with anything that Widel could put his finger on. What twisted Barkah was beyond Widel's comprehension. He decided to push on in the only way he knew how.

"Is Barkah angry at the Masakis?"

"They treat me as a child."

"And you're not?"

"I'm a hunter."

"Are you ready to be a hunter?"

"I'm old enough."

"Well, that's debatable. Oneson is not yet a hunter, and he is older than you."

"Perhaps he doesn't deserve to be."

"If you think about it, he does deserve to be. He has demonstrated his skills."

"If he's so good, let him fight me and prove it."

"That's what you said to Blue, and he beat you in a fair fight."

"I wasn't ready."

"But you started it. He didn't want to fight. Can't you admit you came out second best?"

"I could fight you."

"And do you think you would win?"

"I would.... I don't know. You are much bigger."

"The others you want to fight also are much bigger. And have the killing drums. Would you win against them?"

"Barkah knows.... Why do you ask these stupid questions?"

"Because I want to know why a boy who has known only love and affection hates so much. Why did you go into Joqua's house?"

"To prove I could. The great hunter was supposed to be on guard. I could have killed everyone and nobody would have known who did it."

"But why didn't you go into Joshway's house, or Lurch's. Why not Moremew's or Tonto' or mine?"

"And if I had laid down beside Sayhoo?"

"I would have killed you."

"Joqua did not kill me for laying beside Smalsh."

"If you had chosen to do whatever you were going to do with Coanna, he would have. What were you going to do with Smalsh, anyway?"

"Take her into the forest."

"What for?"

"So she could teach me how to make love with a woman."

"With Smalsh?"

"With any woman I might choose."

"Any woman? Even if they didn't want you? Except for Usula and Noisle who have pledged themselves to Oneson and Armot, there are no women available in the village. "

"I would have taken one anyway." Barkah fixed his eyes directly on Widel's. "But there are women, Ran-ford: Coanna, Love, Penny."

"They're still babies!" Widel shouted. "So help me, touch one of them and you are as good as dead."

Widel was enraged. To have Penny's name spoken in the context of forced sex was too much. He moved to strike the boy and only a supreme effort prevented his doing so. "Put your hands behind your back," he ordered. "I'm tying you to the corner post where I know you'll be in the morning."

"Barkah will not run away."

"That, my young friend, is the least of my worries."

"I've listened to Barkah's words," Widel began, "and since I can't make much sense of them, I'll repeat them to you."

384

Wasmaggi and the six hunters listened carefully. Only Amstay reacted outwardly. His son's behavior tore at the very fabric of Masaki society. To threaten the female children, to threaten the wives, to practically demand an open season on any female was incomprehensible. And when Barkah spoke and challenged the hunters, none knew what to do. An eleven year old boy!

Amstay was crushed. His son. "What had twisted his mind so?" He asked Widel.

"I don't know, and if I knew, I wouldn't know what to do. It is, I suppose, too much killing. I might have more understanding if it was Oneson who lost his mother and favorite uncles. I would expect it of Threesome and Twoman who lost their second father. I would expect some irrational behavior from Penny whose mother, my wife, our medicine woman, was killed by the others. But Barkah lost no family. I just don't know, Amstay. I just don't know."

"Joqua knows one thing," the hunter said. "Know that now Coanna and Love and Penny not safe and one day no woman will be safe."

"What," asked Moremew, "if Barkah have Smalsh? Maybe that be enough."

"That be like feeding jaguar," Tonto offered. "One day food enough. Next day jaguar want more. Then next day even more. So today give Smalsh, then tomorrow Sistal, then Kalo, then one day Coanna and Love. Moremew want that?"

"Not want that. Tonto know."

"Then Tonto say Barkah either go or hunters kill."

That brought the solution to a head. An eleven year old was either to be banished from the village or executed.

"Amstay speak. Is my son. Cutilla and Amstay will take Barkah away. But will not take Sistal and Maltra. They must find new husband."

The thought of losing Amstay was sobering. Lurch would have none of that idea. If Cutilla went, Lurch was certain that Contulla would go, with or without him. Most likely Blue would go with his mother. Then Lurch would have to go.

The hunters could not allow the village to be reduced this way. It would be the death of everyone. So from expulsion or execution, the hunters did what they had done so often; they gave up all suggestions for punishment and sent Barkah home with his father, his father to watch out for the boy and with everyone's hope that Barkah would come to his senses.

Three nights later, Barkah attacked Sistal. Sistal yelled bloody murder.

"Your father's wife?" Amstay screamed. "In his own house? What kind of son are you?"

"You have only one wife, Cutilla, my mother. Other women are not your wives. You say they are, but they only come into our house because they have no one to take care of them. You use them. Why should I not use them, too?"

"They are my wives!" Amstay shouted even louder "You have no...." He fell to the ground, the emotional strain too much even for the sturdy hunter. He could feel the forest crashing around him.

Barkah walked out of the house.

"Where are you going? Come back here."

Barkah turned and laughed at his father, then continued walking. "Barkah...."

The boy did not stop. He walked into the shadows.

Amstay did not follow. "I hope," he shouted, "you meet the jaguar. You don't respect us; respect the jaguar. He will not give a second chance."

With Cutilla hugging him, Amstay sat on the ground by the cooking fire and cried. "Why?" he bawled. "What did we do?"

Cutilla had no answer. Rising up within her was the certainty that her son was dead or soon would be.

TWENTY-SIX

Amstay hunted for two full days, spending the night in the forest. It was an unusual act, and when questioned about it upon his return, he replied simply that he was providing for his family because he was going away.

"And where are you going?" Widel asked, fearing the answer he already knew.

"I follow Barkah."

"Why? What purpose will it serve? He has gone to be on his own."

"If Barkah had raped Sayhoo, what would Ran-ford do?"

Widel knew. "But Barkah did not rape Sistal," he answered with less than full enthusiasm.

"He tried."

"But he's your son!"

"He's a hunter."

"He's a hunter because we need hunters; he's just a boy, not a man."

"Ran-ford, is not choice; is way."

"Amstay, let the hunters decide who will bring Barkah back. Maybe one of the other hunters. A father cannot do what you think you must do."

"The hunters will agree. It was my wife Barkah offended. It is I who must find and...." Amstay let the thought linger before completing it. "I must kill Barkah. It's the way of the Masaki."

"No! It doesn't have to be. There are other ways to punish Barkah for his foolishness."

"What other ways, Ran-ford?"

"I cannot talk you out of this. I'll go with you. Together we'll find Barkah."

"That friend talk. But Ran-ford know this I must do alone. I ask that you look after Cutilla and Sistal and Maltra."

"Will you talk with Wasmaggi, then, before you go?"

"For what? He knows what I have to do. He won't like it, but he'll know. And the hunters know. Even now they wonder why I haven't left the village."

If Barkah had a plan, it did not extend beyond his desire to take revenge upon the village. The hunters had humiliated him; they would pay for that. Blue, of course, would be the first to experience Barkah's rage; then his father for taking two young wives; then Ran-ford. He wasn't sure why Widel must pay except that Barkah suddenly fixated on Sayhoo. Perhaps she would be the one to teach him the secrets of lovemaking. The more he thought about it, the more she became the perfect object of his youthful lust.

He walked a familiar path, one that would lead to a summer camp. He made no effort to conceal his passage, supposing no one would follow. His parents had thrown him out of their house. They would have no further interest in him.

Barkah gave no thought to food, no thought to where he would spend his days and nights, no thought to the ever present dangers of the forest. Ahead of him was the single image of Sayhoo, leading him, teasing him, taunting him. He could see the sway of her hips as she walked, see the fertile, sensual roundness of her belly when she turned to encourage him, see her erect breasts and the protruding nipples that would nurse her child, and before the child, him. His male part became erect and he experienced an acute pain in his testicles. Walking became uncomfortable. He begged Sayhoo to stop, to ease his pain, to touch him and show him the way to her inner place.

Finally, he had to rest beside the old pathway. Slumped on the fallen leaves, he closed his eyes and imagined Sayhoo bending over him. He rubbed himself slowly, and then more vigorously. There was pleasure in his pain; he neither understood it nor cared. He was beyond caring, and when he ejaculated, the pleasure overwhelmed him. It was his first time.

He was exhausted and fell asleep on the very spot of his imagined lovemaking. The images of his desire did not leave him. He dreamed of making love to Sayhoo. He dreamed about Smalsh. He dreamed about Sistal and Maltra. He dreamed about most of the women, but mostly, he dreamed about Penny, white Penny, Penny who soon would have a hair mound to match her mother's and maybe breasts as large.

Barkah awoke with the same pain that had troubled him earlier, his erection more powerful, if that was possible. Sayhoo's image had gone; Penny's remained, and imaging her, he masturbated again. Tales of the wondrous proclivity of the jaguar entered his head. "I am the jaguar," he told himself. "Every woman will know my power."

The thought of the jaguar sobered him enough to realize he was weaponless and defenseless. That could be a deadly mistake. He must make a spear; he must hunt. Suddenly he was famished. And he must find water.

Barkah was not without forest skills. From broken palm branches he fashioned a crude bow, and from palm leaf fibers he made the bow string. With them, fire emerged. Barkah uprooted a young oak, burned off its branches and burned the stick to length. By carefully turning of the stick in the fire, he managed to make a reasonable point. He had his spear. Three days later, when Amstay came upon the fire pit, he would read the evidence and congratulate his son.

Barkah stood little chance of finding meat. He had a much better chance spearing a fish. He headed back toward the stream that nourished the village. Once at the stream he could entice the piranha to the water's edge by beating on the water in imitation of a floundering animal. Maybe the agitated water wouldn't bring the alligators. As confident as he was, he knew he wasn't skilled enough to kill an alligator and get it to shore. If both piranha and alligator showed up, the alligator would eat the fish or else send them scattering. But it was worth a try. Maybe a tiny alligator would appear first.

Spearing a swift and wily piranha was pure luck. Barkah had no experience to speak of, but once having decided to try, his singlemindedness forced him to persist. So focused, he missed his opportunity with a forest deer, completely missed seeing two juvenile alligators, overlooked or ignored a tapir hole near the bank and an egret's nest in the tree above where he stood.

To ignore food was one thing; to ignore an enemy, had one been present, was something else. Although a child of the forest, he was too immature or too inexperienced to be either a successful or a long-lived hunter.

Beating the water was a futile activity. Neither piranha nor alligator appeared. The noise and splashing served only to scare away all potential food; Barkah was reduced to eating nuts and grubs, a common enough diet for hungry Masakis but not a diet fit for the jaguar Barkah convinced himself he was.

If he was disappointed, there was no one to know, and he rationalized his meager meal as the forest's fault. With that tiny measure of false ego, Barkah committed a fundamental mistake, exhibiting a flaw of monumental proportions. To survive in the forest, one must blend with the forest; to prosper in the forest, one must become one with the forest. The forest knows neither right nor wrong; humans make such judgments. The forest neither gives nor withholds her blessings; the people learn to take and use them, or they do not learn and thus invite hardship and death. To blame the forest for indifference is evidence of one's own failure; to blame the forest for that failure gives witness to one's own shortcomings. The wise hunter learns that; the inexperienced, the immature, the stupid hunter does not. Instead of cooperating with the forest, the ignorant hunter fights the forest. The forest does not fight back, it simply ignores the whimpering and impatient fool.

Barkah saw himself as a jaguar only as a sexual powerhouse; he saw none of the qualities that gives the jaguar its place in the forest. Barkah knew nothing first hand about the cat, his one memory lost in babyhood; he could not remember seeing a live jaguar in the wild. What he knew was what he had heard from the hunters and his mother, and the hunters especially enjoyed reciting tales of the frenzied sexual proclivity of the tiger during its brief mating season.

If Barkah had known the jaguar, he would have known its complete identity with the forest, such that the jaguar was like the morning mist, sensed but not seen, floating as if on air, apart from but part of the forest itself. Barkah knew none of the jaguar's qualities; thus, when he called himself a jaguar, he neither assumed nor tried to emulate those qualities.

When Amstay found Barkah's resting place beside the stream, he guessed at his son's efforts and hoped he had caught something worth eating. Lack of fire and bones and entrails suggested otherwise. He discovered that Barkah had crossed the tiny river and was now on the village side of the stream. Judging the day too late to continue, Amstay set about finding his own meal. That he did by quietly sitting beside the water, patiently waiting for some fish or other creature to come within range of his spear. Before long he was rewarded. An alligator not more than two feet long glided along the shore, perhaps one of the pair that Barkah had not seen. Within minutes, it was being cooked.

The hunter was an uneasy, unstable bundle of conflicting emotions. He had his duty; that was clear enough. He was proud that his son had made a fire and had manufactured a spear; he worried that his son had not been well fed. He hoped he would not have to kill the boy, and he hoped when he found his son, the boy would fight strongly and fiercely before Amstay killed him.

Perhaps, he thought, he only would have to wound Barkah. Ordinarily, wounding would satisfy the offense. But rape or intended rape was not ordinary; death was demanded. Perhaps Barkah would travel far away from the village and Amstay would not be able to find him. That was a futile hope. Barkah made no attempt to cover his tracks; indeed, he was heading toward the village. Besides, Amstay was too experienced and successful a hunter to fail at tracking one boy.

After spending the night beside the stream, Amstay let the light of day come to fullness before he crossed and picked up Barkah's trail. Amstay had not slept well, and he went through the motions carelessly and by rote. His resolve was weakening. Maybe Ranford was right; there might be other ways to punish Barkah.

For his part, Barkah was absorbed in plotting revenge upon Blue and then upon the village as a whole, especially the hunters who had embarrassed him. Sometime during the night, he had given up the idea of taking the women one by one. They would come to him gladly when he proved his jaguar power.

Preoccupied with hateful thoughts, Barkah failed to recognize the mist-like figure that maintained a parallel course. The fetid odor of the jungle tiger failed to reach him, the jaguar staying down wind, or he ignored it among the ever-present smells of forest rot. Nor did he discern the jaguar's raspy whistles as the cat breathed in anticipation of the kill.

A true hunter would have been alerted, first by the agitation of the monkeys who sensed a hunting jaguar, then by the quietness of a thousand creatures in the jaguar's path, each as careful as possible not to reveal its presence. To a hunter, the subtle changes in sounds and activity was warning enough. Barkah, if he knew what the changes of sounds meant, ignored them.

The jaguar moved some distance ahead, its primitive brain plotting the boy's course, and sought a tree from which it would leap when its intended victim was underneath.

Amstay had heard the sounds and the lack of sounds, had observed the monkeys, had caught a whiff of the jaguar's foul smell. He held his spear upright. In the forest, the jaguar's attack would come from overhead, the last microsecond warning a growl. Amstay moved forward, his eyes darting in a hundred different directions, his body hunched to take the attack.

Amstay heard Barkah somewhere ahead, not far away but still out of sight. He wanted to call out, warn his son, but did not because shouting might trigger the jaguar's attack. Instead, he began a low whistle, the hunters' warning that danger was near.

Barkah knew the signal well enough, but it got through to him belatedly, and then he misinterpreted it as hunters on a hunt. He didn't want to meet other hunters. Looking for a place to hide, he stopped just short of the jaguar's ambush tree, and when he selected his hiding place, the jaguar had to change its location. Barkah was safe for the moment.

Amstay's intention, once the fact of the jaguar was clear, was to place himself in such a way that the jaguar would charge him rather than his son. Amstay knew Barkah could not hope to survive the jaguar's attack. He advanced cautiously, passing the place Barkah had chosen for his hiding place.

Barkah watched his father, assuming Amstay's carefully measured steps hunted him. Barkah still was unaware of the jaguar's presence.

When Amstay was about fifteen paces beyond Barkah's hiding place, Barkah stepped out behind Amstay. He easily could have speared his father in the back, thought about it, and hesitated.

"You look for me?" he asked instead.

Amstay did not turn around. "Right now I hunt the jaguar."

Thinking Amstay was making reference to him, the boy laughed. "I am the jaguar you seek."

Amstay turned part way around, ignoring Barkah's self-reference. "The jaguar I seek is real. It hunts either Barkah or Amstay. It's very close. Or do you choose to ignore it?"

Still ignorant of the jaguar's smell or whistled breathing, Barkah assumed Amstay's talk was intended to distract him. He knew Amstay was present for only one of two purposes: to kill him outright for attempting to rape a wife or to capture him and return him to the village where the hunters would pronounce a sentence of either death or banishment. Death he could face, as young as he was; banishment, with its shaven head, would be an embarrassment he could not tolerate. To be expelled from the village weaponless and friendless with all the hunters and women and children turning their backs on him was more than he could stand. If he was to remain free to become the human jaguar he knew himself to be, he must kill his father.

As Amstay continued turning, he caught sight of the jaguar in a tree to Barkah's left and slightly behind him. The jaguar was beginning its crouch, preparing to spring. In one practiced motion,

Amstay raised his spear, drew back him arm, and sent the spear into the jaguar's side.

Barkah saw only the raised and thrown spear. Assuming it was meant for him, he ran forward and thrust his own crude spear deep into Amstay's stomach. Only then did he hear the sounds of the cat, mortally wounded but still a threat.

With the spear stuck in its side, the jaguar charged the boy. Amstay had fallen. Barkah tried to free his spear from his father's gut, could not, and before he realized his helplessness, the jaguar was upon him, breaking the boy's neck in one powerful bite. He who would be the jaguar died without conscious pain.

Not so Amstay. Barkah's crude spear, more blunt than sharp, had done great damage. Witnessing the wounded jaguar's attack, seeing his son die, knowing the jaguar would turn on him next, Amstay wretched the spear from his belly and rammed it into the jungle tiger. Even as he did, he slid the lanyard which held his knife up over his head and in a single motion slit the jaguar's throat. He took no pride in the kill. Even had he not been so badly wounded, he would have taken no pride. The jaguar had killed before it was killed.

Amstay was bleeding badly, the pain intolerable. With his left hand, he pressed his stomach as tightly as he could. With his right, planting a foot on the jaguar's side, he pulled out his spear. In spite of his pain, he noted the sex and probable age of the jaguar, its length and weight, and its unique coloring. If he lived, the village would want to know such things.

Only then and after seeking the best possible waiting place did Amstay consider he might die. If he went to the river, a sure and simple way home, once in the water he would die within minutes, his blood a free meal welcoming sign for piranhas and alligators.

Thus he did the only thing possible. He whistled and sang the songs of the animals and birds into the forest, the sounds that called for help.

When the hunters found Amstay, he was unconscious but he continued to make the sounds of his great need. One had to put an ear next to Amstay's lips to hear, but it proved that Amstay never had given up hope.

That single item was the sum of the hunters' observation and reflection about the scene spread before them. Barkah was dead; the jaguar was dead; the order of events unimportant at the moment. Tomorrow someone would return and figure it out. It depended entirely on whether Amstay lived or died. If he lived, he would reveal everything; if he died, the hunters would make of the scene what they could. It all rested in the hands of the ancient medicine man.

There was some talk about making a litter, but cutting tree branches and weaving a mat was time consuming. Instead, Lurch picked up the unconscious hunter and walked toward home. Joqua raced ahead, marking the best trail, wanting to alert Wasmaggi and the women.

Within minutes, Moremew had killed a small howler monkey and had skinned it, the fur used as a dressing for Amstay's wound. At least the outward bleeding had been stopped.

Amstay had been closer to the village than he had realized. Unknowingly or unconsciously, Barkah had led him on a circular route toward the village. When Amstay whistled and sang the animals' calls, Joqua and Lurch were hunting. They had passed the calls back to the village. In the village, Widel had gone immediately to get his bow and arrows; Wasmaggi prevented Widel's leaving, convinced that Widel and Tonto had to organize Oneson and Armot and Blue into a home protection force.

"But those are not sounds of warning, Wasmaggi. They are calls for help."

"Is true, Ran-ford. One hunter is injured. What if he was injured by the others?" Widel deferred to the old man's intuitive knowledge. The "what if" was enough.

Meanwhile, Tonto directed the women and the older children. There was no mad dash to the protection of the forest; the women had long since given up that means of escape. They had proved their willingness to fight, and now Tonto was placing them in strategic positions out of sight but with carefully chosen sight lines into the heart of the village. Once the young children had been concealed, the women took positions surrounding the village.

Lucknew, Pollyque and Tilla took charge of the five youngest children. No matter what happened in the village, the three old women and the children would not return until it was safe, and should the village be destroyed and the other adults killed, the women would assume responsibility for Coanna, Threesome, Twoman, Love, and Penny. It was not spoken; it simply was and would be, and from the three ancient women the children would receive the remainder of their education as the only people in the world. In time they would become the new Masakis and would build a new village. It was as certain as the forest.

When Joqua raced into the village, there was no one to greet him. Instinctively, he knew why, and he shouted out the basic fact of his haste.

"Wasmaggi! Medicine! Xingu! Water!"

Immediately, the women reappeared. Sayhoo went directly to Wasmaggi's hut and began moving medicines and knives to the central fire. Widel and the boys brought wood; the women brought food and water.

With a remarkable conservation of words, Joqua drew a picture of the forest scene. Barkah was dead; a jaguar was dead; Amstay had been speared in the stomach. The how and whys he left unsaid, partly because he did not know the details or the sequence of events, partly because Cutilla would bear the burden of a dead son and a dying husband. He wanted no questions, especially those he could not answer, and he hated being the messenger.

Cutilla stood quietly, absorbed the news, then slumped to the ground, overcome by the impact of what Joqua had said. Had father and son killed each other? That was all she could think. That was enough.

Lurch had carried Amstay the entire distance. If there was anyone Lurch loved, after his wife and son, it was his brother-in-law, Amstay. He was exhausted from his effort, and his eyes were filled with tears, not from the effort but because he thought he was carrying home the lifeless body of his dearest friend. Never along the way had he stopped to check on Amstay, never had he stopped for any reason, not to drink or to eat or even to eliminate his body's wastes, his one purpose to get Amstay to Wasmaggi and to Wasmaggi's medicines.

Stretched before the fire in the waning light, Amstay looked dead, although Wasmaggi detected a lingering spark of life. "Wish for An-na," he said to Widel. "Too much work for old man, and none of women able help."

"I'll take Anna's place, old man. She will help us. Her spirit will help us. What do you intend to do?"

"Clean wound, sew up."

"Not enough. Amstay has two wounds. Surely you know that. One wound on the outside, another wound in the inside."

"How Ran-ford know that?"

"I can smell it. Wasmaggi, this man's stomach has been pierced. That's where the foul odor comes from. You have to cut into him and sew up his stomach first, then sew up the outside."

"Wish An-na were here. Old man cannot do what must be done."

"I'll do it."

"Amstay will die anyway."

"But we'll know we tried to save him."

Wasmaggi forced liquids into Amstay, mostly coca mixtures.

"Your best knife, Wasmaggi."

"All my knives are best."

With Wasmaggi's guidance, Widel opened the wound, slicing carefully. The flesh was relatively soft and yielding, and what muscle he encountered he cut without regard to later weakness. He went straight to the stomach, found the puncture, and enlarged his incision. The blood and stomach contents mixed in an unwholesome mash of brown.

"Water!"

Wasmaggi laced the water with powders and other liquids, and Widel flushed the entire area, moping up with wades of kapok. And when the area around the stomach wound was as clean as he could

397

make it, he took the bone needles threaded by the women with fine palm thread and stitched the wound closed.

Wasmaggi had prepared a syrup-like mixture to spread on the stitching. Widel didn't bother to ask what it was, nor did he ask the nature of the powder Wasmaggi sprinkled in the gaping wound still to be closed. Wasmaggi's knowledge was so vast and superior that Widel never questioned the man's medicines.

When Widel had finished the last of thirty stitches, Wasmaggi spoke. "Glad Ran-ford have steady hand. Would make fine medicine man with right teacher."

For six days Amstay hovered between life and death, Cutilla at his side constantly. To her he revealed the hunt for Barkah, the jaguar, the killings. He did not say anything about Barkah's charging and stabbing him, only that Barkah's spear was in the jaguar. He thanked Widel and Wasmaggi. He embraced Lurch and Contulla and Blue, and one night he was carried to the fire so he could listen to the old songs and stories.

Later, he spoke to his new wives, Sistal and Maltra, and told them he might still be a good husband to them, and he laughed when they said they hoped to be in his bed soon. He asked their forgiveness for Barkah's behavior, and it was given readily.

Then, one afternoon, he asked Cutilla to leave him for a few minutes with Widel. "I wish thank you again," he said. "Never was more Masaki than Ran-ford."

Widel sat with Amstay for a few minutes, their shared silence as much a testimony to their unity as any words could be.

When Widel left Amstay, he went directly to Wasmaggi. "We have to open him again, see what we failed to do."

"No, Ran-ford. Forest take Amstay. We do no more. We gave more life to him; let him go. If he needs help going, I'll do that, but no more."

"I hate giving in to death."

"We were born to die."

The next morning, Amstay asked to be taken out of his house so he could see the mist and the forest in its morning glory. He held

Cutilla's hand and smiled. It was a good day to return to the forest, he said.

TWENTY-SEVEN

Before the mist had evaporated in the obscured sun's heat, Widel become responsible for three women, Contulla, Sistal and Maltra, and when the marriages were formalized, he would acquire burdens he never dreamed possible. If the totality of his situation was not immediately apparent, Wasmaggi made it so.

"Ran-ford will have to make house bigger," the ancient medicine man began that afternoon with a soulful laugh. "Big family is good."

Wasmaggi's subtlety went completely over Widel's head until Wasmaggi added, "And have to make much bigger bed."

It then dawned on Widel just what the old man was saying. Four wives, and each would demand some consideration and attention.

Wasmaggi was trying to make light of it. "Medicine man find medicine to make Ran-ford like the jaguar. Course, jaguar only good in season. Ran-ford good all time."

"It's not a laughing matter, Wasmaggi. Ranford has enough with Sayhoo."

"Contulla and Maltra and Sistal do not please?"

"Damn, Wasmaggi, it's not a question of pleasing. Sayhoo pleases me; I need no other."

"Soon Ran-ford will not have Sayhoo. She gets fat in belly. Ran-ford need others."

"You're not going to let up on this, are you? I suppose this whole conversation is to get to another of your sinister purposes. Let's hear it."

"Wasmaggi only try help."

"Yeah, but so far I haven't heard any help."

"Ran-ford, Cutilla will go to Lurch, be with sister."

400

"Yes, I suppose she'd rather. But what about Blue? She still blames him for some of Barkah's problems."

"I take Blue to live with me. Wasmaggi need help; old man can't get around very well. It will be agreed."

"You mean you've already spoken to everyone and they have agreed?."

"Well, had to find out."

"Okay. That solves one problem."

"Sistal says she will come live with Wasmaggi."

"So you have arranged a match between Sistal and Blue, who, I remind you, is still a little boy."

"Not so little, I think. But it's been agreed."

"What about...?"

"Maltra? I come to her. First, tell Ran-ford about Sistal and Usula and Noisle. Wasmaggi will have big house made; Wasmaggi's house. But in house are to be the three women and Blue and Oneson and Armot, and...."

"And you will teach them about making love and let them.... Wasmaggi, you are a dirty old man."

"Once the village had only one house, when Wasmaggi was small, and all the people lived in that one house, and those people made love. Is natural."

"Your excuse for everything."

"Wasmaggi makes no excuses."

"No. It's a solution. I don't know any other. You do know best."

"Then Ran-ford agrees?"

"There's another choice?"

"No other choice."

"Then, Wasmaggi, I agree."

"Good. I'll tell Maltra."

"Wait just a minute. What about Maltra?"

"She has no one."

"But...."

"And she says she will be your second wife."

"You've asked her?"

"In passing."

401

"You didn't ask me. Did you also ask Sayhoo?"

"You said there was no other solution. Is the way it is. Sayhoo will agree because you will tell her."

"How, for God's sake?"

"Just as you told me. No other choice."

"I didn't say that; you did."

"And you agreed."

That night as they lay on their sleeping cot, Sayhoo reached for Widel. He held her at arms' length. "I do love you, Sayhoo. With all my heart, I love you."

"But you don't hold me."

"Sayhoo?"

"Ran-ford has something to say to Sayhoo?"

"Yes. I can't find the words. The words trouble me, yet I must say them."

"Then speak them. As long as you love me, the words will not matter."

"Sayhoo, there's something we must do."

"What is that, husband?"

"We must.... I must.... There's no choice. You see that, don't you. Not that I want to. It has to be done."

"What must we do?"

"Must...."

"Take a second wife? Is that what Ran-ford cannot say?"

"Yes. How did you know?"

"It is talk. Sayhoo hear. Maltra difficult, but she will be good second wife."

"Thank you for understanding. It's not my choice but there's no other way."

Maltra would be difficult, but in ways Widel could not appreciate at the moment. Maltra was strong-minded, independent and, despite the circumstances that had placed her in the village, strangely secure. She had been raped repeatedly by Luckee and abused by her own medicine man; her entire village had been destroyed and, except for the eight women, its population killed.

402

She had been captured by slave hunters and dragged through countless miles of unknown forest; she had been rescued only to have half of her rescuers slaughtered; she had been made the second or third wife to Amstay as a matter of survival, not of love. And now, because of circumstances totally beyond her control, she was to be the second wife of a man whose color and habits were still strange and mysterious.

It was obvious that Widel's and Sayhoo's welcome on the fourth day after Amstay's death was conditional. Beneath the welcome was the hint of intrusion and, on Sayhoo's part, suggestions of jealousy and resentment. Maltra could not read Widel. His expression and manner revealed none of his feelings.

"Ranford welcomes Maltra," he said. "We have not had an opportunity to become well acquainted, so this is awkward for both of us. You're part of our family now."

"Ran-ford, Sayhoo, Maltra knows this Sayhoo's house and in all things I'm second here. I not interfere between you. I'll try to be good second wife, and I'll be good second mother to Penny and to your unborn child. I ask for nothing for myself, only Ran-ford's protection."

Penny took to the arrangement immediately. She was envious of the other children who had several mothers; Maltra was one more immediate person to indulge her.

As Sayhoo's delivery time drew near, Penny asked Widel why the women argued so much, something he did not know. Straightway, he confronted them. "It's said in my house the women argue. I thank them for not arguing in front of me, but I resent they argue at all. I'll hear your arguments and decide who is right. I'll hear you now."

"Ran-ford, is women's talk. Not what Ran-ford would wish hear. We settle our differences ourselves. I am number one wife, am I not?"

Widel felt as though he had been slammed against a wall. A dominant number one and a subservient number two did not fit into his idea of a polygamous family. The Masakis were oriented toward a democratic wifehood of equals, but the truth came to him suddenly.

In his house there was no equality whatsoever. Maltra was a nonwife. She never was consulted; she was not involved in decisions; she served and cooked and cleaned as she was directed by Sayhoo. All without complaint.

"I have but one wife," Widel said meekly. "You know that I've not taken Maltra as a second wife, although I should. What does Maltra say about the arguing? Why all the bickering and fighting in my house?

"I not Ran-ford's wife; I have no say."

"If you were my wife, my second wife, what would you say?"

"Maltra would say...."

Sayhoo interrupted. "What she would say is, why does Sayhoo not let Maltra share Ran-ford's bed?"

"And what does Sayhoo say in reply?"

"That Sayhoo is all that Ran-ford want and need. Is that not so?"

Widel was caught between the proverbial rock and a hard place. It was true. Sayhoo satisfied him. He loved her deeply and without reservation. It also was true that if he did finally formalize a marriage with Maltra, she had a right to be in his bed. And if the truth was spoken, he had admired her body and her fastidiousness, as though, now that he thought about it, she had prepared for his call.

Why, then, had he not called, and why had he not married her? When the answer came to him, he was a little surprised. In his house, Maltra was meek and timid and displayed none of the strengths he had observed through the many months of turmoil and horror. Then she had reminded him of Anna, and he had been attracted to her. Now she was a mouse and allowed herself to be bullied by Sayhoo.

Widel had to answer, knowing each woman expected an answer, knowing each expected an answer that would be unliked by the other, but before he could reply, Penny entered the house.

"Well, Ranford," she had taken the Masakis' way of addressing parents by their name, "are you going to take Maltra or not? That's what they are always fighting about."

Widel was stunned. What did his little girl know about love and sex? She was too young to have such thoughts. "Penny!" he shouted, but he said no more to her. To the Masaki, such knowledge was natural.

Always natural, he thought. "It's natural that a man sleep with his wives," he announced, "and if a man has two wives, he sleeps with both. It's natural."

And with that said, he walked out of the house.

Once outside, be called back. "Penny, I would talk with you. Now."

Penny appeared promptly.

"Where do you get such ideas?" he demanded.

"What ideas, Father?" using the familiar term, knowing that Widel was into something dark and mysterious.

"You know what I mean, men and women."

"I sleep in your house. Do you think I can't hear or see what you and Sayhoo do? Coanna says it's what Xingu and Joqua do. Love says it's what Sarahguy and Joshway do. And with their second and third wives."

"You are too young for...."

"Look at me, Father. Look hard. I'm not a little baby girl anymore. See? My breasts begin to swell. Twoman and Threesome say they will be like my mother's. And that I'll have hair like hers"

"Oh, my god."

"Soon I'll be a Masaki woman."

"Oh, my god."

That night Sayhoo said she would sleep with Penny in the far corner of the room. "Sayhoo doesn't feel well," she said. "It would be right for my husband to sleep with Maltra."

"But what if I don't want to?"

"It's a husband's duty. We have decided."

As lovemaking went, it was a disaster. Widel felt guilty, as though he was betraying Sayhoo on the one hand and on the other hand failing to give Maltra any measure of affection whatsoever. In five other houses, not knowing what was going on in Wasmaggi's expanded house, men were making love to wives one, two and three. Even old Tonto probably had done so. Maybe Lurch had made love with Cutilla, so recently widowed. It was natural.

Then why was it so hard? Guilt alone did not explain Widel's inadequacy. Was it because Penny listened for the sounds, because no matter what the other children said, he should protect Penny from human knowledge? The sin of Adam and Eve, he thought, knowing their nakedness. But, hell, the Masaki always had been naked. There was not any part of anyone's body that could not be seen in a glance. And were the Masakis immoral? Hardly. Their structure was more rigid than any he knew.

He did not sleep. He had to figure out what was wrong, what had gone wrong. Was Maltra ugly? On the contrary, she was quite handsome, something other than beautiful but very acceptable. Was she fat? No, she was as trim as any Masaki and more so than most. Was she dirty? Just the opposite. She took great care of her body and hair and teeth. No, there was not a thing wrong with Maltra.

Having exhausted all possibilities, then...the fault must lie within. I turned her off, he thought, because I was nothing. I didn't even do my duty by her. For better or worse, she will be my wife. I'll come to love her and learn how to make love to her.

Sayhoo's delivery was prolonged and difficult. The baby was tangled in the umbilical cord. Tilla and Lucknew and Pollyque had taken charge of the birth, but it was Maltra who did most of the work, never leaving Sayhoo's side during Sayhoo's two day ordeal. Wasmaggi was called, an unusual event; medicine men were not present at a birth unless there were strong medicines to be administered or excessive bleeding to be stopped.

Widel spent two days pacing outside his house.

When, late in the second day, toward sundown, Widel heard a baby's weak cries, he rushed to Sayhoo's side. She had not uttered her pain, a proper Masaki through it all, and now was sleeping the sleep of the utterly exhausted. Widel took her hand and held it.

"Does Ran-ford not want to see our daughter?"

"Our...daughter?"

"The baby is fine, Ran-ford. A nice round female. Here. See? Then I'll clean her and she will eat." Maltra held the newborn, already wrapped in a jaguar skin.

"How is Sayhoo?" he asked. "Is she okay?"

"I.... Ask Wasmaggi."

Which is exactly what Widel did.

"Masaki women not have trouble dropping babies," Wasmaggi began. "Your women make much work of it."

"But is Sayhoo going to be all right?"

"She will be, how do you say, okay. But, Ran-ford, she should not be in your bed for much time. And I think maybe she not have another child, not for a while anyway."

"What does that mean?"

"Means not make love for time. Let Sayhoo heal, no matter what she says. And maybe she'll not have another child. Not know, but Wasmaggi have to cut to free baby, and sometimes that ends woman's birthing." Wasmaggi paused before going on. "But, Ran-ford, she will be well and one day be in your bed again, only she may not conceive another child for you."

"But...."

"But she will love you. You have made her mother."

When the villagers had drifted away, Maltra sat beside Widel, the baby in her arms. "Ran-ford," she said, "the baby is not white. Sayhoo wanted a white baby."

"It wasn't in the genes," Widel responded absentmindedly, preoccupied with his conversation with Wasmaggi.

"Not know genes. Who she?"

"It's of no consequence, Maltra. Just that Sayhoo's color was stronger than mine."

"I hope when I give you a child, it is white."

"When...?" Of course, that was a possibility. "Maltra, when you showed me the baby, you said it was our baby. What did you mean by that?"

"All babies belong to family. This baby have two mothers. I'll treat her as my own. And when I have baby, Sayhoo will treat that baby as hers."

"You and Sayhoo are getting along better?"

"We are Masaki wives."

"But you're not my wife, really. We haven't stood before the fire and told the people."

"We will, Ran-ford. Sayhoo and I have agreed."

Once, long ago, Widel had fantasized about having two loving wives, only then it was Connie and Anna, and although he had let his mind run wild in anticipation, he had wondered how it would work and he worried that it would not work at all. Now, because of circumstances he could hardly comprehend, he had two wives, and what once had seemed a magical situation now presented him with realities he wondered if he could handle.

He chuckled at his choice of thought. Handling, physically at least, was not his problem. Emotionally, the reality confronting him was enormous. Was he capable of loving two women? He had unbreakable bonds with Sayhoo deeply anchored in the past. What he and Sayhoo had done come naturally, there's that word again, but it was true. He had no such bonds with Maltra. He liked her; she seemed to like him, but they had reversed his natural order of things: first you find mutual affection, even love, and then you have sex. With Maltra he began with sex, hoping, he guessed, that good sex would result in affection.

"Does Maltra love Ranford?" he asked.

Masaki feelings are expressed openly for the most part. A sincere question requires a truthful answer, one that does not evade or repress the truth. But if the answer is likely to hurt the one who asks, the truth is clothed in kindness and gentle tones.

"Maltra likes Ran-ford very much; respects Ran-ford; is protected by Ran-ford."

"But Maltra doesn't love Ranford?"

"Love is earned, and Ran-ford is trying very hard. One day Maltra will.... Does husband-to-be love Maltra?"

"I find much to love."

"But you don't."

"I want to."

408

"I know that. Love will come to us both; we'll be glad; the forest will be glad."

"I'm not used to the idea of two wives."

"That I know, too. You love Sayhoo first. I'm not jealous because one day you will love me equal with her. You will be proud to say these are my wives, and you will not say this wife one and this wife two, only these are my wives; I love them both."

For a baby whose entry into the world was delayed and whose birth caused her mother great pain, growth came rapidly. She was as healthy as a horse, Widel told everyone, a comparison totally meaningless to a people who had never seen and could not imagine a beast such as Widel described.

Sayhoo progressed into health far less swiftly. Her milk was barely adequate to the baby's needs. And she seemed unable to regain her strength. It was a question of will power, Wasmaggi told Widel, knowing she might not have another child. What she needed to regain her health was a sign that she was well. Widel asked if taking her into his bed would be that sign. Wasmaggi didn't think so. He would prepare some medicines that might help.

Weeks later, late one night, Sayhoo screamed out in the dark. Widel and Maltra rushed to her bedside.

"Leave us alone, Ran-ford," Sayhoo commanded. "Maltra will help me."

Widel left the house and rebuilt the fire. In due time Maltra joined him. "Sayhoo has been made well," she announced.

"How the hell does she know, just like that?"

"Her flow has begun. She's a woman again."

Widel had no need to know more; such female things were not for him, but he went inside to be with Sayhoo.

"Can I get you anything?" he asked.

"There's no need. Maltra has cared for me, and Penny will get what I need." Then she said, "Ran-ford, I am woman now. I worried I would not be woman for you. In six days I'll be in your bed."

In the morning Sayhoo, Maltra and Penny walked to the stream, and while Penny held her half-sister, a distinction she never would make, Maltra bathed Sayhoo until her skin and hair shone in the sunlight. They maintained a careful lookout for the piranhas, but they never appeared. It was the beginning of a good day.

That afternoon the hunters returned, all except Milken. Milken hunted for Tonto and the old wives, mostly within a narrow range around the village. Usually Tonto accompanied her, but today she had gone off by herself, saying she would not go far. There was much worry. The hunters blamed themselves for having allowed Milken to become Tonto's hunter. It was against nature for women to hunt.

There was little the hunters could do in the dark; before dawn they would fan out and search, hoping to hear her calls. The evening fire was subdued and lifeless. Then from the darkened stream came Milken's calls of her return. The hunters rushed to find her. With no call of distress or injury, the women let out an audible, collective sigh of relief followed by outspoken testaments as to Milken's sanity and audacity.

But mostly there were questions. Where have you been? How far away were you? What did you think you were doing? Who do you think you are, anyway? And statements: you are a stupid woman; you should not be hunting alone; you should not be hunting at all. Questions and statements filled with relief for the safe return of one of their own .

"Milken will tell. Please. Let me greet my husband and his wives." Thus did Milken observe the ancient custom, reassuring her family and tightening the bonds that bound her to Tonto and to the two old women.

Milken had intended to hunt the river bank just below the beach. A turtle or a ray would have been enough, something resting in the shallows or on the bank. But when an anaconda, three or four feet long, swam by, the size Milken could easily handle and which would feed them for two days, she tried to spear it. She managed to thrust her spear through the snake, but not in a fatal spot. The anaconda took off down stream, carrying the spear.

Not wanting to lose either her spear or the snake, Milken followed. She lost track of time, but she traveled a far distance. Finally, the snake grew tired, and Milken was able to wrestle it onto the bank and kill it. Foolishly, she had followed the snake most of the way in water. As she thought about it, a water return was not wise, so she went in search of a trail. That's when she found the jaguar, dead and skinned.

At first, she said, she thought a hunter had killed the jaguar, but neither the teeth nor the claws had been touched. Perhaps, she thought, the hunter had been hurt and only took time to skin the animal. She looked for signs and tracks.

And that, she said, shaking and visibly upset, was when she saw the prints of the others, the same prints as the tropas de resgate who had killed her village and had taken her captive.

She was lost in the forest, not completely because there was the stream, but uncertain as to exactly where she was. Now she could not use the river. She would be seen by anyone with one eye. She had to find a trail, a land route her only hope. And while she searched for the trail, a second jaguar was found, and as she studied the jungle cat, she heard, far away, the sound of the killing drums, the sound that had torn her village apart, mutilating the hunters and older women and children, the sound that had killed Tannee and Laiti and Spiker and Mike.

When she found the trail, she ran as fast as she could, leaving the killing drum sounds far behind. She stopped only once; another skinned jaguar blocked her path. That cat was less than half a day from the village. Yes, she had studied the tracks. The others' tracks had not approached the village. "But they know we're here. We leave tracks of our own, and one day they will come for us. I see our tracks, and I see where the others have studied ours. They study our tracks, and I'm afraid."

Milken's revelation was a thunderbolt of despair.

"We'll leave with the morning mist," Wasmaggi said. "We'll burn the houses early and go to the island of safety."

"No!" shouted Widel. "I agree we must leave as soon as possible, but we must not burn the houses. That would be a signal. We must leave the houses, make the others think we are here, in the forest. It will give us a little more time to get away."

The bandeirantes, the cangaceiros, the tropas de resgate were after jaguar skins, Widel believed, but once they had killed all the jaguars, they would come to the village looking for gold or women. Milken was right. It was only a matter of time. The one possible hiding place was the island, and that wouldn't be a safe place for long.

Moremew stood and spoke. "Moremew and Tilla will stay behind with Tonto and Lucknew and Pollyque. We'll make the others think whole village here. We too old for such a journey. We can't keep up. And we wish die in village of birth, not on trail of running away."

No one said anything. There was sentiment for what Moremew said, right up to the dying part. To stay was sure death, perhaps a prolonged and cruel death for the women. The men would be killed outright because they would fight; the women would be wounded, perhaps, and left to die.

"I not born in this village," Lurch reminded the villagers. "I'll fight the others on the trails; I'll fight the others from the island; I'm not running away; I'm leaving here so I fight my way in my forest."

"We all will go, the oldest and the youngest. I'm growing old, but I'll not die here. I don't wish to die in place of birth. I don't wish to die ever, but if must, I die fighting where and when I choose." Joshway had spoken sitting down. He stood. "If have to, will carry Lucknew and Pollyque and Tilla."

"Wasmaggi says all go. I have three young women to help me and three young hunters to protect me. Tonight we'll say goodbye to our village. Now, this old man suggest...."

And it was agreed. Fortunately, only Widel and Sayhoo's baby had to be attended. All the other children were at least six or seven years old.

Especially, Wasmaggi wanted Tonto free to begin the serious education of Threesome and Twoman, each nearing his adolescence. Armot, Blue and Oneson were given over to Moremew for their continued education as fighters. The women would make arrows along the way, careful to leave no sign of their doing so, and bows, not the traditional long bows used for fishing but Widel's short forest bow. And as they traveled, Widel would teach the bow's skill to every woman and child.

Long before dawn, cooking fires were built up and food served, and before the first light reached the camp, before the morning mist began to rise, the Masakis were on their way. Turning back, Lurch felt his heart grow weak. Once he had stumbled here in search of a wife. He had found her, and he loved her. This was his home. On the outside it looked serene and inviting, a picture he would carry the rest of his days. Perhaps, he whispered to the forest, the others will not come. But he knew they would, if not today, then tomorrow. And his adopted village would be no more.

The Masakis were on their march toward....?

Safety, they hoped. Extinction, Widel believed. Theirs was a world lost within a world. He wondered if the lost world would even be noted.

End of Book Two

~

ABOUT THE AUTHOR AND THE BOOK

When Wolley started *The Death of the Jaguar* series, it was to have been one book with that title. The original research revealed a much more complicated story than first was envisioned, and as sometimes happens, the story itself took over the telling.

One book became two. There was so much to tell, so many lives that were and became intertwined, so deep and intense was the relationship between the Masaki people and the land, that two books became three. In a way, the story became unmanageable, yet with continued research, every aspect begged to be told. The original title became the name of the series, the whole story was divided into three complete novels. Each book is a complete story; together the books tell the larger story.

Wolley rebels against the careless, pejorative use of the words "primitive" and "pagan," as though ancient peoples in Brazil and elsewhere are incapable of love and caring, unity and kindness. The history of Brazil brings to light the whole question of "civilization" and who, in view of Brazil's shameful past, slavery, genocide, inquisition and the holy war of conversion, is civilized.

And not only are the original people of Brazil being exterminated, Brazil is destroying its life-giving forests. Another side of the story needed to be told, and Wolley has attempted to do that by making the unknown and the ignored known and appreciated.

~